Bill & Laurie

· After the Glory ·

•After the Glory•

by Helen Topping Miller

APPLETON-CENTURY-CROFTS, INC.
New York

· After the Glory ·

• *One* •

THEY LAY UNDER THE THIN SHADE OF THE CEDAR THICKET THAT SLOPED
down to the river. At the bottom of the rocky slope ran a narrow
creek that not long since had run red with the blood of fighting men.
On the shaly ground that slanted downward to the greener, reedy bed
of the stream the litter of conflict still lay scattered, bleaching and
rusting in the sudden heat of a May afternoon.

Kingman Markland stretched a foot from his prone position and
kicked at a rusting canteen. It had been trodden by a horse and was
flattened in the middle but from the mouth of it crawled a little
lizard, that skittered away swiftly into the ragged grass.

King rolled over on an elbow and laughed loudly, a sudden, whoop-
ing laugh. Beside him his brother Jack jumped.

"What the devil?" he growled. Then he himself laughed thinly,
grudgingly, as though any mirth he possessed was a private and secret
shame, reluctantly revealed. "Can't get over the feeling that some
Yank is going to take a crack at us from those bushes," he said.

King, long, black-haired, lean, sun-weathered and darkened, so that
now he had almost the look of a Latin, sat up and tossed a pebble
after the fleeing lizard. "Look at the little devil go! Reminds me of
General Forrest. Look at that old scoundrel, first he's there and then
he ain't."

"That was Pa's good bay stud horse that Forrest was riding," said
Jack, as though resuming an argument. "I'd never have believed Pa
would give up that horse to any cavalry ever was."

"To Forrest he would. Maybe didn't have any choice," said King.
"A hundred of 'em ride in all armed and tough, even if agreeable, and
a man gives up what they want and doesn't voice any objections." He
lay back on the ground squinting his dark eyes as the sun smote them.
He was twenty-seven years old, and four years of war had not dimmed
or softened the steely insolence in him. He was handsome with arrogant brows and a classic profile, and it was immediately apparent that

he was aware of this, that he dramatized his looks and was always act-ing a little.

His brother, two years older, leathery, more taciturn, ran his hands around his belt irritably. "Can't get used to having nothing," he said. "Not even a cartridge."

"You could have kept your saber if you hadn't thrown it away back there when that Yank knocked you out of the saddle," King reminded him.

"My horse fell on it. He was dead and I couldn't move him so I lay down and the Yank thought he'd killed me and galloped off. Anyway he was out of ammunition or he wouldn't have hit me with a rifle butt. Hadn't we better be pushing on? It's a hundred miles to home yet, and nothing to eat anywhere on the way."

"I don't figure it's that far," King said. "If we can make it to the river by dark I reckon maybe the Larsons would feed us." He pulled himself to a standing position with one fluid movement of his long body. Jack Markland studied his brother meditatively, still sitting in the ragged grass, leaning back on his big flat palms. That boy, he was thinking, could have licked Rosecrans and Thomas by himself if he had put his mind to it. The trouble was that Kingman Markland, steel wire and lightning as he was, had never been able to keep his facile mind at anything.

"Maybe the Larsons won't even be there," Jack objected, feeling bound, as all his life he had felt bound, to throw cold water on his brother's unconsidered impulses. "Maybe their house was burnt when Schofield went through here and the whole lot of 'em run off. Fool around that river and we might run into some Union renegades. Any-way we'd have to cross it twice, and there's likely no boat left anywhere with a bottom in it."

"You want to tramp all that way chewing on sassafras?" grumbled King. "My belly's as hollow as an empty drum right now, and yours rumbles about as loud. All right, if we've got to go slogging through that rough country let's get moving. Might find us a still hid some-where in a bushy hollow."

Andrew Jackson Markland got up painfully. His feet were bare and the fraying fringe of a ragged pair of butternut breeches dangled over bony ankles scratched and insect bitten. Jack had been the first Markland to enlist, riding off after that loud, belligerent Tennessean, Nathan Bedford Forrest, to his father's indignant disgust.

"If he had to ride why couldn't he sign up with a gentleman?" he had growled. "Somebody like Wheeler or John Morgan. Nate Forrest was a slave trader, didn't even have a command till he raised it himself, and they say he can hardly write his name."

But only a few weeks had passed before King had received a letter from his soldier brother. "If you boys want to win this war you come along with me," wrote Jack. "This colonel could win it all by himself if they'd give him enough men and guns."

So King and Morgan, the youngest Markland son, had set out for West Tennessee riding two of Boone Markland's fine horses.

"Billy wouldn't come," they reported to Jack when they overtook Forrest's troops. "He claims the war's a mistake and we ought to preserve the Union. Billy and Pa were glaring and barking at each other like two mad dogs when we left."

"Dumb stubborn young fool!" Jack fumed. "Always had to be on the offside of everything, all his life. He'll fool around and get drafted and have to do all his fighting in Beauregard's infantry."

"Could be that Billy'd go into the Yank army if Pa rides him too hard," remarked King. "He never did have good common sense."

"Boy from our county wouldn't ever take up for the Union," argued Morgan. "But if anybody's that big a fool it'd be Billy."

Somehow they had sweated, gloried, starved and struggled through four years of hard riding and fighting. Johnsonville, Corinth, Shiloh, the river raids in Mississippi and Alabama, Chickamauga and the blood bath of that last bitter year at Franklin and Nashville, fighting always until Forrest's reluctant surrender at Gainesville. There Jack had found King, but although they had searched for two days they had never located Morgan.

"That boy Morgan must have got himself killed," worried Jack as they started up the ragged slope, painfully putting one sore foot in front of the other. "I never even saw him when we were loading all that plunder on the pontoon bridge at Eastport."

"I guess you were too busy herding hogs across that bridge to look for anybody. Last time I saw Morgan was when we rode that last charge into Franklin, then coming back covering Hood my horse got killed and set me afoot. But the last time I saw him Morgan was mounted and firing back, like the rest of us," King said, then added savagely, "Never did see an army go to pieces so quick. When the news came from Appomattox it was like salt dissolving in a rainstorm."

"I never did give up till Johnston surrendered." Jack kicked at a battered saddle that lay belly up, rain-stained and dusty on the slope. Some gray horse hairs still clung to the ragged padding under it.

"That's what lost us the war," he growled. "Rotten leather, no horseshoes, no nails if we'd had shoes to put on the horses."

"You'll see stuff lying around like that for years. Ought to be plenty up on Stone River where they cut up Breckinridge's Orphan Brigade. That must have been some battle, from what I heard. Twenty-three thousand killed when Rosecrans crashed down on Bragg."

They fell silent as weariness and hunger took toll of their young bodies, bodies too long overstrained, underfed. At dusk they came to a dusty road and crossed it, climbing a rail fence on the opposite side.

"No troops came this way, wouldn't be a rail left. Down at Ringgold we tore down a man's crib to build cooking fires," King said. "And not enough to cook to pay for the trouble. This country is going to be uneasy for a long time. I'm for staying off the roads."

Jack spied an apple tree in bloom. "Must be a house yonder."

"Better reconnoiter," warned King. "These hill people might not be friendly. Half of these skinnies up here in the rocks and cedars sided with the Union."

"Never owned any Nigras. Had no interest in the war." Jack took off his faded cap and roughed a hand through his shaggy hair. "I heard a rooster. Wait till dark and maybe we could snag him."

"Come dark and we could be ten miles nearer home."

"Not with my feet, and my insides neither," declared Jack. "Not unless we find another creek where I can wash the fever out of my feet. When I left home I left four good pairs of shoes and some boots. Reckon they're still there if Miss Annie or Sue didn't give 'em away to the hands."

King thought unwillingly of the possibility that his mother and Jack's wife Sue had had no control over the disposing of his brother's shoes.

"We've got to remember the house may have been looted. Thomas was over there. Might even be burned to the ground."

Next morning, when they had slept briefly and painfully under a cedar thicket, Jack resumed his angry worry.

"You reckon Billy was really crazy enough to join up with the Union army?"

"If he did, he's a damn traitor, and if he got wounded I hope he didn't try to hide out at home," King swore. "It would be bad for the folks, and Ma would hide him, renegade or not. I never did understand that boy. He was raised like the rest of us and he's not much younger than me, but he's no more like us than a mule colt raised with a lot of blooded horses. He looks like the rest of us, more like you and me than Morgan ever did, but he never did think like anybody else in the family."

"He read too many books," said Jack. "Even when he didn't have a whisker to shave he'd start arguments, ranting around that Pa ought to free all the Nigras, that it was a sin to own another human being."

"Hell, the Nigras didn't want to be free. Been taken care of all their lives, nothing to worry about, fed and clothed and given houses to live in. And you know Pa, his hands never did wear themselves out working."

"They've got ham down at that house," sighed Jack. "I can smell it frying. If this was still war and we were still mounted infantry with arms, we wouldn't be hungry much longer. Just long enough to go down there and take it away from 'em. Look, boy, I've got to sit down a little. My legs won't go any further and my head feels queer."

"Lean against that tree and get your mind off ham," advised his brother. "We've still got a long way to go and they've likely got dogs down yonder at that house."

Jack sank obediently on the clean grass of the meadow. His face, King noted, was drained and gray, his emaciated body quivering.

"All this green stuff we've been eating has got my bowels all torn up," Jack grumbled. "Wish we could find a cow to milk. I don't reckon there's a cow left in the country now. What we didn't get the Yanks cleaned out after us. These folks around here aren't going to like anybody that wears a uniform. We've got to expect that."

King squatted on the other side of the tree. "Losers are never popular, no matter how good an excuse you've got for being licked. We ought to get home day after tomorrow if you can hold out to travel. Maybe Miss Annie will have a chicken left to put in the pot with some big fluffy dumplings." He leaned his back against the tree and felt the coolness of the green heart of it through the bark. A beetle ambled over the ground and scrutinized him with flat, opaque eyes, then went its stodgy way.

King let worry gnaw at him, wondering if he'd be able to get Jack home, if there would be anything left of home when they finally made it back. The place was set pretty well back in a hill cove off the beaten track, so both armies might have missed and ignored it. He didn't like the way Jack looked, drained green and bloodless by exhaustion, dysentery and hunger.

Jack was the oldest of the Marklands, married to Sue now for eight years and always he had been the toughest, the still, gritty one who broke the wildest colts, the one most dangerous in a fight because of some terrible relentlessness in him, a kind of tight-mouthed deadly thing. His only observable tenderness had been evidenced toward Sue, the fire-top girl he had married. Sue could lead Jack around with a silk thread, the other Marklands grumbled. Now King's only feeling for Jack was an anxious pity. He knew, uneasily aware of the trembling in his own legs, he had to get Jack home soon even if he had to carry him on his own back.

They had seen them on the road; haggard, ragged men in gray, lurching along, one stumbling under the burden of another, wounded, legless perhaps, drained white, half-dead. Sometimes they tottered along in pairs, clumsily holding up a third, often an older man or a boy. Men who had marched off jauntily in time to a drum, or ridden out of sight of home on a prancing horse, as the Marklands had set forth to war. How sickly, sadly, was everything lost! How sourly stank the rotting corpse of glory!

King Markland swore bitterly, beating the uncaring body of the tree with helpless fists. Behind him Jack did not stir. He had sunk into limp, sweating slumber, his mouth open and drooling a little, showing his shrunken gums, his yellowed teeth. King shuddered with involuntary revulsion. That flesh lying there, already wearing the look of deterioration, a carrion look, was his brother, Andrew Jackson Markland, who not long since had been one of the handsomest bucks along the Harpeth River. Deadly as his own pistol, fierce as a white-eyed stallion, a rich young man and staunchly proud. King gave a little moan, rolled over on his own shoulder and dropped off into exhausted sleep.

The foot that prodded him kicked hard. He jerked up, glaring, reaching for a weapon that was not there, dragged himself to his feet, bracing against the tree to scowl at the old man who stood over him, a shapeless straw hat pushed back on a head full of rough white hair.

"Who're you, soldier?" demanded the old man.

King got his breath, slapped sweat from his eyes, unclenched his fists.

"Markland, Lieutenant. Seventh Tennessee. Forrest's brigade. On my way home with a sick brother. Any objection to our taking a little rest on your land? I reckon it is your land?"

"Yeah, it's my land and I got no objection. Where you headed, soldier?"

"Up toward Harpeth Valley. Boone Markland's place. If my brother holds out. He's tramped and starved all the way from Alabama. We'll move on as soon as he gets rested. We're not armed."

The old man hitched up his shabby pants. "Have you seen a young feller out of Pope's army on the road anywheres? About nineteen year old, he was. My grandson. Maw and me raised him. Seen you draggin' up here, thought maybe it might be Herbie. Maw run straight out and wrung the head off a chicken."

"We've seen a thousand soldiers on the road." King softened his tone of defensive belligerence. "Old ones, young ones, sick, wounded, hungry all of 'em. All trying to get home like my brother and me."

"That man looks pretty sick." The old man came closer. "You wait here. I'll fetch the wagon. Still got a piece of a wagon and one mule. Hid him out in the woods or I wouldn't have no mule. You wait. Somebody's got to eat that chicken Maw's stewin' up yonder at the house. Could be Herbie got killed out yonder in Virginia. Two years now we ain't heard nary a word."

"There was mighty little chance to write letters and less chance to send them home." King tried to be reassuring. "Our folks don't know if we're still alive either. Or our younger brother that joined up later. If your boy was with Pope you're for the Union, Mister. My brother and I are Confederates. What do you want to bother with us for? There's no bounty on our heads. We gave our paroles, we're free men." King's voice rose a little, his face darkened.

The old man did not bridle or show offense. "You're men, ain't ye? Fellow humans in trouble. I never took no side in this war. All wrong, I figures, brothers fightin' each other, ruinin' the country all for a lot of Nigras, didn't care one way nor t'other. You wait here, I'll be back." He took a few steps, turned back. "Boone Markland? He's your daddy? I've heared of him. Used to own fine stud horses a while back. You ain't so far from home, boy. Not more'n a matter of thirty miles or so."

"What county is this?"

"Lincoln County, Tennessee. Sixty per cent for the Union. But you're safe, boy. We're decent folks in Lincoln. Don't hold with whippin' no enemy more'n once."

"A generous foe, eh? Our thanks, sir. You haven't told me your name."

"Name's Clark. Proud of it. You set. Set and rest. I'll be back."

He trudged down the slope and King tried to rouse his brother, succeeding at last in getting him into a limp, sitting posture, collapsed against the tree.

"You got to come out of it, fellow! We've been rescued." He slapped Jack gently with an open hand. "An old farmer is coming for you with a wagon and we're going to be fed, all because some little Yank in

Pope's army hasn't come home yet. And listen, Jack," he went on seriously as Jack showed signs of comprehension, "these old folks who want to help us are Union, so you mind your mouth and your manners."

"Some trick in it," mumbled Jack. "Bound to be."

"I don't believe it. The old fellow sounds decent and honest to me."

"Trick in it. Let's move on. Help me up."

With difficulty King got his brother to his feet. But almost instantly a sick, greenish pallor washed over Jack's face, his jaw dropped, he retched and his eyes rolled back and he toppled unconscious into King's arms. When the old man returned, driving a fat high-headed mule hitched to a light wagon, King had to lift Jack into the wagon bed.

"Got a little whisky at the house," said the man, Clark, clucking to the mule. "Know it's good, made it myself. Might perk him up some. How long since you boys et?"

"Gainesville, Alabama," King told him. "Since then only old acorns and sassafras leaves. Country picked clean and gardens not up yet. You're very obliging, Mr. Clark. I hope somebody along the road helps out your boy too."

They had gone off to war jaunty and insolent, sashed and plumed, to the thumping of defiant drums and the cheering of admiring neighbors.

They returned in darkness in the rattling little Yankee wagon, drawn by a snorting Yankee mule. It was three days before Andrew Jackson Markland roused enough to know that he had come home.

• *Two* •

Boone Markland was sixty years old and his boast was that he hadn't a creak in a joint or a gray hair in his head.

"Could have marched and fought as spry as any young feller, would they have had me," he boomed often. "Likely outlasted a lot of 'em. Got lost on a bear hunt one fall up on Cumberland, laid out three days and nights, nothing to eat but hickory nuts, found me a creek finally and walked eighteen miles home, totin' forty pounds of bear meat and my gun. Dogs had been home two days when I got there and my pappy and the hands were out beatin' the brush looking for my dead body."

"Nobody," drawled King from the couch where he had lain for two days, fluttered over by his mother, "was shooting at you, Pa. You didn't tramp in frozen mud for three days with no rations but a handful of moldy corn and a sliver of bacon with skippers in it. No chance to make a fire or lie down or dry your socks before they froze on your feet. After Franklin we marched like that. Men just gave up and dropped beside the road and died where they fell."

"Well, you got hauled home in a wagon," snorted Boone. "Reckon Morgan's making it on foot if he's making it at all. And all three of you left this place riding horses worth three hundred dollars apiece."

"Morgan still had a horse the last time I saw him. They shot Jack's horse and mine fell and broke both front legs."

"Didn't have proper shoes on him."

"Didn't have any shoes on him. About a hundred thousand men, I reckon, left home on good horses and there won't be five thousand ride 'em back. They shot the horses first if they could, or they hamstrung them with bayonets or sabers. Set a man in cavalry boots afoot and he's easy to run down and kill or capture." King rolled over and stuffed a pillow under one ear. Not that anything would deaden the resonance of Boone Markland's pontificating, especially when he stalked up and down a room making expansive gestures to the imminent peril of his wife's bric-a-brac.

"You reckon Jack's ever going to feel himself again?" he demanded now, taking a tall stance, his hands jammed into the pockets of his worn riding pants. "Big stout feller like he is, don't look right for him to be lying there being fed with a spoon."

"Of course he's going to be all right again," declared the boys' mother. She was as small and fleshless as Boone Markland was big and lusty. She was called Miss Annie by her husband and all the servants, and of late years her sons and daughter-in-law too had taken to calling her that. There had been a ribald joke passed around when Boone Markland married wispy little Annie Lou Breen. They said he would have to shake the sheet to find her, and Boone still liked to repeat that jest to his wife's impatient annoyance.

Miss Annie's hair was snow white though she was twelve years younger than her husband. She had a deceptive air of frailty. Never sick, she always wore the pallor of illness, and there were deep purple shadows under her great amber eyes.

"Miss Annie always reminds me of a doe deer," Morgan had once said. "Looks rickety on the legs and scared to death, but she can move like chain lightening and she ain't scared of nothing."

She appeared to be always weary and yet was never still. All her sons teased her unmercifully, lifting her small, light body in the air, setting her on a high mantel or in the crotch of a tree, leaving her there screaming furiously, but in matters of moment they obeyed her with amazing meekness.

Even Boone Markland, though he might roar protest, seldom went against a direct order from Miss Annie. His family knew that Boone never had a mare bred, sold a bushel of corn or changed his shirt without having her advice on the project. Pa was the big noise on the Markland place, but tiny Miss Annie, darting about like some gossamer-winged insect, was the boss.

"Jack," she stated now, whisking a bit of dust from a marble-topped table with her little white apron, "is going to lie right there in that bed till he feels like getting up. And any other of my boys that comes home all wore out and sick from this fool war is going to do the same."

King Markland looked quickly at his father, saw Boone's face darken, saw him as quickly look away. Not a word had been said, but King knew by what was not spoken that Billy, the third Markland son, had gone for the Union. He had had no chance to ask questions because somehow Miss Annie was always on hand to change the subject swiftly and obviously. I'll get Pa or Sue alone, or one of the Nigras, and find out, King determined. But for the present, fed and relaxed, he was content to try to sleep.

Sleep did not come easily since his mind was so full of questions that had, so far, no answers. The house still stood although it had a slightly shabby, neglected look. The grass grew long and ragged in the yard, the shrubbery was overgrown and untended. The stables were there but there was a deserted air about them. He had been too exhausted to explore, too numbed by weariness to make inquiry, but he heard no young colts whinny, no stallion scream, and Ranse, the old horse trainer and stable hand had not appeared, dusty cap in hand, as of old.

"They get all our horses, Miss Annie?" he had asked once and Miss Annie's answer had been a cool cloth laid over his eyes.

"You rest now, Kingman, and don't you worry about a thing. We're going to get along all right now you boys have come home."

Things must be bad, they were all so stubborn about being optimistic, he decided as he burrowed in the pillow. The sun was hot outside, the heavy fragrance of honeysuckle drifted in at the open window. His mother had seated herself at his side with a fly whisk of shredded newspaper tied to a stick.

"Sue's sitting by Jack," she said. "You sleep now and I'll keep the bugs off you. They're worse this summer than I've ever seen them. All kinds of flies, and rats too. Your father says it's so many dead bodies lying all over the country that draws them, but I won't let myself think about something so horrible. It's bad enough to think about boys being killed without letting your mind go wandering on in such a ghoulish fashion." The fly brush stopped in mid-air and, turning his head, King saw his mother's face change and crumple a little, her eyes dim behind her steel-rimmed glasses. "Kingman, you reckon Little Brother is dead?"

She meant Morgan, the last-born, her baby. Spoiled outrageously, Morgan, who had inherited the reckless Markland courage, all the arrogance and belligerence of the clan, had early demonstrated brash young scorn for many of the principles of honor, trustworthiness, generosity and forbearance that went with it.

He said, choosing his words carefully, "I've got no right to think he's dead, Miss Annie, because I don't know. He was riding with Forrest when Thomas chased us back to Alabama, but that was a good while back. We never did know what month or day it was, all the days ran together, some bad, some fairly quiet when we got to draw our breath and clean up our equipment. He could have been killed a hundred yards from me when we were moving so fast and I'd never know unless some trooper rode ahead to tell me, and nobody did. I won't believe he's gone for a good while anyway. It's slow business getting home. I was scared Jack was going to die on me before we made it back. He would have died if that old man from down in Lincoln hadn't helped us out. He was a good old chap, even if he was Union."

"There are a lot that are Union around here now, people who kept mighty quiet when Bragg and Hood and all the rest were up here in this country."

"Now they'll be top dog and make it hard on all the rest of us," King said bitterly. But now, although opportunity offered, he could not bring himself to ask about Billy. William Breen Markland, the odd one, named for their Irish grandfather, and like that taciturn, obdurate old man always a nonconformist, an objector, full of booklore, aloof and stiffened with stubborn opinions.

Miss Annie would still defend this third son of hers, he knew, just as she had always defended Billy when King and Jack picked on him. Just as she had always supplied reasonable motives for actions that the

Markland sons, and Boone, their father, had raged at as unreasonable. When Billy deserted the family table to eat from a tin pan in the yard with the stable boy, Buzzy, Miss Annie insisted it was a gentlemanly, charitable gesture. Hadn't Buzzy and Billy been born on the same day, with Mammy Dory so distracted over two births occurring on the place at once that she hardly knew which came into the world first, Miss Annie's child or her own caramel-colored grandson.

Buzzy had been born light-skinned, and because of this Big Bob, young Rinda's coal-black husband, had beaten his wife half to death and run away. When he was caught trying to ride a barge down river to Kentucky, Boone Markland had sold Big Bob south, the only Negro ever sold off the place. But Buzzy stayed, riding the two-year-old bareback behind Billy, leaving any task to go off fishing with Billy.

"Worthless yellow scoundrel!" Boone Markland stormed. "I should have sold him too."

"You leave Buzzy alone. He can churn butter quicker than anybody," ordered Miss Annie.

So Buzzy was left alone to grow up, his submissiveness owned by Billy and by no one else. Now nobody, not even Billy, could own Buzzy, King was thinking. Abraham Lincoln had seen to that.

"What became of Buzzy?" he asked his mother.

"He ran off," she said, her face changing again like a soft flower closing, her lips graying and straight. "So did Ranse and Ivy and Phoebus. Ranse made off with one of your father's mules and a good Democrat wagon, and Ivy stole every pot and pan and blanket out of their cabin. Ungrateful creatures, after all we'd done for them. I hope they starve to death."

"The Yanks had some Nigras in their army. They garrisoned places with them after they'd taken them away from us. George Litchfield saw two of his father's hands down there at Shiloh. They slipped across the lines at night and begged George for money and tobacco."

"I hope he shot both of them," snapped his mother, her mouth like a trap.

"You know you don't hope any such thing, Miss Annie. If Buzzy walked in here right now all dressed up in Union blue you'd start yelling at Minerva to feed him."

"Well, I'd give him a good talking to first," declared Miss Annie, flicking viciously at a meandering fly. She would not, never, if she died of her own repression, put into words or even into coherent thought her own instinctive feeling about Buzzy. But she had never been able to look at the butter-light, big-eyed little slave without seeing a trick of expression or movement too like her own children's. Now she said meditatively, fanning more slowly, "I disciplined my head and my heart when you all went off to war—"

All, thought King. So Billy did go. But she won't talk about it.

"I said I was no better than thousands of women," she went on, "and if it so be that any of you had to be sacrificed I could bear it. And I have. But it was a glorious day when I saw that little old wagon rolling in, and I hope that poor old man's grandson comes back. I wish all the boys could come back, mistaken and wrongheaded or not. Now"—she jumped up, letting the fly brush fall—"I'm going to fix you a good eggnog and I'll talk your father into letting me put a little authority in it. We've still got a cow though your poor pa about wore his legs off hiding her up in the coves. And we've got a few hens but no rooster. He crowed so much so we had to eat him. We had them hid in Ivy's house with hay piled over the windows but nobody bothered us except some cavalry scouts now and then hunting horses."

"Pa gave that big bay to Nate Forrest. We saw him riding him down at Johnsonville."

"Your father would have given anything he owned to General Forrest, I reckon, after all you boys went fighting with him. He might have given me away but the troopers that came by never gave me a good look, though I fed them every biscuit and crumb of corn bread on the place. Sue was the one they made eyes at."

"The boys were that homesick they'd make eyes at anything young and good looking," King said. "Most of them had left girls or young wives at home."

"Then they should have been thinking that other soldiers might be making eyes at their women," snapped Miss Annie.

"Soldiers didn't think. We took it one day at a time, an hour at a time, or otherwise we couldn't have endured it," King sighed. He had always known how to droop his eyelids and sigh and get around his mother. Boone Markland had kept a few private reservations about his second son, suspecting King of being a sly dog and a rascal around women, but a few lurid memories of his own past had kept Boone from being vocal about it, although he did remark on occasion that King was too damn handsome and plausible for his own good and prophesied dubiously that ultimately King's career would be ended by a bullet from some aggrieved and enraged husband or lover.

They were all handsome, that was the trouble. They wore their dark masculine beauty, their tall slenderness, their imperious manner like glittering chain mail. They were insolent and jaunty and afraid of nothing. Even Jack, who had settled down at last, to his father's vast relief, had refused to be daunted by responsibility. Now here was Jack's son, called Boone-boy, seven years old and growing up as black-eyed, as sardonic and reckless as his father and his uncles.

Though he would not have known how to put this thought into words, there were times when Boone Markland felt like a rough old lion who had whelped a pride of black panthers.

He came striding into the room now brandishing a half-empty bottle like a weapon. "Know what this is?" he demanded loudly. "It's about the last bit of good liquor on this place!"

"Not the very last bit, Pa," soothed King. "I'm betting on that."

"Well, there's mighty little left, I can tell you. Miss Annie says she has got to have some so you boys can get your strength back and you know your mother. When she sets her head for anything she gets her way. She set her head she was going to marry me and by God, she did it! Me, a grown man thirty years old and her a little flippity bit no bigger'n a hummingbird and just as hard to catch and hold on to. There were a lot of surprised people in Dickson County when I set Annie Lou Breen up on a fine black mare and rode off with her, but not one of 'em was any more surprised than I was." Boone grinned, twisting his mouth so that his black beard swished across his front, went to the door and shouted, "Here's your poison, Miss Annie. See you be stingy with it."

"Stingy," repeated a scornful voice beyond the door. "And when did you ever stint yourself on whisky, Boone Markland?" A small brown hand reached for the bottle, and Boone came back and surprisingly dropped into a chair.

King sat up attentively. His father sat so rarely, his great body was so seldom quiet that when it did happen it usually portended something or other. A silence stretched a little until King grew restless and moved to break it.

"Sir?" he said, as though Boone had spoken.

Boone cleared his throat harshly. "I reckon you know what has happened to the country?" he said.

King rose and walked to the fireplace, leaning an elbow on the mantel. His legs still felt weak and shaky, his heart wanted to skitter and thump in his breast, but he kept his voice steady.

"We knew that Lincoln was shot before the surrender. What happens now?"

"Andy Johnson is now President of the United States. Before that he was military governor of Tennessee. Put there by the Washington radicals and the scurvy tribe who call themselves Union Democrats. He was a sorry governor and he'll be a sorry president. He'll try to please everybody and be an honest man, and there's nobody so helpless among a lot of radical scalawags and scoundrels like that gang who tried to run Lincoln as an honest man. They'll throw him out before he's been up there a year. Some of those black Republican senators and cabinet members will try personally to throw poor old Andy out, just because he don't want the South persecuted. But that's all far away. What's here and now is this poisonous rattlesnake of a psalm-singing old devil we've got for governor of Tennessee, William Gannaway Brownlow!"

"So he's back. I thought they had him in jail some place."

"Had him in jail, our people did. Found it made a goddam martyr out of him so they took him out and sent him up north through the lines. Yanks made a hero out of him, then they got sick of his virulent raving, so now we've got him back. Yanks won't have him, and if he died the devil wouldn't have him, so looks like we've got Brownlow for good."

"Some fellow got into our outfit told me he saw Brownlow shoot a wounded boy on the ground, up in East Tennessee. Said his brother vowed he'd kill Brownlow if he ever got near enough."

"He might get near enough but if he's like the rest of us he won't have any weapon when he gets there," growled Boone. "Already they're sending snoopers around to seize every pistol and rifle in the state from our folks that stood for the Confederacy. Before you got home I wrapped up both my pistols and my squirrel and bear guns in muslin and tallow and hollowed out a cotton bale and put 'em inside."

"What if they take the cotton? They could do that. Call it contraband. They're doing it down in Alabama. Taking it for taxes or something."

"Not this bale. It's in the bottom of that old dry cistern out by the cow barn, old straw and stalks dumped in on top of it. It's an old bale—haven't raised any cotton in three years. No hands to pick it. They all wandered off. Glad to get shut of 'em, furnishing 'em, keeping up their houses, always wanting more meal and more meat than what cotton they raised was worth." Boone took out a brown twist of tobacco, whittled off a hunk and eased it into his jaw. "What do you figure to do now, boy?" he asked abruptly.

"What can I do?" parried King. "Not much left here, or so I gather from what Miss Annie's let slip. And is she ever a close-mouthed woman!"

[21]

"I trained her. Trained her good. And when you've got a woman trained to hold her tongue you've done something."

"No horses to break and train?"

"Three colts. Scrubs. Before the war I'd have given 'em away to the hands," snorted Boone. "Not quite three-year-olds. No looks and not much brains. You can do something even with a scrub if he's got brains but these three ain't got the spirit of a woodchuck between 'em."

"Gelded?" asked King.

"All but one. His color's fair. Good bay. I had hopes he'd make something worth keeping, but he won't. Won't fight anything. Boone-boy can ride him. A banty rooster could lick him. Remember how old Duke used to stand on his hind legs and fight the air and bugle so you could hear him halfway to Nashville? This colt's out of Duke but he's meek as Miss Annie."

"And how meek is Miss Annie?" chirped his wife, twisting through the door, a pitcher in one hand, a mug in the other. "Not so meek, Mr. Markland, as you'll discover if you spit on my clean hearth. Take that filthy tobacco out to the barn where it belongs."

Boone rose obediently. "Better drink that pap, King, or she'll hold your nose and pour it down your goozle. And where is my bottle, Madam Spit-in-the-Fire? From the sparks in your eyes you've drunk the rest of it."

"It's in the buttery and there it stays. Jack needs some of this same treatment, and there's just one good dram left." She set the mug down and filled it daintily, and as he had often done, King marveled at the delicacy of his mother's tiny fleshless hands. They moved like the frail amber sticks of a lace fan or the fragile antennae of a butterfly, but move they did and almost too fast for the eye to follow.

Boone gave a barking laugh as he went toward the door. "If a man could breed a colt out of Miss Annie, now," he brayed, "Lord what an animal he would have."

She made a fist no bigger than a walnut and shook it at him. "Be-gone, you low-minded creature you!" she ordered. "Take your vulgar jokes out to the manure pit. They'll be at home there."

Kingman Pryor Markland drank all the creamy eggnog and felt the warmth of it flow through his dried-out veins and aching muscles. Miss Annie, he was certain, had put a doughty nip of brandy into it. Presently he fell asleep.

· *Three* ·

SUE MARKLAND WRAPPED A CRISP BROWN CORN PONE IN A CLEAN TEA towel, blew out the kitchen lamp and let herself quietly out the back door. The steps down from the narrow porch were high and steep, and she sidled down cautiously, reaching for the cistern at the bottom, picking her way gingerly over the uneven rock paving around the pump.

Then the door behind her opened and she stood dead still, drawing back into the shadow of the grape arbor, patting a foot impatiently as a small voice piped in the darkness.

"Ma—ma!"

Sue stumbled swiftly back to the steps. "Boone-boy, you go straight back to bed, you hear?" She gave her small son a push. "Out here in your nightshirt and your bare feet!"

"Where you going, Mama? What you got in that bundle?"

"I'm going to see poor old Mammy Dory. She's sick and I'm taking her some supper. You scoot now! Get straight back upstairs and don't you wake up Grampa or your papa."

"Papa don't wake up. He just lies there all the time," whined Boone-boy.

"Papa's sick. He's sick from the bad old war. Go along now, son, before Mama has to slap you."

"I want to see Mammy Dory. I want her to conjure off my wart."

"Mammy Dory's too sick to worry with your wart. You might catch what ails her." Mammy Dory was dying of being ninety odd years old and worn out and ready for death, but Sue was desperately indifferent to the truth. "You want to swell all up and have to lie in bed like Mammy Dory? Hurry back to bed, now."

Slowly Boone-boy backed up the steps, opened the door into the dark kitchen. Then he skittered out again.

"Mama, you come with me. I'm scared."

"You weren't too scared to come down here. You get gone this minute or I'll come up there and spank you good."

"I'll yell and wake up Grampa. He won't let you spank me," the child threatened impudently.

[23]

"You won't yell because you'll have a dishrag in your mouth like last time, remember? I'm breaking a switch off this bush right now. Hear it crack? All right, scamper. There's a light up in the hall."

He fled then and she waited for a moment under the swarming vine till the rear of the house returned to dark silence. Then she ran, light and fast, down the soft sandy path under the dark trees, past the smokehouse and the empty loom house, across the trodden area where the butchering was always done and where a fetid odor still lingered. Now the path widened until it was almost a street, between two facing rows of whitewashed cabins. All but two were dark. From these, dull, murky light seeped between the cracks of the wooden shutters.

Sue tapped at the door of one lighted house, calling, "It's me, Mammy Dory."

The food would have to be divided and Mammy Dory given a share in case Boone-boy tattled and Minerva contradicted his tale of Mammy Dory being fed late at night. Sue broke the bread in two, left half on the doorstep, carefully wrapped, pushed open the rough plank door and went in.

The air in the dim room was so thick that she choked involuntarily, then gave a startled exclamation. The old Negress was a swollen lump in the disordered bed, her round black face, sunk in a soiled pillow, so puffed and distorted that her small, piggish eyes were lost in it, except for tiny gleams that focused on a man who sat by the hearth. A yellow man, not tall, who wore the uniform of the Federal army and who got to his feet and removed his cap as Sue entered.

"Buzzy!" she gasped. "Buzzy—you've come back!"

Mammy Dory chortled. "Mah grandson, he come back. Big soldier now, got him a gun an' everything!"

"I brung Cap'n Billy's horse, Miss Sue," said Buzzy. "I got it here along with one I stole 'way over the mountain. Old Reb thought he had it hid but I found it easy. Where-at is he, Miss Sue?"

Canny suspicion stiffened Sue's chin. This was Buzzy who had been born on the place but this also was the enemy. His uniform was new.

"He's hid out," she evaded. "You'd better not stay around here, Buzzy. Pa Markland or one of the boys might shoot you."

"Marse Billy in Ranse' ole house," squawked Mammy Dory. "Ole dog he smell out Marse Billy mighty quick."

"You stay away from him, Buzzy!" ordered Sue desperately. "He's not going riding off with you. Not till that knee gets well."

Buzzy shrugged, and buttoned his coat. He spoke gently.

"You let him say, Miss Sue. You let the Cap'n say what all he want to do."

"He can't do anything, I tell you. His knee is still sore and lame from that bullet they took out after the battle of Five Forks. He ought not to bear his weight on that leg at all," she argued.

"He done rode all the way back from Virginny," insisted Buzzy. "It ain't till we crossed the mountain over by Murfreesboro that it got to hurt him so bad he ain't able to stay in the saddle. I brung him in a wagon from there."

"*You* brought him?"

"Yes'm. He made me set him down up yonder by the back gate and go back after his horse. You let me talk to the Cap'n, Miss Sue."

"You let me talk to him first. Mammy Dory, here's a piece of bread."

"Didn't bring no coffee?" the old woman complained.

"There isn't any coffee. You know that."

"Kingdom done come, ought to fetch us a little coffee."

"You wait, Buzzy," Sue ordered. "You wait here till I talk to him."

"Yes'm." He sat back on a stool, very erect, put on his cap again, fingering all the brass on it.

The varmint, the little yellow mongrel! fumed Sue, as she hurried out of the house and flew down the path. Everybody on the place knows that Buzzy's Pa Markland's by-blow, although none of the proud, uppity Marklands would ever admit it.

The cabin at the far end of the line was dark and still, the door closed. Sue crept close to the door and scratched on the panel.

"Billy," she whispered. "It's Sue. Let me in."

There was a fumbling, cautious movement within and the door opened a little way, letting out an ancient Negroid smell, mingled with the sweaty, horsy odor of an unwashed white male.

"They'll hear you. They'll listen," warned a voice from the blackness within. "Get inside. I can't make a light."

"They won't tell. They know you're here, Mammy Dory and 'Nerva too. 'Nerva brought me your message." Sue slipped inside and the door was shut and barred again. "Billy, Buzzy's up there at Mammy Dory's house. He wants to talk to you but I made him let me come first."

"Buzzy!" she heard the creak as William Markland sank back on the cot. "Buzzy never fails. From First Manassas to Appomattox, he never failed me. When I needed Buzzy he was there. Did he bring my horse?"

"He said he brought it. Billy, he's all dressed up in a new blue uniform. A Yankee uniform."

"He signed up back in April. He's been an enlisted man ever since. Now he's detailed with me to be garrisoned here in this county."

She put the bread into his hand. He muttered, "Thanks, Sue," and she heard his teeth crunch into the crusty pone. "Good," he said, then, "Good old 'Nerva!"

Tears sprang into her eyes, stinging there. There was a hard, cold cramp at her throat. Something so wistful and undefended about a hungry man. She still could not endure hearing from Jack or King about those starving times after the surrender.

She said, "Billy, you can't go off with Buzzy. You might ruin that leg forever. You stay quiet here and let me try to talk to them up at the house."

He laughed low, without mirth. "Don't you know I have no choice, Sue? I'm an officer in the army. I go where I'm ordered. I shouldn't have come here at all. It was just an urge I had, not very sensible, probably. Now I have to go."

"If your leg gets infected they'll cut it off in some miserable army hospital. How did you ever get down here, Billy? Buzzy says he put you out of the wagon way up yonder at the back gate."

"Crawled," he said simply. "You wouldn't understand, Sue. After I heard that Thomas and Hood had been through here I had to know what had happened at home. I knew I wouldn't be welcome at the house. I knew Pa would likely turn me out and that if King came back alive he'd probably shoot me. He'd believe he was defending the family honor. You couldn't get me a little whisky, could you? If I had a dram it might ease this pain a little so I could sleep."

Sue sat down beside him, the cot sagging and groaning under the added weight.

"You know your father, Billy, how he keeps everything locked up. Miss Annie had to get mighty fussy to get a little dole for the boys, and he knows they have to get their strength back. Jack's had dysentery so long he's just a skeleton, all sores, and King not much better. They say Forrest fed them as long as he could capture supplies from the Yankees, but even the Yankees ran out because so many of their wagons were burned. So they had slim rations most all the last part of the winter. You let me go to the house and tell Miss Annie you're out here, Billy. You know your mother would never turn you out no matter who you fought for. They're bound to find out now that Buzzy's come back."

"They'll find out. They'll find out the Union has taken control. They'll hate my guts the way things will be from now on," he said.

"Why did you go for the Union, Billy?" she asked suddenly. "I never have understood at all."

"Because they were right! Because the Confederates, God help them, even my own family, were deluded by high-sounding words and explosions of their own touchy pride. Pride and arrogance never won a war, not without steel and ships, money and men behind it. Look at Napoleon."

"Who was he?" asked Sue naïvely.

"He was the Emperor of France, my dear ignorant little sister. And he thought he could whip the world. The South wasted everything— their fine young men, thousands and thousands of them, and their good horses. They gave their country over to ruin. This had to be one country, Sue, it had to be! One and indivisible. I saw it that way. I fought for it and we won."

"Why did you say God help your family, Billy?" she inquired anxiously. "The war's over. Morgan hasn't come back, but he will. I know he will."

"I saw the war, what it would be," he said solemnly. "Now I can see the peace. Except that it won't be a peace, it will be an ugliness and a vengefulness, especially with Brownlow up there at Nashville. He'd have every Confederate officer arrested for treason and hung if he dared. He'd burn every Confederate house in Tennessee. That's why I had to come home—crawl home. Somehow you've got to warn them, Sue. Warn the boys and Pa to keep quiet and swallow any humiliation, any insult, without resentment."

"That's why you came home?" she asked doubtfully.

"That's why I came home," he repeated bitterly.

"And are you going to cling to this stubborn idea not to let your family know you're on the place? Personally," she almost cried, "I think it's wicked and stupid."

He laid a comforting arm over her shoulder. She pulled away a little impatiently and let the arm fall.

"You think that now, Sue," he said, "but later you'll be glad I didn't antagonize the Marklands by a premature appearance. That I didn't lean on pity for a poor wounded boy who foolishly stood for the wrong principles, disgracing the passionately Southern Markland family in the eyes of their neighbors. I don't want pity and I don't want forgiveness. What I have to have is respect, confidence and co-operation, not resentment, if the Marklands are to save anything at all."

Sue shivered. "You sound so ominous. I suppose you are reminding me that you are the conquerors," she said acidly.

"I don't need to remind you. You know we won and it's going to be a bad time for dedicated Confederates who are still full of poisonous bitterness. It may be a lot worse unless you can educate those valiant hotheads up there in the house to be tolerant and to accept things as they are."

"If you think I can make any of them love the Yankees, and knuckle under to people like Buzzy, you're wrong! I couldn't do it, ever."

"But you can try. I admire you, Sue. You've got more courage than any male Markland, and good sense too when you want to use it. You were the only one I dared let know I'd come back because I knew I could depend on you to use your head."

He got to his feet with difficulty, bracing with one hand against the whitewashed wall. The whitewash scaled off and drifted down in dusty snow, sifting up his sleeve, and he shook his arm to be rid of it, tottering a little as the pain in his knee stabbed at him. Sue jumped to steady him and cried in a protesting whimper, "You see, Billy. You can't go!"

He lurched away toward the door. "I have to go. Remember what I've told you, Sue. Do your best. I don't want to see the Marklands having to refugee to Texas any more than you do." He opened the door then and said, low, "Come in, Buzzy."

"You can't take him, Buzzy!" cried Sue. "He's not fit to go."

William Markland's voice snapped with authority. "Corporal Markland, fetch my horse and report here, mounted, in three minutes!"

"Yes suh, Cap'n suh." Buzzy snapped a salute and marched out.

"How dare he take that name?" demanded Sue, as Buzzy closed the door. "How dare he—the impudent little buzzard?"

"Because it's his name. The only name he owns," said William. "Ever think how it would be, my girl, not even to own a name? Buzzy is loyal to me and smart. He'll take care of me. He'll take care of all the Marklands so far as he is permitted to do it."

"We don't need to be taken care of by yellow trash!" she exploded. "Marklands can take care of themselves."

He was fumbling into a coat, propped against the wall. "Maybe I've failed, Sue. I thought I could make you see the danger, the hopelessness. Don't take that belligerent attitude if Buzzy should come back here some day with a squad of Union troops. You could find yourself in that jail up in town and it's a dreary place to be."

"They wouldn't dare!" She was growing shrill.

"They would dare. And worse could happen. Oh, God, can't I make you understand? Maybe I could have talked to Pa. No, he'd just fly off the handle and never understand either. He'd probably try to horse-whip me and then they'd take him and everything he has left. I've tried my best but I'm afraid it wasn't any use. Goodbye, Sue."

She did not look up nor answer. There was the soft sound of hoofs outside on the sandy track, she heard the door open and softly close. She smelled trees and the fresh warm air of summer, knew that William was riding away, but she did not stir till the last faint beat of hoof and jingle of stirrup had died across the fields. Then she rose, carefully closed the door and went stumbling back along the path. She locked the kitchen door behind her as she went into the house and then, as a kind of panic seized her, closed and locked a window that had been left open. She was making the fastening secure when a light flickered over her and starting she wheeled to see King standing there in the door-way, a scrap of candle in his hand.

"What goes on?" he drawled, looking her over, his dark sardonic brows tilted.

Inspiration came swiftly, so ready that it surprised her.

"Yankees!" she gasped. "Yankee soldiers! I went down to Mammy Dory's cabin and a soldier came in. There was another one around too."

King grinned dryly. "Buzzy, of course? And who was this other soldier?"

"It was dark. I couldn't see," she stammered. "You knew about Buzzy being in the army?"

"I heard he'd been up in town for days. And where did you have Brother William hid?" He put the candle down and perched on the corner of the table. He was still very thin and his big dark eyes glittered out of caverns under the insolent Markland brows. "Where did they go? What did they tell you?" he demanded.

"They told me," she flung at him, knowing her deception had failed, "that you and Jack and your father too, could be hanged if you lay a hand on a Union soldier."

"After four long years, these pleasant tidings? No 'Give my love to mother'? No brokenhearted words about the old home fireside and the vacant chair? Callous, wasn't he?"

"Shut up!" she cried angrily. "You're all madmen, you Marklands. You all think you are God."

He sighed sardonically, and the sigh blew out the wan, dying flame of the candle.

• *Four* •

WILLIAM BREEN MARKLAND WAS TEN YEARS OLD WHEN THE SICKENING
bewilderment began to torment him. The occasion had been an accident, the result a shock, because nothing in William's brief education had prepared his young mind for such a problem.

Vaguely, like every other boy reared on a farm, he had known that
there were two sexes. He knew about stallions and roosters although
Miss Annie had erected a wall of protection about her sons as best
she could, out of the fabric of her own modesty and fastidiousness.

William knew too that Negroes did things that white people disdained to do. He was continually having to yell at Buzzy, his devoted
shadow, for vulgarities and breaches of decency that would outrage his
mother.

"Miss Annie have a duck fit, you go in her kitchen with that hole in
your breeches." William always talked like the field hands when he was
with Buzzy and that offended his mother too, when he lapsed into
Negro speech in her hearing.

"Speak like a gentleman, act like a gentleman and Buzzy will learn
good manners from you," she scolded.

"And stay out of Rinda's house," barked Boone Markland. "Even if
the people are our servants they're entitled to some privacy."

"He sleeps on her bed," tattled King, who was twelve then and of all
people the most obnoxious to William. "He and Buzzy, dirty as hogs,
both lying there sound asleep. I saw 'em."

William gave his brother a deadly look that King loftily ignored. He
turned the same glare of malevolence upon Jack when the older
brother put in a scornful remark. "He'll be bringing bedbugs home
next."

"Rinda's house is kept clean and free from vermin, I assure you,"
said his mother stiffly. "I see to that. What I'm trying to teach you all
is that we should try to improve and elevate the standards of our
people, not descend to their level."

William slid out of the house as soon as he could. All his brief life
he had been an introspective little boy, keeping his thoughts and his

bewilderments to himself except such few as he confided to Buzzy. His older brothers had early amalgamated themselves into a team, ignoring and scorning him except when they heckled and tormented him. Young Morgan, whom his mother called Little Brother, had been all his six years a house baby, a "titty baby" as Buzzy disdained the youngest Markland. Almost as tall as William, Morgan was still in dresses, the long-waisted, kilt-skirted affairs with which the masculinity of small boys was offended in those times.

When Morgan tried to tag after William and Buzzy he was always yelled at, ordered back, pelted with small sticks and pebbles till he ran, wailing, to his mother. Morgan wore little white starched collars and white stockings.

"You git dirty, Titty Baby," Buzzy would warn shrilly, "and Miss Annie lick all of us."

So William went his aloof, secret and indifferent way, defying parental taboos and injunctions because Buzzy minded nobody and he had to be as good a man as Buzzy. The one door of Rinda's house was visible from the kitchen and Mammy Dory, who bossed the house and kitchen and every one black and white in it save his mother, was a blabber and a watcher, with a flat maroon eye that missed nothing that went on on the place, and a liver-lipped mouth that instantly reported it. So William and Buzzy escaped surveillance by sliding in at the back window of Rinda's house, landing in a giggling heap on Rinda's bed. On this fateful day Rinda screamed at them and snatched up a green dress spread out on the fraying quilt.

"Y'all git your black foots off my bed!" she yelled. "Git on out o' here. You too, Mist' Billy!"

"That her silk dress." Buzzy apologized for his mother after they had scuttered out and reached the second crotch of the big pear tree. "She bust anybody that touch that dress. It silk."

"Niggers got no silk dresses," argued William. "They got linsey stuff like Sheba, she weave down yonder to the loom house."

"My mammy got a silk dress," insisted Buzzy.

"She steal it, I bet."

"She never! Boss Boone fetch that dress from Nashville, all the way from Nashville in a big poke. You ask my mammy. She tell you true," stormed Buzzy.

"She tell big a lie as you." William slid down the tree and ran very fast back to the house.

It was with difficulty that he got his mother alone. Morgan was always sidling around listening and Mammy Dory, young Minerva the housemaid, or Katsy who made beds and ironed seemed to be forever popping in. But after hanging around most of the afternoon William finally cornered Miss Annie in the linen press where she was looking over the tablecloths that needed darning.

"Mama," he began in a hoarse whisper, "Rinda stole your good silk dress."

Miss Annie laid down her thimble. She had a threaded needle between her teeth and almost she swallowed it.

"How do you know, Billy? What good silk dress?"

"Your nice green silk dress," he persisted. "I saw it."

"But I don't have any green silk dress. I never had a green silk dress, Billy." Her eyes were still wide, but a strange look had come over her face, a taut, apprehensive, frozen look. "What were you doing in Rinda's house? Your father forbade you to go there, just today."

"I saw it," he persisted. "Buzzy told a lie. He said my pa fetched that green silk dress from Nashville. He told a lie." He was vehement, almost in tears.

As too often happened, Annie Lou Markland's stony white anger, the anguished fury that she must repress where Boone Markland was concerned because she was a lady and superior, turned upon her son.

"How often have I told you not to carry tales about the people?" she demanded, shriveling the little boy with the chill lightning of her eyes. "You are not to tattle and you are not to listen, you hear? And if I catch you going into that woman's house again I shall tell your father. Do you want a good whipping with his riding whip? Well, that's what you'll get, sir, if I hear any more backyard gossip from you."

He slunk away then, confused, angry and in torment. Almost he collided head on with Katsy in the hall.

"Get out of my way, nigger!" he shouted at her, ducking around to run very fast out of the house by way of the front door.

It was not long after that, crouched high in the china tree, William heard two black women gossiping over the washtubs that stood below in the shade. Katsy and the lank woman called Pudge, who was married to a stable hand, were sousing clothes up and down in water, scrubbing them with their bony, purplish knuckles.

"Miss Annie, she do right she run that Rinda off the place," Katsy voiced her opinion. "Boss Boone sell Big Bob south, he'd ought to sold Rinda too."

"Boss Boone ain't goin' to do that, for sure," stated Pudge. "He ain't goin' to sell no cow gives good milk, Boss Boone ain't. Miss Annie, she know, she don't say nothin'. Miss Annie hold her haid high. She a lady."

"She bound to know," argued Katsy. "If she look good at that Buzzy, she bound to know who his daddy is."

"Look mo' like Boss Boone than Mist' Billy do."

"Heh!" giggled Katsy. "Look mo' like Mist' Billy than Mist' Billy do, hisself. If them two ain't blood brothers none was ever born."

William stayed, rigid and cramped and miserable in the tree, till his knobby knees ached and ants crawled all over him. When the women left at last he eased himself down silently, avoiding Katsy and Pudge who were hanging clothes on a line and draping some on the gooseberry bushes, and ran away like a creature possessed.

He ran all the way down the lane where yellow dock grew tall and big furry mulleins lifted their woolly heads of bloom. At the plank gate he shinnied up and perched on the top board, then scrambled quickly down again and stood staring fearfully through the bars. Beyond the gate was a pasture and there old Baron, the stallion, was turned out alone, the meanest and handsomest horse on the place. Even his father approached Baron with wary respect and a stout quirt.

The moment he spied the boy the stallion came leaping toward the gate, his head and tail high, his great golden, glassy eyes flashing. He charged at the gate and William backed away fearfully, falling and landing painfully on his skinny rump.

"You git away!" he shrilled at the horse, who was showing what looked like a hundred long, yellow teeth and, between squeals, taking bites out of a gatepost. "You git away, you ole mean horse you." William's roar was a shaky soprano imitation of Boone Markland. "You git away before I peel the hide off you."

He heard a yelp of laughter behind him then, scrambled up and whirled angrily, expecting to confront King, the mocker. But it was Buzzy lying there in the short grass and sweet clover, laughing and rolling over, pulling up sorrel and stuffing it into his mouth. Rage ran hot over William's small body. He was tall for ten then, but he had little meat on him. He would be tall all his days but there would never be an ounce of fat on his slim frame.

He charged at Buzzy, all the confusion and shame and hate in him boiling up till his head and chest fairly bubbled with it.

"You git gone too!" he shouted. "Git away from here. Git out of my lane, you hear?"

Buzzy only laughed louder, spitting out the green leaves, sitting up and clasping his thin, oaken knobs of knees.

"Whyn't you git over that gate and ride ole Baron? Whyn't you let him chaw a hunk out o' your backside? Li'l white boy backside taste good to ole Baron. He hongry," he taunted.

William flung himself upon the darker boy, pummeling him with furious fists.

"You shut you dirty liver-lip mouth, you!" he sobbed, as they rolled and tussled, Buzzy deftly squirming away from the blows, trying to hold William's wrists, cannily and instinctively refraining from striking a white boy.

"You Billy, you quit! You let me up!" he panted. "You gone crazy, you li'l white fool? You want Boss Boone to lick both of us? You want Miss Annie to sell me clear down to Alabammy? Git off me, boy. Quit that blubberin'. Big white boy blubber like a calf!" Buzzy rolled free, jerked loose and staggered up, smacking weed seed out of his shorn, almost-straight hair. "You gone plumb crazy, White Boy?" he finished scornfully. "You gone plumb teetotal crazy!"

William stumbled up, scrubbing his hot wet face with a torn sleeve. Tragedy was in his small dark face, in the black eyes, deep and liquid under proud arched brows. He squared himself in a dramatic stance.

"One thing I know," he announced pompously. "You ain't my brother!"

"Who say?" demanded Buzzy, dry impishness possessing him, as he stood, butter-colored arms akimbo, scrawny legs spread. "Who say I ain't?"

"I say!" screamed William, wrung and burning with helpless rage again. "I say so, double and triple and quadripple and all hell you ain't!"

"Miss Annie wear you out, cussin' me! Miss Annie bust the breeches plumb off your backside with a big switch. Li'l ole white trash what you is, cussin' and fightin' niggers. Li'l ole white trash Billy!"

William choked on his ire. His desperate dread of the things that churned unexplained in his brain tightened his throat and made him sick. He wanted to puke and fought down the turbulence in his stomach knowing he could not risk that humiliating degradation. Because his fists were cold and rigid he stuffed them down inside his pants, feeling the impotent quiver of his thighs and small, sweaty belly. He backed away, taking his authoritarian pose again.

"Ain't any way you could be my brother," he declared scornfully. "Ain't no way at all. You a Nigra. I'm white. I got brothers, they all white."

"I don't want you for no brother," sneered Buzzy. "You mean and biggity. But if I want to be your brother I will. But I ain't goin' to want to. Not never, White Trash Billy. Not double and triple and quadripple never!"

William stalked away then, not looking back. He heard the stallion trumpet angrily and knew that Buzzy was very likely baiting the animal to rage by tossing little sticks over the gate.

"All right—all right!" he yelled back, when he had attained a safe distance. "You make him bust down that gate and he come out and tromple you dead and then my pa'll lick you good!"

He was only ten then but a small, dark horror of something not understood, a darkness, secret and dimly known, stayed at the back of his mind coloring with its boding shadow everything that was familiar and safe so that somehow nothing was as it had been before.

Mopey, they called him then. Sullen, growled his father. Sneaky, jeered his older brothers. Always lingering around somewhere silently, listening, some guarded thing behind the enigma of his eyes. His mother defended him, "Billy's just a little boy, growing too fast. You all stop picking on him."

"Plays with Nigras," disdained King.

"He's lonely. He has to play with somebody," argued Miss Annie.

But there were times when she was uneasy, watching William, wondering what sinister hurting thing it was that he hid, halfway suspecting, then incredulously rejecting the thought that William could have heard sly whispers, that he was mentally developed enough to understand them if he had. Children were supposed to be somehow invisible, to lack awareness. Servants were blithely careless about gossiping in their hearing. And there was the green silk dress. Proudly she had ignored that revelation as before she had ignored other suspicions and other innuendoes. A woman delicately bred held herself aloof, masked her outrage with dignity, accepted, although often with difficulty, the knowledge that men were what they were, lusty, sometimes gross, more than a little disappointing.

For herself, she could be oblivious, forbearing, disdaining to notice or remark, but for her child she wanted no torturing confusion, no dread, no loss. But there was no getting anything out of William. She made many attempts to probe, always without success. He would listen, give vague answers, slip away as swiftly as possible and his attachment to small, impudent Buzzy appeared to grow stronger every year. Miss Annie even considered appealing to her husband to sell Buzzy, and when Boone Markland boasted that Buzzy was going to make a fine rider, a good jockey, she put away discretion.

"Sell him then!" she cried suddenly. "You don't need a jockey. He'll soon be twelve years old. Sell him to someone who needs a jockey."

Boone Markland laughed loudly and harshly, and Miss Annie could feel his eyes boring into her, digging for all those injuries she had struggled so many years to keep to herself because to admit them, even to herself, was to admit an inferiority, a lack.

"Have to sell Billy too, then, if I sold that yellow boy," he snorted. "Know what Billy's been doing ever since you sent him to that woman's school? He's been teaching that little nigger to read. As if he wasn't biggity enough already. Caught them up in the mow not long ago. Billy had one of those little old primers of Morgan's and he was making Buzzy read a page over and over."

"Won't be long till Buzzy can read better than Billy," volunteered Morgan, eight years old now and, his brothers thought, insufferable. "I can read every word in my books—every word."

"When you let go of your mother's petticoat might be we'll make a man out of you," drawled his father.

It was that year, when he was twelve years old, that William got it all straight in his mind about his father, and although the end of sick confusion and the sharp surgery of truth was painful, it was also a kind of relief. Buzzy did it. Out of the turgid pit of knowledge that sly, too-wise small boys accumulate by absorption Buzzy dug up a sort of pity for Billy's protected ignorance.

Billy had argued vehemently that the brother business was bound to be a lie.

"I know darn well that my father was never married to your mother. So when you brag you're my brother you say a big ole lie."

Buzzy took on a look as old as time, as old as Africa, the look of some gnarled old medicine man squatting in a palm-leaf hut.

"You see that hoss there?" He pointed to the stall where Duke, the young bay stallion, son of old Baron, laid back his handsome ears and rolled a savage eye.

"Sure, I see that horse."

"How many colts he got?"

Farm-wise William knew the answer to that. "Five. Two fillies, two young ones and that off-color they gelded."

"That Duke been married to any them mares that fetch them colts?"

"Horses don't get married. They don't have to get married," argued William, but illumination was dawning on him, leaving him frozen, a tall, dark, rigid shape filled with incredulous abhorrence.

"People neither," stated Buzzy loftily. "They just wants to git married and they do, they don't want to, they ain't got to. Man just like a stud hoss—git him a colt any place."

"It's a lie!" strangled William, bounding out of the mow with a jolting thud, landing on his skinny knees and oblivious of the pain.

But now he knew it was not a lie. He was sent to Nashville to school along with his older brothers, and swiftly he hated both the school and his brothers, who ignored him as usual. Once Jack did take up for him when some older boys jumped on him, but after Jack had washed him off and brushed his clothes, he gave William a sound cuff on the ear.

"I had to keep them from licking you because it would disgrace the family," he stated, "but you better get some guts in you, Billy, and do your own fighting or I'll let the next fellow beat hell out of you. You'd better get your Latin and arithmetic better too, or Pa will take you home and put you in the cornfield with the other ignoramuses on the place."

"I know Latin better than you!" stormed William, and this was true. Books he loved. He devoured everything that came to his hand, everything he could borrow. He read the newspapers avidly too, and by the time he was fifteen the country was torn by political strife. Tennessee seethed with internal turmoil and it seemed to William that no man trusted any other.

Jack had gone home, refusing to enter a northern university, and now King packed up and left the school. "Too many radicals in this town," he announced. "Pa wants me to go to the University of Virginia, but hell, I know enough already. There's going to be a war and all a man needs to know is how to ride fast and shoot straight. Fellow can learn that at home."

In 'fifty-seven William went home to attend Jack's wedding to Sue Wetherby. Boone Markland was in a rage at all the stubborn northern asses who were trying to grind the South down under a heel of iron. The house was full of ranting and angry voices raised in arguments. Sue Wetherby's father argued that the Union should be kept intact but by God they had better not meddle with his property. That Henry Clay and John Calhoun should be hung, whereat Boone Markland roared louder than ever.

He was seeing his father very clearly now, William thought, staying back in a quiet corner with a book. Seeing Boone Markland for the bombastic, poorly informed person that he was. Admiring Boone a little for his audacity, halfway despising him but pitying him too. And Jack and King, in William's mind, were merely diminished copies of their father.

Whatever they stood for, William decided, whatever stand they took in their state of belligerent wrongheadedness, he would be against them. Couldn't they see how utterly asinine it was to believe that the agricultural South, with little industry, little steel and practically no ships at all, could win a war? That loud words and brash bravery were no match for cannon and overwhelming man power?

He spent the next years quietly learning to ride well and shoot well. With Buzzy pounding behind him on a limber-legged, jugheaded three-year-old, he rode the country, practicing taking walls and fences, learning to swim his horse across the swiftest deeps of the rivers. At home he was quiet, reserved, respectful. That he was an enigma to his family he was not aware. When his mother tried to draw him out he smiled a quiet answer.

"I want to know more before I take any stand or think anything, Miss Annie."

Two days after Morgan and King had both gone off to ride with Nathan Bedford Forrest, William and Buzzy, William's horse and the jugheaded three-year-old quietly vanished from the Markland place.

• *Five* •

IT WAS A SMALL, SHABBY HOUSE BUILT OF PLANKS STRAIGHT UP AND down, with warping slats battening the cracks. There was a porch like a shelf across the front, with a plank rail that held a motley assortment of tin cans filled with blooming plants.

Two wooden washtubs stood on a bench in the middle of a bare space at the east of the house, and beyond an iron kettle hung on a wooden tripod steamed over a slow fire. The thin mulatto woman who was poking at the stewing mess of clothes in the pot turned quickly as the slat gate creaked open.

Her body stiffened, her flat eyes turned feral, her Negroid mouth pushed out. Her voice snickered with sudden hostility.

"What you want, white man?" she demanded.

King Markland crossed the bare, well-swept space between them. He had put off the tattered remnants of his uniform and wore the light fawn-colored pants, the riding boots, the white shirt of a young country squire. They hung on his emaciated frame loosely, but they gave him a jaunty air.

"Hello, Drusy," he said. "Remember me?"

She gave a stab at a bubbling hump in the kettle, poked the air out of it. "I 'member you too good, Mister King Markland. How come you didn't git kilt in the big war?"

"They didn't have any silver bullets, Drusy. Take a silver bullet to kill a Markland."

"Hmmmpf! Take a silver bullet to kill the devil too. Ain't nobody kilt him yet. How come you walkin' here 'cross the fields, Mister King Markland? Where at all them fine hosses you had to ride? Where at all them feathers on your haid and red sash around your belly? Ain't got no sword neither, ain't got no pistol. Come afoot like a nigger," she snorted.

"The horses went to war, they didn't come back. Where's Lutie, Drusy?"

Her face turned rigid again. She held the stick, worn and bleached white from many immersions in boiling suds, like a weapon.

"How I know?" she snapped. "She ain't here. And if she here she ain't takin' up with no Rebel soldier neither. Somebody what fit to unfree us folks."

"You've been free for years, Drusy. Sam Hilliard set you free way back yonder before the war started," King reminded her.

"Lutie ain't been free. She was property. Mist' Sam done tole me times a-plenty Lutie his property. Like a cow. Like a hawg he own. Now she free. Linkum gunboats come up the river and my Lutie done git free. Now them Yankee soldiers done tote her off. Ain't seen Lutie in a time," she declared mournfully. Then she looked around, an avid slyness in her eyes. "Ain't got no money, is you?"

He laughed harshly. "Confederate money, Drusy. Haven't seen anything but Confederate money for years and mighty little of that."

"Then what you hangin' round here for? Got some li'l ole piece of ribbon in your pocket, think you kin coax my Lutie off to the woods with some raggedy ole fady piece of ribbon?"

"I'm not hanging around," King shrugged, hands in his pockets. "Just passing by. Just stopped to pass the time of day."

"Pass on then," she grunted. "Git gone and let decent folks git on with their business." She flourished her wand, then as he opened the gate again called after him, "Better stick to the road, Mister Rebel. Yankee soldiers meet you some place and you might not git home no more."

Unheeding, King took the road to the west. It was a narrow, twisting track about knobby hills, so lost in bushy undergrowth that it had been little used by either army. He set his feet down irritably, angered by the indignity of travel on foot when for so long he had galloped this road, booted and spurred and arrogant. His legs were still shaky, and he dropped down to rest under a hickory tree where the short grass was already turning brown and the dry hulls of last year's nuts lay about like little abandoned boats with upturned bows.

A squirrel came backward down the tree, waving a tail like a question mark, stopped midway, turned head down and jibbered squirrel insults at him. King threw a dried-up nut at him.

"You're safe, fellow," he said wearily. "No gun and no ammunition."

There was, his father had told him, a plentiful supply of game, since nobody had done any hunting during the war. Ammunition was scarce, weapons had been confiscated, and to fire a shot in the woods these past three years could likely bring a gang of guerrillas charging at you from somewhere.

"Got a little powder and shot hid," Boone said. "A few balls and a little lead to run more for the deer rifle. Might get us a buck some night when you boys get your legs under you."

"Some meat surely would taste wonderful," Sue had said. "When General Wilder's boys took that last sow we had Minerva just hunkered down under a tree out there and bawled."

"Cowpeas go poorly with no fat meat to season them," sighed Miss Annie. "When I think of all the sides of bacon I used to dole out to the hands I get right weak and squawmy in my stomach."

King was feeling a trifle gaunt and sweated now from long hunger, which had been but scantily appeased at his mother's meager table, but he dragged himself up and tramped on. It might be that the Olivers would have a ham left and undoubtedly he would be asked to stay to supper. Also if old Colonel Oliver had a horse left he might be lucky enough to be driven home by Miss Winnie Oliver in the yellow-wheeled trap he remembered.

The Oliver house was up a sloping lane that climbed a ragged hillside and King had to stop to rest twice before he reached the top. There, he was thankful to see, the house still stood, apparently unmolested. All along the road from Alabama they had passed one blackened fire-gutted settlement after another, both armies having wrought destruction, the Federal troops being most savagely vengeful after they had hounded Hood and Forrest southward. The Oliver place looked neglected. Paint was peeling from the clapboards and one of the posts supporting the narrow front porch leaned a little.

A wagon to which two lean mules were hitched stood in front of the house and as King toiled up the last slope of the drive he saw an old man and a girl drag a heavy trunk out through the front door and stand, breathlessly panting, the old man mopping the sweat from his beard and thinning hair.

The girl gave a little cry as she saw King approaching.

"Grandpa! It's King! It's King Markland. King, come home from the war." She ran swiftly down the high wooden steps, her wide calico skirt billowing, her hair, wheat-gold and fine, flying out of the pins and falling to her shoulders. "Oh, King!" she exclaimed, "I'm so glad you're still alive, so glad you came home!"

He took her hands. "I'm alive, Winnie. I came home."

A bright blush spread over her face, she disengaged her hands and pushed the hair out of her eyes. They were very blue with light, gold-tipped lashes and her light brown brows had a tilted, questioning lift.

"We hadn't heard. Not a word. But no one comes here any more. It's King, Grandpa." She raised her voice a little, taking King's elbow and leading him toward the house. "King Markland's come home."

King said, "Howdy, Colonel Oliver. How are you?"

"Puny," wheezed the elder. "Mighty puny. Well, now you're here, young man, you can give me a hand with this trunk. Winnie here, she hasn't any more muscle than a kitten."

"What goes on?" inquired King. "Who's going traveling?"

"Got to get away," declared Oliver. "Got to get clear away."

"We're leaving. All of us," said Winnie. "Mother and Grandpa and I."

"Get a hold here, young man," ordered the Colonel. "They've got two more trunks upstairs both heavier than this one. I dunno what all they got in 'em—hefts like tombstones." He gave a desperate heave at one end of the trunk and the frayed old leather handle broke in his hand. He lurched back, almost sobbing. "Now you see," he complained childishly. "How can I get it loaded? Damn Abraham Lincoln to hell!"

"You mean all your hands are gone, Colonel?" King was recovering from his first startled confusion. "There's nobody here to do this but you?"

The old man staggered back, took an indignant stance, glaring out of pale eyes sunk in dry folds of skin under ragged white brows.

"Would I be doing this nigger job if there was a Nigra left to do it?"

he demanded irritably. "Not a hand left on the place. All run off after this damnable Union League or whatever they call the foul abomination. Now I'm left alone to get these women to a safe place all by myself. And I can't do it. I can't do it." It was a wail.

"But why are you leaving? And where do you plan to go?" King persisted. "Those animals don't look as though they'd hold out to travel far."

"Cornfield mules. Old and worn out. Ready to die like me. No, they won't go far. They'll likely drop in their tracks but they're all I've got left. Eight fine horses—all gone. Six stout Nigras, all gone too. Even Sudie. Been in this kitchen all her life. Old—almost as old as I am. Gone off after the damn Yankees!" stormed the old man.

"Reckon we can heave this thing in, end over end? You and me?"

Winnie began to cry, small pale tears beading the golden lashes, her mouth quivering. "We don't know where we're going, King. Somewhere south, Grandpa says. And he says we have to leave right away on account of Governor Brownlow."

King's legs were about to buckle under him. The long hot walk, the climb up the hill made him realize how weak he was still.

"Could we sit down a minute?" he asked. "You need to rest too, Colonel. You're mighty red-faced and sweated."

"Come in the parlor. It's cool there." Winnie got her grandfather by the arm. "I'll fetch you a cold drink from the cistern. Grandpa"— she stopped and turned back apprehensively—"you didn't put that stuff in the cistern yet, did you?"

"No. No, not yet." He had sunk into a chair in the stripped, bare-looking parlor and sat collapsed and quivering, mopping his face. "But I'll do it when we leave," he shouted after the girl. "Nux vomica!" he told King with a grin of dry malice. "I'll fix it so any vile Yankee drinks from my cistern will get plenty sick."

King took a chair near the door, looking about at a place that had been familiar all his life. A room that he remembered as filled with candlelight and laughter, with the music of fiddles and banjos, with the silken swirl of girls' skirts, the perfume of their hair, the starlight in their eyes. Now faded rectangles on the wall showed where pictures had been taken down, the windows glared tall and naked, the floor was uncovered and dusty.

"Who did this, Colonel?" he asked. "Who stripped your house like this? Which army came this way?"

The old man lifted his head. "Why, no armies ever came through here. We heard of 'em, off to the west and south too, our troops and the Yankees too but no soldiers ever did show up here. Sort of out of the way, this place is."

"Then who—this looks like the looted places I saw in Alabama. Houses had been robbed of everything movable," King said.

"We did it. We stripped this house ourselves. Mary and the girl and me. After the last Nigra took off in the night, after I saw that piece in Brownlow's paper, we packed and hid things. Hid 'em where they won't find 'em, the scalawags." The Colonel chuckled mirthlessly, beating his knee with his fist. "Got a lot of stuff in these trunks. Makes 'em mighty heavy. Take all we can, Mary said. Reckon it will be a good long time before we come back."

Winnie came in then with two tin cups slopping water. "I washed these cups. Mother packed away all the glasses. This water is good and cool. Drink all of it, Grandpa, you look so hot."

"Winnie"—King put the cup aside after draining it gratefully—"sit down and tell me just what you mean to do. I'm all confused."

She spread her hands in a helpless gesture. They were darkened and rough, he saw, not the frail, lily-white hands that he remembered.

"Grandpa says we have to get away," she sighed. "He says the radicals will kill him, that there'll be nobody to protect Mother and me and that dreadful things will happen to us. We don't know where we're going, King. At least Grandpa hasn't made up his mind."

The old man's hands were twitching, his mouth worked nervously. He jumped to his feet.

"Have you seen Brownlow's newspaper, young Markland?" he cried. "Have you seen that foul, treasonable, radical sheet printed by a man who calls himself a minister of God and who is now Governor of Tennessee? God help us all! Show him the paper, Winnie. Or did you burn it as I ordered you to do?"

King shook his head. "No, I've never seen Brownlow's paper."

"It's an old copy. I think Mother wrapped the sugar bowl in it." Winnie hurried out.

King sat down opposite the Colonel and sat frowning, leaning his chin on a closed fist. Once he had thought himself halfway in love with Winnie Oliver, but that was in the days when they were all young and carefree, when there were good horses to ride, smart coats and natty beaver hats, gay waistcoats and polished boots. When every girl worked at being a charmer in huge fluffs of skirts ruffled to the waist and adorned with ribbon bows and little roses, with lacy bodices that revealed white shoulders and just a whisper of a sweet rounded bosom.

Now the world seemed made of flatness, drabness and weariness. Life was as savorless as the makeshift food his harassed mother put upon her table, and King was uncertain if the capacity to care for any good woman again was left in him. All he was feeling now was a bewildered anxiety concerning the old man in the other chair, drained gray and obviously tormented by some unexplained terror.

"You read that paper you'll know why I have to leave this state, young Markland," stated the Colonel. "Andrew Johnson was bad enough, turncoat Southerner, no real principles, no character, no education. Then there was Lincoln, no education either. Andrew Johnson kept this state neither bond nor free, but he was a decent, well-intentioned blunderer. You couldn't hate Andrew Johnson, you could pity him for being the deluded person he is, but you didn't despise him. But this poison Brownlow—you read your Roman history. You read about Nero and Caligula, young Markland. But they were gentlemen compared to William Gannaway Brownlow! A man who works anathema in the name of God!"

"How did Brownlow ever get to be Governor of Tennessee, Colonel?"

"It was last January, after our boys were run out of Nashville. Then the Union men decided to set themselves up a government in Tennessee. They called a convention, about five hundred of 'em I heard, and most of the meeting they spent fighting among themselves, but they got together long enough to declare Secession null and void, vote for abolition and set up two elections, one to ratify what they'd voted and the other to elect the state officers they had picked."

"So they shoved through an election and Brownlow got elected, but what about Andrew Johnson? Hadn't he been military governor?"

"He was anxious to get rid of the job," said the old man. "He'd been elected Lincoln's vice president in 'sixty-four. Brownlow hates Johnson—called him all kinds of names in that paper he printed in Knoxville. The election was a farce. Nobody voted but a lot of Union blue-belly renegades, mostly from East Tennessee. Decent Union men —sounds curious to my own ears but there were some thinking men didn't like Brownlow—they thought the election was illegal but it suited the government up in Washington. Lincoln wanted Tennessee back in the Union, wanted some kind of state government. Civil government. Well, we got it but it's not civil. And it's not military either because what bloodshed and destruction happen from now on won't be perpetrated by soldiers, fighting for what they believe. But it will come—you'll see. That's why I'm getting clear away."

Winnie came back then, followed by her mother, a still-young woman with only a few feathers of gray in her thick brown hair. Mary Oliver looked harried and spent and as she passed her father-in-law, sagging in his chair, she gave him a look of patient exasperation.

She held out a welcoming hand. "Kingman! Winnie told me you'd come back. God be praised some of our boys were saved."

"Young Carter?" he inquired, taking her hand.

"We never heard. Not a word."

"Not since Shiloh," added Winnie, who had returned holding a crumpled sheet of badly printed newspaper. "Here, Grandpa," she said, spreading it on his knees.

"Things were pretty bad at Shiloh," said King, offering Mary Oliver his chair. She dropped into it with a weary sigh.

"They're still bad," she said. "You knew I lost my husband at First Manassas? Drew brought him back, walking all the way with Carter laid limp over the saddle. That was when my boy went—young Carter and Drew together, and they've never been heard from since."

"Drew might have been impressed into the Union army," King suggested. "They picked up a lot of Nigras who were separated from their masters and their outfits. And it takes a long time to walk home from a war, especially if a man happened to be wounded or put in prison. I thought Jack would die on me before we made the last hundred miles."

"So Jack's home too?" asked Mrs. Oliver. "And Morgan?"

"We've heard nothing of Morgan. He was with us all along the river but when we turned east again we lost track of him," King said.

There was in this desolate house, as at home, no mention of his brother William, he noted. So the Olivers also knew that a Markland son had turned against his own kindred. They would never speak of it. No one would ever speak of it, these people who in the good days had been their friends. Death brought a kind of nobility but William had not been noble enough to get himself killed. He was alive and back in home territory, but his name would not be spoken in the hearing of any living Markland.

The Colonel was smoothing the newspaper across his knees with angry strokes.

"Listen to this, young Markland!" he almost shouted, his voice breaking with the senile urge of his fury. "This is Brownlow's *Whig and Rebel Ventilator*. 'This war is not ended,' he writes. 'It must be pursued if it exterminates from God's green earth every man, woman and child opposed to the Union south of Mason and Dixon's line.'"

"That was printed before the surrender, Pa," Mary reminded him. "You can tell by the date."

"Yes, but what does Brownlow advocate now?" he shrilled. "I had that paper but it made me so goddam fighting mad that I burned it. I'll tell you what he encourages these radicals to do. I learnt it by heart. Kill their neighbors if they were rebels, he says. Kill them secretly without noise and bury them in the woods like brutes."

"Pa," expostulated his daughter-in-law, "you know that man is crazy. You know people aren't going to do any such things now that the war is over, even if he says do them. Not even Union people. Why a lot of Union people right here in this county didn't even vote for Brownlow."

"I don't know any such thing," he persisted stubbornly, red patches burning under his hollow eyes. "Anyway, I'm not waiting around to see you proved right or wrong. Young Markland, you reckon you've got rested enough to help me with those trunks?"

Winnie twisted her hands together in helpless desperation. "King, can't you persuade him? He doesn't even know where we're going. We only have a little money and we can only carry a little food and almost no corn at all to feed the team."

"Once we get across the river among Southern people we'll be taken care of," argued the old man, standing shaking and wild-eyed as a warlock, his fists clenched.

King said quietly, "Colonel, the Southern people you're talking about across the river are in worse straits than you. They've lost everything. Even their homes, a lot of them. There's no food. Nobody could make a crop. If they did make a little, one army or the other took it or trampled it or dug trenches through it. That Freedmen's Bureau moved in in some places to feed the Negroes and they found they had to feed a starving white population too."

"You see, Grandpa?" begged Winnie. "We entreated you, we implored you—but no, you have to get across that river."

"And how were you going to cross the river, Colonel?" King pursued. "There's not a bridge nearer than Chattanooga that hasn't been destroyed and the Yankees are there too. All the ferries have been sunk and the railroad torn up. The Yanks will build it back and the bridges too—but not today and not next week either."

The old man's body seemed to shudder all over in an angry convulsion. He ground his teeth audibly, smote his fists together and lifted them in the air.

"I'm going, I tell you!" he screamed. "They won't bury me in the woods and rape my women. I'm going. If nobody will help me I'll do it alone."

He scuttled out to the porch and began tugging at the heavy trunk. Mary Oliver flew after him and Winnie screamed, "King!"

King ran but he was too late. Moved by some inhuman power of rage Colonel Oliver had dragged the trunk to the steps and there it went toppling down thunderously, splitting open, the lid flying off, carrying the old man with it.

There was blood on his head and his breast when at last, panting and struggling, they dragged the wreckage off his body, freed him and carried him into the house. Winnie flew for more water and Mary sobbed, "He made me pack all the blankets."

"It's no use, Mrs. Oliver," King said, gently laying a limp, broken hand straight. "He's not breathing."

• *Six* •

HE WAS A STRANGER IN HIS OWN COUNTRY. SUDDENLY, OUT OF THE shadows into which they had discreetly retired at intervals, the town seemed full of Union men. Union Democrats, conservatives, quiet men who had deplored the war and its divisions, its rancors and outrages, now walked in security. They could be differentiated from the Confederate sympathizers, now in tragic eclipse, by their forthright manner, smacking sometimes of triumph and arrogance. They had had a time of unease when Bragg and Hood had been all over the country, but now things were decisive. They were on the side of the winners. Now power was theirs and those who had kept their political complexions cannily obscured wore no more airs of apology.

There were some, William Markland knew, as he regarded a crowd around the courthouse door, who were turncoats, adventuresome opportunists, and a few who were knaves, shaping their convictions to circumstance. Undoubtedly there were people, friends of his family, who labeled him with a disdainful, unsavory brand, but he knew that he could have taken no other stand. Not believing as he had believed, not dedicated as he had felt himself to be. But because few here had shared his faith in the Union he felt himself now a stranger. Almost an interloper it seemed at times, in a town only eighteen miles from where he had been born.

After the bullet had been removed from his knee he had been certified as eligible for discharge by the army surgeon and advised to go home.

"I'd rather stay on duty, sir," William had said then. "I have no home to go to."

So they had detailed him to this garrison company of Colored troops posted to protect the western approaches to the state capital.

William Brownlow was still dubious of the hotly Confederate regions out Memphis way and also halfway suspicious that civil war was again imminent in divided Tennessee.

William had two white lieutenants under him and an illiterate sergeant of Scandinavian ancestry, and the opprobrium of such a command was lightened a little by the awareness that at least he was near home and thus would have some foreknowledge of what could be expected to happen if any sudden reprisals were contemplated.

He was sitting on a bench in the courthouse yard, the cane he still needed propped beside him, when Buzzy found him. Buzzy had a complaint.

"Them white lieutenants don't know how to git along with Colored folks, Cap'n Billy. Not quality color like some of us boys. Boss Boone he ain't never cussed me nor called me bad names. How come that white man got a right to kick me around like I was a low-down cornfield hand. And he say I ain't a corp'ral no more. I got to be a private. You make me a corp'ral, Cap'n Billy, how come he unmake me?"

"It's the army, Buzzy." William's leg was aching, likely it would go on aching with the slow misery of an abscessed tooth for the rest of his life. He was resigned to it as he had resigned himself to a hitching gait, the pain that grew worse in the saddle, the awkward canes that were always falling or slipping on mud or wet cobbles. The pain made him a little irritable. "It's the army," he repeated. "You wanted to get into the army all the while we were up there in Virginia, so now you're in and you'd better not run off. You've seen what happens to deserters."

"You know sump'n, Cap'n Billy? I saw my mammy. She livin' out yonder on the edge of town, done took up with a no-good yellow man name of Caucus. My mammy say my grandma mighty poorly and she reckon she 'bout to die. I'd ought to go home, Cap'n, my grandma think a heap of me."

"You saw Mammy Dory six weeks ago, Buzzy. You know she's

mighty old and sick and I guess she'd be glad to die. But she wouldn't be glad to see you arrested and shot for deserting the United States Army so you'd better get back to your post and make up your mind to be a good private."

"Cap'n Billy," confessed Buzzy, "I'd done been gone 'fore now 'cept you know they took my horse. I come all the way over here to ask you would you give me the loan of your horse so I could see my poor old grandma on her deathbed."

William put on a stern face. It had always been difficult to be grim with Buzzy. It was like giving orders to a squirrel that might sit up and blink bold eyes at you, then whisk away about his own affairs without a backward look.

"Once and for all, Buzzy, the answer is no." He put a flick of anger into his tone, hoping for the emphasis of surprise. "I'm still an officer and you're still a private in this army. You can't have my horse. You know I need him. How much attention would those bumble-footed boys pay to me if I tried to give them orders limping around on two canes?"

"What they got all them black-trash soldiers for anyhow, Cap'n Billy?" Buzzy wanted to know. "Don't know which is their left foot, don't know nothin' at all. That white lieutenant rip the stripe off my sleeve, he don't know nothin' neither. Can't none of us boys understand nothin' he say. Talk some kind of ginny talk."

"People up east talk like that, Buzzy. You heard those New York troops, men from Brooklyn. They complain that they can't understand us either. That sergeant we have is from Minnesota. They speak an old country language up there, a lot of older people do."

Buzzy put on an abject face. "Cap'n Billy," he pleaded, "you git me out of this ginny soldier outfit. You let me go back home where I belong. Ain't I always belong to you back home? Ain't I always tend your horse and keep your boots shined all over Virginny, all that fightin' and retreatin' what we done? Ain't I fetched you home when you git wounded, when the white folks ain't paid you no mind at all? You let me git back with you."

"I know, Buzzy. You've been faithful. That's why you'll be a good soldier now. You didn't have to enlist, remember? You wanted to wear a uniform and you got it. Now I won't let you disgrace it." William employed his most pontifical manner, knowing the same baffled and exasperated feeling he might at launching a feather against a stone wall.

Buzzy was not to be talked down. He grew solemn. "Cap'n, you and me been back home. We knows Boss Boone ain't got no more niggers. They all run off. My mammy say ain't anybody left 'cept 'Nerva and my ole grandma. How Boss Boone goin' to run that place without no hands? Who goin' to clean that stable, milk a cow? You reckon Mist' Jack or Mist' King do that? You know they ain't. You'd ought to think 'bout Boss Boone a little bit. He your own pappy."

William reached for his canes, lifted himself to his feet, standing very tall.

"Listen, don't be a fool, Buzzy!" he snapped. "If you run off from this garrison you know they'll catch you. They might hang you right here in this courthouse yard to show those other boys that once they're in the army they have to obey regulations. I'd hate to see you hanging from one of those big trees yonder with a rope around your neck."

Buzzy stood, heavy lips pursed, his brow creased so deeply that it gave him a simian look. Then he gave a quick shrug. The squirrel, William was thinking dryly. The swift feral gesture of withdrawal.

"I'd hate to see me hangin' yonder, too," he agreed with a flicking grin. "One thing sho', though. 'Fore they hang me they got to catch me."

He was gone then as quickly as a dark drift of cloud evaporating. He went so quickly that a little of his body odor lingered on the hot, still air of July to mingle with the scent of trampled grass, of ordure and the greasy reminiscences of some cook's frying pan.

The crowd around the courthouse was in constant flux. Countrymen and townsmen, Negroes, grave older citizens. They stood in pairs reading the written paper posted beside the courthouse door. As fast as two would end their scrutiny of the long document two more would move up, some reading the written words silently, one man even following the lines with a tracing forefinger.

William limped nearer, keeping apart from the moving men, aware of the precarious support of his canes. He was in uniform and more than once a sly kick from a Rebel sympathizer had sent him tottering. They knew him, that was the trouble. They knew him, these Southerners, to be Boone Markland's son, the young sprout who had turned his back on his own people.

"What's the broadside this time?" William inquired of another trooper at the foot of the steps.

"Property listed for unpaid taxes, I understand, sir," replied the soldier in a clipped New England accent.

"A legal form of confiscation," remarked William, but there was a quick chilly grab of apprehension at his nerves.

He hitched up the steps as rapidly as safety permitted, waited in line to win his place before the posted notice. On a long piece of foolscap two parallel lines of names were written in a bold black hand. William's eyes scanned quickly the lower lines. The name of Markland was not written there and he breathed in relief. Somehow Boone Markland had escaped this first attempt at humbling and impoverishing the vanquished. But a little higher in the alphabetical list was a name he remembered. Estate of Colonel Carter Oliver, Sr. Two years delinquent. Total indebtedness to the state three hundred dollars.

Once, William recalled, the Olivers had been considered wealthy. The old Colonel had fought in Mexico with General Winfield Scott, and young Carter, his son, had been one of the first to enlist in the Confederate cavalry though he had been then, so William was certain, more than forty years old. There had been a grandson, still another Carter Oliver, a wastrel of a boy, younger than William, who had been sent to Virginia to be educated and had come home spouting hatred of Abraham Lincoln and all abolitionists. And there had been a girl. A pale, precious young thing, jealously chaperoned everywhere by her old fire-eater of a grandfather.

Seeking the bench in the shade again William tried to feel sorry for the Olivers. The Oliver place had been a handsome estate before the war, a place aloof, as the Olivers were a bit aloof, but the Marklands had always been welcome there, especially King. But then King had always been able to make his own welcome. A handsome devil, and he knew it. William thought bitterly of his brother. He tried to believe that he had hated King, but a homesick heaviness within him told him that this was untrue. It had been only envy that tore at him when he had compared himself to his jaunty, nonchalant older brother.

His nostalgia increased as the day waned, and he began wondering if Morgan had ever come home, or if he had been given up for dead. Sorrow pressed on him, knowing how grieved Miss Annie would be at the loss of her favorite son. Sue had assured him that his mother was grieving for him, William, and because desolation was having its way with him, he took what comfort he could from that assurance—small comfort for a man convinced that he could never go home again. He struggled to his feet and hobbled out to the street, back to the old warehouse that had been taken over as headquarters for the troops he was detailed to train. It was when he passed the little brown frame house on the corner, where the minister's widow was reported to live, that he heard the girl scream.

He saw her then in the widow's backyard where hollyhocks grew tall. She was struggling with a Negro soldier for possession of a Dominique rooster and screaming wildly, while the fowl added raucous squalls to the din.

William pushed open the gate and limped in, his canes swinging widely as he hurled his body forward.

"Hands off that chicken, soldier," he ordered sharply.

The trooper loosed his hold on the clawing legs of the rooster, stepped back frowning.

"It confuscate, Cap'n," he argued. "It confuscate for the Newnited States Army, suh."

"The war is over, soldier," stated William sternly. "Or didn't they tell you?"

"Yessuh, Cap'n, but they done tole me to confuscate Rebel stuff, all what we kin eat," argued the Negro.

"He's my chicken," blazed the girl. "I raised him. He's a pet. They took all our hens but they shan't take Cicero."

"You're dismissed, soldier," snapped William. "Get out of here and tell your sergeant Captain Markland gave you the order. All right, move," he barked. "Get back to your barracks and stay there."

"Lieutenant sho' git mad at me if I ain't confuscate nothin', suh," grumbled the trooper as he shambled away.

William bowed to the girl, awkwardly. "In the future, Miss, I'd suggest you keep Cicero out of sight. A fat chicken is difficult for a Colored confiscator to resist."

She looked him up and down, clutching the nervous fowl under one elbow. She looked about eighteen years old, a figure lithe and tall with light-brown hair and eyes that held sparks.

"You're a Yankee," she said. "You don't talk like a Yankee."

"I am an officer in the United States Army, Ma'am. A soldier can also be a gentleman. Better shut that rooster up somewhere as I advised."

"But he crows!" she cried desperately. "No matter where I hide him they'll find him." She came a little nearer. "Haven't I seen you before, Captain?"

"That might be," he admitted, "I was born and reared less than twenty miles from this town. However, I've been away at war for four years. Long enough for you to have grown up," he added gallantly.

"Then you're a Southerner. I knew it." She tucked the fowl's exploring beak down, gave him a mildly admonitory cuff. "Be quiet, Cicero. Your life has just been saved. You should be grateful. I'm Angela Wood," she went on. "You may have known my father. He was a minister in the church down the street for most of my lifetime. He was killed at Stone River."

"I'm William Markland," he told her. "On detached duty here, training troops."

She frowned a little, tossing her head. "Not militia? Brownlow's hound-dogs people call them."

"No, not militia. These are regular army troops."

"The war is over," she said. "Does the hatred have to go on? You conquered us, so why do you have to hate us too?"

"We had to hate while the war lasted, because a man has to hate before he can bring himself to kill his neighbor, or perhaps his friend, as happened too often in this war. Men made themselves hate, now perhaps when they've nurtured the poisonous strangeness for years they find it hard to get rid of. And the ignorant and bigoted have no wish to be free of it. What is happening in Tennessee now is more mob violence than war."

She stood musing, remembering. "I knew a Markland. His name was Morgan. He came here to school for a while. That's why I thought I had known you. Are you Morgan Markland's brother?"

"An older brother. Morgan was the youngest son."

"He went with the Union too?"

William shook his head. "I was the only black sheep in our family. Morgan rode with Forrest. When last I had news of Morgan he had not yet come back from the south."

"Morgan was a handsome boy, and did he know it! Very dashing, and all the girls were mad about him. I do hope he comes home. I remember that Morgan used to get into fights. There were people for the Union and he used to taunt them and there would be brawls."

"That was Morgan," he said, smiling. "I had one argument with Morgan before I left to enlist with Sheridan. It happened in the kitchen at home and he threatened me with an iron skillet. Our old cook threw cold water on him to calm him down. May I wish you good day, Miss Wood? And do something about Cicero, will you? I might not be around the next time a trooper tries to confiscate him."

She held the rooster out, studying him, his flaming comb, his rolling beady eye. "I don't know what to do with him, Captain. Really I don't. He's so lonely since they stole all our hens."

"You could eat him." The boyish grin that was rare and sudden lightened the darkness of his face.

She sighed. "That's what my mother says. Mother and Aunt Ella are both disgusted because I won't have him killed. They wanted to kill the hens when all the troops came, but I wouldn't let them, so now they remind me every day that the troops ate chicken and we eat dried codfish when we get any meat at all. My mother and my aunt sew for people, but you know how it is, perhaps. Nobody has any money and Governor Brownlow is inciting people to hate and persecute everybody who had any one in the Confederate army."

"By all means then eat Cicero. With plenty of gravy and some dumplings."

"We haven't any flour, but perhaps Mother can make some out of meal. Captain, I do thank you. I can't invite you in—I'm sorry."

"Naturally," he said, "you could not invite me in."

"I'd love to ask you to dinner when we eat Cicero," she went on in a rush, flushing a little. "I know it would be all right with Mother because you're Southern and a gentleman, and you did make that horrid man leave me alone, but Aunt Ella! She still keeps a Confederate flag pinned inside her bosom and once she wrote a letter to President Jefferson Davis, inviting him to bring his family here when he was running away after the surrender. I know he never got it and Mother worries for fear the Yankees may have got hold of it. She expects them to come and arrest Aunt Ella any day, now that Brownlow is stirring up so much animosity."

"Undoubtedly I'm outraging her Southern sensibilities by hanging around here in this uniform," William said dryly, balanced on his canes. "So I'll say good night, Miss Angela."

"Good night, and thank you again, Captain Markland," she called after him.

She hurried to the back door and, opening it, confronted two stiff-faced women who had lurked anxiously behind the thin window curtains.

"Don't say a word," she ordered peremptorily. "He was a Yankee but he was a gentleman and he saved Cicero and me from being mistreated. He's a Markland from down the county and I like him."

"No man in that uniform could possibly be a gentleman," her aunt snapped. "No matter who he was or where he was born."

• *Seven* •

Sue Markland bumped the cooling iron back on the stove and tried another with a wet, hissing forefinger. She hated this menial job of ironing, but Minerva was continually complaining lately of a bad pain in her back.

"Minerva's getting old," said Miss Annie, who was always ready with excuses for everybody in the house, Sue was convinced. Everybody but me, she thought bitterly. Everybody but me and Pa Markland. Jack was too weak to work yet and Boone-boy was too little to carry in wood, and now here were these two women to wait on and a wedding to fix for.

Not that Mary Oliver and her scared wisp of a daughter didn't try to be helpful. The trouble was that they had been waited on all their lives, managed and protected, and their eager inefficiency made Sue want to bite her knuckles and scream. She had been irritated for days, it seemed to her, and nothing mollified her, not Miss Annie's gentle briskness, her calm acceptance or Boone Markland's ebullient good humor, his slightly tiresome jokes.

She whacked the iron down grimly on the back breadth of a skirt. The cloth was worn frail and she hoped the fragile thing would hold together till she got it pressed.

"Why does she have to wear her mother's wedding dress?" she demanded of her mother-in-law. "She won't dare sit down in it. This old silk is ready to split in a thousand places."

"Wouldn't you have wanted to be married in your mother's wedding dress?" inquired Miss Annie, beating eggs vigorously. "We were so lucky," she always said when she broke an egg, "the army foragers didn't come often so we've still got some hens and the cow."

"My mother was married in a green bombazine thing, the skirt so tight she couldn't bend her knees," said Sue. "Ruffles clear to the waist—little old black silk ruffles. I wouldn't be buried in it, much less married. And there's no sense in King marrying that girl anyway. You know he's not in love with her, even though he puts on that affectionate show. She's got about as much spirit as a pint of buttermilk.

He's just being gallant and you know it, Miss Annie, and you're letting him spoil his whole life."

"Well, there is a little expediency about it, I'll agree," sighed Miss Annie, sifting a little flour gently into the foaming eggs. All the flour in the house nearly gone, Sue was thinking. I heard her scrape the bottom of the barrel, but she has to bake a wedding cake! "Certainly Mary Oliver and Winnie couldn't go on living there alone, and while we are always glad to help a neighbor and do for those in distress, we are hard put now to do for ourselves. So little planted and Jack laid up again."

"He just hurt his back lifting that heavy coffin. And there was mighty little neighborly help offered when they buried that poor old man," snapped Sue.

"People are so uneasy," said Miss Annie. "No one knows who their friends are any more."

"Because all the people who were for the South are scared to death. That poor old Colonel Oliver was literally frightened into his grave! Not," she added grimly, "that he hadn't reason to be."

Hadn't she talked and talked, trying to warn them all since William had come back in June? Hadn't she kept her promise to him? But everything she had said had seemed to go in one Markland ear and out the other. Poor Billy had crawled back dragging that wounded leg to bring a warning to his family, and though she dared not speak his name she had dropped hints enough. And in her eager desperation she had stirred King's cynical suspicions anew.

He had faced her alone one day. "Who are you quoting, Sue, all this doom you are prophesying? It has the smell of our wandering brother, William. Did he foresee all these persecutions you are suggesting because he knew damned well he was part of them, one of old Blue-belly Brownlow's lick-rump hounds?"

She had flared at him. "Can you buy Miss Annie one teaspoonful of baking soda anywhere? Only yesterday that Marvin at the store wouldn't credit you for a pound of nails. Ten cents worth of nails. If you can't see for yourself what things are coming to, there's no way I can open your eyes. You'll be blinded forever by your stiff, stupid Markland pride. You'll still believe that the Marklands are better than anybody when you're running on foot for Texas with everything you own on your back."

"I'm marrying me a wife," King had grinned audaciously. "I'll let her carry what we own on her back like a squaw."

"Marrying a wife, when you're not even able to provide for yourself,"

Sue had flung back angrily. "That girl will carry no burden for you, my fine strutting rooster. You'll have to carry her."

But there was no quenching King, and Jack was almost as indifferent, except that along with his maddening helplessness he had a passive acceptance of futility. "What can we do?" was his argument. "We have to get along somehow—though how is a question I can't answer."

Now Jack was back on the bed, moaning and reeking of his mother's homemade liniment and as his wife smoothed the last breadth of Winnie Oliver's wedding dress, she knew with sick heaviness that that might likely be the way with Jack from now on. At least so long as his mother was at hand to run with hot bricks and plasters, with eager sympathy and passionate defense for her elder son, so grievously injured by the cruel war.

I wish Morgan would come back, Sue was thinking as she shook out the fragile, yellowing silk. If Miss Annie had Morgan to pet and fuss over maybe I could make Jack stand on his feet and act the man. Aloud she said, "Well, Miss Winnie can be elegant for one day in this, even if she has to live on turnips and sassafras tea from now on. You know there hasn't been a furrow turned on that Oliver place this spring, Miss Annie, now it's too late to plant even if those feeble old mules could pull a plow."

"They were always thrifty people and counted mighty well to do." Miss Annie sprinkled a little nutmeg into her batter. "Mary says old Mr. Oliver spent days before he died hiding and burying provender." She poured the batter into a greased pan and Sue promptly raised her voice loudly.

"You, Boone-boy!" she called. "Come here this instant and bring in some light wood for your grandma to bake with. Scamper now!" She threatened with the butter paddle as the little boy whined a protest. "Bring in enough to fill that box or I'll warm your breeches good!"

"I can fetch it, Sue. He's so little—"

"You will not, Miss Annie! Move, sir! If your grandma carries in one stick, that's the stick I'll use on you." She faced the older woman sternly. "Miss Annie, you're spoiling my family rotten out of the mistaken goodness of your heart. My boy has to face bad times—tough, miserable times such as your children never knew. I've got to put some gimp into his gizzard, make him face life like a man, and I don't want to have to fight you and Pa Markland to raise him."

Miss Annie blinked, tucked in her lips. "Very well, Sue. I'm sorry I interfered. And if you'd rather I didn't take care of your sick husband—"

"Now look, Miss Annie, don't you get your feelings hurt. It's just—Oh, my Heaven, can't you see? Somebody in this family has to face reality. Somebody has to be strong enough to take what's coming—what's bound to come. Hard going, trouble, privation. Why does it have to be me? Jack gets sulky and King laughs. Pa Markland pooh-poohs it all and you pucker up to weep. It has to be me, all alone. I won't let it break Boone-boy because he's been made too precious to face living. I won't let it destroy Jack either if I can help it. Miss Annie, you know that the best thing we could do, Jack and I, would be to go clear away somewhere and start all over."

"Oh, no! Oh, no, Sue!" Miss Annie flung out her hands in a despairing gesture of protest. "You can't leave us! How could Mr. Markland run this place with no help at all? And I think he'd die if you took Boone-boy away from us. He'd simply die of heartbreak and discouragement. You think about your father-in-law as a rough, noisy old man who isn't afraid of anything or anybody, but he's not like that deep inside. He's sensitive and kind, and though he may not show it when he's hurt the pain is there. I can see it."

"Still," argued Sue, "he ought to want what's best for his sons and be glad to see them standing on their own feet."

"But we made this place for our sons," insisted Miss Annie. "Thank you, Sweetie." She stood aside while her grandson flung down an armful of wood. "Now don't fetch any more till I get my cake out of the oven. You might make it fall. Run out now and play."

"Lemme lick the bowl. You promised," reminded Boone-boy.

"Stand over here then and don't stamp your feet. Sue, I was saying—"

"I know, Miss Annie. You made the place for the boys, and Pa Markland cried when they all rode off to war but no one knew that but you. You've told me. But the place now—what is it, if it's going slowly to ruin."

"Mr. Markland," stated his wife stiffly, "has done all one man could do. One man alone—and not a young man any more."

"He's not old," disputed Boone-boy. "Grampa ain't old. He gets mad if you say he's old."

"He's not used to hard work because until the war came and the people began drifting away, he never had it to do," Miss Annie went on. "But he was out there in those fields—with a hoe, and the only thought he had was to make something and save something for his children. Now—if all he wins for that endeavor and sacrifice is ingratitude, Sue, I think it will kill him. He will be old. He'll wither away and die."

"Nonsense!" snapped Sue. "Pa Markland is a sensible man, sensible and practical. He'd admire independence in his sons. I know he would."

"Just where," inquired her mother-in-law coldly, "would you go? And how would you go? There's so little money left. I wasn't too happy when Mr. Markland bought so many Confederate bonds but the boys were off fighting, doing their part. I couldn't oppose him."

"Uncle Billy was a Yankee," put in Boone-boy, running a red tongue over a spoon. "Mammy Dory said Uncle Billy was a Yankee fighting on the Lord's side."

"Hush, Boone-boy!" warned his mother. "I've told you you mustn't repeat what you hear out in the quarters. Mammy Dory is a sick, silly old woman. She doesn't know what she's saying."

"She knows all right," persisted the child. "She says she's free and I asked Grampa and he said he reckoned she was but he'd have to go on feeding her, free or slave."

"Boone-boy, you get out of here! You're getting your grandma all upset. Go and help Winnie cut the flowers."

"She says she's my aunt." He dabbed sticky hands on his faded breeches. "Have I got to have her for an aunt, Grandma?"

"When she is married to your Uncle King she'll be your aunt and you must be very nice to her and speak politely."

"Will that old Mrs. Oliver be my aunt too?"

"No, she won't." His mother lifted a hand. "Did you hear me tell you to get out of here, Boone-boy? I'm sorry, Miss Annie," she said hastily, when the boy had scampered out, "we forgot to warn him not to talk about his Uncle William. I didn't even know he remembered William. Mammy Dory stirred that up, the hateful old creature. She should be thankful you're willing to take care of her now."

"She nursed all my children. She was Mr. Markland's nurse too. She'd never leave us and she doesn't realize what she's saying."

There it was, the inevitable excuse. Mammy Dory knew what she was saying, all right. And very likely she had already let the family know that William had come back and gone again, and Buzzy with him. Sue draped the long dress carefully over her arm and went through the house to the big parlor where Winnie Oliver was handing long sprays of althea blooms up to King. King stood on a kitchen chair awkwardly stuffing the flowers into a vase on the mantel.

"Oh, no—not that way," Winnie was protesting. "Arrange them

loosely, King. Make them look delicate. Oh, I'm so sorry all the roses are faded. I always wanted bowers of roses at my wedding."

"You can have them if you'll wait till next spring," Sue put in brusquely. "Your dress is finished but you'd better be gentle with it. This old silk is mighty frail."

"Oh, thank you so much, Sue. You're so clever. I'd never have been able to do it right, never in the world." Winnie pressed her cheek against a fold of the yellowed silk. "It still smells of the lavender and rose petals," she sighed dreamily, a soft flush coming and going on her pale face.

"That dress will be too big for you." Sue studied the small waist, the almost nonexistent bosom. No more meat on Winnie than on a pigeon. "You'll have to feed her up, King," she said. "Some of these rough winds we get in winter might blow her away."

"I'll tie a knot in her hair so she can't go out the keyhole." King got down to survey his handiwork. "For old Nigra posies they don't look too bad, but 'Nerva says they'll close up at night."

"The buds will open," said Winnie optimistically. "Anyway there won't be time in the morning to cut fresh ones."

"There aren't any more. I robbed every bush. Miss Annie used to have flowers all over the place."

"Miss Annie used to have Phoebus to take care of them," Sue reminded him. "We used to have great fields of corn and wheat too, but we had people to plow and reap and hoe and now there aren't any."

Winnie dropped into a chair, the wide folds of silk laid carefully over her knees. "How can we go on living, Sue?" she asked plaintively. "On and on—no change—for years and years."

"We have to go on and we will!" Sue was grim. "And you'd better learn to lift an iron and the rasp of a washboard too, my girl, if you're going to be Mrs. King Markland."

"Do you have to be so nasty?" demanded King of Sue later. "Can't you let the poor child alone? She's had trouble enough already."

Sue looked him up and down, green fire glinting in her eyes. "Knowing you—" she had her chin up and her face was so pale that all the golden freckles sparkled, "knowing you, Brother-in-law, I'd say that the poor child's troubles were only just beginning."

Mary Oliver and Annie Lou Markland wept all through the brief wedding ceremony. Boone Markland cleared his throat raucously half a dozen times, and Boone-boy, bullied into a starched collar by his mother, twisted and tugged at his flowing tie, snatching off the offending piece of unaccustomed elegance the instant the minister said Amen.

They ate the wedding cake and drank toasts to the wedded pair, Boone Markland having spiked the weak punch his wife had contrived from berry juice sweetened with brown sugar. Miss Annie, excited and teary now, fluttered about in her old gray silk dress with a brisk kind of competence, but her decisions were slightly confused by sentimentality. She wanted everyone to be comfortable and healthy and happy, but also she wanted to be the one to arrange for their comfort and well being, and with wistful eagerness she wanted credit for her ministrations, too.

Jack was always reminding his wife that Miss Annie had been mighty brave. Hadn't she lost her two younger sons? Definitely William had to be counted lost and two months had gone by since the surrender and not a word heard from Morgan. Sue could respect Miss Annie, even admire her courage, but certainly she had no wish to find herself in such circumstance that she would need to lean on her mother-in-law. Winnie would do enough of that.

Studying the face of King's bride, paper-white save for two small, burning patches of crimson, her tremulous mouth and wistful eyes— eyes that searched every face for encouragement and commendation— Sue was confident that Winnie was going to be a family liability. Mrs. Oliver was an aloof, amiable woman, but a woman born to be mastered, with no more initiative than a gentle cow. All the Olivers had been reported to be stout bottle men and it was rumored in the neighborhood that Mary's husband, the second Carter Oliver, had gone tearing off to join the Confederate cavalry roaring drunk and spurring his horse till the blood ran.

Sue looked at King. He was already red-faced and laughing too loudly from too many trips to the punch bowl and once, when Boone Markland brought out a fresh bottle to renew the concoction, King took the bottle from his father's hands and downed a huge gulp, wiping his lips with the back of his hand.

"If we'd had a few gallons of that at Franklin, Pa," he said, giving his new wife a pat on the back so vigorously that Winnie tottered off balance and had to clutch at Jack to steady herself, "things would have been different."

"Hold on, fellow," advised Jack. "Don't go beating on the poor gal already."

"Just a love pat," insisted King, pulling Winnie against him and hugging her so hard that she squeaked small mousy protests. "Get your bandboxes together, light of my life, we have to start on our honey-moon."

A look of sick, utter fright made Winnie's blue eyes darken. Her mother saw it and gathered her daughter up quickly. "She has to change," Mary Oliver argued hastily, "but we're all packed. Oh, dear! I do wish it could have been different. I always thought of Winifred as being driven off in a handsome carriage with a fine pair of black horses and people throwing rice and roses."

"We had a carriage," whimpered Winnie, "but you let Grandpa burn it. You let him destroy everything."

"I couldn't have stopped him, daughter, you know that. At least we have a house left to live in and"—she gave King a motherly smile—"a big strong man to take care of us."

They went upstairs, and Miss Annie began bustling around gathering up glasses and plates and piling them on the tray Minerva held ready.

"I don't know—" She seemed to be talking to herself. "I don't know how it will turn out. You were so impulsive, King. Oh, I hope—I hope—"

Sue cut in sharply. "King, let that bottle alone! Do you want to be disgracefully drunk on your wedding night?"

"Might help," drawled Jack, reaching for the bottle himself. "Did you get drunk on your wedding night, Pa?"

"Not me," laughed Boone Markland. "I didn't dare. Miss Annie would have busted my head for me."

"I hope Winnie has a stout broomstick handy," said Sue viciously. Then she gathered up her skirts and ran up to her room. She didn't want to see the bridal party leave in the Oliver wagon drawn by the woolly old mules. She heard a trunk being bumped down the stairs, heard her name called and shut her ears, dragging off her dress, the last decent one she owned. She put on a limp and shapeless faded calico.

It was all horrible! King had thrown away his whole life, and none of the Marklands had made a move or said a word to halt what to her was merely a sentimental, impulsive gesture. True, Boone Markland had been very quiet and a little grim all day. True, Miss Annie's eyes had held anxiety and speculation. It was all part of the mistaken, passionate loyalty that had made the stupid war inevitable. The touchy pride of caste, the sanctity of property and of women. A man must sacrifice to defend them both no matter if the sacrifice destroyed him.

She had heard only one comment from Boone Markland concerning his son's hasty marriage.

"The places join down yonder there at the creek. Some day it will be a handsome property."

She heard the wagon rumble off, smelled sweet potatoes baking, and knew that Minerva was putting together some sort of an evening meal, but Sue flung herself across the bed and determined not to go down again, no matter how insistently they called.

She was half asleep when she heard Boone Markland shouting and a little scream from Miss Annie. She jumped up and ran. King was drunk and had let the mules run away, she was certain, probably they were all killed.

She burst into the parlor and stared.

Union blue! William?

"No!" she gasped. "No!"

Miss Annie came rushing up. "He scared me to death too," she cried. "It's Morgan! Morgan—home from the war!"

Morgan, grinning jauntily, hale and as insolent as ever.

"Took these clothes off a dead Yank, sis," he explained. "Didn't think Miss Annie would like it if I came home naked."

• *Eight* •

CAPTAIN WILLIAM MARKLAND LAID DOWN HIS CARDS.

"Gentlemen," he said, "a man who quits when he's winning is a cheap scalawag, but it is now three o'clock in the morning and reveille at my barracks will blow in less than three hours. I seem to have had a surprising run of luck tonight—"

"Luck?" chortled the jowly elderly man at the end of the table. "Boy, I'd say you had luck come and sit in your lap! Goddammit, you've mighty near cleaned me out." He took a wallet from a greasy inner pocket and thumbed through a thick pack of limp bills. He was the county assessor, who had slid into office in the last abortive farce of an election, and William had heard talk in town of his venality and dirty work with known Confederates.

"Me too," sighed a corpulent fellow whose every word was a wheeze.

[63]

"Was you fighting a war over there on the Rappahannock, Billy, or learning to make these picture ladies behave? Never see a man draw so many queens. Ought to be a heller with the ladies. How do I stand, boys? Count 'em up. I figure the military got into me close to a hundred dollars."

The county official slammed down four bills, scowling. "There they lay, Captain! Boy, you remind me of your pappy. Old Boone could sit us out all night till he up and married Annie Lou Breen. She turned old Boone mighty respectable and mighty poor company. How come your pappy got himself all mixed up with these here Jeff Davis scoundrels, Billy? You had better sense. Should have talked old Boone out of taking the wrong side. Sooner or later them fellers up at Nashville are going to start bearing down on us boys out this-a-way, and we'll have to go out there and sell old Boone out."

William put his winnings securely away in a deep pocket. He retrieved his canes and stood erect. "You can't sell him out, Mr. Fletcher, if he keeps his taxes paid," he said.

"Yeah," said the fat man, who William knew had been elected to the Tennessee legislature riding on Brownlow's coat tail, "but how's he going to keep 'em paid? Can't sell nothing unless he takes the oath, and can't get any credit any place."

"Course, there's one way," observed Fletcher, lifting a jug from the floor, tilting it and taking a deep pull at it. "Old Boone could deed his property to the captain here, Billy being his own son, that fought for the Union and come home crippled. Might be arranged, did we take the right steps in the right direction."

"And the right steps would cost money, no doubt?" suggested William dryly, hating this pair of buzzards who were waxing fat picking the bones of the defeated. He had gotten into this game deliberately, taking a chance on losing what he had saved from his pay. That he had won had been unexpected good fortune.

The third man at the table, a lean young doctor named Carson, lately come west from Nashville, barked a brief laugh.

"More money than you will ever see, soldier," he remarked, "if I know that crowd, and I think I know them."

"Case like that has got legal aspects can't be overlooked," said Fletcher, "and legal aspects can get mighty tangled. Need a good lawyer, a shrewd lawyer to straighten 'em out."

"And if the lawyer happened to be dishonest and a friend of a judge with greedy fingers, that would be a help too," drawled the doctor. "You've got a lot to learn about things in this state, son. Well, gents,

I'm taking my leave. I about broke even, I think. Now I forego the pleasure of your company to attend to all the dysentery that is sapping the courage of our noble troops at the garrison. Been living too high off the hog and drinking too much of this raw, homemade liquor."

"I ain't in favor of giving those boys weapons, I ain't in favor of it at all," remarked the legislator. "The Secretary of War up yonder has already had a letter from me to that effect. You take even a good Colored boy—and we've all known good Colored boys—good house boy, always knows his place, you put a rifle and a bayonet in his hands and he figures he ought to use it. No sense or experience to learn him better."

"Got to get plenty of whisky to keep him in mind that he don't have to take any sass from white folks." Fletcher lurched erect, belching loudly. "Had me a good boy. Tended my horse. When Lincoln signed that proclamation I gave him his manumission papers, paid him wages too. Slipped off one night and now he's up yonder strutting stripes on his sleeve and making white men get off the sidewalk. I dunno. I wasn't for slavery, not in this part of the country anyhow. But I dunno. Billy, you keep that cash you got hid. Word gets around."

"Yes, sir. I intend to. Good night, gentlemen." William took his leave.

As he went out the door he heard Fletcher say, "Good boy. Took guts for him to stand against his folks. Had a lady mother. Now I don't reckon she'll let him darken her door."

William limped back, keeping to the middle of the shaded street so that no sullen lurker could spring out of a shadow and waylay him. There was hostility on both sides now, and hate was in the air like a poisonous gas. Every man was now the enemy, anyone the potential victim, and to carry money was to take a long risk. He had trained himself to balance and draw his gun quickly, also he was on familiar ground, which gave him a little advantage. The trouble was that the county was filling up with strangers, vultures gathered for the kill, and when the railroads were repaired there would be more of them.

Railroad and bridge repairs, they said, were going ahead very slowly. The freed Negroes were not to be depended upon, most of them expecting to be fed free by one agency or another. And most of the returned soldiers were too weak and emaciated to do a hard day's work. Money was still scarce, too much of it in the hands of a few, and there were men abroad who would kill ruthlessly for a dollar or two.

The sky was very dark, without stars, and the July heat still pressed down, no coolness coming with the approach of dawn. William's heavy uniform coat was a weight on his shoulders, sweat ran down his sides and stung his hands as he bore upon his canes. Often of late he had found himself wishing he had let them take his leg off. The men who limped around on wooden pegs, or the new cork and steel contraptions the doctors were reported to be obtaining for men able to pay for them, seemed to get about better than he did. There was the promise that the shattered knee would eventually stiffen and bear his weight without the wincing stab of pain, and he had to be content with that hope and be thankful that he could still ride a horse.

He walked by the Wood house where all was dark and silent, but in there soon the girl, Angela, would be stirring, combing her brown hair, putting on one of those prim frocks with all the buttons down the front. He had seen her twice since the affair of the confiscated chicken. Once he had been riding the town road toward the river when he had overtaken her, walking very fast with a basket on her arm. She had stepped off the road and stood breathing rapidly, a flush on her cheeks.

"Oh!" she exclaimed. "I'm glad it's you, Captain. I'm bound I won't be scared but sometimes I catch myself running."

"This is a lonesome stretch of road," William had reminded her. "You shouldn't be walking here alone." He wanted to swing down gallantly from the saddle but he knew that without help or a high place from which to mount he could never get back on again.

"The Harpers, up the road, send my mother work to do," she explained, "and they pay in bacon and meal and things we need, so I have to walk out to fetch and carry."

"Give me your basket," said William. "It looks heavy."

"It is heavy. Five pounds of wonderful bacon, and Mrs. Harper put in a cabbage as big as my head and a little poke of meal. Oh, thank you, Captain. My arm was getting really numb."

"Wait a minute." He surveyed the situation. "There's a rail fence over there. Could you climb up on it? If you could you could ride behind me. It's a long walk to town."

She drew back. "Oh, thank you—I couldn't! It's generous of you to carry my basket."

"Meaning that you can't afford to be seen riding with a Union officer?"

She stiffened a little. She was not a pretty girl, William was thinking. Her nose was too proud and her eyes had too much coppery fire in them. She had a judicial mouth and brows that must have been a legacy from her preacher father, so facile were they to condemn. She was not pretty. She was beautiful.

"I meant that it would be unfortunate for you to be seen riding with the daughter of a Confederate soldier," she said coolly.

He jerked his mouth sideways, his impatient Markland brows bent darkly. "To hell with that! I'm sorry, Miss Wood, but all this niggling factionalism makes me boil. Get up on that third rail there and don't let your petticoat get caught and throw you. Come along, do what I tell you!"

Her lips tilted impishly. "I see I am to be taught discipline along with the rest of the Southerners."

"I'm a Southerner. Any Southerner knows that the first attribute of a gentleman is courtesy to women. Watch where you step in that Jimson weed. We used to kill snakes along this road, a thousand years ago when I was a lad. Now that's a smart girl," he said as she mounted the fence, not looking at him. "Now give me your hand. Turn around—be careful." The horse sidled close uneasily, and she flattened herself against the rotting old rails, nervously. "Don't worry. The Count won't shy. He's used to me, lurching on and off."

"Is that his name—The Count?"

"His father was a Duke. They were all nobility on the place in the old days. Now, put your left foot in the stirrup. Easy! I won't look at your ankles. Now, can you give a little jump? Whoops—get both your arms around my waist and hold on," he ordered. "You're an impostor, Angela Wood," he remarked when she was up, light as a bird. "You're not so helpless. You've done this before."

"My father served four churches. I rode with him often. Here, let me have the basket—only—this gun—"

"Wait, I'll shift it." He took his heavy cavalry pistol out of his belt and swung it to the front. "I vaguely remember your father," he went on as The Count ambled down the road. "We weren't very pious people at home. Miss Annie liked to go to church, but she'd been raised a Catholic by her devout Irish parents. They thought she was doomed to perdition when she married a roaring Presbyterian like my father. Miss Annie is my mother," he explained. "We call her that."

"Mother was Episcopalian. Her father was a Bishop down in Alabama. Aunt Ella still reads Morning Prayer every day and makes us repeat all the proper psalms. But Father was a Methodist so I had to be baptized Methodist too. Mother was always reminding him that John Wesley was Church of England all his life. What will you do if we meet somebody? If we meet some Union soldier?"

"You," he bantered, "will be assumed to be confiscated."

"Not my bacon. I'd fight all the Yankees before they could take away my bacon."

"The way you fought that trooper for your rooster? It's a wonder poor old Cicero wasn't pulled in two."

"We ate him. Mother stewed him nearly all day and still he was tough."

"You gave him the wrong name. You should have called him Nate Forrest. Thomas and Schofield beat on him for months and still he was tough," William said.

"Sam Hood was the worst," retorted Angela. "Over at Franklin he slaughtered thousands of his men so uselessly. Everybody around thought he had gone mad. He even had General Lee bring up his artillery and fire a hundred rounds into a trench full of dead Yankees— not a single living soldier in it."

He felt indignation in the quiver of her arms, heard it crackle in her voice. "The follies committed in this war," he observed, "will be the wonder and bewilderment of generations of unhappy youth who have to study history. And one of the most idiotic acts of all is that I'm here and being paid to try to make soldiers out of a lot of poor ignorant, good-natured country Negro boys. All they're supposed to learn is how to threaten and intimidate. For that I'm a poor teacher."

"You were wounded. They should have let you go home."

He said it again, "I have no home any more." She was perceptive enough not to protest or question. "I had three brothers in the Confederate army," he continued, quite certain that she knew it already.

She sighed. "At least, it's over. Perhaps the wounds will heal. Though my Aunt Ella will never be reconciled, never—if she lives to be a hundred and fifty."

At the edge of town she insisted on alighting and he sat still in the saddle and watched her go off down the dusty street, a neat little figure in that prim dress, her hoops swaying over the toes of her shabby little shoes and kicking up a gentle dust in her wake. He had followed then at a discreet distance, saw her safely into the parsonage as a woman tall and iron gray as a cannon came out and took the basket.

That night he had drawn five pounds of flour from military supplies and very late he had carried it to the brown house, slipping in quietly to lay it on the kitchen doorstep. On a scrap of paper he had written, "From a friend of the parson."

He was sitting on his favorite bench before the courthouse late the next afternoon when she came walking by. She moved very briskly, a little parasol over her head, and as she passed him she dropped the open parasol low over her face and behind the screen of it slipped a little packet of white cloth into his hand. It was warm and fragrant and when he opened the cloth he found a still-hot fluffy biscuit. So she had guessed the donor of the flour. He was grateful for the first hot home-cooked food he had eaten since the beginning of the war. On his brief visit home in June Sue had been able to smuggle in nothing but cold corn bread. He ate the biscuit slowly, watched by a hungry drooling hound, who leaped at every scattered crumb. William rubbed the dog's ears and gave him the last scrap.

"Times have been tough all over, hey, fellow?" he said. He felt suddenly fine. He felt light and buoyant and young again and his knee forbore for a little to remind him that at twenty-five he would be forever, undoubtedly, a lurching cripple.

He wondered if he was in love, if this floating feeling was what happened to a man when the right girl came along? Now, on this sultry night, hitching himself along the dark street, he tried to call back that happy feeling, to concentrate upon himself, William Markland, and upon a girl with brown hair and eyes with a topaz shine. On the realization that the war was over and that the future could hold a promise, as he limped toward his shabby quarters, with six hundred dollars in United States currency in his pocket.

The trouble was that lonely and deserted as was that narrow street, a small ghost walked too close, too hurtingly close. It was almost as if he could reach out and touch another hand, small and brown and quick, with bony fingers that could be both deft and gentle, the hand of another courageous woman, Miss Annie, his mother.

There in that smoky room, with those men who had at the same time excited his youthful audacity and repelled him, he had become aware of his mother abruptly. Of Miss Annie, her clean starched dress that always rustled, her brisk, affectionate, indomitable way, her tricks of making her men do what she wanted them to do. All but her son, William. With him, when it came to matters of principle, she had failed. Perhaps because she had been too proud to weep. If she had cried, he wondered, could she have prevailed, would he have gone off proudly mounted like his brothers, to battle for her Holy Cause, instead of slipping away with Buzzy in the night to ride with Sheridan alongside her enemies?

It was ended now, the last card played for the Confederacy. But here in her own country, here where she had spent most of her life, the enemy of Miss Annie still shuffled the deck, still dealt from the bottom if cheating meant advantage. William limped into his quarters, let his canes fall and dropped onto the hard cot, his strength failing him, as he thought with raw nostalgia of his home.

The rocking chair that creaked, the old yellow bowl in which, for as long as he could remember, Mammy Dory and Minerva after her had beaten up yellow corn bread. The grape arbor where blue globes fell to be trodden into delightful squirtings by small, dirty feet. The wasps and hornets that lurked there too. Goose grease and lemon toddy for a cold, and his father's bellowing call to rouse laggards in time for breakfast.

And then he remembered the jowly, repulsive, tobacco-and-whisky-pickled man, Fletcher, saying, "Sooner or later they're going to bear down on us boys and we'll have to go over there and sell old Boone out."

He lay wide awake till day came, carried out his morning routine woodenly and as soon as he was free went as fast as he could to the courthouse.

The interior of that building was ugly and odorous now, full of loafing Negroes and poor white trash. All the officials, squatting in old armchairs in the dingy offices, were strangers. To a man, they had hard, suspicious faces, and even the blue uniform got William no respect.

"What you want, soldier?" demanded the man in the front office.

"I'm William Markland." He drew himself up and put on his drillmaster attitude of impatient grimness. "I want to pay my father's taxes. The name is Boone Markland."

"Where at? What district?" The man did not stir.

"You'll find the name there in your book. Find it. If there are penalties I want to pay those too."

The collector slouched up, slammed open a heavy book, grumbling, then another.

"Ain't no Boone Markland. Only one Markland. Annie Breen Markland."

"My mother. That's the property. How much does she owe?"

"Two years delinquent. Ought to be posted for sale. Ain't got around to it. You'll have to wait till it's posted, boy. Bid it in at the courthouse door." The man sat down again.

"And be outbid by some carpetbagger? Figure up the indebtedness. I have a right to clear it if I pay all the penalties. That's the law," bluffed William, hoping he was right.

"Markland's Secesh. All of 'em Secesh. What are you doing in that uniform?" demanded the man.

"I fought in this uniform for four years. I've got a right to wear it. Get those figures together. I want them now."

"In a hell of a hurry, ain't you? Maybe you ain't got that much money. Take that two per cent—it gets compounded—devil and all to figure." He chewed a pencil, scrawled laboriously, scratching out, erasing, adding audibly. "Four hundred and eighty-seven dollars, I make it—and thirty-eight cents."

"Here's the money. Count it. And I want an ironclad receipt. No monkey business," said William grimly.

"What'd you do? Rob a bank up there in Virginny? Better rob another and buy you a few good properties. Some mighty fine places going cheap, if you got cash to lay on the barrel head."

William folded the receipt tenderly, patted it into his pocket. It looked legal enough. Somehow he would send it home. Buzzy! Buzzy would welcome that mission.

"I saved your home for you, Miss Annie," he said low to himself as he limped down the steps. "Maybe that pays back a little."

• *Nine* •

THE MULES WERE SLOW AND STUBBORN AND THEIR DELIBERATE PLODDING moved King Markland to wrath. With a heavy hickory gad he beat on their bony haunches but the only result was an irritated jerk of a hard tail, the toss of a jug head, and small hoofs set deliberately in the furrow with no acceleration.

Sweat ran down King's back and dripped from beneath his hat. He wiped his face angrily with an already damp sleeve. The sleeve had a button off the cuff and kept flapping down over his wrist and in a sudden fury of annoyance he tore the cuff off and half the sleeve with it. Winnie would be tearfully apologetic if he told her about the missing button. She was mistily, abjectly sorry about so many things; the burned biscuit, the fire allowed to go out in the middle of cooking a meal because she had found an old book of poetry that had belonged to her Great-grandmother Carter—and "Oh, King, listen to this verse. Isn't it sweet? I could read poetry all day long."

She was always sorry, but the devil of it was that repentance for Winnie never took on the aspect of improvement. She flurried around by candlelight to make the neglected bed, scolding herself meanwhile for being such a bad housekeeper.

"You ought to leave me, King. Really you ought."

Of late, through this scorching August, while the sun beat on the fields making sedge grass and thistles dry and brittle, King had let a traitorous thought slip into his mind in response to this often repeated self-castigation of Winnie's. Maybe if he were smart he would leave. Maybe he had been a fool to walk into this marriage in the first place. Jack had said so, mincing no words. Now Jack was slogging around behind his father trying to get the Markland place going again with small help and no encouragement from Brother Morgan.

Morgan, it had been soon apparent, had come back from the war ready to take up living exactly where he had left it off when the bugles blew. His only explanation of his delayed return was that he had taken a notion to see the country, had traveled around down south awhile, eventually deciding to come along home. In the Federal uniform looted from the dead he had slipped into a detachment of Union troops, come north in comfort with a wagon train, won most of the money the other soldiers had, and taken quiet leave of the outfit on a dark night. Now he wore his good clothes, teased his mother and Sue incessantly, and kept up a childish war of words with Boone-boy who admired and emulated him.

"There should," he announced blandly, "be one Markland gentleman left."

When Jack stormed that even gentlemen had to eat and that corn still had to be gathered and wheat ground plowed and harrowed, Morgan gave a mocking shrug, saddled the three-year-old stallion and disappeared for two or three days. When he returned he lugged in heavy saddlebags and dumped their contents on the kitchen table.

"Coffee!" she exclaimed, when he led his mother to survey his spoils. "And white flour and sugar! And even tea! Morgan, where in the world?"

"Money," he grinned insolently, "will buy things, my dear Miss Annie. Even from Yankees. Now the gentlemen in the family can eat."

King went home often. There were no work animals left at the Markland place so the Oliver mules had to be loaned for the field jobs, Jack and his father coming over in turn to help King in his attempts at reclaiming the overgrown Oliver acres. But this morning King was trying to plow alone, and already the palms of his hands were stinging and his shoulders aching from the jolting of the plow through the stubborn sod. He hated it, that was the trouble. He had hated the breakfast that he had had to help cook, the watery mush, the bacon dug out of the old root cellar where the Colonel had buried it, so rancid now that even the odor of it frying was obnoxious.

Winnie had cried a little, but that had not softened him this morning, because there was an uncomfortable, unsatisfactory night to remember. Winnie would never, King was convinced, be a real wife to any man. To her, marriage was poetry, kisses in the moonlight, being together, touching hands, all delicate, all fastidious. For the rest, it was nasty, it was horrid, it was terror to her and sobbing, and the contrite pleadings that followed were ceasing to move him any more.

"I will try, King. I promise," she whimpered.

Now, dropping down in a shady spot close to the sagging fence, King knew that he was tired of that too.

If her mother had stayed—but as soon as the transportation was available Mary Oliver had gone south to a sister in Mississippi. The sister was a widow too. They would comfort each other, and after all young married folks were better off by themselves, and it might be that once she got down Corinth way Mary could find her lost son's grave. King learned then about the money his mother-in-law had so craftily kept hidden.

"She had to hide it, it was all she had, her little hoard she had saved, dollar by dollar," Winnie wailed. "You don't know about my father and young Carter after him! Always liquor and gambling, always every cent spent unless Mother took it when they were asleep, took it and hid it. She earned it by her awful patience with her husband and her son. And she didn't dare let Grandpa know that she had it or he would have given it to the Confederacy."

"You don't have to argue with me about it, Winnie," King protested. "It's her money. Let her spend it. But I wish she'd stay."

Mary Oliver might have been able to teach her daughter a little about duty and responsibility, about being the head of a household rather than a spoiled and petted child of that household with no responsibility. That childish business might be all right for a girl of fifteen but now Winnie was twenty-four and as immature in her attitude toward life as Boone-boy.

He looked wide at the hostile ground, so much of it, and all to his mind withdrawn into itself, old and intolerant of him, defying the plow, offering him a vicious challenge. The strength of his young muscles, already weakened by war, against old rocks, old briars, old grass grown matted and grim. What was he doing here anyway? He was no dirt-digging farmer, sweated, callused and stodgy, content with seeing seed emerge into leaf and an ear of corn grow where none had grown before.

Jack was adapting himself, not happily, but the ebullient determination of Boone Markland carried Jack along. And Sue, King knew, was doing mightily helping Miss Annie keep the Marklands fed and clean and halfway content with the meager living offered now to a people who had for so long known the comforts of plenty and ease, made possible by the service of black hands.

Sue had been a belle once, too, even more courted and popular than fragile little Winnie. There had been a time when King knew that he could have married Sue Wetherby. He had been the fickle one then, looking the field over, not too eager to be tied down, expecting Sue or any other girl to wait contentedly till King Markland had sowed all his wild oats.

That Sue had heard some kind of tale about the bright girl, Lutie, he knew, but in those wild, free days before the war white women learned to overlook and ignore the casual affairs of men and became more or less reconciled to seeing ivory-skinned babies born in the slave quarters. There had been Buzzy. Had Miss Annie let her temper fly and thrown her wedding ring in Boone Markland's face? Miss Annie was a lady and if she was hurt she never admitted or revealed it, wise enough to know that there was an outlaw thing in every man's blood that no wife could ever hope to capture or tame.

On a sudden irritated impulse King jumped up from the shady fence row and strode out to the field where the mules dozed with drooping heads and sagging hips. He unhooked the trace chains from the plow, tossed them over the hames and, mounting the off mule, headed for the barn, leaving the plow in the furrow. He fed the animals, tossing some old hay down from the mow, waiting briefly for a clink that often revealed he had dug into another of the old Colonel's hidden caches of provender, silver or household ware.

Hadn't the senile old fool known that if the guerrilla prowlers did come marauding and looting, the barn would be the first place searched, unless they began their orgy of destruction by burning the building? He wondered how many times the old man had panted up that ladder sequestering his possessions with the naïve trustfulness of a pack rat. What he could not hide, the Colonel had destroyed, including all the saddles and the Oliver carriage.

In the kitchen Winnie was bending over a washtub dabbing at a froth of white petticoats. Her face was fiery red, her hair hanging limply over her ears. She dried her hands on an already damp apron and faced her husband with a look of harried desperation.

"You didn't find any soap, did you?" she questioned. "I know he hid some somewhere, a whole keg of soft soap. Mother told him we would need it wherever we went but he shouted at us that the wagon was already overloaded and we could get more soap."

"No soap," said King, pouring water into a basin and sloshing it over his heated face. "I reckon he buried it. We'll find a little heap of rocks some place and under it will be the soap, same way we found the vinegar keg and the rock salt. It's not in that root cellar. I looked."

"Please don't waste water," begged Winnie. "I've pumped and pumped till my arms are killing me. The cistern is low too. Surely it will rain before long."

"Why don't you leave off wearing all that white stuff?" demanded King. "Miss Annie and Sue said they put away all their ruffled duds long ago. Too much trouble to keep clean."

"Oh, but I couldn't!" she protested. "How could I be properly dressed? I only wear three anyway. I used to wear seven petticoats—always. I can't go around all limp and horrible, King, I just can't."

"Who's going to see you? Maybe Miss Annie has some soap. I'm going over there. I'll ask her."

"You're going—and leave me here all alone?" she cried, aghast.

"Unless you want to go with me. It's a long walk in this hot sun."

"Walk? Oh, I couldn't! But how can I stay here alone? Suppose some Yankees came or some awful free Negroes or somebody?"

"Lock the door. You'll be safe unless they burn the house," said King callously. "Anyway, I'm going to borrow a horse from Pa and go to town," he added. "I've got an errand there."

"I'll have to go. I'd never dare stay here alone. You'll have to wait till I finish this and change my dress."

"Leave that stuff to soak. I've got to shave and change clothes. Get your primping done and take along a parasol. That sun is red-hot today." He stalked off, leaving her complaining and fluttering. She would be an hour at least, arranging her hair, choosing a dress and hat and the stuff that went under the dress. He picked up the iron tea-kettle from the stove, felt it for warmth, tramped off with it.

In their upper room the bed was unmade, the slop jar had not been emptied. He carried that down, grumbling impatiently, demanding as he passed through the kitchen, "Any soap anywhere at all? I can't shave without soap."

She handed him a gourd without a word. She was angry too, he knew, but her temper was a frail thing, like the wrathful shrilling of a sparrow. He ignored it as he ignored all her moods of late.

"Old brown stuff." He scowled at the soap. "Miss Annie knows how to make soap that's hard and white."

"Miss Annie! Miss Annie!" she screamed at him then. "Miss Annie knows everything. Everything except how to raise sons to be gentlemen."

He looked at her with his sardonic brows tilted. "And what would you do with a gentleman, pet? Let him wear unironed shirts, sleep in an unmade bed and eat half-cooked food off half-washed dishes?"

"You don't want a wife. You want a slave!"

He nodded, his mouth quirked, the insolence that always maddened her a mocking mask on his face.

"Might trade you off for a smart yellow gal. It's an idea," he taunted.

Miss Annie exclaimed over them as they walked into the cool Markland house, hot, flushed, angry and dusty.

"My word, Winnie, you look ready to drop. Walking over a mile in this awful heat! Sit here and take this fan and I'll fetch you a cool drink of my raspberry shrub."

"I do feel faint." Winnie's voice was a sick whisper. "I never have walked that far in all my life."

"You might as well get used to it, Winnie," Sue said dryly. "You might as well accept things. We're all poor-white now. We have to learn to live like them. No wonder you got tired, walking in those little thin slippers!"

"But I haven't any other kind of shoes. Oh, thank you, Mrs. Markland." Winnie took the beaded glass and held it daintily to her lips.

"You sit here and cool off," said her mother-in-law. "Sue and I are putting up pears. Morgan found some sugar in town and we decided to save what we could for winter."

"Oh, how clever you are," approved Winnie. "I do wish I was smart. All our fruit is just lying on the ground rotting. Old Sudie always did it, and since she left it has all gone to waste."

"It's blisters, not smartness, sis," remarked Sue. "Just turning to and getting the job done no matter how much you hate it."

"But I wouldn't even know how to begin," defended Winnie. "I don't know how to do anything and King gets so irked with me."

She ignored Sue's lifted shoulder, the dry twist of her lips. "You'll have to excuse Miss Annie and me, Winnie." Sue retied her apron with an irritating gesture of competence. "The doggone syrup boils over if we take our eyes off of it."

Winnie was glad to be left alone to relax in a comfortable chair. If only she did not have to go back! If only she could stay here where there was order and calm and people to do the dreadful housekeepy things that baffled her, kind people who cared what happened to you. The old Oliver house had become a monstrous nightmare of a place where always some wretched task needed to be done and things not done mounted into catastrophe. This, she was thinking, relaxed and meditative, waving the fan languidly, was King's home as much as it was Jack's. They had the right to be here. What a blessing, she nursed the wicked wish, if Grandpa Oliver's tiresome old house would burn to the ground!

In the barn King found his father and Jack hammering a tire back on a wagon wheel. Jack looked at his brother.

"You look beat." He straightened up and dropped the hammer. "Can we borrow your team and wagon tomorrow? Miss Annie says she's mighty near out of wood. And we could use a hand on the saw too."

"Swap you for the loan of a horse today," King said. "I want to ride into town."

"Better stay away from town," advised Boone, straightening up with a grunt. "Unioners and Nigras have taken over up there. Man could get in bad trouble."

"You don't keep Morgan away from town," reminded Jack. "He went off this morning riding the only good horse we've got."

Boone Markland scrubbed sweat from his eyes. His father was beginning to show his age, King observed. There was a sag in his wide shoulders that had not been there before. He was more subdued, less noisy and impatient.

"I never did get a bridle on Morgan," he said heavily. "He was his mammy's boy. Got into trouble she took up for him. Now if he gets into trouble he manages to get himself out of it. You boys might not be so lucky."

"Meaning we can't hold our liquor like Morgan?" asked Jack.

"Meaning we don't know all Morgan's tricks," said King. "He could always talk himself out of anything, duck all the dirty jobs. Even in the cavalry he was good at it. Got put on reconnaissance patrol or riding courier when we got set afoot in the mud to advance against some red-hot Yankee entrenchment."

"Got home with shoes on his feet and money in his pockets." Jack took up the complaint. "Now Miss Annie thinks he hung the moon. Waits on him hand and foot."

"He pets her and fetches her presents," Boone sighed. "Women like that. Always telling her how smart she is. She knows she's smart without being told over and over."

"Anything left here that a man can ride?" persisted King.

"That gelding. He's broke and shod but he's got no speed and not much wind. Any time you geld a colt he gets fat and lazy, so he won't give any trouble though he won't be three till fall. He'll ride. That saddle up yonder is fixed up," Boone pointed. "I put new leather on the stirrups and a new pad under it. Don't heat him up or hitch him where those buzzards can steal him. Every time Morgan rides that bay into town I look for him to come home afoot."

But Morgan did not come home on foot. He came, very late, when his mother had turned gray-faced and tense-fisted with worry and Boone Markland had tramped the room, muttering for three hours.

"It's the horses you're worrying about, not the boys!" Miss Annie stormed at him.

"A horse can't take care of himself. Those boys are grown men, been through a war," defended Boone.

It was getting on for dawn when Morgan rode in quietly.

He had brought King home, braced limply behind him. King was bandaged and bloody and almost unconscious. Winnie, who had been lying wide awake in the big bed upstairs, heard voices and came flying down. She gave a little shriek and fainted away.

But nobody paid any attention to Winnie.

• *Ten* •

IT HAD BEEN THE MUSIC THAT DREW AND MADDENED HIM.

He had had a little too much to drink. On the outskirts of town he had met a friend of his youth, a shattered young-old man who had fought with Johnston and Hood and known the torment of defeat and the sick, sad death of glory. Now this spent and embittered veteran lived with a whining mother and a doggedly industrious father who cut wood for a scanty living and had no sensitive scruples about peddling it to the radicals, whether they were black or white.

The friend, whose name was Ransome, had made no effort at adjustment since the surrender and spent his time loafing on a sagging porch.

"Cussing the Union and ready to run and hide if they come after him," his mother grumbled. "Got ambition enough to tilt that jug and that's about all."

Twilight was falling, the days were getting shorter. The gelding was a jolting mount and King had been glad to slide out of the saddle and join Ransome in tilting the jug, ignoring the fact that except for the homemade liquor and the heady relaxation it produced they had nothing whatever in common.

For two hours, till the hot summer dusk pressed down, they refought the war, berating all the colonels, the generals and the enemy impartially till Ransome grew blurry in his speech, then drowsy. King was beginning to feel a gnawing within that reminded him he had not eaten since early morning, also his smoldering irritation with his lot was beginning to flare again, breaking out in a burning resentment against Winnie.

He would, he fumed, show Winnie that she was not the only woman in the world. Anger made him reckless, with a lusty male fever for conquest, and the whisky fired this slowly simmering rage into arrogant rashness.

The gelding stood dozing under a mulberry tree. The horse should have been fed and watered but when King took a dizzy look at the cistern it appeared a long way off to his wavering sight. Riding with Forrest they had watered their animals at any handy creek, ridden them long and hard, sometimes for a day and night without rest. King lifted the jug and sloshed it around. It was empty. In disgust he hurled it out into the bare, swept yard, gave a parting grunt at Ransome who had fallen into a drunken slumber on the dirty boards of the porch, untied the horse and got himself with some difficulty into the saddle.

The tents of the garrison company were pitched on a slope running raggedly down to the river and King made a wide detour around them, guiding the gelding to the water's edge near the still-charred ruin of a bridge. While the horse drank he dozed in the saddle, dimly aware of the shack settlement beyond, of the slattern makeshift shelters, the murky fires, the dim smoky lights. Not aware at all of the prowling, hostile figures that hung back in the trees or of the yellow boy who had slipped out of the garrison bivouac and who was following him, eyeballs big and uneasy in a taut face.

It was when he turned back from the river that King heard the music. It was swamp music, primitive as the creeping of dark, secret creatures through tangling vine and sucking morass. It was a music as old as creation, old as the Nile, the mourning sob and keen and arpeggio of a people despised and rejected since time began. In mud huts in the shadow of the palaces of the Pharaohs, in the reeking deeps of slave ships, the moan and timbre and ululation of it would have been the same, the melodic plaintive heartbreak of a homeless people.

There was the hollow beat of slapping palms and a liquid note of sorrow, high and eerie, and lost like water poured from a failing jug. And over the monotonous percussion, the occasional high shrilled timbre of lament, rose the clear soprano of a woman. No word that could be distinguished, only the flutelike tones rising and falling, poignant with old sorrow.

King jerked up the head of his horse sharply. He had heard that voice before. Bought with some purloined bit of finery from his mother's bureau that same singing had soothed the young, wild fevers in his blood as the girl herself had satisfied his other flaming need.

"Lutie!" he shouted aloud, digging his heels into the flanks of his mount. "Lutie!"

Footsteps pounded beside him. He heard a voice yelling, "Mist' King! Mist' King!" That voice too struck a familiar note but King was too befuddled to recognize it. When the yellow boy who had shouted tried to seize the bridle King whipped the horse and almost ran him down.

Then out of the shadows they sprang at him, dark, panting shapes with white eyeballs rolling and knives flashing.

"After my woman!" snarled a black man, who hit him with a rock, numbing his arm. "Let me at him. I cut his thote!"

King laid about him with the whip but more of them appeared, and by sheer weight of numbers they pulled him off his horse. Struggling wildly he saw a heavy rock upraised in a black man's hand. He ducked swiftly, thrusting an elbow into a throat, a knee into a groin. The same old furious kind of fighting that had served him so many times against an entrenched Union line. Almost, he thought he heard old Nate Forrest shouting, thought he could hear the thud of gun butts against skulls, the horrid yells, then a knife got to him. He felt the hot burn of its thrust and went down almost under the feet of a strange horse.

Then out of the mist that swam into dull vision, he heard an officer shout. "Lift him easy! Lay him over the saddle."

There was a familiarity about that voice too but darkness was closing in on King Markland. When he roused again it was day and he was

[80]

lying, bandaged and weak and nauseated, on a bed in his father's house.

In the parlor the three Markland men faced each other, tight-lipped, eyes wary.

"All right!" Boone boomed through the silence. "Where did you find him?"

Morgan was not on the defensive. He stood, relaxed, smiling a little while the other two glared at him.

"I did not find him, sir," he replied in his best military manner. "It was Buzzy who found him."

"That yellow—" Coarse epithets fumed from Jack's lips.

"Buzzy found him and ran for Billy. Our brother, William, who happens to be a Union captain, sir. He and two other officers broke up the fracas but not before those black devils had cut King up pretty bad. Billy put King over the saddle and took him to a Yankee doctor, who patched him up. Then he sent Buzzy to find me," explained Morgan.

"And where were you?" demanded his father.

With a languid gesture of pure insolence Morgan took a black cheroot from a pocket, lit it elaborately.

"I, sir, was sitting in on a little game. And I was spoiling the despoilers. It happens that our brother William had seen me before. He knew where to look. So between us we loaded King on my saddle and I brought him home. Naturally Billy, out of respect for your prejudice, did not want to bring King home himself. It was fortunate that I was in town."

"Prejudice?" barked Jack. "What about you? Have you turned radical all of a sudden?"

"I keep an open mind, Brother dear," drawled Morgan. "We are indebted to Brother William. But for his intervention King would now be carrion, probably dumped into the river."

"We want no favors from Yankee turncoats," blasted Jack.

"The favor we received happens to have saved King's life," returned Morgan, unperturbed. "If that's worth anything to you." He walked away, deliberately, turning back at the hall door. "I'm going to bed. King won't die. But you may as well know what he was doing in that shack town. He was looking for a yellow woman named Lutie. You may remember the wench, before the war she belonged to Sam Hilliard."

"Where's King's horse?" demanded Boone.

Morgan smiled again and there was a kind of mockery in the smile, a gleam of impudent delight. He seemed to be enjoying their futile fury since now it was not directed at him.

"Buzzy," he said, "will bring the horse home. And a word of advice to you two fire-eaters. Buzzy wears a Union uniform. Any offense committed against a man in that uniform is punishable by imprisonment, even by death. I have been thus carefully instructed. I pass those instructions on to you."

He had not seen his mother come quietly down the stairs, so that now she stood just behind him. Obviously she had been listening. She put up a hand and stopped him as he started past her.

"You saw Billy." It was a statement, not a question.

"I saw Billy," he told her gently. "He rescued King from a gang of angry Negroes who might have killed him."

She flung her hands over her face. "I won't have it!" she wailed. "I won't have it. All of you standing here, hating him, despising him! Your own flesh and blood!"

Morgan came back into the room. "Look, Miss Annie—" he dug into his pockets, pulled out a thick wad of bills. "Hold out your apron. Money. Nice, green, good Yankee money. I took it away from those Yankee scalawags. You can buy things with it."

She only looked at him dazedly, flung out her hands in a pitiful gesture, letting the money fall to the floor. Then she ran out of the room.

"She'll calm down," said Boone, "but I wish she hadn't heard about Billy. She broods about him all the time and there ain't a thing we can do. He picked his path. He's the one threw his family away, every living thing we stand for."

"We'll never live him down," grumbled Jack. "For two bits I'd head out for Texas."

"You'd find the same thing in Texas," said Morgan. "Black men top dogs, white Southerners being pushed around. It's here. It's our defeat. We've got to live with it."

Jack blazed at his brother. "You fought for the South! How many times are you going to surrender, for God's sake?"

Morgan gave a little shrug. "Any time it appears to be the profitable, expedient thing to do, Brother Jackson, any time at all. Good night, all—or should I say good morning?"

"He came home in a Yank uniform." Jack turned to his father with bitterness riding his face. "Before I'd have worn a rag of their cursed blue I'd have walked the roads stark naked."

"He's young," his father sighed wearily. "He's only twenty-two years old. He'll learn sense. Maybe he'll have to learn it the hard way, like King yonder."

"Hard to figure that out. King must have been mighty drunk. He used to be wild but he was never a teetotal damfool before. Though that girl upstairs would drive a man crazy, even if he was in love with her, and you know and I know, Pa, that King never was. Didn't have to marry her—Lord no! She's got no more fire in her than a dish of cold mush. You can't explain it, King throwing away all the common sense he was born with, marrying a limpsy crybaby like that Winnie. King couldn't explain it himself."

"All he told me," said Boone, "was that he thought it was the right thing to do. Those two women—nobody to take care of them."

"The old lady took herself off fast enough once she got Winnie off on King's shoulders. Had money hid out too, King told me. I reckon now we've got that place to see after too, Pa. Might as well get some sleep."

Annie Lou Markland did not sleep that night. She sat beside King's bed sponging his face with cool water, watching the bandages so that they did not slip, murmuring soothingly to him when he tossed and muttered. He had been badly slashed under his right arm and there was a stab wound in his breast but it had not gone deep, the knife having glanced off the breastbone. There were great purple bruises on his head and face and one of his eyes was swelled shut. A heavy boot had landed on his mouth and his lips were puffed and fluttered when he breathed. His breath still reeked of the raw whisky he had drunk.

Winnie came tiptoeing in once, looking so white and transparent that Miss Annie's gentle heart was touched for the girl. She made Winnie sit in a rocking chair and gave her a cool drink.

"He'll be all right," she whispered. "He's hurt bad but he's strong. He'll get over it."

Winnie's eyes were enormous and in them was a look of stunned incredulity.

"I heard them talking," she said in a strangled whisper. "I couldn't help it. This door was open and they have such loud voices. I heard about that yellow woman. It isn't true, is it?"

Miss Annie sighed. "My dear," she said low, "you married a man. So did I—and so does every woman. We can't really understand them, and because understanding can hurt and destroy us a little in our own eyes, we don't even try. We feel wronged and won't let ourselves believe that they need more than gentlewomen have to give, even when we give willingly. I'd forget it all if I were you."

"How can I?" whimpered Winnie. "Miss Annie"—a spot of color burned in her drained cheek and her eyes glittered in the wan candle-light—"I won't live like my mother. All her life—forgiving. All her married life hoping for a change, for a little peace, a little happiness. Miss Annie, my mother was glad when my father went off to war. You hear—glad! And when he was killed she put on black but she did not grieve. People said she was brave, but she wasn't. She was at peace. All the dreadful time she had known was ended. When young Carter went she cried, but after that she was like another person. She had no more horrid nights ahead, listening for a horse to come crashing home toward dawn, for the shouts and oaths of drunken fumblings, the humiliations. Oh, I know. I was young but I suffered with her, lying all drawn up in a scared cold knot in bed, too frightened to stir from my room. Miss Annie, King is your son and I love him but I won't live like that!"

Miss Annie sat, sunk small and desolate in the chair beside the bed. "Maybe this will end the wildness, Winnie. Maybe this will be the cure. Now you go and sleep. You can tend your husband later while I rest."

Winnie rose and there was a straightness about her as of a white candle. Her eyes flashed.

"I don't know if I'll want to touch him again—ever!" she said, grimly, and marched out of the room.

Dawn was blue-gray behind the curtains when Morgan came in.

"I'm staying now, Miss Annie," he said. "You get some sleep."

"No—no," she protested. "I'm all right. I want to take care of him."

Morgan bent without a word and picked her up bodily, a little dis-mayed by the lightness of her small frame. She struggled and cuffed at him affectionately but he only laughed.

"Forget I was a sergeant in this here mean old war, Miss Annie? When I give orders somebody moves." He carried her into his own room, straightened the pillows and covers one-handedly, laid her flat on the bed, crossing her hands on her bosom, pressing her eyelids down with gentle fingers, all the while grinning boyishly. "Go to sleep now. This merry little ruckus is over. Pa's snoring already. King will feel worse than the devil in the morning, mind and body. Let him suffer. Do him good. He could have been killed tonight. Next time he might not be so lucky. Maybe this will teach him a little sense." He took off her shoes, dropped them beside the bed.

She opened her eyes and put up a small brown hand, clutching at his shirt. "Billy—you saw him?"

"It was dark, Mama."

"He's all right?"

"Stiff knee. Got a ball in it at Five Forks. But he can ride."

"Will you take me some time. Just you and me, Little Brother?" There was heartbreak in the question.

He hesitated. "Things are—mean up there, Miss Annie. No place for a lady."

"I'm his mother."

"I'll see. We'll talk later. You sleep some now. Don't worry. Just remember you had four boys go to war and all of them got back. Not many mothers were that lucky."

"I know. I'm thankful. On my knees." But he had gone and softly closed the door.

She could not sleep but obediently she lay still. Day grew brighter, she heard the morning sounds beginning. The half-grown chickens squawking to be fed around the back door, Boone's heavy boots slogging down the stairs and Boone-boy clattering after, full of shrill questions, Boone's bumbling answers. She heard Sue come out of her room and speak to Morgan. Sue had kept discreetly in the background last night. This had been Markland trouble, King's affair and Winnie's, Sue had no part in it.

Miss Annie slipped out of bed, gave her disordered hair a pat or two, straightened her apron and put on her shoes. Quietly she went down the stairs. In the kitchen Sue was filling the kettle and Minerva, tight-mouthed and with evasive looks, came in with some wood.

"You set table, Miss Sue," Minerva ordered, with the casual freedom of an old servant. "I cooks sump'n to eat."

Sue said, "Make Miss Annie some coffee first thing you do," and went into the dining room where she began rattling knives and forks in a drawer. Minerva laid light wood on the fire, moved the kettle over it, then she crooked a cautioning finger.

"You come, Mist'iss—outside."

Bewildered, Miss Annie followed the woman out, and under the grape arbor Minerva made a great clatter with a wooden bucket at the cistern pump. Over the racket her voice was barely audible.

"Miss Dory's house—he there. You go, Mist'iss."

Annie Lou Markland made herself remember not to run down the sandy path to Mammy Dory's cabin. She knocked at the door, looking about her first with a flare of defiance. This is my old servant's house, she's sick. I have a right to be here. Then the door opened a narrow crack and her throat contracted so that what issued was little more than a squeak.

"Buzzy!"

He pulled her in gently and shut the door. He was in uniform. Not clean and not new any more, one button missing from the tunic.

Mammy Dory was jabbering in the bed. "Mah boy come back! Mah boy come back!"

Buzzy pulled out a chair. "Sit down, Miss Annie. You lookin' faint. Mist' King? He—"

"He'll be all right, Buzzy. And thank you for helping him."

"I brung his horse back before day. I rode most all night. It was so dark and that colt was plumb wore out, Miss Annie, I ain't able to git him off a walk. I done put him up and fed him. Ain't nobody heard me," Buzzy assured her. "I'll sleep here some today and git back to camp tonight. Kin I sleep in Ranse' ole house, Miss Annie?"

"Oh, yes—yes—and I'll bring you some breakfast. But how are you going to get back, Buzzy? Back to camp? It's so far."

"They'll come for me. Cap'n fix it up. And Miss Annie, he tole me to give you this. Not to nobody else, Cap'n say. Give it to Miss Annie and don't tell nobody." He took a soiled paper from the inner mysteries of his apparel and laid it in her hand.

"Buzzy—" She stared at him. "Who—who—?"

"Cap'n Billy, Miss Annie. Cap'n Billy Markland, that who."

"Oh, Buzzy!" She bit her lip, tears standing in her eyes. "It's all wrong. You ought to be here. Both of you. Both of my boys—"

"Yessum," gulped Buzzy. "I don't like that ginny army no way but Cap'n say if I run away they hang me."

"You go and get some sleep. But wait for your breakfast. I'll bring it myself," she announced firmly.

The loom house door was open and she slipped inside and sat down weakly on the weaver's stool, spreading the rumpled paper out over her knees.

She had to read it through three times before its meaning came clear. The taxes! Paid in full, the paper said. Billy had done that and Boone Markland must never know. Jack must never know.

"They'd sell everything on the place to pay this money back," she told herself. "Jack would throw it in Billy's face. Oh, my dear son. My dear, dear boy!" She pressed the tax receipt against her cheek, then folded it carefully and hid it in her bosom.

· *Eleven* ·

KING LAY FOR TWO WEEKS IMPATIENT AND FULL OF GLOOMY ANGERS
while his wounds slowly healed. The deep cut under his arm had been
trampled full of filth and too hastily treated so that now there was pus
and inflammation that frightened Winnie, although Miss Annie attacked it calmly enough with hot linseed poultices and swabbings with
turpentine and raw corn whisky.

"When they were little they were always getting cut and bruised and
once Jack shot himself through the foot. I thought that hole would
never heal. I used to pull a soft rag through it, all the way through,
soaked in oil to keep it clean. It did close after a while. You might as
well get used to it, Winnie, if you mean to raise a family," she said.

"I don't know—" began Winnie faintly. Then she flushed and
flounced out of the room when King gave a dry, barking laugh.

Miss Annie went on talking to cover up an uncomfortable awkward-
ness she did not entirely understand. She could sympathize with Winnie for being hurt and insulted by King's drunken action but she was
more than a little puzzled by the harshly synical attitude of her son. It
was as if he were lying there blaming Winnie for everything that had
happened, and being amused by her furies and resentments.

Sue had complicated the situation too by setting herself up as King's
champion. That Sue was being extra solicitous of King's comfort, seeing that his food was the best that could be achieved from their lean
supplies, having his sheets fresh and cool every morning as a kind of
backhanded slap at Winnie's inefficiency, was clear to their mutual
mother-in-law. The puzzling angle was that Winnie seemed not to
care very much, but when Annie Lou thought it through she could
understand that too. There was a transparency about Winnie that
went deeper than physical fragility. It was as though Winnie's slim
white body was a crystal case which enclosed but did not protect her.
Inside you could almost see her thoughts and emotions turning like the
works of a watch, impelled by the fine hairspring of her own small,
stubborn self-importance.

Winnie had been wound up to spin out her life in only one way.

Somebody would always have to take care of her, keep her precious, and by a sad succession of disappointments she had been repeatedly bereft of that demanded support and protection. Three Carter Olivers had let Winnie down, one after the other; her furious old warlock of a grandfather, her drunken father, her worthless brother. Then she had been abandoned by her mother and now King, her husband, had defected.

Winnie came into King's room dutifully when the others were too busy to sit by him but she pulled her chair as far from the bed as possible and sat there fanning herself languidly, answering in grudging monosyllables when King attempted any conversation.

Chiefly he slept, the sheet pulled over his ears against the annoyance of a few flies that slipped into the darkened room. Then Sue would bustle in briskly, close the blinds tighter, give Winnie a dismissing look, half pity, half disdain, switch out the flies while she chattered to King. But Winnie appeared to be unperturbed, pulling herself into her pale shell and all the quivering antennae of her vanity in after her.

Miss Annie noted these maneuvers quietly, saying nothing, until it became obvious that Jack was becoming resentful of his wife's possessive concern for King. When she saw the simmering anger, thinly concealed on the face of her eldest son, Miss Annie decided to spend more time in the sickroom.

All summer Jack had been drawing in upon himself more and more, a brooding aloofness in him being broken through now and then by snappish flares of indignation. There was so little left, his mother knew, so little to interest or enthuse a young man. Only a life that was little now but an arid, demanding treadmill, offering small promise of reward. War had swept him away in its excitement, then war had turned ugly and mean, and bugles and flags had not been enough to keep spirit alive in men who suffered through it. And now home had been degraded into ugliness and meanness too.

No longer were there Negro men to carry on the grubby work in field and pasture, no longer the fine horses, the rich crops, and she sensed that to Jack's impatient eyes the future held little that was better. Once he had been full of plans and excited about working them out, but now nothing seemed important enough to concern him, and the flickering of his jealousy was obvious.

"I wouldn't make so much over King if I were you, Sue," Miss Annie launched boldly one morning. "No use to irk Jack. I know you don't mean a thing by it but a touchy husband is as unpredictable as a powder keg."

"Winnie makes me so mad!" fumed Sue, snapping viciously at the beans she was shelling. "King needs to be encouraged and she just freezes him."

"Jack needs encouragement too," suggested his mother. "He used to be so smart about fixing things. He laid all those wooden pipes to bring the spring water down to the stables, but now there's little to farm with, and it's dismal trying to work with those poor old crow-bait Oliver mules. When I think of all those fine fat mules we had once—"

"They wore them out hauling artillery," Sue said. "They wore out the mules and the horses and the men. And they came mighty near wearing out the women. Miss Annie"—Sue flung out her hands, scattering beans in a tinkling shower—"do you realize I'm only twenty-five years old? And Jack's not thirty yet and we're old, old people."

"You don't look old to me." Miss Annie smiled and tried for lightness. "That color hair won't turn gray till you're really old. Now mine—it's been gray since I can remember and it was black as Jack's once, that shade of black that looks blue when the sun strikes it."

"It's pretty now, Miss Annie, with your black eyebrows and those long lashes."

"Irish. Irish eyes, rubbed in with a sooty finger, my mother used to say."

It troubled Sue that Jack did not talk to her any more. Only the desultory, unimportant scraps of commonplace conversation that might ensue between two people not acutely interested in each other. When he came in at night he was always tired and his first act was to kick off the heavy, dusty shoes that he kept limber by smearing them with axle grease. The shoes had been cobbled for slaves on the place, and that idea was in the loathing kick that Jack gave them.

Every morning he stamped back into the shoes again, gave his too-long hair a swipe with Sue's rubber comb and frowned at his whiskered face in the mirror.

"A hell of a handsome brute!" he snarled at his reflection on a hot morning when King had been two weeks in bed.

Sue, scrabbling into her heavy white cotton stockings, perched on the high edge of the bed, gave him an intent, examining look.

"You can be a handsome brute," she said crisply. "You've done it before."

"What for?" He gave his sweat-stained suspenders an irritated hitch. "So I'll look pretty slogging along a corn row? Those mules don't wear looking glasses under their tails. They don't even turn an eye to see who's beating on their rumps, whether I'm black or white. Put me some cold bread in a poke, Pa's determined to go over to the Oliver place today. Says we're duty bound to help out King and Winnie when they're in trouble."

"Why don't you take Winnie along? She could cook up something for you over there. I should think she'd want to know what is happening to her house."

"I've got the key," Jack said. "I know what's happening to the house. She left it in a mess and nobody has cleaned it up since they walked out of it."

"Well, one thing's certain," snapped Sue. "I'm not going over there to clean up her dirt. Nor Miss Annie either. So don't you mention it downstairs. Winnie might flare up anyway."

"I've never seen her flare up at getting out of doing anything," grumbled Jack. "Just so nobody crosses over that line she draws around her own private vanity and conceit. No Markland gets inside that line, not even King. King least of all, I'd say." His face darkened. He prodded a button through a buttonhole. It fell off and he swore unhappily at it. "You know, Sue, I don't believe King is any more married to Winnie than I am. Really married."

"Hush!" She flushed a little, though there were times when the rigid prudery of the age irked her more than a little. "King's got little to say"—she let hasty malice scorch away her inhibitions—"running off to a shanty town after a yellow bitch."

Jack laughed, short and ugly. "You nice, delicate white women. You should have got a little taste of the war, of what some of those women down in Alabama and Georgia got. Something should have happened to you so you could comprehend the hell life has been for young men these last years. You stood off and said, Oh, how dreadful! Just like a schoolteacher seeing a nigger beat a jackass. But there never was any common denominator and I don't suppose there ever will be. The women will be the ones to keep the war alive. The men who fought in it would like to bury it deep and stamp on the grave but you women will convince yourselves in a few years that the whole damn hellish mess was very sad and romantic."

"What has all this tirade got to do with your brother getting himself half-killed, running after a Nigra slut?" she demanded.

"Because," he balanced himself on the balls of his feet in the door, grinning at her one-sidedly, looking impudent and dangerous and handsome in a Satanic fashion, "because the thing that sent King helling off to town was the same thing that has sent a million odd men into wars since time was. Because men need more than good women can give them and though they don't know exactly what it is they want, they know that they want it enough to fight for it. What they want out of any kind of fracas is to prove to themselves that they are men. Not many do. But the wanting is there, deep under."

"You talk like Billy, out of a book," scorned his wife, "and if you don't shave that beard off pretty soon I won't sleep with you. I'll move into the company room with Winnie."

"You'd freeze to death." He scrubbed his face with slender, callused fingers. "What's wrong with my whiskers? They keep the flies off my neck."

"They make you look as old as General Nate Forrest."

"Poor old Nate's brush was getting mighty grizzly by the time we got to Alabama."

He went pounding off down the stairs and Sue heard her small son's bare feet thudding after his father. The smell of cooking drifted up. Ham. Abruptly she knew that she was hungry. She knew that Morgan had money from somewhere, that he made mysterious contacts in town and that presently food appeared on the Markland table. Morgan was in the dining room when she went in. He sat at the table sopping corn muffins in red gravy.

"Ham!" Sue exclaimed. "You baffle me, Morgan. Where on earth did you find it?"

He grinned at her over the edge of his cup. "Money, my pet, nice Andrew Johnson money. It goes anywhere. It buys things. It has no party and no politics and no passionate prejudices. All those stupidities sneak out the door when money comes in the window."

"That ham was looted from some poor Confederate family, I'll wager."

"Might be. At least I didn't loot it. What we confiscated was very swiftly devoured. More likely it was stolen from some officer's mess. Those uniformed Union officers do themselves very well. But ours did too, when they could. There was one old colonel in Schofield's outfit who carried along his own pepper mill and a china slop jar with morning glories on it. Sit down and have some grub."

"I'll go help. Has Miss Annie had her breakfast?"

"You know our Mama. She can't be persuaded to eat till every chick, child, man and woman on the place has been fed."

"That's why she's poor and thin as a grasshopper in winter. I'll make her come and eat with you," Sue said.

Jack came in and pulled up a chair, looking with interest at the food on the table. "I don't know how you do it," he said grudgingly. "It will likely land you in jail if they don't shoot you but it takes a lot of worry off the old folks."

"You mean that for slightly curdled approval, no doubt," Morgan said dryly. "For that parsimonious bit I say thanks, and I promise that when they get me in jail I'll give them a false name and swear I was one of Sherman's bummers. Sherman and an avenging Jehovah are a holy alliance in William Brownlow's fermenting mind. Too bad he can't call Beast Butler his own too. Butler would make an excitingly evil Holy Ghost."

"We can use another hand at the Oliver place today," Jack said, with some sternness. "It ain't good for Pa to work too hard out in this hot sun."

Morgan finished his coffee, spooning the brown sugar out of the bottom of the cup. "What makes you think King will go back there?"

"But it's their place," argued Jack. "It was a fine farm before the weeds and sassafras took it. Once it's cleaned up and seeded—"

"She doesn't want to go. She's satisfied."

"Satisfied to let Sue and Miss Annie and 'Nerva do for her," said Jack.

Sue came in, dropped into a chair. "I heard you," she said. "Miss Annie says every house ought to have one lady."

"And I say she goes back where she belongs," persisted Jack, "and the sooner we can help King get the place in shape so they can live off of it, the better."

"What can I do? I'm no farmer," argued Morgan.

"Neither was I. You can swing a scythe. You can learn, anyway. And you can go out with me right now and help me get some guns out of that cotton bale in the barn cistern. Those Nigras in town might come hunting King. We've got to be ready."

But when in midmorning they drove the slow mules up the slope to the Oliver house it was quickly apparent that they were too late. Morgan, who had ridden the gelding ahead of the wagon, came charging back.

"My God, there must be twenty of them!" he cried.

Horses were standing about under the trees and they could see men running in and out of the house, loaded with booty.

"White men. Guerrillas," growled Boone. "Low down white rascals. Get along, Jack. I want a shot at them."

"No, Pa—they're too many," protested Jack, "and they've got rifles."

"Stay back here, Morgan, you crazy fool!" Boone shouted, alarmed abruptly as a gun cracked up near the house.

Morgan circled back, the horse snorting nervously. "We took that many plenty of times down around Huntsville," he argued. "Knock down two and the rest will run. Give me your squirrel gun, Pa. I'll creep around through the brush on this side. Jack, you go the other way and they'll think they're surrounded."

"I say no," said Boone, "and I'm no coward. They'd charge down here, kill us all and steal the mules. What plunder they'll take ain't worth it."

"Damn. I'm going anyway!" stormed Morgan, sliding out of the saddle. "Give me that rifle." He snatched it out of the wagon bed, dropped a handful of cartridges into a pocket and disappeared in the screening brush.

"They'll kill him," fumed Boone. "Likely they'll burn the house too." He flogged the mules into a trot and turned the wagon off the road into a thick clump of cedars. Jack had jumped out and caught the gelding. He ran up and handed the reins to his father.

"Give me the shotgun. Maybe I can pick off one or two." He snatched the weapon and vanished into the thicket.

Boone Markland shook angry fists at the air impotently. "Damn fools! Got to be heroes!"

There was one gun left, a heavy old bear gun that delivered a ball less than a hundred yards but with deadly impact when it landed. Boone looked to the load and prime of it and let himself down stiffly at the rear of the wagon. Cautiously he tied the mules and the horse, then moved through the cedars till the house came into view. He could see a man on the porch rolling something into a bundle—Winnie's white lacy things, strapping them with a belt.

The grass was very high and Boone Markland was back again in his old bear-hunting days when the game was more wary, less vile. He rolled into a little gully, then hitched out of it, hating the grass that would wave and rustle as he crept through it. Ten more yards. A shot to his right cracked suddenly and by the smoke Boone knew that it was Jack who had fired. Two ragged, whiskery men leaped off the porch and started running in that direction and one stopped to aim and fire a rifle. Boone was certain that Jack would be long gone from that spot, but the attackers' brief pause gave him his opportunity. The old bear gun roared and the outlaw with the smoking rifle dropped like a stone. Boone was kicked backward by the recoil, rolled ten feet into the gully.

A bullet spat the ground above him, and off to the left Morgan's rifle cracked. The second rider who had run down the slope pinwheeled in air and rolled over and over. His gun flew wide and Boone watched where it fell as he rammed another load into his heavy weapon and cautiously crept up the slope.

From the house there came a sudden fusillade of yells and shots, then the strangers rushed out, firing wildly, and went crashing off through the orchard, urging their mounts away from the road. The Marklands waited a little, then when it was obvious that the looters had departed, they ventured out boldly and surveyed the scene.

"They thought we had 'em surrounded." Morgan kicked at one body. "My God, Pa, you mighty near blew this scoundrel's head off with that old blunderbuss."

"Told you I'm not dead yet," chortled Boone, slapping the butt of the old gun affectionately. "Told Nate Forrest when I gave him old Duke to ride that I could shoot better than any boy I'd raised."

"Now I reckon we've got to bury these buzzards," grumbled Jack. "Ground's as hard as iron too."

"Anyway they left two guns. But they rode off all the horses, led the ones hadn't any riders. Pa, why don't we put these skinnies in the wagon and dump 'em out at the fork of the road back yonder? Warning to any more that get bright ideas."

"Somebody might see us and we'd end up in trouble," objected Boone. "Though I never laid eyes on either of these hounds before. No, we'd better plow 'em under some place."

"Smoke!" cried Morgan, breaking into a run up the hill. "They set the house on fire."

It was a reluctant and smoldering fire, kindled in the kitchen, and Jack soon doused it out with Winnie's abandoned tub of sour suds.

"Can't tell what they took till she comes over here," said Boone, as they looked over the rooms where senseless destruction had run rampant. Mirrors had been shattered, beds stripped and feathers were everywhere from slashed ticks and pillows.

"She won't come," Jack said. "She'll never come near this place again. You'll see."

She did not come. Not for years. Much had happened, much had changed, before ever again Winnie Oliver Markland entered the old Oliver house.

• *Twelve* •

THERE HAD NEVER BEEN, SO WILLIAM MARKLAND WAS CERTAIN, A MAN in love so bewildered, baffled and frustrated as he.

As the heat of summer waned and a few faded leaves drifted down on the dusty streets and lawns, William was more certain each day that he was in love with Angela Wood. He had had no wish to fall in love and definitely no desire to let his heart become involved where so many barriers of political prejudice existed. He had been for so long alone, severed from every old relationship and not too happy with the new, that he had come to reconcile himself with a life of solitary aloofness. There was drama in the idea, and William, steeped for so long in books, had liked that dramatic aspect of his situation, the coloring of mystery and romance it gave to his lonely days.

He thought of himself as a lone conquistador, riding the fields of his youth, a detested conqueror, proven right and resented for that rightness, eventually restoring prosperity and happiness to those who disdained and rejected him. It made nice melodrama with which to soothe an often smarting ego, when people whom he had known all his life looked past and through him as though he were so much thin air.

There was ugliness and division and hate seething in Tennessee and he was part of it, an instrument of it, a tool of Andrew Johnson and of William Gannaway Brownlow, and because he commanded a black troop the opprobrium in the minds of Southern people was worse. Samuel Arnell's bill, disenfranchising for fifteen years any white man who had in any manner aided or served the Confederacy either as an officer or a financial abettor of the Rebellion had been passed by the hand-picked radical legislature.

The same bill disenfranchised the great mass of returned Confederate soldiers for five years. There were conservative Union men in the state who regarded Brownlow's government as illegal and there had been a demand for an election in which all white men should vote, but Brownlow had shouted that any such call would be considered an open declaration of war.

Now in the sultry death of summer a campaign for the election of Congressmen had stirred again the smoldering rages burning under the hot skins of Southerners, and the mission of the military was to keep those fires damped down and the population properly controlled and intimidated. And to be in power, as William knew sadly, was to be despised and obnoxious, which was a dreary fate for a young man who could not put a girl out of his mind.

He had ridden the river road many times since he had overtaken Angela there but obviously she was going on no more errands to the Harper farm, and although he made it a point to ride past the old parsonage several times each week he got only an occasional glimpse of her.

Once she had been gathering vegetables in the ragged little garden and she had snatched a big onion out of the ground and waved it at him as he let his horse amble by. But almost immediately he had heard the door clap shut and a woman in black had appeared on the door-step to stand glaring after him.

On Sundays he saw Angela walking primly to church between the aunt and her mother, faded women who looked alike with narrow mouths and white, close-set ears. He sat on the bench in front of the courthouse one Sunday so he could be near enough to rise and bow and see the flick of raw color over her face but although he made his most courteous obeisance, sweeping off his black hat, he got only stony looks from the older women and a nervous twitch of Angela's eyelids that offered frail apology for the rebuff. They were on guard against him and there was little that he could do about it. The last gift of food he had left on the parsonage doorstep had stayed there, ignored, for days. Later he had seen the parcel lying in the street, fought over by two lean dogs and a skinny Negro child.

Putting his squads through manual drill in camp William found his mind wandering as he remembered the feel of Angela's arms around him on the river road, the lavender and rose-leaf scent of her petti-coats as the jolting trot of the horse tossed them, the lilt of laughter in her voice. He had been wondering if she ever thought of him when he found himself confusing his bumble-footed troops with contradictory orders and caught the eyes of his lieutenants upon him sharply. Even Buzzy began to be worried and, still counting himself a privileged character, he lost no time in making his anxiety vocal.

"How come you don't yell loud at them black trash, Cap'n Billy? Their guns is dirty and they don't even keer. They say if the white Cap'n don't keer, how come they got to worry? Cap'n Billy, pretty soon I got to whup some of them no-good soldiers. They talkin' that the Cap'n don't want 'em to shoot good, so they won't shoot no Rebels."

"Why should they shoot Rebels, Buzzy?" William was always patient with Buzzy, knowing how precariously thin was the mulatto boy's loyalty to the army and how difficult Buzzy would be to catch if he decided to arrange his own personal separation from a military career. Also Buzzy's desertion would undoubtedly involve the Markland family, and so far, while so much suspicion boiled in the country, William was grateful that the Marklands had been able to continue in at least partial obscurity.

"They say we got to shoot Rebels, if they try to vote," argued Buzzy, "or if they mess with us Colored or the army. They say we ought to shot Mist' King when he come down here messin' around after that Lutie woman. You reckon somebody goin' to shoot Mist' King, if he come back? Maybe I better git back home and tell Miss Annie not to let Mist' King come to town no more?"

"He's not likely to come again, Buzzy. He got hurt pretty bad. Boss Boone won't let him come again."

"Boss Boone"—Buzzy drew on twenty years of experience—"ain't never told his boys much they put to their mind. You know Mist' Jack and Mist' King do what they please to do and don't give no nevermind to nobody. I could go back home easy could I git me a horse."

"I could put you in the guardhouse too, but I'd hate to do it," said William tersely. Buzzy was lucky, he was thinking, Buzzy still considered that he had a home. He was forever arguing that he was needed there, that once Boss Boone got over his big mad about losing that jughead horse Buzzy had ridden off to the army, Boss Boone would be glad to have a stout boy to help around the stable.

A few days later Buzzy tried a new approach to the same old theme. "Mist' Morgan, he done come to town," he announced one afternoon. "Mist' Morgan tell me a lot of white trash done tore up that house where Mist' King been livin' with that Oliver gal, set it afire too. Mist' Morgan and Boss Boone put the fire out and killed two of them white skinnies too. Boss Boone blowed one man's haid plumb off with his ole bear gun."

William worried more than a little about that. Guerrilla bands were loudly labeled as Confederate scum by the radical element in power, but there were shrewd rascals out for advantage who knew how to use these lawless skulkers for personal gain. If the two men who had been killed had friends or connections in high places there could be trouble brewing for the Confederate Marklands.

He warned Buzzy solemnly. "Don't talk about this in camp, you hear? Don't go bragging that Boss Boone killed anybody. You could get the place raided, the house burned and Boss Boone hung."

"You tell Mist' Morgan not to talk then, Cap'n. Mist' Morgan messin' round them ole Yankees all the time."

"You're a Yankee, Buzzy, a Yankee soldier. And I'm a Union officer," William reminded him.

"Just the same," insisted Buzzy sadly, "them ole Yankees and ginny soldiers ain't our kind of folks."

"A retrogressed Yankee," William gave Buzzy a sidelong punch. "You eat their grub, Buzzy, and take their pay. The least you could do would be to be loyal to the flag."

"I done followed that flag too far already, Cap'n," sighed Buzzy. "Halfway 'round this here world and gittin' shot at. Whyn't that ole flag go home and let us soldiers git some rest and good vittles? Ain't you sick of ole beans and corn beef, Cap'n? They be boilin' 'lasses pretty soon down home. Wish I could git me some of them good ole 'lasses on a biscuit."

"I know a place where they make good biscuits." William toyed rashly with a mad idea. "Have you any old clothes, Buzzy? Old worn-out regular farm clothes? Pants and a ragged shirt?"

"Ain't got no breeches but these here. Gittin' raggedy too. Shoes gittin' raggedy. All that fours left and by squads right we got to do all the time. What you want, Cap'n Billy? Want some hen roost robbed? I find me some ole clothes. Find me a washin' hangin' on a fence some dark night."

"You'd get shot at. You're not black enough, Buzzy."

"If I burn me a charred stick I git black enough."

"You could always put the clothes back when you got through with them," mused William, thinking aloud, letting reckless impulse run away with discretion. "You know that little brown house about a block from the courthouse? Where a preacher used to live?"

"Gal live there, don't she?" Buzzy asked boldly.

"A girl lives there, yes."

"Seen you ridin' by, three-four times. Seen her wavin' at you."

"She only waved once."

"She waved. You ain't looked back. Sittin' up too straight, hat pull down, big Yankee Cap'n, struttin'. I seen you, Mist' Billy."

"All right, you yellow scoundrel, you saw me." A warm glow was running swiftly through William's blood. "She makes good biscuits. If a poor hungry Colored boy, with no home any more on account of the bad war, should knock on that door and say he was hungry she might slip him a biscuit."

"And then," said Buzzy, "I slip her the note."

"Buzzy, you are a diplomat and a man of brilliant intellect."

"You ain't never teached me them big book words, Mist' Billy."

"You're smart enough without any more teaching. When is the next pitch dark night when it would be safe to raid a clothesline?"

"Moon wane right now, be dark till midnight next week. Cap'n, if I wear them clothes in the daytime some nigger's goin' to see me and cut my throat."

"You won't need to wear them in the daytime. You can put them back inside of an hour."

"And if that ginny lieutenant see me, he put me in the guardhouse," persisted Buzzy.

"We'll see that you don't get into the guardhouse, Buzzy." William grew wistfully reminiscent. "We've always been stout friends, haven't we, Buzzy?" He was happy. Some of his harrowing doubts, the uncertainties that had annoyed him were miraculously lessened. She had waved at him. He would not himself consider the dismal possibilities. That Aunt Ella might slam the door in Buzzy's face. That having received his surreptitious billet-doux Angela might crumple it up and throw it in the fire. That even if she read the note, which he was now frantically composing in his mind, nothing else might happen, ever.

Too well he knew that never would he be welcomed in that little brown house. The words not meant for his ears, spoken by that half-drunk dirty politician had never died in William's mind. His mother was a lady. Now I reckon she won't let him darken her door. Would there ever be a door he would be welcome to darken, here in his own country, the land where he had been born? Was he a fool to hope? William buried his face in his hands. Buzzy looked disturbed. His pale face with the lavender shadows, the lips, only a little shaped to Negroid fullness, quivered.

"Cap'n Billy," he said, sorrow in his voice, the deep, mystic, half-incredulous sorrow of the rejected. "Cap'n Billy, I got to say this. I ain't never goin' say it again. I know how you feel, but you know and I know who is my pappy—"

"Dammit! No!" shouted William, springing up.

"Don't git mad, Cap'n, don't git mad," pleaded Buzzy. "Ain't no use to git mad. What I'm tryin' to say is—how come I always know what you want me to do? How come I know what you thinkin' when you don't tell me? How come I got to go where you go? How come you git hurt, I hurt too? Because part of you is the same as part of me, Cap'n."

"Shut up! Get on away from me and shut up."

"Yessuh, but you better sit down, Cap'n, or you fall down and all them folks up yonder on the courthouse steps they see you fallin' and they say there that Yankee Cap'n drunk again." Buzzy pushed William back to the bench, handed him his canes. "I'm goin' now, Cap'n Billy."

"Come back here," ordered William sharply. "Now what was all that fool talk about knowing how I feel?"

"That gal. That little white gal." Buzzy's teeth flashed in an impudent grin. "Whyn't you git you some unarmy clothes, Cap'n, and knock on that door yourself? You want me to rob some white folks' clothesline for you? Look, Cap'n, why don't I go back home and git your clothes? All them good clothes you done had to wear 'fore we went off to war, all them stylish pants and coats with silver buttons on and fancy shirts? Boy, did you strut, Mist' Billy! Ain't no more stylish white man than you ride out to court the gals then. I can git 'em. 'Nerva, she steal 'em out for me."

"They're probably not there any more, Buzzy. Miss Annie has likely given them away or the other boys are wearing them."

"Ain't nobody ever wore your pants. They all taller than you. Only one on the place could wear your ole pants was me," Buzzy recalled.

It was true. Of all the slim, long-legged Marklands William had been the shortest, standing just a fraction under six feet. Even Morgan had topped him by half a head, and Jack and King had each loomed almost a head taller. Miss Annie's smallness had striven to impress itself upon one of her children but had not succeeded.

"I couldn't go into a house unless I was invited and knew I would be welcome, Buzzy. And I wouldn't be welcome in that house," he said.

"Them ole ladies, they look at all us boys like we trash in the mud!" growled Buzzy. "Mighty few white folks give us a friendly look. One ole man he spit on my foots. I ain't told him he git put in jail if he do that but that sergeant say, next one spit on me, let him know."

"You've let me know. Now forget about it. Things are bad enough without stirring up trouble."

"When I find them clothes I let you know, Cap'n, but if I git in trouble you got to git me out. That ole guardhouse ain't got no good bed nor nothin'. Just a ole plank got to be scrubbed off with lye all the time."

"Haven't I always taken care of you, Buzzy? Just as you've taken care of me?" demanded William.

"You ain't had to do no courtin' for me, Cap'n. That diff'unt. That kind of complicated."

William got his canes braced and heaved himself erect. Hating his handicap, he knew that he should be grateful that the military let him remain in command. Sam Hood had fought the final, calamitous battles of the Confederacy one-legged in the saddle, and there had been Union officers who refused retirement because of maiming wounds, but William suspected that it was his tactful handling of Negro troops that kept him on the Federal payroll. The Lieutenant from Brooklyn frankly admitted that he could not tell one black man from another, that they changed their adopted names every roll call, answered for each other and laughed at the officers behind their backs.

"You must remember that for several generations they have had no names, Lieutenant," William had placated. "There is no legal way for a Negro to acquire a name so he chooses one that piques his fancy. If he gets tired of it, there's no law to compel him to keep it unchanged."

"That mulatto boy has the same name as you, Captain."

"He was my property before the Proclamation."

"How did it feel to own another human being, body and soul?"

"I fought to free Buzzy," William said. "Does that answer your question?"

"Hard to figure you out, you Southerners."

Now, gripping his canes in sweated palms, William looked at the crowd that was gathering about the courthouse door. "What goes on over there?" he asked a passing man.

"Tax sale," the other snarled. "The radicals are bent on ruining all the decent people in this county and running us all out of the state."

William limped quickly nearer. Most of the crowd were strangers, newcomers into conquered territory, dry-eyed, thin-lipped speculators, eager to witness the rape of a province, ready to profit by it. In the background other shabbier citizens glowered and growled among themselves: the local property owners, the "Secesh," despised and menaced by the men in power in Tennessee.

Already the clerk, a sheaf of papers in his hand, was beginning to rattle off in an almost unintelligible singsong the boundary "calls" of property seized for unpaid taxes. The bidding was slow, the customers cautious.

"That piece ain't on no good road. Never make a profit on it."

"Bid a dollar an acre. Land's worth that just to hold the earth together."

William watched as property on which men had spent their lives, black men, white men, was sold for sums so low as to be fantastic. Then the clerk began another description. Six hundred acres. Buildings fair. Land arable. Past due taxes, five hundred and sixty dollars.

"This here farm the estate of the deceased Colonel Carter Oliver. Sole heir to date, Mrs. Winifred Oliver Markland."

"That's the place guerrillas burnt," a man said to William. "Ain't been worked since the war. Gone to sprouts and sedge grass. Bid fifty dollars!" he shouted.

"Fifty dollars an acre?" questioned the clerk.

"Haw—fifty dollars for the whole durn property."

"One hundred dollars," called out William recklessly.

"Raise you fifty," came another voice.

When the sale was completed, no more bids being offered, Captain William Markland of the United States Army was the tentative owner, for a price of two hundred and fifty dollars, of the old Oliver place.

"What you figure to do with that piece of bramble and sassafras?" inquired the first bidder. "Give you a profit of fifty dollars on it right now."

"There's still the right of redemption," William reminded him.

"Ain't much chance of that. Secesh property. Even if they get the money together, which ain't likely, court throws the case out. Happens all the time."

"Maybe I'll live there," said William with a dry grin.

Now, he was thinking heavily, King would hate him more than ever.

• *Thirteen* •

THE EIGHT MEN WHO RODE UP TO THE GATE WERE ALL KNOWN TO BOONE Markland. Three were men of some respectability, quiet men who had made no secret of their Union sympathies before the war. The others were hard-faced, political hangers-on of the type numerous now in the county. One, a man named Jeff Nichols who had been an itinerant horse doctor, was now sheriff of the county.

Boone was turning the grindstone for Jack to put an edge on a plow-point, with Boone-boy standing on tiptoe pouring water over the stone from an old coffee pot, when the riders halted outside the gate.

They did not dismount. The horse-doctor sheriff raised a shout.

"Open this gate, Markland. This is the law!"

Jack put the plowpoint down and walked with truculent stiffness toward the group. Boone wiped his sweated hands on his breeches, gave a quiet order to the child.

"Get in the house, Boone-boy! Go find your mamma."

"What those men want, Grampa? What they come here for?"

"I don't know. Go find your mother. You keep to the house," ordered Boone, striding toward the gate.

"Open this gate, Boone," ordered the sheriff. "Git that chain unlocked before we bust it. We're ridin' in."

Boone pushed his dusty old hat back. "What you want here, Jeff?" he asked with a tinge of contempt. "I've got no colts to be gelded nor critters with colic."

"This ain't no critter business, Boone. This here is law business," barked the sheriff.

"You've got a warrant I suppose, to come on our property?" demanded Jack.

"We've got warrants, eight of 'em. Loaded and holstered. We're searching this place, Boone, unless you're willing to give up that boy of yours, peaceable. Mought as well give him up because we're going to take him, peaceable or not. You unlockin' this chain or do we bust down the gate?"

Boone came near to the gate. Jack was taut with rage and it dismayed and angered him even more to see his father's calm and almost indifferent attitude.

Boone was saying, "I got four boys, Jeff. And a little shaver seven years old. Or are you looking for some Colored feller? None here any more, just two old Nigra women."

The sheriff ignored this. "Gimme that there!" he ordered a man who rode beside him, a slack-jawed countryman with an evil face. Slack-jaw took a short-handled hatchet from his saddle, pulled his horse around and neatly chopped free the hasp that held the gate chain. Then he got down, dragged the gate back and the eight rode into the yard.

"This him, Sheriff?" asked another man, crowding his horse against Jack and forcing him back against the fence.

"All look alike," said Nichols. "You King Markland? King's the one we come for."

"King?" demanded Jack. "What do you want with King? A gang of crazy Nigras cut him all to pieces a while back. He's still laid up in bed."

"None of those Nigras got hurt, Jeff, but they beat my boy and trampled him, like to have killed him," Boone said. "Some of your Union officers saved him, saved him from being beat to death and his throat cut. You can ask them. King's been lying up in bed for two weeks, his mother nursing him."

"Figured you'd lie for him, Boone. Figured you'd hide him out." The sheriff had alighted and stood braced, belligerently, his hands on the butts of two heavy pistols.

"I ain't hiding King. Why should I hide him? He ain't done anything. What you picking on King for, Jeff? He never did any violence to anybody. He's lying up yonder in his own bed, got a bad rising in his side, been there going on three weeks now. Been a mighty sick boy."

"I reckon," drawled Nichols, with contemptuous irony, "that them two dead men the wild hogs rooted up over yonder on King's wife's place just died quiet and natural with no violence being done to 'em?"

"I reckon," put in the slack-jawed man angrily, "that Bart Hoople, was my wife's first cousin from down in Lincoln, reckon he just naturally blowed out his own brains. Got tired of livin' and buried hisself over yonder in that plowed field. Sounds reasonable!"

Boone drew himself up haughtily. Jack shouted a warning.

"Pa!"

But Boone did not heed. "I blowed that feller's brains out," he announced. "They were guerrillas, twenty of 'em. Mounted and riding out to burn and destroy. They attacked us—Jack and me. We went over to help King out on his plowing, him being sick so long. They looted the house and set it afire. We defended ourselves. Any man would defend himself if he was attacked by a gang like that."

So, he left Morgan out of it, Jack was thinking with a tinge of bitterness. Pa drags me into it but he leaves Little Brother in the clear.

Aloud he said, "How were we to know they were kin to decent people? Decent people don't start in to loot a house and then set fire to it."

"Ain't burnt. It's standing right there," argued Nichols.

"It's not burnt because we put out the fire, and we buried those dead men after all the rest rode off and left them lying where they fell," stormed Jack. "You county officers taking up for guerrilla raiders now, Nichols?"

"My wife's kin ain't no guerrilla!" shouted Slack-jaw. "If he was there he was on business."

"You said you found him there. His business was smashing up everything that couldn't be carried off and then burning the rest. Fine business for any man's kin to be mixed up in," snarled Jack.

The sheriff looked a trifle uncertain and disgusted. "Looks like we can't never learn you Secesh that the war's over," he said sadly.

"When mounted outlaws ride the country, burning and robbing, the war's not over!" Boone shouted. "A man's got a right to defend himself if he's fired on, no provocation at all. I figured we did them men a kindness when we buried 'em, when all the others left 'em where they fell. I killed that man at a hundred yards with an old bear gun that belonged to my pappy, and I'm telling you straight, Jeff Nichols, that you'd have done the same if they rode through your place and took shots at you, you minding your own business."

"Want we should tie 'em up, Sheriff?" asked a red-whiskered man. "Don't look like you could take 'em peaceable."

The sheriff pursed his lips, gnawed his mustache. "I reckon you know I got to take you in, Boone?" he said, unhappily. "It's my legal duty. It'll be better for everybody if you go along peaceable."

"You can't take us without a warrant," defied Jack, his face tight and livid with impotent fury. Desperately he was remembering his rifle, hid in the oatbin a hundred feet away. Remembering other times of violence down in the valley of the Tennessee River, on the bloodied hills of Alabama and Tennessee. Tight places, outnumbered, surrounded, where he had met an enemy bent on his destruction and had fought free. Always he had fought free. All the Marklands had fought themselves free. Had all that bitter conflict been endured only to bring him home to be dealt with violently and unjustly by a gang of political scalawags bent on winning favor by the destruction of the enemies of other scalawags in high places? "You come here properly, with a legal warrant, and we might listen to you," he said coldly.

"I told you we fetched all the warrants we need. Looks like we got to use 'em." The sheriff drew his pistol. Instantly every man in the crew drew a weapon. A dozen guns were leveled at the Marklands, standing gray-faced and unarmed in the slanting sunlight.

Abruptly Jack sprang, caught the top rail of the fence, swung his legs in air and kicked the red-bearded man in the face. The man went down like a poled ox and a half-dozen startled shots went wild, splintering the planks of the barn, and the rails of the fence. Jack found himself pulled down, heavy feet pressing his shoulders to the ground and as he fought he blinked up through sweat and glared into the angry face of his own father.

"Lie still, you hot-headed fool!" ordered Boone. "You could have got us both killed."

"Turn me loose!" yelled Jack, writhing sidewise, beating with furious fists on his father's knees. "Turn me loose, I tell you."

Boone Markland jerked his son upright.

"Turn him loose, Boone. We can handle him," ordered the sheriff.

"I'll handle my own get, Nichols!" Boone gave Jack a hard cuff on the side of the head. "He'll come peaceable."

The red-beard, sloshed into furious awareness by a thrown bucket of water, charged through the group. "Lemme at him!" he screamed, kicking Boone aside. "Lemme at the son of a bitch!"

He slammed a flat blow at the side of Jack's head with a pistol turned menacingly on Boone. "I'll deal with you too, you damned old Secesh traitor!"

But Boone was too quick. With bone-breaking strength he had the ruffian's arm twisted behind his back, shoving him backward.

"I'm trying to keep down trouble, you crazy fool," he raged. "All right, Nichols, if you're in command here and got any guts to do your job, take us into town!"

"Tie him up—that young one," ordered Nichols importantly. "You aim to come quiet, Boone, or do I have to rope you like a steer?"

"I've got to tell my wife," said Boone. "Maybe there'll be a judge in town with a smattering of brains, or has justice been hamstrung forever in Tennessee?"

"You'll be lucky if the judge ain't minded to hang the both of you," snapped Nichols. "That young squirt of yours, resisting an officer in the performance of his duty. Rope that feller good, boys. I got to go along with Boone to the house."

Behind him Boone was aware that Jack's limp body, tied hand and foot, was being flung across the saddle of a stolid horse. Miss Annie, pale as chalk, was waiting at the door.

"Jeff Nichols, you should be ashamed of yourself!" she stormed at the sheriff. "As many times as I've had a good meal cooked for you here on this place. You bring my folks back here safe, you hear? Fighting your own neighbors like they were wild Indians! Mr. Markland, I rolled up some clean shirts and underwear for you and put some corn bread and sweet potatoes in. You'll get hungry before you get home."

Dimly Boone noted the stark, terrified eyes of Winnie, Sue with all the flame of her coppery temper blazing from her face, Boone-boy's appalled, big-eyed terror. Boone-boy came rushing up and gave the sheriff a savage kick on the shin.

"You hurt my papa, you ole devil Yankee you!" he screamed.

Gently Boone lifted the child and put him into his mother's arms. Gently he bent and kissed his wife.

"We'll be back," he promised. "Don't you worry."

Afterward, riding a jolting nag led by another man he tried to remember how long it had been since he had kissed Miss Annie. Her face had felt cold and tight as glass.

They slogged the dusty, deserted road in silence. Before they reached the river Jack had come to and leaned, retching and moaning, against his father's body. Three men turned off at the bridge.

"Reckon you won't need us no more, Sheriff. About feedin' time."

They rode away without a backward look and Boone's eyes, following them, held no malice or resentment. Countrymen, ignorant, fanatic, prejudiced, impressed into a scurvy job by a petty official. For the four who remained alongside, sorry scoundrels, he had only contempt.

"I got to lock your boy up, Boone," Nichols said when they approached the center of town. "He ain't minded to act peaceable. But you can stay to my house till the prosecutor decides whether you can get bail or not."

"I'm not leaving my son, sick and stunned like he is," declared Boone indignantly. "You lock me up with him."

The sheriff sighed. "Well, if you say so, but remember I tried to make things easier for you. Not that you ain't guilty of murder by your own admission, but there's circumstances ain't proved and I don't like unproved circumstances. Rear up in the middle of a trial and knock your case all to hell."

"What you're meaning is, if they hang me you don't want any part of it on your conscience," drawled Boone. "You right sure you got any conscience, Jeff, or did you swap it off to Brownlow's radical mob for that tin badge to wear on your shirt?"

"I told you, I was trying to do the right thing!" barked the harassed horse doctor. "If you got no appreciation for decent treatment it's no skin off my rump."

There was only one bunk in the odorous cell into which the Marklands were shoved, Jack reeling blindly and held erect by his father's strong grip. Boone laid his son flat on the sorry cot and turned back as the door swung shut with a heavy clang.

"If you're feeling so magnanimous all of a sudden, Jeff," he shouted, "send a doctor to tend this boy. Might be that blow cracked his skull. His eyes don't look right."

"Save us a length of rope," jeered the red-bearded deputy, standing, grinning and still wet, in the corridor. "Leave him die where he lays, old man, and he'll be purtier to bury."

There was a bucket half-full of stale water in the cell and Boone took off his sweated shirt, dipped and wrung it out and pressed the cool, wet cloth over the dark swelling on Jack's head. His eyes were already closed and he licked his lips and gagged and muttered incoherently. Boone clenched his fists and beat them impotently on his own chest, snarling words that would have appalled Miss Annie. He shook the bars of the door, roaring maledictions like a wounded lion, and the prisoners in other cells began yelling too.

"Cuss 'em, old man! Cuss their rotten, nigger-loving guts!"

Then a quavering voice from the next cell was lifted shrilly. "That you in there, Boone Markland?"

"It's Boone Markland," Boone answered, startled. "Who are you?"

"John Lawson, Boone. Your neighbor. Thought I recognized your bellowing. What you locked up for?"

"Sheriff figures I shot Abe Lincoln."

"You never did it, Boone. I shot Abe. Blowed his brains plumb out of that gorilla head," chortled Lawson. "Then a low-down carpetbagger thief took title to my place and tried to run me off. I filled his breeches full of buckshot. Hit him where his brains were, like they learned us down in Lincoln County. Who'd you kill, Boone?"

"I killed one looting skunk and directly I get out of here I'll kill a few more," stormed Boone recklessly. "They half killed a boy of mine. He's laying here now, plumb out of his head."

"Well, you got you a boy." Lawson choked a little, as though helpless fury strangled him. "You can look at him. You don't have to think about him flung out on some hill somewhere for the buzzards to pick at like my Milo. Or drownded in a bloody muddy river like my Johnny. Got blowed up down to Mobile. You ain't had your land took away from you like me, land where my grandpappy fit the Cherokee and died with an arrow through his gizzard. You ain't got no cause to bellyache. Might be they'll hang both of us but the world's gone to the devil anyway. Ain't much inducement to keep living, breathing the same air as Brownlow, not to mention Seward and Sherman and that whole pack of contumacious, contemptible, Judas-cursed radicals."

A deputy tramped in and stood truculently, hands on gun butts.

"Shut up in there, you mess of goddammed yap-mouthed Rebels! Shut up before I come in there and learn you not to low-rate your betters."

Boone Markland sat down wearily on the single stool. It was rickety, one leg loose, and teetered perilously. He buried his head in his hands and let desolation take him. Taxes. He had not thought of taxes. For years, when he had money he paid up, sometimes as much as a five-year levy. No land had ever been sold at the courthouse door, no decent Tennessean would bid on the property of a citizen in distress. Now they had forged this new weapon with which to cudgel and destroy men already vanquished.

Lawson's place, a rich, well-tended river farm, seized from him for a few paltry dollars. Lawson had never owned slaves but his sons had fought for the Confederacy. Maybe at this moment Boone's own home was in peril. He had deeded it to Annie when King was born, handing her the deed grandly, his gift in payment for his two strong, handsome sons.

The thought was anguish and Boone bit back the bitter groans that pressed up from the pain in his breast. Then Jack stirred.

"Pa?" he muttered. "That you, Pa?"

"It's me, son." Boone went to the bunk, wiped Jack's sweated face with the still-damp sleeve of the shirt. "You lie still. You got hit on the head."

"Where are we?" Jack tried to raise his head, closed his eyes again and moaned. Boone felt the swollen place on the boy's scalp gingerly. It throbbed under his fingers and a little blood stained them.

"We're in jail, Jack. Locked up like felons by white-trash deputies, with them cussing us through the bars. This is the peace, Jack. The peace you fought for."

"We never fought for any Yankee peace, we fought against it," muttered Jack. "My mouth is mighty dry, Pa."

"There's no water here fit to drink. A hog wouldn't drink it." Boone went to the door and shook the bars till they rattled. "There's a sick man in here needs a drink of water," he shouted when the red-bearded deputy appeared.

The man grinned maliciously. "Want water do you, Reb? All right, here's water. Drown yourself in it." He seized a bucket that stood on a bench outside the cell, lifted it and flung the water through the bars.

Boone was drenched and much of it splashed on the cot where Jack lay.

Boone did not speak. He stood and glared till the snickering tormentor backed off, flinging back, "That'll learn you, you old devil you!"

"Some time," Boone said then, slow and deadly, "I'll see you again."

"Dance pretty when you do, old man," taunted the red-beard. "You'll be dancing on air, Markland, and there won't be no fiddles playing."

· *Fourteen* ·

IT WAS ONE OF THOSE VERY DARK NIGHTS THAT COME LATE, BEFORE THE birth of the autumn-bright harvest moon. The stars were very few and far, and all about the earth was shrouded in purple-black secrecy, aloof and hostile, full of small stirrings and cracklings.

The gelding was nervous and snorted as he ambled the dim road. Sue patted his neck and spoke low and soothingly to him, holding a tight rein. Once when an owl swung down silently, a movement, a whisper of feathers on the air close to her head, the horse shied and Sue had to clutch the saddle horn quickly, almost dropping the rifle.

She and Boone-boy had dug the gun out of the oatbin in the dark, loaded it in the dark, blowing the dust from the muzzle. She hoped it would fire if she needed it and not burst in her hand. At least she was confident that the gelding was not gun shy. There had been shooting when Morgan rode him to Winnie's place the day of the guerrilla raid, surely enough gunfire then to accustom any animal to the noise of shots. Thinking of Morgan made her skin prickle and anger burn in her throat and stiffen her hands.

Just when he was needed most Morgan had not come home at all. Hour after hour they had waited, terrified, Miss Annie a bloodless wraith pacing from window to window, King groaning and cursing on the couch where he lay, still hot and weak with a low fever. When he had been trampled in that Negro melee some filth had gotten into a wound and it still drained, fetid and angry, in spite of Miss Annie's poultices and bandages. They had waited, listening and tense, Winnie running to the door every few minutes to stare through the darkness down the road, but still Morgan had not come.

"If he's in town he has heard about it by now," grumbled King. "They couldn't drag somebody like Pa off to jail without everybody hearing about it."

"You don't even know that they took them to jail," Winnie cried. "And you certainly didn't make things any easier for them if they are in jail now, you stirring up all that trouble in town."

"Oh, shut up," King muttered wearily. "I told you a hundred times I was drunk. No man knows what he's doing when he's drunk."

"You knew!" shrilled Winnie, white-lipped. "Yelling that slut's name out for everybody to hear."

"Who said I yelled her name?" He rose on an elbow, livid with fury.

"Buzzy said so. He was there. He ran and brought your brother to save you from being killed. Buzzy told Mammy Dory you were yelling for that Lutie and her man was going to cut your throat. And Mammy Dory told me," announced Winnie triumphantly.

"Hush up, both of you!" ordered Sue, bluntly. "Miss Annie has enough trouble without you two fighting all the time. Miss Annie"— she turned to the little woman who still stood at the window as though she had been frozen there—"I'd feel better if we had a gun in the house. Do you know where Pa Markland would have a gun hidden?"

"I know!" piped up Boone-boy, whom nobody had been able to persuade to go to bed.

"Last I knew they were in a bale of cotton in the old cistern," King said, "but Pa must have taken them out. They had guns over at our place."

"I know," persisted the child. "In the oats! I saw my papa hide a rifle in the oats."

"Come along then, Boone-boy." Sue moved with alacrity, thankful for something definite to do. "I'll drop you over in the bin and you hunt us out a gun."

"Barrel down, boy," reminded King. "Don't pull a gun out by the barrel."

"I know about guns," declared Boone-boy loftily. "I can break 'em and load and everything. Grampa showed me."

"You'll need a lantern." Winnie started for the rear of the house but Sue interposed.

"No—no light. I don't want to show a light out there. And you lock the door after us. Come on, son."

"You're going alone? Out in that awful dark?" asked Winnie.

Boone-boy looked scornful. "My mama's not skeert. She's not skeert of anything."

[111]

It was while she was crouched in the pitch black quiet of the stable with Boone-boy rustling and grunting beyond the plank wall of the bin that Sue knew what she had to do.

"I found one," whispered the boy excitedly. "Shotgun. Take it easy, Ma, by the stock."

"Find another," ordered Sue, lifting the heavy weapon and feeling abruptly inadequate with the cold weight of it in her hands.

He dug up the rifle next and Sue took it from him, waited till he scrambled out, then stood both guns against the planks of the bin.

"Now," she whispered conspiratorially. "You help me saddle that gelding. I'm going to get help for Grampa and your daddy and I'll take the rifle, but don't you tell your grandmother till I'm gone, you hear?"

"You going to find Uncle Morgan? Uncle Morgan will get my pa and Grampa away from those bad men, won't he? Lemme go with you, Mama," he begged.

"No, you have to stay here and take care of your grandmother and Winnie because Uncle King's too sick. Help me get that saddle down and stay away from that colt's heels."

"Aw, I know how to act around a horse," complained the boy in disgust. "If that geld wasn't so tall I could put the bridle on myself. Those stirrups will be too long for you, Ma. If I had a light I could shorten 'em."

"Never mind, I'll manage. I've been riding horses since I was smaller than you. I won't get thrown."

The gelding blew out and swelled himself up when the girth was tightened, and Boone-boy pummeled his hard body with his fists till the animal relaxed and gave a resigned sigh.

"Grampa kicks 'em. My legs ain't long enough," he said. "Pull that throat latch tight, Mama."

"I am pulling it," panted Sue, "but he wants to lick my hair. Shove that keg over here, Boone-boy, so I can get on. Now you take that shotgun to the house and tell Uncle King I've gone for help. You won't be afraid?"

"Hell, no!" scorned her son, shouldering the heavy gun. "Does anybody come messing around this place I'll blow his head off."

"Don't you dare fire that gun, Boone-boy! It would kick you clear across the yard. And don't be using bad words either. Prop that door back, then get going. I'll wait out here till you're safe inside."

"If Grampa had had this ole gun I'll bet those mean Yankees wouldn't never have hurt my daddy," declared the child as he trudged toward the house.

Sue rode out of the yard. The gate had not been fixed since the sheriff's gang had forced it, and she walked the gelding out to the road, then urged him into a jolting canter. She rode astride, her skirt bunched up over her knees and she knew that that would be a scandal by daylight. She recalled that by carriage the town was at least four hours distant, but now the nights were longer and there was always the chance that she might meet Morgan on the road. Just what Morgan could do in the desperate situation was a bit vague in her mind but waiting long in that dread-haunted house with Miss Annie wearing a death's-head face and Winnie whimpering and complaining had been intolerable. At least it was a relief to be out alone in the dark with only the soft notes of late-nesting mocking birds and the occasional grunt of a wandering groundhog in her ears.

Along the road the old rail fence, once overgrown fragrantly with honeysuckle and trumpet vine, was nearly all torn away, burned by the two armies that had ravaged this countryside. The skeleton stones of a blackened chimney dim against the sky were all that was left of a farmhouse where two Confederate spies had hidden, according to a lurid story. Union cavalry had overrun the place and burned the buildings and there had been a day of panic on the Markland place when the riders in blue were reported less than four miles away. Musing on that memory Sue suddenly pulled the rein so hard that the gelding snorted and stopped dead still.

Cavalry. Union cavalry. Billy! Captain William Markland of the United States Army. Why hadn't she thought of Billy?

If anyone had a chance to extricate the Marklands from their desperate situation it would be Billy. Not Morgan, who by his Confederate record would be assumed to be as guilty, as vulnerable to persecution as Boone Markland and Jack. Sue slammed her heels hard into the horse's flanks and urged him into a jarring lope. Her skirts flew up and down, the pins tumbled out of her hair so that the snood blew away and curls fell over her shoulders and across her face.

It came to her like a breath of icy wind that King's misadventure had happened at night near that garrison camp, that she could be running into danger and it might be wiser to wait for day, so she slowed her mount and let him amble quietly while she watched the eastern sky for some pale hint of approaching morning.

A star was burning very brightly there now, and a slow, cool breeze began stirring the grass and weeds in the neglected fields along the road. There was a sharp smell of cool water and she knew by the moist suck of the gelding's hoofs that she was nearing the river, remembered that the road ran close to the river's edge for a mile or two before it reached the outskirts of the town.

She smelled apples then and surmised that she was passing an old orchard, and suddenly from the trees a bird began to sing and far off an excited rooster crowed. She pulled the horse into the deeper shadow of the apple trees, let him reach and nip at the lower branches but held the rein taut so that he could not get his head down. It seemed hours before a wan, sickly greenish light began to seep thinly over the landscape, not bright enough to let forms come clear but at least it diluted the shadows. Then a pale, lime-green line shimmered along the softly rolling land to the east and Sue began putting her dishevelment into some kind of order, shifting to perch sideways in the saddle, smooth her rumpled skirts. Her hair was hopeless so she twisted it into a plait down her back oblivious of the curling tendrils that fluffed around her cheeks and ears.

The light grew brighter and trees and bushes took on definite form. In a farmyard up a slope a little way a lantern winked in the hulking shadows of buildings that had escaped the shattering of war. Birds twittered, flying about excitedly, and her horse dragged down a low-hanging apple from the tree overhead and crunched it, slobbering and jerking the bit, flinging drops of moisture back on her restraining hands. She clucked to him, pulled his head up, but he was reluctant to leave, backing and nuzzling the branch, hunting more apples. She hit him hard on the head with the long end of the rein, tugged him around and headed him back to the road.

There he broke into a brisk trot, scenting the river and wanting water, and she let him go, guiding him down to the edge of the stream where the bank was firm. Hearing him drink made her thirsty herself but she did not dare get down for fear she would not be able to mount again. Her stomach began to hurt hollowly too, reminding her that none of the Marklands had been able to eat after Sheriff Nichols' invasion. Minerva had cooked supper but even Boone-boy had picked nervously at his food, frightened and upset by the tension of the others.

I hope Billy can get me a cup of coffee when I find him, she was thinking—adding uneasily, if I find him. She knew that he had been in town when King was attacked but nearly three weeks had gone by since then and the troops might have been moved on. She caught herself praying as she rode slowly into the outskirts of the town. Lord, let him be here, make him listen. But what if Boone Markland and Jack refused to accept help from William? Sue had heard the bitter words when Billy had saved King from that vengeful mob and knew their continuing angry resentment. Morgan had silenced them then. She hoped Morgan would be available now.

That brought another confused, angry thought. Where was Morgan, where did he go, where did he stay, when time after time he failed to come home? Always he had a jaunty, insolently evasive excuse, always he brought home money—won at cards, so he claimed. Morgan had been a Confederate soldier. Why was he tolerated, why could he ride boldly into the radical camp and return unmolested when Jack and King had both been beaten? Morgan had better help and he had better have some answers ready when she saw him again.

She had no idea where the troops were camped but from Morgan's report of King's escapade she knew they could not be too far from the shanty town, the scrabble collection of makeshift huts and shelters where the gangs of dislocated, homeless Negroes had gathered. That sorry rendezvous of confusion and misery would be on the outskirts of the town so Sue avoided the main streets and skirted around the established area by back lanes and alleys, stared at sullenly by a few early rising blacks and poor whites, smelling hungrily the odors of frying bacon that seeped from the scattered hovels she passed.

Would there be tents and a flag, sentries to challenge her, deny her the right to see the Captain? She had a hazy idea of the military, having seen little of it save the few detachments of Confederate cavalry that had appeared at the Markland farm, been royally entertained and given the best of everything, and who then usually repaid that hospitality by requisitioning more horses, more hay and grain.

She glimpsed the shack town then, huddled on a slope above the river, crazy shelters of slabs and rough planks, ragged tents with rusty stovepipes jutting from the rear. Dark figures moved in that noisome jungle and she nervously urged the horse into a trot, almost running down a man in army breeches and a soiled undershirt who was trotting ahead of her on the road, jerking on the sleeves of a Federal uniform jacket as he trotted along. He jumped, turned, rolled big eyes at her and yelled.

"Miss Sue! Miss Sue!"

"Buzzy!" It was a cry, a sob of relief, a hysterical outburst that released her tension and terror. "Buzzy! Oh, Buzzy, it's you."

She reined the gelding in and Buzzy came alongside and laid a hand on the saddle leather.

"Miss Sue, what you doin' here?" he asked anxiously. "This here ain't no place for a lady like you."

She was sobbing so much that she could hardly speak, and her whole body shook with a nervous chill. This was Buzzy—part of home, Buzzy who had belonged till the war worked its savage destruction to home ties and loyalties. "Buzzy—it's Boss Boone and Mister Jack. The sheriff came yesterday and took them both and they beat Jack unconscious. I rode all night to find Billy—your Captain Billy."

Buzzy's wide eyes bulged even wider. With one agile leap he sprang up behind her.

"Git along, Miss Sue. Git goin' you hoss! We find the Cap'n. Mist' Morgan too. Miss Sue, they got Boss Boone in that jail? They got white folks in that jail, they say they goin' to hang some what killed some Unions. I heared it. Niggers hears all the white folks' talk. Turn here, Miss Sue. I reckon I got to wake up Cap'n. Reckon he ain't feelin' so good. Last night they had a big fight."

"What kind of a fight, Buzzy?"

"Just a cuss and hit fight. Not no guns. Mist' Morgan and Cap'n Billy fightin'. The officers took Cap'n Billy's gun, didn't want him to hurt nobody he was so mad. Mist' Morgan got his nose busted—bloody all over. They never knowed Boss Boone got took. They too busy fightin' each other. Right yonder," Buzzy pointed, "that ole house where Cap'n Billy stay at. Miss Sue, you let me go in and git him up first."

"But why were they fighting, Buzzy? Because Billy went with the Union?"

"No'm, don't reckon. They was fightin' over some li'l ole white gal. And it shore was a mean fight."

• *Fifteen* •

SHE WAS IN TERRIBLE DISGRACE.

Neither her mother nor Aunt Ella would speak to her when they went to bed long past midnight, although her mother had turned at the last and given her a sad, reproachful look. Earlier, Angela had stormed at them, all the green fire in her eyes alight and blazing, scarlet cheeks flaming.

"Why are you blaming me?" she demanded. "Can I help it if what men do doesn't please you? I've known Morgan Markland ever since we were in school. You thought it was fine when he first came calling here, all dressed up and riding a fine horse. You said he was one of our Confederate heroes, you even made tea and brought in those poor little dry cakes. You said it was like old times having gentlemen come calling again."

"When he came calling like a gentleman of course we approved," stated Aunt Ella icily. "But that other one, that Yankee in his vile uniform. You were very sly about that, Miss. We should have known— that flour on the doorstep."

"You ate it," reminded Angela maliciously. "You were very glad to eat it. And before that he saved me from being abused by a Colored soldier, and he brought me home safe from the Harpers' when you know very well I might have been attacked."

"If we had known it was Yankee flour it would have gone into the street along with his later insulting donations," snapped her aunt. "That was deceit and you were a party to it, young lady. So were those notes that came by the back door, that you hid till your mother got possession of that last one. A disgusting, familiar note from a Yankee! And the boy who brought them was no poor, hungry lost slave, he was one of their abominable soldiers. I found that out. I took the trouble to find out. And I spoke a piece of my mind to that captain. He knows exactly what I think of his outrageous conduct."

"For which piece of insolence fortunately you are not in jail this minute," flared Angela.

"The idea!" Aunt Ella flounced her black alpaca, making all her petticoats rattle. She had to boil corncobs to starch them now but starch them she did, picking up the dirty cobs in the henhouse, scrubbing and boiling them. "They would never dare put a Southern lady in jail. Not for trying to protect an innocent and ignorant girl from vile attentions."

"I resent that word, Aunt Ella! Nobody ever offered me any vile attentions. William Markland was a gentleman and so was his brother."

Her mother spoke up then, more with gentle sadness than with rancor. "You will admit that there was much conduct tonight, Angela, that could hardly be called the behavior of gentlemen? Morgan Markland coming here, decidedly under the influence—"

"The fellow was drunk!" snorted Ella. "Definitely, disgustingly drunk. The house reeks yet of alcohol and his filthy tobacco. And no gentleman would use the language he employed when he walked out that door."

"After you invited him out the door, sister," reminded Mrs. Wood. "I do not condone his actions in the least. For the son of a well-born and prominent family he was certainly guilty of indelicate conduct."

"Boasting, in this house, the home of a man who gave his life at Shiloh for the Cause—boasting that he had spent a whole day playing cards with radical scum like that Josh Fletcher and Doctor Grimes. Men whom no decent person would condescend to recognize on the street."

"Morgan was boasting that he had won their money, Aunt Ella," Angela suggested. "He thought he was doing something praiseworthy. He called it despoiling the Philistines."

"It was contamination, even breathing the same air with such creatures. I sorrow for his mother. And then to shout profanity—profane insults to a respectable, delicately reared girl like you—from our very doorstep—" Ella paused, panting with indignation, her face stiffly gray except for two purple patches on her cheekbones, her eyes looking ready to come plumping out of their sockets.

"He wasn't insulting me," defended Angela, permitting herself a nervous giggle at the sight of Aunt Ella, all swelled up and ready to explode. "He meant it for a compliment."

"Profanity never complimented any one, daughter. I can imagine what your dear father would have to say about that."

"Morgan said that I was his girl—and that he'd come to see me any time he goddam pleased," quoted Angela impudently. "And that was what made his brother William mad."

"Watching this house. It has gone on before. Oh, I've noticed. Even before that yellow boy started coming to the back door on one flimsy pretext or another. Claiming to be separated from his family and hungry. When I think of the bread you wasted on that wretch when all the time the army was feeding him. Giving you sly looks so you'd manage to smuggle in the note he was carrying and slip it into your bosom. Shameless—utterly shameless!"

"They were very nice notes, gentlemanly and polite. And you needn't order me to give them to you, Aunt Ella, or you either, Mother, as I shall never do it." Angela's eyes blazed defiantly.

"I don't know what to think of you, Angela," sighed her mother. "Deceiving us. Seeing this Yankee—"

"He was born right here in this county. Anyway we've all got to be Yankees now. There's no Confederacy any more. It's dead and the dead ought to be buried—buried and forgotten!" cried the girl. "Oh, I know you think that's heresy, especially you, Aunt Ella—keeping that silly little flag in your bosom."

"Don't you dare defame our flag," shrilled Ella. "You callous, immoral creature! Yes—immoral, Carrie, for no one with morals and honor could possibly say the things your insolent daughter is saying. Thank Providence your poor father never lived to see this tragic day."

"If he had lived," said Angela coldly, "he would have been the first person in this town to take the oath of loyalty to the Union. He didn't want the Union destroyed. It grieved him to his heart and you both know it. You were the ones who thought Jefferson Davis was a god, not he. He said, and I heard him, that Davis was a weak, deluded man, that it was tragic that the South must depend upon men whose minds were confused, and obstinate in their wrong-headed confusion. Events," stated the girl, with a flare of her dead father's gift for pungent phrase, "have proved how right my father was in his thinking. Even his death was the result of their stubborn stupidity and hollow pride."

"Angela, Angela," mourned her mother. "You must not say such things. What if you should be heard outside this house? Don't disgrace your father's memory with such reckless remarks."

"If he were alive he'd be making the same remarks himself," persisted Angela. "Maybe even from the pulpit."

"How can you sit there, Carrie Wood, and listen calmly to such words from your own child's lips?" fumed Ella, pacing the floor. "No doubt you are quoting your friend, the Union Captain, Angela. Treason to the South, the South that bred him, is not so strange and appalling coming from a traitor to his own family. Why doesn't he go home when he has a mother less than eighteen miles away? Because she repudiates him, as does every loyal Southerner in Tennessee."

"Because everything that has happened has proved that William Markland was right, and all the rest of his family wrong," argued the girl stubbornly. "People are never forgiven for being right—never."

"At least I don't see how he can be forgiven for picking a horrid fight with his own brother right in our front yard," said her mother. "He has made us all objects of shame and embarrassment before our neighbors."

"William hit Morgan because Morgan swore in my hearing," Angela said. "And if William hadn't hit Morgan I think that you would have slapped him yourself, Aunt Ella. You were certainly mad enough to do it."

"I assure you, Miss," said Ella stiffly, "that I had no desire to engage in an unseemly brawl. My only wish was to get the drunken creature out of this house, get back inside and lock the door before we suffered further humiliation. I should have gone instead and fetched the sheriff and had them both locked up. If either of them ever sets foot on these premises again that is exactly what I shall do."

Angela gathered up her skirts and tossed her head. "Then," she said, her chin set grimly, "I shall have to meet them elsewhere. I've already made up my mind that if I'm ever to meet any men at all that's exactly what I shall have to do."

"You are utterly depraved," flared Ella. "Carrie, say something! Are you going to sit there and snivel and let your only child challenge your authority in such bold fashion?"

Mrs. Wood rose wearily and picked up a candle. "I think that too much has been said already. Angela is angry now. We will all be able to think more calmly in the morning. I for one am going to bed before the sun comes up."

"I shall not be able to close my eyes," snapped her sister. "I shall sit here and read the Prayer Book and pray for this wicked, misguided child as her father would do if he had been spared."

"I think," said Angela, "that my father would have thought it an exciting fight. Except that Morgan wasn't able to stay on his feet very long and most likely now has a beautiful black eye. Those Marklands always did fight like tigers even when they were small boys. I suppose that's the reason they came safely through the war."

She marched away to her own room and closed the door firmly. She was still tingling a little and aghast at her own temerity, but there was a kind of wild singing in her blood and a humming in her ears. He was jealous—jealous! William had been jealous, furious because his younger brother had been received in the house. The fact that Morgan had been drinking was only an excuse. William had been jealous and he had wanted to hit Morgan for being there at all. Two men, fighting over me, sighed Angela deliciously, falling back on her bed and kicking her heels in the air in gay abandon.

And she had warned them, those good, gray guardian women. She had challenged them to restrict her any longer. She had been dreadful but it had been exhilarating and now she was all aquiver with the heady stimulus of her rebellion. Now she would walk out boldly alone and if she saw Captain Markland on his usual bench in the courthouse yard some sundown she would stop and speak to him and let who pleased glare condemnation.

She would even, if she could manage it, go and take the oath of allegiance to the Union. She was not sure whether young people were allowed to swear allegiance, but she would find out. She was young and the young marched with the living, accepted what was unavoidable, what was true, rather than huddling in secret to bewail the past in sackcloth and ashes. A past that was forever dead now, except that women like Aunt Ella would never let it die. For years, she knew, women like her aunt would be weeping over the corpse of that lost Cause they refused to bury. Weaving wreaths of sentiment and tears, exaggerating every glory, fiercely denying every error and deluded mistake.

Morgan Markland had said that he expected things to get worse before they got better. There were too many scalawags in power, too many men violently inclined, both black and white. Violence understood and respected only violence, he had said blandly, and Aunt Ella, grimly chaperoning her niece, had nodded passionate agreement. Aunt Ella believed that the South should have repudiated the surrender, should have stood firmly for secession no matter how cravenly it was deserted by its own army. Morgan had advanced a bit of resentment on his own at that point.

"It was the South who deserted the army, Miss Crabtree. We were eager to fight, but where were the weapons and the ammunition? We were barefooted and hungry. General Lee fought Richmond for supplies harder than he fought Useless Grant. They could have balls for the officers and banquets, with the leavings of the feasts generously carried to the hospitals where wounded men lay on cold floors without even blankets to cover them, but the army lay out in the mud fed on wormy bacon and parched corn and half the time the cartridges we got wouldn't even fit our guns."

"You do not look underfed, Sergeant Markland," Miss Ella had stated firmly.

"I fought under a foraging commander. Old Nate Forrest robbed one Yank supply train after another. It was after the surrender that things got tough. One of my brothers had a hard time recovering after he walked home from Alabama. Some time we'll see an end of persecution and a decent government in this state, but not yet."

"A horse-doctor sheriff! Drunken scalawags in our legislature," snorted Miss Ella. "What can you do about outrages like that when they juggle the law so that you cannot even vote?"

"There are, Miss Crabtree," Morgan had quoted then, "more ways to kill a cat than choking it on butter."

He was, Angela was thinking now, lying on her bed and staring into the sultry dark, somehow fascinating in his handsome insolence. There was an undismayed jauntiness about him, a brisk, sardonic recklessness quite different from William's patient gentleness. William was always talking patience, that all things passed, that the ugliness would end, but there had been times, riding home from the Harper farm, when she had wondered if he really believed what he said so confidently. The Marklands were reputed to be fire-eaters, all, and she had wondered if William's attitude was not a bit spiritless until last night.

Last night, striding in at their gate, rigid with fury against his own brother, he had certainly fought spiritedly enough. Only Aunt Ella's strident threat to call the sheriff, and the intervention of two other officers, had cooled the enraged battling of the pair. Then William had coolly lifted the prostrate Morgan and, helped by the mulatto boy who had been his messenger before, had loaded Morgan on his horse and led the animal away. He had been followed by a ragtag trail of black soldiers and town loafers, and Angela now admitted to herself that it had all been pretty horrible, that she could not in fairness blame Aunt Ella for her ire nor her mother for shedding reproachful tears at being thus humiliated.

But no girl who had lived through four years of manless loneliness, uncourted and sternly chaperoned, could fail to be thrilled at having two handsome and dashing young blades fighting over her. The question that kept Angela Wood awake till broad day flared in at the windows was—which was the right one? Would there be an answer to that puzzle in her mind? Would there be a sign? How had her own mother known when quiet George Wood came along that he was the right man for her heart?

Her mother had run away to marry the poor young preacher from Alabama whom Grandfather Crabtree thought highly unsuitable for his daughter. If she herself decided to run off with one Markland or the other, certainly her mother could have little to say.

Of course Aunt Ella would fume and storm but who would listen to Aunt Ella? Aunt Ella was nothing but a sour old maid. Nobody would listen to her, certainly not Angela, if she were far away and married to a Markland. But which Markland? The sun blazed in at the window but still she had no answer to that question.

• *Sixteen* •

BUZZY SLID OFF THE SADDLE BEFORE A HIGH, SHABBY OLD HOUSE.

"You let me go in first, Miss Sue. You let me go in and wake 'em up. Mist' Morgan ain't had no clothes on when we put him in that bed."

"Morgan's in there? You said that they were fighting."

"Yessum. Cap'n and me fetch him back here and wash him up. He ain't felt so good. Somebody," he stated soberly, "done slipped Mist' Morgan some mighty poor liquor. He ain't acted the way he do, if he be himself."

"Hurry, Buzzy. Mister Jack had a hard blow on the head. If he's over there in that jail he may need a doctor."

"Anyhow they ain't hung nobody yet. They rings that courthouse bell when they fixin' to hang somebody." Buzzy bounded up on the battered porch of the house the army had taken over to quarter the white officers. The door was locked but he shook it twice, up and down and sideways, kicked the lower panel and it swung open. Behind him he could see Miss Sue slumped wearily in the saddle. The gelding sagged too, head down, one hip high, sweat a brown patch under the saddle blanket.

In a room to the left the two Marklands lay stretched on army cots. Their clothing, Union blue and a young planter's nattier apparel, was flung over the back of a chair, but William's pistol belt was carefully hung at the head of his cot.

Buzzy went to the bunk and shook it hard. "Cap'n Billy! You gotta wake up. Us got trouble, bad trouble!"

William blinked, scrubbed his eyes and swung his bare legs off the bed. He looked dazedly at his brother, stretched out on the opposite bunk, rubbed a hand over his forehead and groaned, "Oh, my God."

Buzzy kept on shaking. "It ain't him, Cap'n. Mist' Morgan ain't the trouble. It Boss Boone and Mist' Jack. They done been took."

"What?" William jumped up, lithe and pale in his underwear, dark hair standing in disorder on his head.

"Miss Sue out there," persisted Buzzy. "She done rode all night to fetch you. Sheriff come yisti'day, Miss Sue say, took Boss Boone and Mist' Jack. Sheriff say they done shot somebody."

"Hand me my breeches," ordered William. "Easy. Don't drop everything out of the pockets. Who did the sheriff say Pa and Jack shot?"

"Miss Sue don't know. She just heard a little bit. Somebody knocked Mist' Jack down with a pistol, she say, and he ain't knowed nothin' when they drug him off. Miss Sue thinks they in jail. Might be they git hung, Cap'n, but ain't no bell rung."

"Not even reveille yet. Where have you been? How'd you find Miss Sue?" demanded William, twisting into his clothes.

"I been down the road courtin' a gal, Cap'n. Seen Miss Sue on the road when I was hurryin' back to camp. She mighty wore out and hungry, Cap'n, but she say for me to fetch you to git Boss Boone and Mist' Jack out of that jail."

"Wake that fellow up," said William, pulling on his boots and waving one toward the other cot. "Maybe he knows something about this."

"Reckon he sober by now, Cap'n? I don't want Little Brother fightin' me." Buzzy advanced timorously toward the bunk where Morgan lay sprawled on his back. "His eye mighty swole up, Cap'n. Nose too."

"Wake him up and fetch a pan of water for him to wash up. He won't fight anybody. Not today." William was grim.

"Yessuh, Cap'n." Buzzy laid a gingerly hand on Morgan's naked shoulder. "Mist' Morgan! Mist' Morgan! Cap'n say you wake up now. We got trouble."

Morgan jerked, gasped, choked, and his lips fluttered. "Whu—whuh —whuh—" He tried to sit up, fell back again, then rolled erect and glared through bloodshot eyes. "What the hell?" he shouted.

"Get on your feet. Wash your face," ordered William, buckling his belt. "Pa and Jack are in trouble. Sue rode all night to tell us."

Morgan pressed his hands over his eyes and moaned. "God, my head! Where am I, anyway?"

"In my quarters," said William coldly. "We brought you here last night after you'd made an unmitigated ass of yourself. Get your clothes on. Sue's out there waiting."

"Sue? How'd Sue get here? And what did you hit me with, Billy? My head's ready to bust." Morgan groped about, Buzzy handing him his garments, a piece at a time.

"It that bust-haid whisky hit you, Mist' Morgan," said the boy. "Cap'n Billy, he knock you down but he don't tromp you none. You got that sleeve on the wrong arm. Here, let me turn it round. That a purty eye Cap'n hung on you," Buzzy giggled. "Gals sho' goin' to know you been in a fight."

"The old lady threw me out," raged Morgan. "The desiccated, whey-faced old virgin. Keeps that girl shut up like that house was a convent. You didn't have to hit me just because she threw me out, Billy."

"I hit you because you were drunk and foul-mouthed around my girl," stated William sternly.

"*Your* girl! By gad, sir—"

"Get your pants on and shut up. Then you take Sue somewhere, get her some coffee and find out what the trouble is. Take care of her horse, too. Buzzy and I have to show at roll call, then I'll meet you and we'll see what has to be done. No damned radical sheriff can keep our father in jail," stormed William, slapping on his hat so hard the gilded acorns jingled.

"Who the hell do you think you're giving orders to?" demanded Morgan angrily. "I'm not in your goddam army. And how come you've turned rebel all of a sudden?"

"Oh, quit acting the fool, boy," snapped William wearily. "The Marklands are in trouble. You're a Markland. I'm a Markland. It's our trouble. Sue's been sitting out there nearly half an hour now. She had the guts to ride all night to tell us, and she's not even a Markland. Button your breeches and get a move on."

"Some day we'll settle whose girl that is," Morgan flung after the military pair as they went out. Then he grew thoughtful. Pa in jail, and Jack too. Light seeped slowly into Morgan's numbed brain. Somebody had found those bodies, too hastily buried on the old Oliver place. Some member of that looting gang of marauders had gotten the ear of the sheriff. But I was in that, he remembered, if I had been at home they'd have taken me too.

A bit of broken mirror was propped against the shelf that served William as a washstand. Morgan regarded himself dubiously in its cracked surface. Lord, what a mess! He had been summarily disciplined by his older brothers in earlier years but no Markland had ever hung an eye like that on him before.

He scrubbed his face and smacked back his hair with wet palms, buttoned his jacket with a shrug, kicked the door open and went out. The slanting morning sunlight made him blink and grimace as it smote his inflamed eyeballs but he put arrogance in his stride as he stalked out to the tree-shaded street where Sue still sat, leaning wearily forward in the saddle.

She said, "Hello, Morgan, Billy told me you'd look after me and this horse. He's mighty tired and so am I. Help me down. They told me to sit right here till you came."

He held up his arms and she slid into them, her legs quivering under her. "You were mighty brave to come alone, Sue," he said. "Tell me what happened as we walk along. I'll get your horse taken care of and you too." He thrust an arm through the bridle rein and the tired gelding followed them as they walked the grassy strip at the edge of the street. Sue held up her skirts with one hand, clutching Morgan's elbow with the other.

"I don't know all of it. We were in the house when Boone-boy came tearing in yelling that some bad men said Grandpa had killed a man and they were going to take him off and hang him. There were eight of them, but that Jeff Nichols was the only one I recognized. Miss Annie gave him the rough edge of her tongue when they took your father away and Nichols looked mighty shamefaced and hangdog about the business."

"It's that raid at Winnie's place," said Morgan. "Jack was right. We should never have left those dead men on that land. He wanted to dump them somewhere along the road but Pa talked him out of it. He said it would get us into trouble but it seems trouble caught up with us anyway."

"You were in that as much as Jack was," Sue reminded him. "Jack fought them but somebody hit him an awful blow on the side of the head with a gun. He was limp as a rag when they took him away."

"Been better if he hadn't fought back," Morgan said. "We have to fight 'em, Sue, but we have to be smart about it."

"Like you?" She was acid. "Hide out and let somebody else take the blame?"

"I wasn't hiding," argued Morgan. "I was carrying on secret operations that you wouldn't understand, Susie, my gal. Very profitable operations. Helps Miss Annie no end, the way I operate."

"But you're here and Jack is lying over there in that jail. At least I hope he's there, and I understand this much—from Buzzy's report your secret operation involved some girl, and you must not have done too well at that."

"I was doing all right till that strutting Fed brother of mine tangled himself into it. No, Susie, no girl is mixed up in my operations. It's a kind of club. Some of us young fellows who want back what the Yanks took away from us. We lure them into our lair and take it back painlessly, for us. Wait here, while I get this nag fed and watered in that stable. How did you ride all night on Pa's old saddle? Why didn't you put on proper gear?"

"It was dark and we were in a hurry. Boone-boy and I got the guns out of the bin and I took the first saddle we got our hands on. Hurry, Morgan, I'm beginning to be scared. All those people are staring at me."

William found them in the dingy dining room of the little hotel where Morgan had ordered breakfast for Sue and himself. It was a scanty meal consisting only of gray slablike biscuits, fried salt pork and two eggs swimming in grease, but the coffee was hot and strong and Sue felt her weariness relaxing a little.

With William came two other white officers in blue and at the door Buzzy waited, all his brass and buttons shining. William's dark face was set in formal military firmness above the gilt emblems on his collar. He made a little bow, some of the old Markland mockery showing in the dry twist of his lips.

"My sister, Mrs. Andrew Jackson Markland," he said to his companions. "Lieutenant Perry, Lieutenant Gore. You've met Sergeant Morgan Markland already, I believe."

"To our loss," declared Lieutenant Gore. "If Sergeant Markland could be imprisoned indefinitely it would contribute to the morale of the United States Army and also improve my personal finances."

William pulled up some chairs for the three of them. Sue felt uneasy. There were people about, there were turned heads and whispers. People were wondering about these Marklands, passionate Confederates as they were known to be, drinking coffee with officers of the garrison company. And a Negro garrison too, she was thinking unhappily.

"Now," William began, "I have to know all the facts about this fracas Pa and Jack were mixed up in. I have to know what happened before I make a sortie on that jail."

"It wasn't just Pa and Jack," Morgan said. "I was there too."

"And King?"

"Not King. He's still got a bad rising under his arm from that fight he had over here when the Nigras rushed him. It gives him a fever every night and he gets dizzy and can't walk or ride."

"Those men who were killed—who actually killed them?"

"Could have been me," said Morgan. "We were all shooting. But I think Pa got one with that heavy old gun of his. They were looting the place, just a gang of guerrilla hoodlums on horseback."

"Now hear this," said William sternly. "When I talk to the sheriff,

Pa didn't kill anybody. Can you remember that, Brother Morgan? You didn't kill anybody. Nor Brother Jack. You'd better remember that or I'll black your other eye."

"They killed themselves then and just lay down in the furrow and buried themselves, not wanting to be a trouble to anybody," drawled Morgan cynically. "They were guerrillas, I tell you. We had a right to defend King's property when he couldn't protect it himself."

"The army," stated William sternly, "is stationed here to protect all property and to preserve the peace."

"Like hell!" sneered Morgan. Then in a slightly startled voice, "Billy —you can't—"

"You would be even less attractive with two black eyes," declared his brother, rising to his feet. "Now come along with us. And if you are questioned you will simply answer that those men were looting and committing depredations in that house."

"They tried to burn it. We put out the fire. Look here, Billy, you can make me hold my tongue but what are you going to do about Pa? He won't keep quiet. He'll brag and defy those fellows. You know Pa."

William drew on his gloves. They were very clean, Sue noted, and she wondered who washed them for him. Did Buzzy do it, or was it that girl Buzzy had babbled about, the girl for whom William had blacked his brother's eye?

"We'll take care of Pa," he was saying. "Sue, you stay here. Stay off the street till we come back." And they were gone, one of the lieutenants handing some money to the landlord as they went out the door.

Sue finished the eggs, her own plate and Morgan's, then leaned her chin on her hand and sank into weary drowsiness, her bright hair drooping over her fingers.

When the three officers, followed by Morgan, entered the sheriff's office they found only a dirty deputy, half asleep in a chair, his feet propped on the window sill. He informed them that the sheriff had not come in yet.

"Out late last night roundin' up some murderin' Rebs. What you want with Jeff, Captain? I'm in charge here till Jeff comes back. Might not come all day if he gets a call off some place. You tell me your business, I'll see what can I do for you."

"I'll tell my business to Jeff Nichols," said William stiffly. "You know where he is. Get word to him to meet me at his jail in thirty minutes."

"Look here, Captain"—the deputy's muddy heels crashed to the floor—"you're in command out yonder but you don't run this here courthouse nor the jailhouse neither. Tennessee ain't under no martial law."

"It could be," remarked William. "If it's established that the civil authorities can't keep the peace and control these bands of marauders, President Johnson would declare martial law in Tennessee, even if Governor Brownlow refused to co-operate."

"Yah, reckon old Andy would be plumb pleased to put this state under the army jest to spite Brownlow," conceded the deputy. "But we ain't had no trouble so fur keepin' the peace. Got a whole jail full of disturbers locked up back yonder now. You listen you can hear them yellin'. Ain't fed 'em yet. Act just like critters when they ain't been fed."

William's face tightened grimly. "Didn't you hear me say I want to see the sheriff right now? Send somebody to find him, unless you want me to put an order out. I doubt if Nichols would appreciate being brought back in custody by a squad of troopers."

The dirty man scowled and spat. "Now wait, young feller, you ain't foolin' me none. I been around this here county a long time. You're one of Boone Markland's wild boys and that feller there's another of 'em. And ole Boone is one of them Secesh we got locked up back yonder. If you got some trick worked out to get your pappy loose after he done confessed to a cold-blooded murder I kin tell you right now you can save your breath and bile. You may run them scabby niggers out yonder but you soldiers ain't running this county. Not while there's men around with guts to see you don't do it."

"I didn't come here to argue with you, fellow," said William. "I came to see the sheriff. Looks like I'll have to send a squad after him. I'm no defeated Confederate to be persecuted by you bullies. My authority in this area comes from the Secretary of War in Washington, and I mean to exercise it."

The deputy growled in disgust. "All you Marklands always was a lot of biggity blabber mouths, lording it over other people. Put a uniform on any one of you and there ain't no enduring him. Eph!" He removed his quid, opened his mouth and shouted, "You, Eph!"

A Negro came in the door and leaned against it. "Yeah," he said. "What you all want?"

"Find Jeff and git him in here. I got no patience to deal with no Markland, Fed or Rebel. Allus did make theirselves believe they was sons of God instead of the kind of sons they is!"

"Easy, Morgan," warned William, as Morgan's jaw muscles tightened and his fists knotted. "Don't waste ammunition on one stinking little target."

"Let him hit me," urged the deputy. "Whole litter of Marklands back there in them tanks would suit me fine. Looks like somebody put that young dude through the corn sheller already. Nobody ever fetched an eye like that home from a Sunday school picnic."

Cautiously the two lieutenants ranged themselves alongside Morgan, put a firm grip on his elbows.

"Let the army take over, son," advised Lieutenant Gore. "Nothing gained by starting a ruckus with civilians."

"I'll smash his filthy lying mouth for him," muttered Morgan.

"Turn him loose," ordered the deputy. "Let him try it. I got plenty men can handle any Markland ever whelped."

Jeff Nichols broke the tension then, walking in calmly, hat on the back of his head. He spat out the straw he was chewing and looked the group over casually.

"What goes on here?" he asked, with studied indifference. "What do you officers want?"

"We want the Marklands, Sheriff," stated William with military crispness. "Both of them. They happen to be military prisoners on parole, and they are in custody of the army till released. You've got no right to hold them."

"Looks like you got one already," drawled Nichols. "How'd we miss him, Pete? He was into it, like as not. Must have been hid out."

"He's under military detention, as you can see," said William. "Now I want the others. Fetch out Boone Markland and his son, Jackson."

Nichols scratched himself. "You're a Markland yourself, Captain. This here has got the smell of fish about it. I ain't turnin' no prisoners over to you. Not till I got a damn good reason."

"Too bad," William shrugged elaborately. "Nothing to do but bring a force here and raid your jail. I have orders to put under arrest any guerrilla outlaws in this area. I found these men at the scene of a guerrilla raid and put them under parole till I could investigate their story of being innocent victims of an attack. My orders come from Washington, and as I suppose you know, they supersede the civil authority. Morgan Markland, you were present when the guerrilla band raided the old Oliver place on the twenty-third of September. You were armed and firing, as you admitted to me. Two men were killed there. State to the sheriff who killed those two men."

The pressure on Morgan's elbow increased to the point of agony. He had a moment of wrathful bewilderment, then something in his brother's face gave him his cue. He almost grinned.

[130]

"The army shot those men, Captain," he answered. "When they refused to surrender, you and your troopers opened fire and two men were killed."

• *Seventeen* •

BOONE MARKLAND WOULD NOT SIT DOWN. HE PACED THE NEAT, MONASTIC room that was William's quarters, his great body quivering with fury.

He had been led, stumbling, fuming and protesting between the two lieutenants to this place and being seen in the custody of Union officers on the street had been a worse outrage to Boone than being taken to jail by a county posse. Jack had been half carried by Buzzy and two stout troopers and laid on a cot. Now Sue sat beside him sponging the dark, savage bruise on his head with a damp cloth. Leaning against the wall Morgan stood silent, still wearing the ghost of a grin.

The drama, the trickery, the magnificent bluff had appealed to the brash, outlaw strain in Morgan. That this was a Union victory did not dismay him. He was beginning to concede that Billy was not too bad a Markland, that the same streak of reckless bravado was in him, uninhibited by the Union blue.

Boone kept shouting, "I tell you I won't go along with it. Making a fool and a liar out of me in front of a gang of scurvy rascals and an ignorant lout of a hog doctor like Jeff Nichols. I shot that feller and I saw the ball hit him and smash his skull just like I've seen it hit a bear many a time. You—" he whirled on William angrily, "you're the liar. Making out you were there, letting on you put Jack and me on parole. Where's the rest of the gang? Why ain't you brought them in? That's what people are going to start asking. Not that I give a damn if it ruins you. I disowned you the day you rode off to fight for the Union!"

Sue's eyes blazed. "Billy saved the two of you and he saved King from being killed! You admit it may ruin him, yet he took that chance to keep his own people from being dragged through a rotten farce of a trial, and like enough from being hung. If you can't appreciate that, Pa Markland, you can at least hold your tongue and not abuse your own son. I'm grateful to Billy for getting Jack out of that filthy jail and I wouldn't care if he was Ulysses Grant or Sherman or even old Brownlow himself."

"They'd have had to give us fair trial, Sue," muttered Jack.

"Hah!" snapped Sue. "A fair trial in their rotten court with a rigged-up jury and a whole mob of skinnies bought and paid for to swear lies against you. You talk like a fool. If they didn't hang you you'd be run out of Tennessee like a lot of poor people we know about already. Everybody knows that Brownlow's sworn he won't stop till he's run every Confederate out of this state."

Boone was not mollified. He turned his ire upon his youngest son. "You!" he barked. "Standing up there lying in your teeth like a dirty politician, letting on I never fired that gun."

"Worse than that, Pa." Morgan was apparently unperturbed. "I made 'em believe you didn't even own a gun. I had to own the rifle for there it was, hung on the saddle Sue rode over here. I told 'em I fired it and that was the truth. I did fire it and I reckon I killed one of those men."

"That ain't the way you made it out," argued Boone. "You let it lay where Billy laid it, that the army was there and wasn't satisfied with our story that we was defending our own family's property."

"Confederate property, Pa," Morgan reminded him. "You know it can't be legally defended, nominally defended at any rate in Brownlow's state."

"Any man's property can be defended. That's in the Bill of Rights," put in Jack, "but I reckon Abe Lincoln knocked out The Bill, too, when he scuttled the Constitution. Hold your hand on that spot, Sue, and press hard. It keeps my head from aching so bad."

"He ought to have a doctor," worried Sue.

"I'll have a doctor for him," William said. "The best we can find around here."

"I reckon—" Jack struggled to sit up but Sue's pressing hands restrained him, "I reckon you intend to keep us locked up." He glared angrily from two swollen eyes and his lips drew taut in a bitter grimace.

"You have to stay in custody, all of you," said William. "Otherwise the sheriff's gang will pick you up again and that time I might not be able to free you. So unless you are willing to obey my orders I'm helpless to do anything for you."

"But what about Miss Annie? She's there alone, nobody but King and him sick, and Winnie's worse than nobody," Sue reminded him.

"I shall make arrangements to send you all home under military protection and surveillance. But it can't be done quickly and you'll have to be patient. Remember, this is all a rash operation, desperately undertaken for the honor of the Marklands. I'm taking risks myself, but I'd be a sorry Markland if I could stand back and let my father and brothers be hauled up in a makeshift, loaded court and charged with murder."

Boone Markland squared himself. "We're all Marklands here. All but Sue—"

"Sue's a better Markland than any of us," stated William.

"Could be. Could be. But I say it now and I say it plain, William Breen Markland. I'd rather take my chances in court than be beholden to any Yankee alive—son or no son. And since 'sixty-one you're no son of mine."

"Pa Markland, you're an ingrate," said Sue. "Open that door, Buzzy, and let Jeff Nichols take him. Morgan will swear he fired that old blunderbuss, if that's what he wants, he'll swear he killed that Hooper fellow. You could be thinking about Miss Annie a little. You could be remembering how she's feeling instead of sitting here mouthing a lot of foolish abuse. What would it do to Miss Annie and Boone-boy too, if something awful happened to you?"

"She'd rather see me hung dead than a traitor to the South," said Boone, but it was apparent that he was halfway trying to convince himself. The pain of the turmoil ridged his face and made his mouth quiver a little. Sue went to him and took his hand.

"Don't you see, Pa, that we couldn't bear it if dreadful things happened to you? Not any of us. Not Billy, though you do set yourself to despise him. We're Marklands and the Marklands are a clan. Maybe we're all mad and stubborn and wrong, maybe we fight among ourselves and work ourselves up to hurt each other, but if anybody outside threatens any of us then we're a clan all roused up to fight like tigers to defend any Markland alive."

"Good girl," said William. "That puts it on record for all of us, Pa. Now let's move. You need something to eat and Jack must have some attention."

Jack sat slumped on the cot, his head in his hands. "Damned if I go along with this," he growled. "You can take us now because you've got men and guns to do it, Bill Markland, but there have been a lot of rash Yanks who've tried it before and nobody ever held a Markland for long when he wasn't willing to be held."

"You didn't want to be in Jeff Nichols' jail," his wife reminded him. "I didn't see you come charging out of there till you had help, my fine bragging husband."

"All this gets us nowhere," declared William wearily. "Pa, you have to go along with me without argument. I'm sorry, but that's the way it has to be. You've got to be kept under guard for your own protection. Morgan, you stay with Jack and Sue till I come back with a litter and some bearers."

"I can walk," shouted Jack. "I won't be carried to your rotten guard-house nor worked on by any of your Yankee doctors. I can walk and I'm walking out of here right now and taking my wife with me. If Morgan wants to act the fool and go along with your crazy scheme and Pa too, that's their business. You've got a horse here, Morgan? You sure didn't come afoot from home. Sue brought the gelding. Let's move and see if gallant Captain Markland of Sheridan's Cavalry has the guts to stop us. Maybe he'll have us shot down in cold blood the way he claims he shot the raiders on King's place. Come on, Sue. Give me a hand."

"No!" screamed Sue, flying to him as he tried to get to his feet. She held him desperately as he wavered. "Morgan, help me," she said, as Jack's knees buckled and he collapsed limply on the floor.

"Lay him flat. Keep his head down," ordered Boone as his younger sons tried to lift their unconscious brother. "He's fainted, that's all. Get some water, somebody."

"He must have had a concussion," William remarked, when they had straightened Jack's legs and covered him with a blanket. "I'll get the doctor. He mustn't move. I'll station a guard here so that nobody will bother you till I get back. Sue, Buzzy's waiting outside. Call him in, will you?"

Buzzy's eyes rolled nervously as he eased through the half-opened door, his rifle trailing. These were all his white folks but around them was such an atmosphere of tension, distrust and resentment that Buzzy could feel it pressing on his dark hide as so many times back in those war-torn Virginia thickets he had sensed the chill, creeping blanket of fear.

There was Cap'n Billy, gray-faced and stiff and very military and over against the wall was old Boss Boone, glaring at Billy, wearing the thunderous face Buzzy had flinched before so often, way back home. Miss Sue and Mist' Morgan were fussing over Mist' Jack who looked half dead to Buzzy's frightened eyes. Miss Sue was crying and dabbing water on Mist' Jack's face while Mist' Morgan rubbed his hands, hands that looked mighty dry and cold to Buzzy.

"He daid?" he got out in a gulping whisper. Then he ducked his head from old habit. "Howdy, Boss Boone," he mumbled, backing against the wall also from old habit, waiting for Boss Boone to hurl some hot blast of wrath at him.

William took the rifle from the yellow boy's uncertain hands, inspected bolt and load, handed it back with military abruptness.

"You are to guard this door, Private Markland," he ordered brusquely. "No one is to leave this room till I and the other officers return, you understand?"

Buzzy gulped again, managed a wobbly semblance of standing at attention. "Yes, suh, Cap'n suh." Then he added anxiously, "Mist' Jack—he ain't daid?"

"He's not dead. I'm getting the doctor. And no talking from you while you're on duty."

"Yes, suh, Cap'n suh." Buzzy squared himself militantly against the door, jerking his cap lower over his eyes, and for a long minute he tried not to look at Boss Boone's scowling and flushed countenance. Boss Boone, he suspected, was getting all blowed up ready to call him a yellow bastard and order him to put down that gun and get away from that door. Buzzy tightened every muscle waiting for the old man to start yelling at him, determined at all costs to stand his ground. Wasn't he free? Wasn't he a soldier of the United States Army and wasn't there a law that said nobody better start any meanness with a uniformed man in blue or the army would deal with him bad and sudden?

But Boone Markland did not speak. He only grunted, a sound eloquent of contempt and rage, then he set himself down on a hickory chair as though his legs were plumb tired and wouldn't hold him up any longer.

It was Sue who said hesitantly, "Buzzy?"

Buzzy swallowed hard. "You heard the Cap'n, Miss Sue. I cain't talk to nobody."

"Oh, this is all silly and stupid," she said. "Our own family, our own people. Look, Morgan—he's moving his eyelids. He's coming to."

Buzzy took one forward step anxiously, remembered his duty and stiffened again at the door. The sun was getting high and beginning to glare in at the uncurtained windows, where only tattered remnants of blinds hung askew, fly-specked and rain-stained. Outside was the pungent smell of October, of leaves getting ready to call the summer ended, of ripe corn and apples fragrant on the trees. Back home it would be a good time, Buzzy thought, mist on the ground and persimmons ripening, possums running at night and foxhounds baying in the light of a swollen autumn moon.

Suddenly Buzzy felt like cutting a pigeon wing and yelping gleefully, hoping that Cap'n Billy would send him home. Doggone, that would be a great day! Corn pone again like 'Nerva knew how to make it, crusty and brown and greasy around the edges.

Secretly he nursed a hope that Cap'n Billy would let him take Miss Sue home, and would keep Boss Boone under guard here some place for a good long time. Back with Miss Annie Buzzy could really enjoy himself—although there would still be Mist' King—but it might be a good long spell before Mist' King would get on foot again and meanwhile Buzzy could tend Miss Annie's cow and hens and eat 'Nerva's good corn bread and pot liquor. Thinking about it the boy leaned his shoulders hard against the door and almost dozed off. He had had a wild night yonder in the scrabbling settlement where the dislocated Negroes had their shacks, and likely he would be in the guardhouse right now if the Marklands hadn't gotten into a mess with the law. It was his name spoken sharply that snapped him alert again and made him grip his weapon tighter.

"Buzzy!" Morgan, long silent, now spoke commandingly. "I think I'll just take that gun away from you and walk out the door."

Buzzy's eyeballs bulged and his teeth clamped till he could hardly force his voice through his rigid lips.

"No, suh, Mist' Morgan. Don't you do that, suh. I don't want to shoot nobody but I put on guard and got orders and I got to shoot if anybody try to take my gun."

"The Captain didn't order you to shoot anybody," pursued Morgan, a glint of gleeful mischief in his eyes. Buzzy knew that shine of old. When Mist' Morgan git that devil grin in his eyes a nigger had better run. Buzzy had an inspired spasm of inventiveness.

"'Tain't no good, Mist' Morgan. Some more us boys outside. Do they take you you git flang in the guardhouse right quick."

"He's lying," remarked Boone at the window. "There's nobody outside."

"They ain't showin' theirselves. They right clost to this door," improvised Buzzy desperately. "We got to pertect you, Mist' Morgan. If you git outside that sheriff git you again and then can't nobody git you a-loose."

"He's right, Morgan," said Sue. "Let the boy alone. Let Billy handle this. Billy knows what he's doing."

"All Billy knows is he's getting a vindictive sort of satisfaction keeping us shut in here," said Morgan, his moment of reluctant admiration for his brother forgotten. "It must be his idea of an elegant joke. First he beats me up. Then—with my help, I'll admit—he ruins us by implying to Jeff Nichols that we've been under suspicion, and on parole, of all goddam crazy ideas. If Jeff wasn't the ignorant old rascal he is he'd never have swallowed that guff. You may be able to see some trace of family loyalty in it but I can't any more. We disowned him for taking up with the Union, now he salves his injured vanity by humiliating us."

"The humiliation," said Sue hotly, "happened when I saw my husband and your father dragged off like criminals by that posse. I suppose it wasn't a humiliation to your father to be locked up all night in that filthy jail? Why"—she flung out her hands—"do you always think the worst of your brother?"

"So far the worst seems to be what meets the eye," Morgan said, moving slowly along the wall, so deliberately that Buzzy gripped his weapon tighter and hot water came into his mouth. "He got Pa and Jack away from Nichols, he put on that show so he could hold all three of us. What gives you any idea he's going to let us go home free? It would tickle his pride mightily to keep us shut up somewhere the rest of the summer. Buzzy!" He raised his voice in peremptory command. "Give me that gun before I take it away from you and brain you with it."

Almost Buzzy screamed. "No, Mist' Morgan, no!"

"Grab it!" ordered Boone Markland, plunging forward, huge and clumsy as a bear.

Buzzy gave another scream, animal-shrill with panic. Sue's sharp cry tore the air as Morgan plunged.

The gun, wavering frantically in the Negro boy's tense fingers, went off with a hollow sort of thud. Boone clutched his belly.

"Son of a bitch!" he yelled as he toppled sideways.

Morgan clutched at Buzzy as the gun fell smoking to the floor, but Buzzy tore free and was out the door, running wildly, all the raw terror in his being putting fire into his heels.

· *Eighteen* ·

BETWEEN THEM JACK AND KING MARKLAND CARRIED THEIR MOTHER DOWN the slope from the family burial plot. Already up there among the cedar trees sympathetic neighbors were shoveling damp clods into the raw, new grave.

Miss Annie was gray and limp, her dark eyes sunk in great hollows in her little heart-shaped face. Her sons made a cradle of their hands and she leaned against King's shoulder, clutching his coat, her small feet dangling pathetically. Behind them Sue and Winnie led a scared and silent Boone-boy between them; the thin, sad procession of the Marklands, all who remained on the place to mourn the master.

Three days ago Morgan had disappeared. Morgan and the stallion, the best and fastest horse left to them, had vanished suddenly in the night. All the weeks while his father lay fevered and sickened from the bullet wound in his stomach, Morgan had paced the house like an angry panther. The others could almost see the violence growing within him till it fairly poisoned the air they breathed.

Now the Negroes whispered fearfully that Mist' Morgan Markland had gone off to find and kill Buzzy, that Morgan had been seen in one squalid settlement after another. That he was half drunk and crazy and that sooner or later he would be found lying beside the road with his throat cut from ear to ear.

That had been in late November, now December was upon the earth with a sky like a leaden blanket and cold winds swirling little spits of snow against the horizon.

Through the long days while Boone Markland was slowly dying, through all the wretchedness of blood and pus and moans and bitter curses, Miss Annie had stood like a rock, a tiny, valiant figure, refusing discouragement, defying death, exaggerating every sign of improvement, insisting that Boone would be back on his feet by planting time. Wasn't he stronger than any of his sons? King had had the strength to recover from the fetid abscess on his ribs and Jack was almost himself again although he still suffered violent headaches and there were days when he shook with chills and seemed a bit vague and dazed in spite of Miss Annie's quinine, blue mass or other remedies. But now Boone was dead after lying for a week in a stupor, and abruptly all the strength had gone out of her. They had almost seen it go in that moment when Boone shuddered away his last breath, running out of her like wine from a glass overturned, leaving only a pallid crystal emptiness and dark and bitter dregs in her deep eyes.

They reached the kitchen door and Boone-boy, glad to be released from formality, ran ahead to open it.

"Go ahead, Sue," ordered King. "Fix her bed. We'll lay her down to rest."

His mother lifted her head and her voice came, as from far away but crisp and firm. "I saw him. Up there on that hill. There were three of them, on horses and he was one. Billy—I saw Billy!"

Over the top of her head Jack and King looked at each other bleakly. Their mouths drew tighter as they edged past each other to enter the door.

Miss Annie raised her voice sharply and brought her palm down with a brisk smack on King's head. "Answer me!" she snapped. "It was Billy, wasn't it? He came to see his father buried and he stayed far off—but it was Billy, I know it."

"You lie down now, Miss Annie," Jack said, as they reached her bed. "You lie still and rest and Sue will have 'Nerva fetch you a cup of tea."

She would not relax but lifted herself on her elbows and brushing aside Sue's hands she kept her eyes like gunsights on her two tall sons.

"Leave my bonnet alone, Sue," she ordered. "You two pay attention to what I say. I want him to come here. Billy has a right to come here to his own home."

"He wouldn't come, Miss Annie," argued King desperately. "After what happened to Pa, Billy wouldn't show himself on this place."

"You notice that he stayed behind the boundary fence," muttered Jack, bending to unlace his mother's worn little shoes. They were scuffed very thin and there was damp grave clay on the heels.

Miss Annie sniffed. "That's all ugly, hateful nonsense. Sue said Pa's getting shot was an accident. She said Buzzy got scared when Pa and Morgan started after him and it was an accident the gun went off."

Jack straightened with a rasping sigh. Pain was riding him with an iron spur, his head rang with it, his eyeballs were dry and hot. There were times when agony flashed like flame over his body so that his tongue tasted of copper and every nerve screamed protest.

"Mama"—with an effort he colored the old childhood name with gentleness—"it was no accident that Billy put a Nigra to stand guard over Pa and Morgan and me. A Nigra that we'd raised here on the place and had never been able to teach any sense at all. A Nigra with a loaded gun. And it was no accident that Billy gave that boy orders not to talk to us or let one of us go out the door. Sue heard him. I was sick and didn't hear him give that order but Morgan did, and Pa too. Billy had some wild notion of holding us till things cooled down and Morgan went along with it at first, then he got tired of it and got his temper up and wanted to get out of that place."

"Billy was trying to keep you all in that room to keep you clear of Jeff Nichols and his hot-head deputies," argued Sue. "It was no wild notion and it would have all worked fine if Morgan hadn't acted the fool and got Pa all stirred up. Now Morgan's acting the fool again and likely he'll get himself killed by some bad Negroes if the Yankees don't catch him up in something and jail him."

"Oh hush, Sue," begged Winnie, tearfully. "Such dreadful talk before your mother when she's already had all she can bear."

"Go get her some hot tea then," directed Sue, bluntly. "That will help her feelings more than you standing there bawling."

Winnie burst into sobs, then ran out and King said, "Leave her alone, can't you? She can't help being tenderhearted. Maybe Miss Annie ought to put her feet in hot water. Her hands feel like ice."

"I'm not sick," said his mother. "It's in my heart, the hurting. Deep, where no medicine ever can cure it. Hate makes wounds that no remedy will ever ease. And you boys keep that hurt in my heart burning, keeping your brother away, away from his dying father and his grieving mother."

"Mama," said Jack, "nobody kept Billy away. He didn't even offer to come. He sent us all home with some of his troopers to help with Pa, and white officers riding guard on us. And after that we never saw him again. You know that Pa never did forgive Billy for taking up with the Union. Over and over Pa said that Billy was no son of his. He said it to Billy's face. We heard him. Sue heard him—"

"I was ashamed," Sue said. "Ashamed of all of you. I told your father I was ashamed. It was Morgan's fault that day, getting your father all stirred up. There was a devil in Morgan. There has always been a devil in Morgan. Sometimes I think there's a devil in every Markland alive. Get on out of here now, you two, and let me get her quiet so she can get some sleep."

"I can't sleep," protested her mother-in-law. "I'll just lie here seeing him up there on that hill in that blue uniform. He had his hat off and he looked so handsome."

"You're going to sleep, Miss Annie Markland, if I have to give you laudanum." Sue was grim. "You're going to forget all this misery and nobody is going to remind you. You know Pa Markland wouldn't want you grieving yourself to a shadow. Look at you now. Not an ounce of flesh on your poor little bones." Sue pushed the men out and slammed the door. "I'll see she drinks some hot tea," she told them, "and maybe after a while I can get that old black dress off of her and get her to sleep. King," she said abruptly, "if you're so concerned about Winnie, why don't you take her home where she belongs? You've got provender over there and there's no call for you to stay here any longer now poor Pa Markland is out of his suffering. We can get along and food is getting scant here, you know that."

King looked uneasy. Always his had been a dominant, determined nature, inclined to impulses that were not always wise, truculent under frustration, but now he was uncertain and troubled.

"She won't go," he said. "She's afraid. Ever since that guerrilla gang came over there she's had a horror of the place. I can go and fetch some stuff from over there, trouble is I don't know where the old man hid most of it. The old Colonel was crazy as a coot before he got killed and he buried stuff all over the place. I'll hitch the mules and drive over this afternoon. Lord knows what's happened there since Pa and Jack were over. Maybe they've already come back and burned the house."

"We'd have heard about it," Jack said. "Those wandering Nigras that slip in and out of Mammy Dory's house would have brought word of it. That will be a good place when it's worked right, King. And you're better off than we are here, at least you've got a span of mules left."

"If they live through the winter. They were old and broken-down long ago or the army would have got them. What puzzles me is, what happened to all the money Colonel Oliver was supposed to have had. Winnie says her own father ran through a lot of it, and she thinks the Colonel gave the rest to the Confederacy, but he was supposed to be rich once." King was gloomy.

"Pa was supposed to be rich once too." Jack pressed his fingers over his aching eyeballs. They felt hot and bulging and there was a pushing pain in the back of his neck. "God," he groaned, "you reckon I'm going to be tormented by this thing forever? Fight through a war and then get my brains addled by a low-down lout of a deputy sheriff?"

"A good stiff drink would ease you," advised his brother. "Winnie said Morgan had some corn hid out in that press in his room. Could be a dram or two left."

"I hate to get on that stuff. Look what it did to you and it makes Morgan wild. Where the devil do you reckon that scudder went, anyway? Mad as a tinker, never has given a cuss for anything or anybody."

"He'll come back," said King. "Morgan always shows up better off than anybody. He won't kill Buzzy. He won't even find him. Billy got Buzzy far away quick, is my notion."

The old Oliver place still stood intact when King drove up the slope through the cedars in the bleak afternoon, but desolation lay over it like a blight. The front door of the house was open and as King entered the rancid odor of charred wood was still strong in the half-stripped, echoing rooms. Beds had been torn up and feather mattresses slit, every drawer and cupboard was open and some of Winnie's clothes lay about trampled on the dusty floor. The garments she had been washing on that fateful day when King had had his erratic urge to leave lay about the kitchen in dried lumps, some greened with mildew.

"Lord, what a mess," King groaned aloud as he surveyed the scene. Sue would know what to do about it but Winnie would be pathetically helpless, full of apologies and self-reproaches, content with her own inadequacy. Why hadn't he married Sue, King was wondering. His fault, for she had been halfway in love with him before she turned to his brother. That was because of Lutie, and what had he wanted with that yellow slut? Why was she lurking about in the back of his mind now, making him feel resentful against his wife, making this ravaged house that had been Winnie's suddenly abominable?

Abruptly he went charging through the rooms in a petulant sort of fury, gathering up Winnie's scattered clothes, wadding them in dirty bundles, kicking the mildewed garments out the open door, tossing the rest into the wagon. When his irritation had worked itself out he remembered that he had come to retrieve some of the provisions the old Colonel had squirreled away in weird hiding places.

In the old root cellar, screened behind rotting bales of hay, were a few jars and crocks of lard and old apple butter, molded on top, and some jars of preserves turning brown. Two or three times he had raided this cache, now he went back to it half expecting to find it had been already looted. The plank doors had been thrown back, one or two bales were overturned, but obviously the alarm had occurred before the outlaws had had time to explore thoroughly.

He carried what was worth saving to the wagon, getting himself well smeared with black cobwebs from the musty cave, closed the door of the house and headed for home. On the way he pondered the idea of selling the place, certain that Winnie in her present mood would raise no objection. Northern radicals, he knew, were drifting into the state buying up distressed properties or taking them for unpaid taxes.

Taxes! That thought brought a jerk of panic. Why hadn't he thought about taxes? Likely the old Colonel in his senile condition had entirely overlooked the taxes. Certainly the property had earned nothing since the war with which to pay off any obligation.

Darkness had fallen when he drove into the yard at home. Jack was just emerging from the barn, and inside it Sue was perched on a milking stool beside the one Markland cow. She pushed back her bonnet and got up wearily as King led the mules in, chain traces jingling.

"She's slowly going dry," Sue said, giving the cow a gentle whack on the rump and looking ruefully into the bucket. "She should have freshened last spring. How did you find things, King?"

"Bad. Everything gone to wrack and ruin. I brought home a little stuff—lard and so on. Sue, I just realized we've forgotten one thing that could ruin us all. We forgot about taxes. They're selling people out for taxes all over the country."

Sue grasped his arm so abruptly that some of the milk slopped on her skirt. "King, don't tell Jack. He's in a bad state. His head is killing him, so I sent him in and told him to go to bed. Don't mention taxes tonight, please. Sometimes I'm frightened about Jack, afraid there's some pressure we don't know about. Afraid it might drive him out of his mind."

"You go along, Sue, I'll tend to everything out here." He gave her a reassuring pat. "Tomorrow I'll ride into town and find out how Pa's affairs stand—how we all stand. I should have remembered about taxes long ago but Pa always ran everything, he never talked about business, not to me at any rate."

"You won't get into trouble in town, King? I couldn't stand any more trouble, and just one more blow would kill Miss Annie. She's frail as a moth right now."

"I'll keep clear of trouble, I give you my word. Send Boone-boy out here, he can help me unload the wagon."

"'Nerva will be glad to have some lard again," she sighed as she headed for the house.

When supper was finished and Winnie and Sue had settled themselves before the fire, Sue contriving a patch for a pair of her son's breeches, Winnie's pale hands lying as usual useless in her lap, King tossed a log on the andirons.

"I'm going to tell Miss Annie I'm going into town in the morning," he said, brushing dust from his coat. "She knows there are things about this estate that have got to be set right. Maybe she's worrying about them and it will free her mind to know that she has people to look after her."

"She slept a little, then she cried some, but she wouldn't eat any supper," Winnie said.

"I'll come too." Sue laid down her work. "I don't suppose you could finish this, could you, Winnie? No, I reckon you couldn't."

"I'd try but I'd make an awful botch of it," Winnie sighed.

"She sewed the buttons on my shirt on the inside," King said, with a kind of tired resignation.

"I know I'm a burden!" cried Winnie. "But I do try—I do! It's not my fault I was never trained to do anything."

"You're not old. You can still learn," Sue said. "And for goodness' sake don't start crying. At least you could be pleasant to look at if you can't do anything else."

Winnie's eyes flashed sparks. "You stand there and let her pick at me all the time," she flung at her husband. "You could at least defend your own wife."

"Oh, my Lord, Winnie, forget yourself for a minute, can't you?" fumed King. "Sue's carrying the whole load now and she's got a sick husband to worry about too."

"She has a drunken husband," shrilled Winnie. "I know a drunken man when I see one. He was stumbling drunk when he went up those stairs before supper. I lived with drunkards all my life, I know when a man is drunk."

"I hope he was," retorted King. "I hope Jack was blind, stinking drunk. I can't think of any happier state right now than being drunk and dead to the world."

"Well, don't you try it," warned Sue. "It's all ours to carry now, King, the whole burden of the Marklands. You know it's no use depending on Morgan for anything."

"Miss Annie spoiled him rotten. The rest of us picked on him because she kept him a baby too long. It made him rash and crazy. She's awake. Light the lamp, Sue." He went in and sat on his mother's bed, taking her chilly hand in his big palm. "I'm going into town tomorrow, Miss Annie," he told her. "I'll go in and see to all Pa's business affairs. Now he's gone somebody has to attend to things. Do you know where he kept his papers?"

"In that bottom drawer in that big chest over yonder." Miss Annie raised herself, holding his arm. "King, you'll see Billy? You'll tell him I want him to come home?"

"If you say so, Mama, but I'm telling you again it won't be any use. First thing I have to find out is how things stand about this place—the taxes and all that."

"Taxes?" She sat up very straight, her eyes brightening with some of their old determined fire. "Sue, look in my press and fetch me that old black reticule. The one with the beads on it."

When Sue had brought it and moved the lamp nearer the bed Miss Annie rummaged busily among old letters and scraps of paper in the faded old bag. "There!" she cried triumphantly, pulling out a document. "The receipt! I hid it. I was afraid to let your father know I had it. He was so stubborn and so bitter."

King stared at the tax paper bewildered. "This says you're all paid up, Miss Annie. Even for this year. How did Pa ever pay it?"

"He didn't pay it." There was a shine of almost malicious glee in her eyes. "He couldn't have paid it. And I never saw any money after I married your father. Billy paid those taxes. He sent me that paper by Buzzy, that time Buzzy brought King's horse home after King got beaten by those Nigras."

"That's one worry ended, anyway," Sue remarked. "They can't sell this place out from under us at the courthouse door."

King was silent. He handed the receipt back to his mother, who tucked it away again, still wearing her small, dry smile.

"Showing off again," King muttered to Sue, when they had left the room. "Like riding up here to Pa's burying."

"He saved you all," flared Sue. "Sometimes I think there's no decent gratitude in any Markland alive. We could never have paid it. Almost five hundred dollars. We couldn't even have paid five dollars. You know that, King Markland."

But King's dark sullenness did not relent. In moody silence he examined his father's papers and he was still at it when the women went wearily to bed. When Sue rose at dawn he was already gone and Winnie worried that he had not come to bed at all.

He returned very late to find Sue and Winnie still up. He stalked in, his face thunderous, and flung a crumpled piece of paper into Winnie's lap.

"The Carter Oliver property you inherited is gone, Mrs. Markland," he announced with vicious emphasis. "It was sold for taxes in July."

"Sold?" gasped Winnie. "You mean—somebody bought it—somebody else owns my grandfather's place?"

"It was bought," he clipped out the words, "by Captain William B. Markland. For two hundred and fifty dollars!"

"Billy?" cried Sue. "Did you see him?"

"No, I didn't see him. They've moved out. The whole stinking troop has been moved out. If I had seen him, by God, I think I'd have broken his neck!"

• *Nineteen* •

THE MEETING IN THE MAURY COUNTY COURTHOUSE HAD BEEN GOING ON
for two hours when Morgan Markland slipped in and dropped into a
rear seat. Outside a raw wind was blowing down from the higher pla-
teau where winter snow lay rotting, and Morgan realized on his long
ride east that he had been a fool to leave home without his heavier
clothing. Halfway he was convinced that he had been a fool to leave
home at all, that the fury that had driven him had been a piece of the
same odd madness that had possessed him at times, destroying his
control and driving him into reckless and often dangerous flight.

It had beset him in the army and three times when the outcome of
some skirmish enraged him he had caught himself pounding hell-for-
leather away from his outfit, tearing through the country, once finding
himself inside the enemy lines. He had always returned, contriving
some suave and ingenious excuse, resolved never to give way to the
stupid frenzy again, but when the wild impulse came he never seemed
to have the power to resist. No one at home knew how he had fled
from that bloody battle outside Nashville, outraged and insane over
General Sam Hood's tragic blunders, how far he had wandered wearing
the borrowed blue uniform, until news of Johnston's surrender sifted
through the Union lines.

For weeks after that he had passed himself off as a Union private
separated from his command. It had been a rash adventure and the
daredevil in Morgan had gloated over the ease with which it had been
possible to deceive tough officers and even tougher troopers of the line.

It was the sight of his father lying there, gasping and vomiting blood,
of his white-faced mother devotedly standing watch over Boone Markland's slow dissolution, that had made the whole scene at home
abruptly intolerable. That the other Marklands accepted it with what
to his mind seemed stupid and cowardly patience, had inflamed him to
the point where the only relief was escape.

Back in his seething brain had been a desperate determination to
find and somehow wreak vengeance on the two who had brought about
this misery. Riding through the night he had had only one idea, to find

[146]

his brother William and the Negro, Buzzy, and shoot them both dead. But although he had ridden as far west as Memphis, then south into Mississippi, although he had questioned a score of Union officers, he had never been able to locate the post to which William's company had been transferred.

Of Buzzy there were a hundred rumors, but no facts. With the amiable facility he knew so well, freed Negroes were eager to supply glib and erroneous information. The ones in town who knew Buzzy were wary, evasive, loud with assurances that Buzzy had taken himself far away. He had killed a white man, hadn't he? Shot Boss Boone Markland, hadn't he? A Colored boy who shot a white man wasn't going to linger around to make known his contrition for that act. He was going to put the big road under his feet and mighty fast.

Undoubtedly, with the canniness of his race, Buzzy would eventually find William again. But now, resting his tired legs and aching loins on a hard bench in the courthouse at Columbia, Morgan was certain that his chances of finding William's vanished command had become slim.

He had not been idle all this time. He had worn good clothes when he left home, he had expropriated the best horse, the handsomest saddle and bridle. All the circuitous route of his travels he had stopped at decent taverns, because there the officers and the Northerners who had come south to pick the pathetic bones of the conquered were to be found. There was always a game to be gotten into, usually to the profitable advantage of an ex-Confederate soldier with a jaunty manner, a casual approach and fingers swift as lightning.

He had money in his pocket now, the trouble was that there was little to buy with it. No new breeches to replace the fawn-colored pair he had worn so perilously thin. At Memphis he had found his former commander, General Nate Forrest, and made himself known, but old Nate was so busy building up a shipping business he had no time and little desire to reminisce.

By that time Morgan's fierce drive to go charging over the country was beginning to abate. Now, two hundred miles eastward, he was growing anxious. Three weeks away, the thought of what might have happened at home was starting to gnaw at him. His father might have died or even his mother, frail little spark that she was. Indomitable courage had always possessed her but Morgan knew how fiercely a burning spirit could erode physical stamina. When he had been at his bravest and most belligerent, when he had fought most savagely, there had always been a kind of physical collapse afterward. He had seen whole companies, exhausted by that letdown aftermath, fall to the ground shaking with bone-racking chills.

Certainly they were thinking hard things of him at home. His mother would defend him if she were able, but he knew Jack and King. He had had twenty years of Jack and King, their blasting sarcasm, their scorning blows, their heavy boots. Even William and Buzzy yowling, "Titty Baby!" Because of these torments that had tried him from childhood his protective shell of arrogance had hardened like glass in flame till there was now an untouchable aloofness about him. Now the unease came from within.

He had been impressed into attending this meeting today by the men with whom he had played cards all night.

"Old Gid Pillow's going to preside," sneered a Union officer, "and it will be a spectacle seeing grim old Gideon talking on the side of Andrew Johnson and peace and order."

"They're all singing the same tune now," put in a cotton buyer. "War's over. Everybody forget the whole thing. We're good boys now, even if we were out to blow all you fellows to hell last year. Let us back in the Union, hang Brownlow, and let us all vote and go on beating up niggers."

"Look at the way things are going in Kentucky," said a captain from Indiana. "Confederates practically taking over. Every man who fought with Robert E. Lee a hero—every Union man a thieving skunk. You'd swear it was secession over again. As for Andy Johnson with his piddling attitude, placate the rebel states, get 'em all back in the Union, no revenge, no persecution—I say to the devil with him! If those radicals up in Congress don't boot him out of there the army ought to go up to Washington and do it."

"What's the purpose of the meeting?" Morgan tried to maintain the fable he had fostered in this town, to assure anyone who was dubious about him that he was as good a Brownlow man as any of them. "What do the rebels want to promote now?"

"Old A. O. P. Nicholson's going to make a speech. He'll call on everybody to support Johnson, forget all past animosities and urge all the Confederates to admit they were licked fair and accept the fact and get busy being patriots. Not all the speeches that can be brayed over the whole country will save Andy Johnson."

"The scheme is to get Johnson to intervene in Tennessee," remarked another local man. "They know he and Brownlow hate each other like two polecats in the same bag, and these fellows would like to see martial law in this state, all Brownlow's elections and legislation declared void and their own treasonable conservatives put into power. Curious business, seeing men like Gid Pillow and Nicholson and Neill Brown —red-hot Confederates all of them—supporting Johnson while Brownlow and his crowd are itching to break with the President and support the element in Congress that is out to get him impeached."

The courthouse was chilly. A big, rusty iron stove on one side roared and crackled and every now and then a man rose from his seat nearby and heaved in another chunk of wood, making a great clatter with the poker. The stovepipe glowed red-hot half its tilted length and Morgan forgot to listen to the oratory wondering what would happen if that shaky length of sheet iron came clanging down, scattering sparks and soot. He made bets with himself as to which of the listeners sitting near would jump for the windows, which sprint for the door and who of all the group would be cool-headed enough to avert a conflagration. But although the speaking went on with rising emphasis and emotion the pipe stood intact. Slim feathers of smoke leaked from some of its joints and swirled languidly about the four slightly lopsided and smoke-grimed kerosene lamps of the suspended chandelier.

Abruptly Morgan jerked erect and asked himself what he was doing in this place. What did he care what happened to Andrew Johnson or William Brownlow? They were the men in power; Johnson by the fortuitous accident of tragedy, Brownlow by fiercely aggressive determination. They enjoyed the emoluments of power so let them be content with the risks and responsibilities. Johnson voiced a fatuous kind of mercy for a conquered people and because of it stood now in peril of repudiation. Brownlow had a heart of granite. He proclaimed himself a man of God, but Morgan knew Brownlow's God was the avenger of the Old Testament.

All the grim tales Morgan had heard, half listened to, repeated gloatingly by the Union men he had been consorting with, suddenly emerged out of the vagueness of his thinking and became menacing, personal and deadly. Tales of Confederates ruthlessly thrust out of their homes, stripped of everything, arrested, turned out practically naked in a hostile world—what reason to believe that the Marklands had escaped? Just because they had been lucky till now did not mean that their luck would hold forever.

He slipped out of the building, flipped a dime to the boy who had been holding his horse and sprang into the saddle, wincing a little as his threadbare seat hit the icy leather.

An officer with a thick brown beard that smelled of chewing tobacco came up and laid a hand on a stirrup.

"Well, what did that yawping crowd in there decide? Are they going to march on Washington to keep old Andy in the White House?"

"Same old guff," said Morgan. "Like all politics, more wind than bullets."

"Be around tonight? You ought to give me a chance to win my money back."

"Sorry, I'm pushing on. Getting a bit worried about my family." Morgan pulled up the stallion's head, gave him a prod with his heel and cantered away.

Almost a hundred miles to go. Once he had ridden almost that far in one frenzied day and night when the Confederate Cause was crashing down in the final dust of dissolution. Then his horse had been shot under him by a Union sniper, and for days he had walked. Too many days. Never, he had vowed, would he ever walk again so long as a beast with four legs remained afoot in the country.

On the road he met a train of wagons and pulled aside to let them pass. The animals that drew the outfits were mixed, a span of oxen trailing in the rear, horses and mules slogging slowly ahead. The driver of the lead wagon halted his team.

"Howdy, Neighbor!" he called. "How far are we from water?"

"Not far," Morgan told him. "I forded a shallow creek three miles back. Where you from, Mister?"

"From up in Sumner County. Heading for Texas, I reckon, if we can hold out that far. Had a good feed and grain business up home but this year there wasn't any crop to speak of and them Yanks up in Nashville taxed me out of business. Them two wagons behind me lost their farms. We figure we can't be no worse off in Texas, if we get there. Where you heading, boy?"

"Home. Up Harpeth way. You think those oxen back there will make it to Texas?"

"Outlast my team, likely. Don't take much feed for an ox. Just so he gets him a cud and can lie down to chaw it, he'll live to a good old age. That span belongs to a widow-woman. Lost three boys fighting with Longstreet and Johnston and outlaws killed her husband and burnt their house. She's tough and she's got a twelve-year-old boy tougher than she is. They'll make it to Nacogdoches if they have to travel afoot. She's got kin there, she says."

"Any news from up your way?"

"Nothing different. Everything the same. Brownlow riding a cast-iron horse in a red-hot saddle, anybody don't agree gets trompled.

Maybe the same in Texas but might be some warmer there. This sets in to be a cold winter. Well, goodbye and good luck."

"Thanks. Same to you." Morgan waited in the saddle, touching his hat politely as the other wagons ground slowly by, the frosty ruts crunching under the wheels.

The woman who drove the last wagon, sitting high under the bowed top, had a worn and embittered face, and the thin lad who walked beside the oxen, whacking their bony rumps with a goad, gave Morgan an envious look.

"Mighty fine to be ridin' the road, you ole Yank you," he snarled.

"Take it easy, fellow," Morgan grinned. "I'm no Yank. I fought with Forrest's Seventh Tennessee Cavalry."

"What did ye get licked fur?" shrilled the boy. "Whyn't you no-good Johnnies run them Yanks clear to Pennsylvany so Ma and me could stay home?"

"We tried, son. We busted ourselves trying."

"You ain't busted. You've got a hoss."

Morgan rode on faster, not looking back. Those wagons had sharpened a panic unease in him, and he met others as he drew near to the ford of Duck River. Some halted to talk and the complaint was always the same. Taxed out, run out, lost my business, lost my farm. "Won't be anybody left in Tennessee that was for the Confederacy, if Brownlow and his gang have their way."

Morgan caught himself watching the road anxiously till darkness fell. After that, if he saw a campfire burning in some sheltered spot, he rode by calling a halloo.

"Lost my folks," he would explain when a stranger answered.

They wouldn't start out in winter, he told himself. Not unless they had to, not unless they had nowhere to go. All the next day, after a brief uneasy nap under a rock face he warmed with a fire, he felt the panic riding with him. Then the panic took to itself abruptly another point with which to goad him. Angela. Angela Wood!

That little brown house, he was certain, had been the property of the church. If some strange new preacher came down from the north Mrs. Wood and her sister and Angela would have to move. He had to know what had happened to Angela so he headed into town first instead of turning south on the homeward road.

There was something vaguely hostile in the atmosphere of the place as he let the stallion trot along the almost deserted streets. A wintry wind had risen and was sending blackened and broken leaves skirling in the gutters and sanded paths before the low buildings. There were no Negro soldiers lounging about, and but few townspeople. They hurried bent against the wind or averted their faces as though the sight of a young man riding a fine horse was somehow a hurtful offense.

At the hotel no one appeared to take his horse so Morgan hitched him to a tree and strode inside.

"How about some food and a bait of oats for my horse?" he asked the man who slumped half asleep in an armchair behind the desk.

When the man lifted his head Morgan saw that he was a stranger. The stranger reached for the shabby book.

"Who are you? What's your name? Where's your horse?"

"Where's Murphy? He knows me."

"Moved out," said the other. "Moved day after Christmas. I run this place now. Name's Greene. Where's your horse? Take him back to the stable and maybe somebody there will feed him. Write your name here."

Morgan pushed the book away. "No, I think I won't. I'll move on." He turned and stalked out. Definitely he was not going to write a name in that book, a name undoubtedly already inscribed on the radical blacklist. A name that Jeff Nichols or one of his hard-mouthed deputies would be delighted to read there.

The courthouse looked shabby and neglected, the door shut. Around that door weather-stained posters flopped drearily in the wind, each one a public notice of some family's distress. He had an itch to see what names were written on those placards, but he had no wish to venture into Jeff Nichols' lair. The small brown house was only a block away and he rode up boldly and tied his horse to the fence.

There was a stir of white curtain at the front window as he went up the path, and even before he knocked the door was opened and Angela reached both hands and drew him quickly inside.

"Oh, Morgan!" she exclaimed. "Where have you been? I was sure you must have gone off to Texas or somewhere. Come back to the fire. Oh, Aunt Ella—here's Morgan come back."

Miss Ella Crabtree stood like an iron-gray sentinel in the door to the inner room where he glimpsed a feeble fire.

"I see," she said grimly. "After what happened on your last visit, Mister Markland, I am surprised at your boldness in coming here again."

"I was worried." Morgan mustered all his easy charm. "So many people have been in trouble lately, I had to know that you were all right. As for that affair, Miss Crabtree, I present my profound apologies and assure you that it will never happen again."

"I'm sure it will not happen again," snapped the spinster, "because you will not again be welcomed to this house."

"Oh, but he will!" cried Angela, cheeks flaming. "Morgan will be welcome in this house so long as I am in it, Aunt Ella. If you don't like it, you can be the one to leave." She turned abruptly and put both hands on his shoulders. "Morgan, I've made up my mind. I will marry you any time you say!"

• *Twenty* •

THE STUNNED LOOK ON MORGAN'S FACE COMMUNICATED ITSELF TO MISS Ella. She sniffed loudly and disdainfully.

"Nonsense!" she snapped. "This man has no intention of marrying you, Angela Wood."

Morgan looked down into the eyes of the girl who was almost in his arms. What he saw there, desperation, a raw anguish, desolation, moved him to put his arms around her quivering shoulders. She was a pretty thing, even in her dowdy, made-over dress of some elderly gray stuff and she was the girl he had been dreaming about for forty miles of road, well, thirty miles anyway.

"Certainly I intend marrying Angela if she will have me, Miss Crabtree. I've just come a long way from the west to ask for her hand, again," he added tactfully.

Miss Ella went to the inner door and raised her voice. "Carrie! Come in here and tell your daughter we'll have none of this foolishness."

Angela gave Morgan a quick push. "Outside!" she whispered. "We can't talk here."

"You'll need a coat."

"No matter." She hurried him out and slammed the door behind her. "We have to get away from here. Is that your horse?"

"He's tired. I've ridden from Columbia since noon yesterday and he can't go much further. Wait—I'll lift you into the saddle. I'll lead him. He won't be frisky." He swung her up, stripped off his own coat and handed it to her. "Put this on. Weather doesn't bother me since the war. Now, where do we go?"

"Anywhere, away from here. I know—Father's church. The back door isn't locked. Luxton's guerrillas broke the lock when they came through here."

The little church stood back in a small hickory grove on a bare trampled piece of ground littered now with torn paper and dry, drifting leaves. Angela opened a door into a bleak, chilly space behind the pulpit. The floor was strewn with scattered pages torn from the big Bible and in one corner someone had made a bed of hay and dry leaves covered with a ragged Confederate overcoat.

"Whenever I come in here I'm thankful my father is dead," she sighed, shivering. "They kept horses in here once when some cavalry scouts came through. Mother and I cleaned it up after that but when we knew Father wouldn't come back we didn't care any more. Sit down, Morgan. And don't look so bewildered and so trapped. You don't have to marry me."

He frowned. "But what if I want to marry you?" he demanded, dropping beside her on the bench.

"You don't want to marry me. You were being very gallant and you came in the nick of time and carried it off pretty well even if I did sort of take your breath away."

"Why not let me decide what I want to do?" he protested. "It was a bit sudden, I admit, and I don't think I came up to the mark exactly, but you said you had made up your mind."

"I had to say it. You were a savior. A white knight riding up at the fatal moment to rescue me from being pushed into something dreadful, something I can't even bear to think about. I had to be bold and abrupt and very likely you're sitting there despising me for being so forward and cheap and throwing myself at you, without a word of warning."

"I could never despise you, Angela. You know that." He reached for her hand but she drew it away gently.

"No," she said. "Not now. Not till you hear the rest. We have to go away, Morgan. The church wants the parsonage. There's a minister coming from Indiana the first of the year, and he has to live in it. So Aunt Ella has decided that she and Mother are going back to Alabama. There are still some relatives down there and one of them, a cousin, has some money she is willing to lend to Aunt Ella for transportation. Aunt Ella is sure she can get a job teaching school down there and pay this cousin back and she thinks that Alabama is still the South and that there won't be so many Yankees down there."

"Doesn't she know that carpetbaggers and Yankee missionaries are flocking into Alabama? Things are worse there than here, from what I've heard traveling around."

"It would be no use to tell her, she wouldn't believe it. She says Alabama was Southern when they left there, that she came to this half-Union state just on account of Mother, and now that the Union is in control she won't endure it any longer."

"I hope she doesn't delude herself that the Confederates control Alabama." Morgan picked a long sliver from the bench and began to break it into small pieces.

"She dreams up things and then believes them. You can't change her mind and she has Mother completely intimidated, and now that she has this money promised—"

"So now she plans to drag you all off to Alabama!"

"No, not all of us. Just my mother."

"And what did she decide was going to happen to you? Before I rode up on my white charger, I mean?" asked Morgan angrily.

"I am to stay here and be married."

"But when I appeared, an available candidate, I was informed very coldly that I was not welcome in your house!"

Angela drew a long breath. "You weren't a candidate. Not an acceptable candidate. You see, the bridegroom has already been chosen."

"By you?"

"Not by me. Would I have hurled myself at you in such hysterical relief if I had picked somebody else?" she asked.

"Then who is this buzzard they've picked out for you? I gather you aren't too happy about it."

She gave a shudder, leaning against him a little. Her hand, on his, was cold as ice. "It makes me shiver even to think about him. Not that he isn't a gentleman—or he was when men had the opportunity to be gentlemen. It's Mrs. Harper's brother, Morgan. Her old bachelor brother. He's forty at least and kind of fat. But he was with General Longstreet's army and that makes him a hero in Aunt Ella's eyes, even though Longstreet never did really win any victories. But he wants to marry me and he still has money and a house so Aunt Ella thinks it's a wonderful chance to get me settled for the rest of my life so she and Mother won't have to worry."

"Why, the old goat!" snarled Morgan. "How does he know he'll keep his money and his house if he fought with Longstreet? No Confederate is actually safe or his property either so long as these radicals run the country."

"Oh, he protected himself. He took the oath, though Aunt Ella doesn't know it. She'd think that was black treason to the South, but he very cleverly assured her that he was safe from being molested. And you know Aunt Ella."

"I don't know Aunt Ella!" Morgan snapped. "All I've had from Aunt Ella so far is one withering blast after another. She doesn't want to know me and she has fought to keep you from knowing me."

"Aunt Ella believes what she wants to believe. Even if she suspects the truth about Elmo—that's his name, Morgan—Elmo Shinn."

"Great Caesar! Old Elmo Shinn! Why, I've seen him around all my life, always sidling and showing that toothy, oily smile of his. Courting favor with people like old Josh Fletcher and Squire Armitage. He used to be a slave trader. Does your Aunt Ella know that?"

"Oh, he gave that up long ago, he says. Of course he'd have to when there weren't any slaves any more. Now he buys horses and mules when he can find any and sells them to farmers who have lost all their stock."

"Broken-down old army stuff, no doubt. Requisitioned all over the country and worn out in the service. He'll fatten them up a little and get a high price, and the first time a farmer tries to plow with one of Elmo's mules it will drop dead in the furrow," sneered Morgan. "Once a tricky trader, always a trickster. And your Aunt Ella thinks he's a gentleman?"

"He fought for the South. She thinks anybody who fought for the South is a hero," said Angela.

"I fought for the South and to her I'm not a hero, I'm a scoundrel."

"It was all right, Morgan, till you came to call when you'd been drinking," Angela told him sadly.

"I'm betting that Elmo likes his dram as well as the next man. Anyway, he's old enough to be your father. Can't they find a Confederate hero, at least heroic enough to suit Aunt Ella, somebody your age?"

"They haven't found anyone. They say all the young men are so wild now since the war and that a settled, older man will make a better husband. Anyway I have to give Elmo his answer right away because they can't keep the house much longer and Aunt Ella expects the money to arrive from Alabama any day now. And Mother reminds me that Elmo was a member of Father's church, that he gave fifty dollars every year."

"Slave-trade money, dirty money, the hypocrite."

She shivered again, moving closer. "Of course my mother only wants what is best for me. I'll soon be twenty years old. She wants to see me cared for and secure, so she says. Anyway I'd surely hate to get to be an old maid like Aunt Ella. She could have married an older man, Mother told me. He was a widower with a fine plantation down in Alabama but he had four children and Aunt Ella had dreams about a romantic young lover so she said no to this widower and then no young man ever asked her. So now she's bitter and warped. And do you know, Morgan, Aunt Ella's not really old. She's only thirty-eight."

Morgan's laughter barked, so that a rat busily gnawing away somewhere in the frame walls of the church scurried and squeaked.

"Perfect solution!" he exclaimed. "Marry Aunt Ella to Elmo Shinn. Then everybody lives happily ever after."

"But what becomes of Mother and me?" She was plaintive. "Aunt Ella will have the money—we haven't any. That cousin can't afford to lend it to someone who might never pay it back. Aunt Ella has made it very clear that she has arranged all this very cleverly to take care of all our futures, and Mother's helpless to disagree. So Mother says we're lucky Aunt Ella is so resourceful and it's fortunate a substantial and respectable man like Elmo Shinn wants to marry me. So I suppose I shall have to say yes. There's nothing else to do!"

Morgan Markland drew a long breath. A small, reluctant, warning knot tightened in his stomach, he felt a backward, restraining pull of nerves. This is a trap, shrilled a small voice in his brain, this is what King blundered into impulsively, now King is bound and disillusioned and miserable. And yet here was a girl, desirable, wistful, softly feminine, a girl in trouble. Morgan told himself that he was a Southern gentleman but all the time the same inner voice was urging him not to be a fool.

Damn it, why couldn't she have been born with a squint eye or buck teeth and stringy hair? Why did her body have to be so tender and appealing, her eyes so full of bewilderment and heartbreak? Morgan set his jaw hard and tightened his hands into aching fists. He struggled to drag words out of his throat, casual words, something comforting but definitely noncommittal, something that would let him walk out that door yonder still free, but free also from nagging twinges of conscience or uneasy memories of the desolation and dread in her eyes.

Some words came out. Raggedly, as though jerked out like lengths of iron chain, tearing at his throat, hoarsely, because caution was still trying to strangle them.

"There's something you can do, Angela." He heard his voice sounding strange and gleefully malicious to his ears, gloating over him because here was the trap and it was hurling him into it, because he was a Markland and a Southerner and a maid in distress had blue eyes with tears in them. "There is something you can do. You can say you'll really marry me!"

Snick! The trap was sprung. Morgan felt a cold wave wash over him. Angela gave a little shudder, and although it was intended to be maidenly and delicate, he sensed a kind of ecstatic relief behind her small protest.

"Oh, no! I couldn't. You don't want to marry me, Morgan. You're just being gallant, trying to save me from Elmo Shinn."

"And you don't want to be saved from Elmo Shinn?" One small chink of light, the way of escape opening a fraction of an inch. Then it closed again with a finality as solemn as a tolling bell. No hope, fellow, you got yourself into this.

She gave another quivering shudder, drawing into herself, tucking her hands into her sleeves. Her fingers were blue, he noted, and so were her lips. The old shack of a church was like an icehouse.

"It would be like being saved from a fiery dragon," she whispered. "It's the way the heathen offered their maidens to Moloch and Baal. It is the same, isn't it, except that those maidens died and I'd have to go on living with him. He has hairy wrists and ankles—horrible!"

"I have hairy wrists." Morgan thrust out an arm. "Most men do. In the army the men with no hair on their bodies seemed to get hit first, or if they got sick they died."

"You don't have to marry me, Morgan," she said quickly. "I didn't bring you here to put a noose around your neck."

"You didn't?" He laughed, not very mirthfully. "I'd have said that that noose got flung over my head two seconds after I knocked on your door. Didn't you make a bold statement that you had decided to marry me?"

"Now you're angry at me!" she choked. "Don't you see that it was— all put on, Morgan? I had to get back at Aunt Ella. I had to show her she wasn't running my life. I wanted to shock her and she was certainly shocked. She doesn't know right now what to think or do. Neither does Mother. Poor Mother. I hate to oppose her but I had to show them that they couldn't just push me into a marriage that I hated."

"But where are you now?" He got up, limbering his frigid feet, thrusting his hands into his pockets. "You say you won't marry me and that you won't be pushed into marrying old Shinn. And they say they can't take you with them to Alabama. What's left to do, Angela?"

She buried her face in her hands. "Oh, I don't know. I don't know what to do. You don't love me, Morgan, you know you don't. You're half angry at me this minute for getting you into this. You're making a grand generous gesture, but all the time you're thinking it's a stupid thing to do."

"Stop deciding what I'm thinking." He was brusque. "The point is, what are you thinking? If you're thinking that you're willing to marry me to escape from Elmo and your aunt, then why drag out the argument? I have to tell you that I'm not much of a bargain. I drink and I gamble and I fought with Forrest so I'm one stripe below a pole-cat here in this county. I haven't any money—mighty little anyway."

"Oh, stop low-rating yourself, Morgan Markland. Any girl would be honored to marry you, if she thought you wanted her. If you loved her," she added faintly.

"Love. That's a word with two handles. Nothing one-sided about it. If it's lopsided everything spills out and it's all wasted." He was getting in deeper and deeper but now he did not care too much. Not with her eyes on his face like dew-wet flowers, her lips half open and tremulous, her hands trembling in her lap.

"You're trying to make me say it," she cried. "It's not fair! You want me to say that I fell in love with you the first time I saw you. You want all the advantage, you men. Well, I won't say it!"

"Has Elmo said that he loves you?" It was almost a taunt but Angela was too upset to notice the cynical note.

"Oh, no." She was quick. "He was very formal and very pompous. He asked Mother first and then he asked me for the honor of my hand in marriage. He told me he'd be good to me and that I would want for nothing so long as he lived."

"So I come along and tell you that I might not be good to you and you may want for a lot of things, especially if I get arrested or chased off to Texas."

"I wouldn't care!" she exclaimed. "Mother came to Tennessee with my father in a wagon, with one bed and a washboard."

He dropped down beside her on the bench and put an arm around her shivering shoulders. She cuddled against him crying softly into his shirt.

"What can we do?" she whimpered.

"Get married, I suppose." He pushed her hair back from her damp face and kissed her forehead casually. "If Aunt Ella isn't on her way here already with a posse and a shotgun."

"She'd never think of this place. Though she might if she saw your horse out there, Morgan. We'd have to run away."

"And no place to run." He kissed her again, finding it more delectable this time as she responded eagerly. "There's home. But I don't know what's going on there. I've been away nearly three weeks. My mother has two daughters-in-law there already, but it's a big house. When do we run?" He tweaked a lock of her hair, drawing her head back so he could kiss her again, a prolonged and ardent kiss. "We can't wait around till that preacher from Indiana gets here, that's certain."

"I'm afraid to go back home. I don't know what they'd do. They might even lock me up."

"Not after you're definitely married, they won't. There's old Squire Armitage. I've played poker with the Squire, he'd fix us up if we can catch him when he's sober. Then there would be nothing they could do but put a curse on us, and who's afraid of that?" he teased.

She giggled. "Nobody. Morgan, I want to see Aunt Ella's face. I can't wait to see it when we tell her."

"I can live a long and happy life if I never see Aunt Ella's face again. Here, put your arms in these sleeves. You're cold as ice. After we get this business over we'll go and get your clothes."

"Oh, Morgan, you said you wouldn't be good to me and here you are taking care of me already."

"Because it appears to the naked eye that you haven't got the sense to take care of yourself." He buttoned the coat up to her chin. She flapped the dangling sleeves over her hands and giggled like a child again. Then she turned grave.

"You're the one who'll catch his death of cold. In that thin shirt."

"There were some cold days down around Huntsville when I didn't even have a shirt. Let me count my money, gal." He jingled some silver in his palm and flipped one gold piece in the air and caught it again. "It appears that the Philistines must be despoiled again shortly. All right, come along. We'll find the Squire and get the deadly deed over."

"Morgan, you're sure? Sure you won't be sorry?" she begged anxiously.

"If I disappear some foggy dawn you'll know I've taken a few days off to be sorry. Pin up your hair. Don't be a straggly bride."

She obeyed meekly, adoring him with her eyes. It was Morgan all the time, her shaken heart was assuring her. It couldn't have been Billy. No, not Billy. But what if Billy had not vanished so suddenly? No matter. I'm marrying Morgan. Not Elmo Shinn with his hairy hands and greedy eyes. Morgan. Morgan Markland of the Harpeth Marklands.

Morgan Markland brought his bride into his mother's house in the middle of the night. A cold and hostile night with spits of gritty snow in the air.

King, opening the door, nightshirt stuffed into his breeches, black hair standing on end, exclaimed, "Good God!"

Miss Annie, in a faded wrapper, kissed the scared bride and hurried out to brew a pot of tea and poke up the fire.

They told Morgan then that his father had been dead for two weeks.

• *Twenty One* •

THE TENNESSEE RIVER, PUSHING TO JOIN THE OHIO UNDER THE MUDDY bluffs of western Kentucky, was swollen and sullen with the winter rains on this cold dawn of a February morning.

On the sloping shores where water had run down and frozen in little pools of glassy ice a few shanties huddled, with rusty stovepipes thrust up through the roofs, or leaning stick chimneys. A plank landing thrust out from the reedy bank, and it was from this landing that the ragged soldier had leaped aboard while the grunting, grumbling deck hands tossed wood aboard.

The boat was a mongrel craft not too long converted from its earlier military function. What had been an Eads gunboat built to carry war up the Cumberland or the Tennessee was now stripped down into a carrier of hogs or lumber or occasionally, as now, a transport for shifting troops. The soldiers had come aboard at Johnsonville, at what Forrest had left of that river landing. There were sixty of them, all more or less dispirited, all but this newcomer, this ragged scarecrow of a straggler who, as soon as he was safely aboard and the boat had shoved off again, began patting juba with his feet and humming gaily through his teeth.

"What you so happy 'bout, Bright Boy?" demanded an ink-black corporal with bloodshot maroon eyes. "What you doin' back here anyhow? You git loose, whyn't you stay loose? Ain't you heared what the white folks goin' do? Ain't you heared us is gittin' sent out west to fight Injuns?"

Private Buzzy Markland did a dance step, his disreputable shoes flapping.

"I done found my Cap'n Billy," he gloated. "I walk a million miles and I don't git sump'n t' eat for 'bout a hunnerd days, I reckon. Folks say, Boy, yo' outfit long gone from here, you ain't never goin' catch up, but I catch up. I find my Cap'n."

"You a deserter. You lucky you ain't been shot 'fore now."

"I ain't no deserter. I got put on special detail. That's what the Cap'n tell me, special detail. 'Fore I gits loose from that detail you boys done got moved on."

"If you ain't a deserter you a straggler anyhow," argued the corporal.

"I ain't no deserter. I come back, didn't I? I walked and I begged rides from white folks movin', I even drove an ole cow 'bout forty miles. I'm plumb bound to find my Cap'n Billy and praise be, if I done find him!"

"Cap'n ain't pay you no mind," growled the corporal. "Ain't pay nobody no mind since we come aboard this yere ole piece of a boat. Jest stand there starin' at the river."

"He pay me mind do I walk up smart and salute," insisted Buzzy. "You see."

"He bust you in the head with that pistol, he do right. Shacklin' all over the country like some ole Johnny Reb straggler."

"You watch, he don't bust me no place. You watch." Buzzy tightened his belt, buttoned what buttons remained on his torn and weather-stained jacket, snapped his cap over his eyes and strutted aft to where the officers sat hunched in cold misery on a wind-swept bench. He faced the tall dark figure at the end, saluting sharply.

"Private Buzzy Markland reportin' aboard, suh!" he announced in a voice that had a faint quiver of uncertainty in it.

The tall captain jumped to his feet. "Great Scott! Buzzy! Where did you come from?"

"Dickson County, Tennessee, suh, where at you special-detail me, Cap'n suh."

"How did you get here? How did you find us?" persisted William.

"Cap'n, I run and I swum and I clum, but I find you. I bound to find you," gloated Buzzy.

"Come over here." William got him by the elbow, led him to a sheltered spot on the lee side of the cabin. "Now tell me what became of you after you fired that gun?"

Buzzy turned a pale lavender and his eyes clouded and closed till they were mere damp slits in his pallid face.

"Cap'n, that wasn't no way my fault! Mist' Morgan he come at me to take my gun away and Boss Boone he come at me and I'm scairt and I holt that gun too tight and it go off," panted Buzzy. "So then I run and hid out. I hid out a good long spell. Then I started out to find you.

You leave a wide track, Cap'n Billy. Boy know how to trail, a army ain't hard to find."

"You know that Boss Boone is dead, Buzzy?"

A little ripple of terror convulsed and paled Buzzy's face. "No!" he cried.

"Boss Boone died and you killed him, Buzzy. Maybe it wasn't your fault. Most likely it was mine, leaving you there alone while I went for the doctor. I knew Morgan and I knew my father. Violent men. All the Marklands—violent men." William seemed to be talking to himself.

"You sho' you' pappy dead, Mist' Billy?" Buzzy asked imploringly. "Boss Boone a mighty strong ole man. Don't look like one little ole bullet kill him."

"I saw him buried," William said, "the day our orders came to move. The lieutenants rode out with me. Buzzy, you and I are outlaws now. We can never go home."

"You reckon they hang me, Cap'n Billy?"

William shook his head. "You were in uniform under orders. They were in my custody. The law, such as it is, is on your side. They won't hang you. They won't hang me, but there may be times before we die that we'll wish they had hung us to free us from our own consciences."

"I ain't never wish I been hung, Cap'n. Man git shot—that military, that honorable, but gittin' hung is a mighty trashy way to die," philosophized Buzzy. "I sho' am sorry 'bout Boss Boone. He one fine ole man. I sho' do hate it that that ole gun go off. These here ole guns we got now is all wore out anyhow. Wore out in the war before we gits 'em. Been a good new gun it ain't gone off sudden and hurt Boss Boone. You been home, Mist' Billy? You seen Miss Annie? She mighty grieved, I reckon."

"I saw her at the grave. I didn't go close. They carried her down the hill. Jack and King carried her."

"Mist' Morgan, he still mighty mad at me, I reckon."

"He wasn't there. He showed up at the post, I heard later but I'd been called in to headquarters then and you were gone," William said.

"After that gun go off and I see Boss Boone grab his belly and yell I got long gone, Mist' Willie. I run so fast I catch myself mighty near to Nashville with my heels smokin' 'fore I stop. What we do now, Cap'n?"

"We're being landed at Cairo. Then we'll be sent down the Mississippi River to a new post. You've got no equipment, I see." William studied the ragamuffin figure. "I'll try to get you fitted out when we land. You're still in the army. You enlisted for two years. Get back up there with the other troops."

"Got to be in the army," sighed Buzzy. "Do I go home Mist' King, he shoot me and Miss Annie bust a skillet over my haid. You lemme have a gun, Cap'n? Git me a good gun do you find one. It that ole gun's fault Boss Boone got killed."

Soon after William heard laughter at the bow where the Negro troops huddled, squatting on deck away from the searching winter wind. With lighthearted adaptability Buzzy was already forgetting all that was tragic in an abrupt transition from gloom to gaiety. The blame had been fixed. The gun was at fault. But for that old gun Boss Boone would not have died.

William went below to the steamy, low-ceilinged cuddy where the company equipment had been dumped, dug out the dilapidated carpetbag that held the company records, spread the sheets out on a table under the swaying dimness of a lantern. Buzzy's record had to be corrected, brought up to date. With his knife William scratched out the words "Absent Without Leave" and "Presumed to Have Deserted" and wrote on the lines "On special assignment, Captain's orders. Completed and returned to ranks, February 18th, 1866."

All his life now William was certain he would have the job of protecting Buzzy from himself, of keeping him out of trouble with women and the law, refereeing his fights, patching his wounds. Even if this company were broken up and scattered through the other regiments of the present standing army he knew that somehow he would have to keep Buzzy near him, to keep him out of trouble. And it came to him that there could be times when he himself would be thankful for one devoted friend. When their term of service ended, what then? Unless he re-enlisted he would be adrift in a lonely world. A fierce nostalgia for home began to press upon him. Never to go back again, never to see Miss Annie again, or Sue. To this he had sentenced himself and Buzzy.

The torment was that he had been sincerely trying to save them, those wild and valiant Marklands, save them from themselves. He had blundered and likely there would be no forgiveness, only unending resentment. Not from Miss Annie perhaps, and not from Sue, who had been so ready to stand against the others and defend him, but certainly from his brothers he could expect no quarter.

King and Morgan were both unreasonable and violent in their hatreds. Jack was slower but at times even more deadly, more obdurate. He had had a few brief interludes of casual friendliness with Morgan in town but that had been only recklessness attracting recklessness, and now that would be ended. King was unpredictable. There was his sudden impulsive marriage to Winnie Oliver, certainly unplanned, a flash of arrogant gallantry, now no doubt regretted. William had heard enough from the Marklands during that confused and stormy morning in his own quarters in town to know that Winnie was already listed as a family liability.

Suddenly William struck the table hard so that the ink jumped and spattered from the bottle. Winnie! Winnie Oliver Markland. Not till this moment had he remembered that paper he possessed, that tax deed to Winnie Oliver Markland's inherited property. All along it had been his determination to return the document, resigning all claim to the place, though even now he was not sure how he should go about it legally and he did not know how to find out. But he knew that it had to be done immediately. Undoubtedly King had already learned the truth, and another outrage was being charged up to the black sheep of the Marklands.

He rummaged through his gear, came up with the creased and rumpled paper, and read it through carefully. The law provided for a period of redemption with penalties and interest attached, but from what he had seen of the old Oliver place on his last visit to the neighborhood there was little hope in his mind that King would ever be able to raise any money to redeem it.

Still it was a good property—and now, William was thinking, it could be his own, a home again, a foothold in the country where he had been born. Most men would argue that to surrender it would be stupid, yet he knew that he had to do it. He hunted out a long manila envelope, and signing his name on the tax deed, slid it into the enclosure. Then, getting paper and pen, he began a letter.

"My dear Brother Kingman—"

He stopped there, thought better of the idea, tore the page up, and wrote:

My dear Sister Winifred:
    I have not had the opportunity to welcome you into the family but I congratulate my Brother on winning so fair a helpmate. I have no wedding gift for you but last Summer while at the Court House on business I had the good fortune to be able to prevent your Property, inherited from your Grandfather, from being sold at Public Outcry for unpaid taxes. The Document I enclose surrenders all claim I may have upon this Property which is henceforth your Possession, your Heirs and Assigns forever. Your Husband will know what steps to take to clear the Title. I shall be in the field for eight months moving at the direction of the Commander in Chief,

so I leave that detail to Kingman, who I am sure will attend to it Properly. I should have sent this Document to you sooner but have been on the move for some time. Respectfully yours, Dear Madam,

William Breen Markland, Captain, USA.

He added his regiment and company numbers, also the headquarters address; not that he expected any reply but this was business and needed the stamp of official dignity. Then he limped up the steps to the afterhouse where the mailbag hung, ready to be locked and tossed ashore when they stopped briefly at Paducah. He dropped the envelope in, turned his back quickly. At least he had done the decent thing. Most of his pay for three years of fighting and part of his winnings from those Yankee card sharks had gone to make his family secure from the ravening carpetbaggers. He did not regret it. His only hope was that he had not bought more resentment with that money. Obligation, unwillingly acquired, he knew could be a bitter burden.

None of the troop were allowed ashore at Paducah and this produced considerable rebellion and some bitter complaints. Kentucky resented and rejected Colored troops, and had entered into agreement with Washington that none would be stationed within the state.

"They didn't secede in 'sixty-one," grumbled Lieutenant Gore. "Now they're turning the whole state into a Confederate province. If Robert E. Lee showed up in Frankfort they'd elect him governor right now by public acclamation."

"They feel the way they do because so many dishonest and tyrannical Union men were put in command here," declared Lieutenant Perry. "We've got to keep these boys aboard somehow, Captain, for two days and nights, till the transport gets here to take them down river. You'd better watch that blabber-mouth yellow boy of yours or he'll slip ashore and some young Secesh blood just home from Appomattox will slit his throat for him."

Very likely, William was certain, every Colored soldier aboard knew by now that Buzzy had killed a white man. Buzzy would be the big man, ignoring restrictions. Buzzy was as difficult to contain as quicksilver. He called the boy into his official cubbyhole and issued an order.

"Buzzy, I'm making an aide out of you. Hereafter, till we start down river you'll stay close to me, obey my orders, run my errands and sleep where I sleep."

Buzzy looked dashed. "Cap'n Billy, you fixin' to git my haid bash in some of these dark nights? Boys up yonder won't like it, do you make aide out of me, with stuff on my sleeve and wearin' a sword."

"You'll get no braid on your sleeve and no sword. You're under detention, Buzzy, for being absent without leave for weeks. You'll shine my boots, take care of my equipment, fetch me my meals and do whatever I tell you to do."

"Mist' Willie, ain't you forgettin'? I'm free."

"You're a private in this army! I'm your commanding officer. Stand at attention when I speak to you."

"Yes, suh! Cap'n suh!"

"Now go out and pass the word that any boy who slips off this boat at night will probably be found floating face down in the river in the morning, with a bullet in his head or his throat cut." William was grim.

Buzzy's shoulders sagged and his lips pushed out.

"Mist' Willie," he said plaintively, "I done beg you to git me out this ginny army. Ain't no good place for nobody to be, you or me neither."

William looked at the boy long and sadly, the same bleak homesickness making an ache within him that lay liquid and bereft in the Negro boy's eyes.

"Where would we go, Buzzy?" he asked, expecting no answer. "Where would we go?"

• *Twenty Two* •

IT WAS SPRING WHEN WILLIAM RECEIVED THE LETTERS.

The company had moved south into Mississippi, to a small town not far from the river, where a railroad was being projected into Alabama. They arrived on a rainy March day, chilly and dispiriting, and there was nothing about the place to raise their spirits or give them any confidence whatever in the wisdom of the officials at Washington.

"We're supposed to guard the construction of this damn railroad," grumbled Lieutenant Gore. "But where the devil is the railroad? If they've even begun grading for one, the roadbed's sunk deep in the mud by this time."

"See that low black embankment up yonder? That's the railroad," said the other lieutenant. "There'll be timbers and steel dumped off somewhere on the water front and we're supposed to keep the stuff from being stolen and carted away before the engineers get here. Meanwhile"—he pulled a boot out of the sucking mud with a hollow sound —"how do you keep a tent peg from floating away by itself before you get a rope tied to it?"

"You write a letter to the War Department, Lieutenant," William said. "Maybe by next October you'll get an answer."

"Sixteen boys showed up on sick call this morning," said Gore. "The minute it gets hot down here there'll be insects to eat us alive and like enough yellow jack and smallpox and every other foul disease. Why did we fight to drag country like this back into the Union anyway? Who wants it? A dozen Negroes to every white man, and not one of them wants to work, white or black. How are they going to get a grade on that roadbed? Black women carrying dirt on their heads in baskets, the way they do in China?"

"We don't have to build it, Lieutenant, we just have to protect it. But we've no snap job at that, for those few railroad ties they've got stacked up down yonder are going to look mighty good to some fellow with no sills under his shanty, or a barn burned down. Mount four men on guard down there, Lieutenant Gore, with orders to shoot in the air if anybody comes prowling."

"If those boys get scared they're likely to shoot up their own tents, or get some of us in the back and run," growled Perry. "It was never like this up on the Rappahannock."

"We weren't educated about mud at West Point either," complained Gore. "But we fought a whole damn war in the mud, far as I can remember."

Buzzy had a complaint too. It rained, and the tents leaked. The blankets were sodden, and mildew attacked boots and equipment overnight.

"And how come these niggers down here don't know we won the war, Cap'n?" he fretted.

"They're just poor dislocated Colored people, Buzzy," William explained. "Keep your mouth shut, don't go bragging, attend to your duty and you'll have no trouble."

"Up home," the boy sighed, "it plowin' time. Boy, I'd sho' like to git my bare foots in a furrow again, see a ole mule floppin' his tail, Miss Annie's chickens followin' along to pick up the grubs. You reckon Mist' Morgan ever learn how to hold a plow? Mist' Morgan he ain't never liked to git hisself sweated up much and spoil his good clothes."

"When you're hungry you can learn fast, Buzzy."

"Dis here ole Mississippi mighty cold for springtime. Both your blankets they git wet, Cap'n."

"Hang them by the fire then and dry them out."

"Yes, suh." Buzzy shuffled sullenly to obey.

Some day, William was certain, he would look about for his reluctant aide and Buzzy would not be there. The boy had already demonstrated his ability to travel swiftly over the country and arrive at his objective and now all his talk was of the Harpeth country, of home. That there might be violent Marklands there waiting to deal harshly with him obviously did not cloud Buzzy's nostalgic dream.

The mail call came at noon on a sunny Saturday. Buzzy sped as usual to worm his way into the line. He had never yet received a letter and William doubted if Buzzy could read one if he got it, his brief haymow education having proceeded only halfway through the primer, but he was always eagerly optimistic. This day his eyes glittered and bulged a little as the mail clerk put two envelopes into his hands.

"Captain's mail. Don't drop them in the mud."

"No, suh." Buzzy stuffed the missives inside his coat, and sent mire flying as he ran back to the Captain's tent. "Mail, Cap'n," he announced with a flourish.

William took the envelopes, both soiled and worn from much handling and forwarding through military channels.

"From home, Cap'n?" asked Buzzy eagerly.

"We'll see." William slit one envelope with his knife.

A paper slid out into his hand, the folded document, the same tax deed he had mailed weeks ago to Winnie Markland. A small scrap of paper had been pinned to it with a rusted pin and the few words scrawled on this fragment leaped at William in all the anger with which they had been written. He recognized his brother's angular hand.

"You wanted this bad enough to steal it," King had written. "Keep it and be damned."

"Bad news, Cap'n Billy?" Buzzy ventured, seeing the dark spasm of hurt fury tighten William's face. "That from home? They still mad at us back home?"

"Still mad at us, Buzzy." William tore King's insulting message into bits, but put the deed carefully away in his dispatch case.

He cut the flap on the other envelope. The handwriting sent blood pounding warmly through his rigid muscles. His mother! She had signed herself formally, Annie Lou Breen Markland.

But there was no formality in the letter.

My darling Boy: [Miss Annie had written, hastily, crookedly, obviously with homemade ink] I am writing this in the loom house and I don't know how I will get it in the Mail. The boys [here something was scratched out messily as though Miss Annie had begun some revelation that she had later repented] the boys don't go to town often. We only have the Colts now and one old mewel. [Spelling, William remembered, had always been a bit of a mystery to his mother] The other mewel dyed. We let Jack take the Geld and buggy. I just hope it holds together till they get whare they are going. I was shurely glad to find out whare I could send a Letter. You write to your Mama now and let me no if you get this Letter. All as well as common only Mammy Dory dyed last winter. We shurely miss your Pa and Boone-boy. The Girls are fine only Morgan's wife in a family way. You write to your Mama who loves you. No use this War going on forever. Your loveing Mother, Annie Lou Breen Markland.

A tight lump strained to the point of tears in William's throat. He traced the rambling, smeary lines tenderly with a forefinger. Pokeberry ink! How many times had he seen his mother stew up the juicy berries that he and Buzzy brought in in vinegar and whisky, straining the fluid carefully through a fold of cloth? The one steel pen in the house had always been sacred to his father's laboriously posted farm and slave books. When William went away to school and had a pen of his own in a fine green holder he had felt very important.

Buzzy was studying his face anxiously. "What Miss Annie say?" he asked. "That from Miss Annie ain't it?"

William read the letter again frowning a little. "I can't understand some of it, Buzzy. She writes about Jack taking the gelding—and the buggy—and that they miss Boone-boy. Jack must have moved out."

"Mist' Jack and Mist' King ain't been gittin' along good?"

"She doesn't say. But she does say something about Morgan's wife—" Morgan's wife! A stab of unease struck at William's heart. A picture of that moon-washed October night came back to haunt him. Of Morgan reeling out of that parsonage with Miss Ella Crabtree's outraged shrilling following him, of that confused and embarrassing fight, of Morgan yelling at him next morning, "Your girl—by gad, sir—"

Angela! Why, he demanded of himself, hadn't he written to Angela? In the chaos of turmoil and trouble, his father shot, Buzzy disappearing, hot angry quarrels with Jack and Morgan before he had sent them home, he had not even had an opportunity to get word to Angela, or to tell her goodbye when his orders to move had come.

He had been too tormented with worry and remorse over his father's suffering and death to think about his own concerns. Now, if Angela had married his brother on a rebound, it was, William berated himself, no more than he deserved. But that she had been halfway in love with him William was almost certain. There had been so little chance to talk to her, no opportunity to be with her at all. Those gray dragons, her mother and aunt, had seen to that.

Buzzy interrupted this painful thinking again, inquiring wistfully, "That all Miss Annie write in that letter? Mist' Jack done moved and Mist' Morgan git married? Who he git married to?"

"I don't know, Buzzy. I hope he didn't steal my girl."

"One I tote all them notes to?"

"My mother didn't say who Morgan had married. But she did say that your grandmother had died."

Buzzy gnawed a protruding lip. "She pretty ole, my grandmaw. I ain't never told her goodbye and now she daid. Now we ain't got nobody much, is we, Cap'n?"

"We've got ourselves, Buzzy. I've got you and you've got me."

"I bet Miss Annie wish I'd come home," stated the boy boldly. "I bet she see me walkin' in that ole kitchen door right now she yell 'Buzzy, you lazy dog, you git me some lightwood kindlin' right now!' That what she'd say."

William nodded grimly. "And then when King came in and saw you there he'd order you off the place and out of sight and tell you if you didn't move fast Morgan would shoot you."

Buzzy puckered his brow quizzically. "If I rub down his horse and shine up his boots good, Mist' Morgan change his mind," he said shrewdly. "Mist' Morgan ain't never liked to git his good clothes dirty. Got him a wife now, reckon he won't be ridin' round so wild no more, drinkin' and gamblin'."

"He'd better not," snapped William with sudden ferocity. "He'd better treat her well or by God I'll throttle him!"

"You got to go home to do that, Cap'n," Buzzy said hopefully. "Whyn't we both of us go home? This ain't no war army no more. It's a sit-around, draw-ration, shoot-crap, grumble army. Boys all tryin' to pick fights, officers all homesick. Jest form fours, count off, police up this here area."

"It's still the army. You wanted it. You got it. Do your best for it."

"Eleven dollars a month," brooded the boy sourly. "It don't last but one day. What they got us down in this ole Mississippi for, anyways?"

"Because the people in Washington need us here to guard this railroad construction."

"Who in Washin'ton? Linkum daid, all them big generals gone home. General Sherman and General Grant, they don't care where we at. You reckon they even know we alive, Cap'n Billy?"

"Probably not," admitted William. He was knowing now the sting of hurt conceit. If Morgan had married Angela, then he himself had been nothing more to her than a passing fancy, a handsome officer, a whim with which to defy her female jailers, a sop to her girlish vanity.

But what had he had from her after all, beyond casual friendliness? A chance meeting or two, a passing smile or wave of the hand. And she had had from him a long silence. She could not be blamed if she had wearied of being ignored. Why was he harrowing himself before he knew the truth? And how was he to know? He could not write, except to his mother, and his Markland pride would not let him ask whom Morgan had married, although to Miss Annie that would appear the natural thing to do. He could imagine Morgan's gleeful gloating, if he had scored a victory over Brother Billy, when that brother evidenced any sign of resentment.

It was a relief when marching orders came late in April, shifting the company again, this time to a post in Georgia.

All the Southern states were beginning to seethe with fury at the carpetbag governments. To be an officer of a garrison post was to be a hateful kind of police officer, ordered to keep white men from the polls, uphold the freedmen in their insolences, be respectful to the radicals and their cheap arrogant politicians.

William despised the assignment and grew short-tempered, even with Buzzy, who wore an increasingly withdrawn and secret air, said little, and bore himself with disturbing circumspection.

It was no surprise to Captain William Markland to discover on a late May morning that Private Buzzy Markland had disappeared.

• *Twenty Three* •

By THE TIME THEY REACHED THE SOUTH FORK OF THE FORKED DEER RIVER the gelding had begun to limp a little. The left rear tire of the buggy developed a jingle and Boone-boy had commenced to fret peevishly.

"Whyn't we stay home, Mama?" he whimpered. "What we want to come here for?"

Sue had a patient answer ready, although the reply had no roots in her heart. She had hated leaving the Markland place as much as Boone-boy, she had even wept about it, but always in secret. Jack was discouraged enough already, gloomy enough, without having her tears added to his burdens.

"Because there were too many people there, Boone-boy," she told him. "Because the farm won't grow enough food to feed so many of us."

"Why didn't Uncle King go away then and Uncle Morgan? Why I got to have so many aunts? Why didn't Uncle King go home and take Aunt Winnie with him? I don't like aunts that cry all the time."

"Uncle King and Aunt Winnie lost their home," Sue explained for the tenth time. "And Uncle Morgan and your Aunt Angie have no place to go. Papa does have a place to go. A place where he can get land for us to live on, and work to do. Papa is going to help cut timber and build a railroad. We'll have a nice home some day, and you'll like Texas."

"I won't like it. Why do we have to sleep outdoors all the time? I don't like that li'l ole tent. I like my bed in Grandma's house," persisted the boy.

"I liked my bed there too," admitted his mother. "And I liked chairs to sit on and a stove to cook on, but I want to go where Papa wants to go and Papa wants to go to Texas."

"Uncle Morgan says they got wild Indians in Texas. And bears. A big ole bear could come in our tent some night and eat me up."

"Papa would shoot any bear that bothered us and then we'd have bear meat to eat and a big warm bearskin to sleep under. You and I would scrape the skin and play we were real Indians," prattled Sue, trying to drown under a rivulet of words the piteous crying in her own heart. I'm afraid. Oh, I'm afraid. Oh, Miss Annie, why did you let us go? Couldn't you see this strangeness in your son, growing and growing? His odd moods, the frightful headaches, the agony that paralyzes all his senses, the darkness that comes over him when the pain strikes?

She knew well that nothing Miss Annie could say would have changed Jack's grim determination. Not after Morgan had brought a wife into the house. Jack had been stiff and difficult after that, saying little to the family but grumbling loudly to Sue after they had closed the door of their room.

"Stays away—not caring if his father lived or died and then comes galloping in as lighthearted as if he'd won the war, bringing a wife along for us to feed and Miss Annie to wait on."

"She's a good little thing," Sue defended. "She tries to help all she can." But inwardly she was thinking: Morgan doesn't love that girl. Somehow, like King, he was trapped into this marriage.

Morgan had treated his wistfully eager young wife with an amused, gay, often cynical manner that bewildered even his mother. He would leave her without a farewell and return jauntily, offering no explanation, no excuse. Always he brought food home in his saddlebags, or he tossed a ten dollar gold piece nonchalantly into his mother's lap. He brought whisky home too and that frightened Sue since Jack and King drank with Morgan in the stable. Whisky made Morgan more sardonic, given to biting remarks that stung even though the others laughed at them; it made King sullen and Jack grew unpredictable, even after one drink. After she had found her husband lying face down in the barn twice, Sue grew resigned to the migration and in the end she had been a little glad to get away from the Markland house.

But not from Miss Annie, who had worn a stricken face and an air of tragic resignation, and not from tearful old Minerva. From the continual tension brewing between the brothers, threatening to erupt any hour into quarreling and violence.

Morgan had in the end supplied them with some money—a loan, Jack insisted. And King had finally agreed that Jack should have the gelding and the buggy. Miss Annie had offered more blankets than the rig would hold and she and Minerva and Angela had cooked for days.

"It's cool yet. Things will keep," she argued. "But I do wish you had a wagon. So much here you could take with you."

"Too slow, Jack says," Sue explained. "It's six hundred miles to where Jack wants to go. With a horse and buggy we can drive it in four weeks, he thinks, even resting the horse on Sundays."

"King says," put in Winnie, "that he never heard of this lieutenant from East Texas that Jack thinks is going to help him get located when you get there. And you know, Sue, that King and Jack were in the same regiment all through the war. You don't think it could be a delusion or something? You know there are times when Jack isn't—well, exactly himself since he got that blow on the head."

Sue bristled. Winnie could always stir a flare of antagonism in Sue although for her mother-in-law's sake and to keep peace she strove loyally to control it. Winnie could do it just by being Winnie. Always limp and undependable, always the pessimist, thinking of no one but Winnie.

"Jack," Sue retorted stiffly, "may have times when pain masters him

[174]

but he would never drag his family all that distance following a dream."

"So many people going off to Texas," said Miss Annie. "Just last week the Lawsons, the last of our good neighbors. That poor man and all those girls and no son to help him."

"But they had a covered wagon," said Winnie. "Jack and Sue will have to sleep on the ground."

"Jack slept on the ground through the war," argued Sue. "I'm as strong as he is. Whatever Jack can bear I can bear too and so can Boone-boy."

But it had not been easy. Now here at the Forked Deer River they were only a little more than a hundred miles on their way and already six days had passed. There was that clinking tire now. Tonight the buggy would have to be unloaded and backed into a stream and left there all night so the wheel would swell. Then, as laboriously again in the morning, it must be dragged out again and all the food and clothing and blankets, damp with spring dew, packed away. But thus far the banks of the river had been high and rocky, the water fast and turbulent, and although Jack got down and walked, searching, he found no sign of a ford.

Dusk was beginning to thicken, the greening fragrant dusk of spring, when he returned from his last exploration, sweating, gray-faced and angry.

"Looks like we'll have to follow this damn river all the way to the Mississippi. White water and deep everywhere I've sounded."

"Can we drive the horse right across the Mississippi?" asked Boone-boy.

"A river a mile wide and a mile deep? Sounds likely doesn't it?" snapped Jack.

"How would the child know if no one tells him?" interposed Sue.

"Going on eight years old. Goes to school. Well, I've told him. Does he have to ask questions all the time?"

"Little boys can't learn unless they ask questions," said Boone-boy. "Grandma says so."

"Might as well camp here." Jack took the bridle to lead the gelding off the dimly visible road. "Too dark to go on. At least there's water if I can get down to it without breaking a leg."

"I can get down, Papa," volunteered Boone-boy. "I won't break a leg—but I can't carry that big ole bucket."

"You stay with your mother," ordered Jack. "I don't want to be fishing you out of that river in the dark. Hunt some wood for a fire while you can still see."

"If there was a snake I might not see him but I could still see a bear or an Indian." Boone-boy was jauntily brave. But his mother was not brave at all.

Even when the fire leaped red and the smoke-blackened kettle steamed over it, when the April moon came up delicately riding a chiffon cloud on her silver keel, when the mocking birds sang deliriously in the great trees bordering the river, Sue could not shake off a chilly oppression that made every shadow a menace, every bird a homesick reminder of happier days.

The river clucked, sucked, snarled and splashed over the rocks that impeded it. It was, she decided, rightly named. Down from the higher ground of the Cumberlands these waters plunged like frightened forked deer, but surely there would be quieter levels ahead as the land sloped gently toward the greatest river of them all. They had crossed the Tennessee on a crude ferry, hastily built of pine logs and slabs by some free Negroes, poled across by the power of their dark bodies. It had taken all Jack's strength to keep the nervous gelding from plunging off the shaky craft into the stream. What would it be like when they essayed the crossing of the vast Mississippi? And once on that distant shore, what then? Would there be any roads at all through Louisiana? Spring, she knew, was a time of bottomless mud, quagmires, holes filled with roily water on almost any road, and Louisiana was reported to be a land of bayous, many small streams and swamps. Lying in the little tent on a blanket Sue caught herself digging her fingers into the earth as though she would tear from it the answer to all the apprehensions and anxieties she had never put into words, lest she tear away what valiance was left in her husband's spirit or put fresh fears into the heart of her staunch little son.

The next day dragged off from a late start. They had to move slowly because of the gelding's strained leg and the loose tire that threatened to fall off the rim at any moment. Jack stumbled and slid to the edge of the river, fetching water up for the horse, and came back with his breeches dripping mud and his face like thunder. The road followed the stream for four miles with no break in the high banks and no slowing of the current. It was past noon when they reached a little village where a rusty cannon lay tilted on broken wheels beside the single street.

The few houses had doors standing open and Negro children stood in them, staring, half naked. A litter of young pigs scurried squealing across the road, causing the horse to shy nervously. When a tall mulatto in a faded pair of Union breeches came shambling near, his bare feet making squishing noises in the mud, Jack reined up.

"Where do we cross this river, Mose?" he asked loudly.

The Negro drew himself up with chilling dignity. "Name ain't Mose, white man. Mah name William T. Sherman, Junior."

"All right, Sherman, which way to a ferry or a ford?"

"*Mister* Sherman to you, white man," was the frigid reply, "and there ain't no ferry. We fords this here river five miles north and she mighty high right now."

Sue sat clutching Jack's elbow, begging him by silent pressure not to let his temper rise. Boone-boy sat hunched very small beside her.

"Where can I find a white man?" demanded Jack. "Any blacksmith in this town?"

The Negro shook his head. "Ain't any blacksmith. Ain't any white people neither. Just us free Colored."

"But there must have been some white people here?" Sue said, keeping her tone polite. "Those houses—"

"They left, Madam," stated Sherman pompously. "They done head out for parts unknown. Seven families, all head out."

"Drive on, Jack, please," she begged. "There are bound to be people further along this road."

"I'll have to pour some water on that wheel. Would one of your Colored citizens lend a man in distress a few buckets of water?" he asked the mulatto, acidly.

"Well yonder," the man shrugged a shoulder, ambled away.

"For Heaven's sake don't be so sarcastic!" Sue protested. "There's no slavery now and we're far from home and helpless."

"*Mister* Sherman!" snarled Jack. "I'd Mister him!" He unslung the bucket from the rear axle, rummaged a blackened kettle out of their packed possessions, handed it to the boy. "Here, make yourself useful. Move. The quicker we get out of this dead and gone place the better."

"But why did all the white people go away, Papa?" Boone-boy trotted after Jack. "Over there is a pretty, big house but black people are living in it."

"Why did we move away?" countered Jack. "Because the Yankees won the war. Because they're trying to take over the country and make the black man a king and the Southerner a slave."

"Will we be slaves in Texas, Papa? I don't want to be a slave. Buzzy's daddy was a slave and Grampa sold him down the river. Mammy Dory told me so. Can they sell us if we get to be slaves, Papa?"

"We won't be slaves in Texas. Pour that water slow now and don't waste it. It's going to be hot today. That wheel will dry out fast." Jack sloshed the borrowed water anxiously. The sun was mounting to its zenith and mist rose from all the pools and reeds along the river's edge. The horse slumped in the harness, resting his lame leg. Black children, wearing only brief faded shirts, hung about, their big dark eyes curious. The gelding pawed and stamped as a horsefly nipped him and the little Negroes scattered like partridges. Boone-boy laughed to see them run and was scolded by his mother.

"We mustn't anger these people," she said. "There are many of them and only three of us."

"But why don't they like us?" Boone-boy puzzled as they drove on. "'Nerva's black and she liked me. Mammy Dory liked me. She used to hug me all the time till she got too fat and sick."

"They've been taught not to like us by wicked white people." Sue strove to explain what was still not clear in her own mind. "Wicked people from up north who wanted Negroes to like them and hate us."

"Damn Yankees!" Boone-boy quoted his uncles bluntly. "We ought to get some guns and chase them clear into the ocean."

"We tried that," said Jack. "Did you see that Parrott gun lying wrecked beside the road back there. I was there the time we abandoned that gun when we were chasing the Yanks north after Shiloh."

The boy's eyes widened. "You were here? In the war? Right here on this road, Papa?"

"Right here. Riding a good horse then. Gray Knight. He was brother to The Count, that bay that Billy stole when he went off with the Union."

"Billy didn't steal that horse any more than you stole Gray Knight," Sue argued. "They were your own horses. Pa Markland gave them to you."

"Pa would never have let a horse go to the Union cavalry and you know it. Billy left in the night and Buzzy with him."

"Where's Gray Knight now, Papa?"

"Probably a heap of bones in a gully picked clean by the buzzards. He broke a leg when we were retreating from Franklin, and I had to leave him where he fell."

The bad wheel was quieter now, the gelding stepped out a little faster under Jack's urging. He still favored his lame hind leg, not resting his weight upon it, lurching one-sidedly when he trotted.

"Did you look at his shoe?" Sue asked, further on. "He still limps mighty bad."

"Shoe's all right. When that rock rolled under him back there a way, he must have strained a tendon. He ought to be taped up and kept off it, but we can't stop now. I should have brought along some of Pa's liniment. Ranse used to bandage 'em and cure 'em in three days."

"Suppose he gets so he can't travel?"

"Suppose he keeps on traveling," Jack flared back. "He's got to travel. We're not even out of Tennessee yet. We'll have to cross part of Mississippi and some of Louisiana. God, when I was riding this country with Forrest I never expected to come limping back!"

It was two days later when they had crossed south into Mississippi that Sue saw black people working in a vast field of cotton, hundreds of Negro men, it seemed.

"Jack, look!" she cried. "Soldiers are out there in that field with those hands. Union soldiers."

"Freedmen's Bureau," he told her. "They have to feed all those Nigras so they lease them out to landowners, then they have to appeal to the army to help 'em keep the Nigras at work." He laughed. "That's their Yankee freedom for you. Ever see a soldier standing over one of Pa's hands, over Ranse or Phoebus or Buzzy with a gun? Well, they wanted it, now they've got it."

An elderly man with lieutenant's stripes stood near the road, regarding them curiously, and a little way down the field a very young boy in blue poised his gun nervously.

"Yankees," whispered Boone-boy, aghast. "Will they hurt us, Mama?"

"No, they won't hurt us. And they won't let those black men hurt us, either."

But hardly had she spoken than the terror happened. So suddenly that Sue could never quite order it all in her mind afterward. The shouting, the terror, as all at once there was a gustily breathing swarm of black humanity climbing over them, the whistle and slash of Jack's whip as he laid it about him, the struggle and grunts and curses and blows as he was pulled to the ground. Boone-boy snatched the whip from his father's hand, raining blows on sweated black faces where yellow eyeballs glared. Jack was still on his feet, fighting, and the soldiers were shouting and running. The Negroes wanted the horse. There were six of them, huge, sweaty, fiercely belligerent.

Sue struck at the dark hands that tried to drag her out of the buggy. She kicked and screamed, and was vaguely aware of the aging officer laying about him with the flat of a pistol, of the shouting coming nearer and yelled commands and loud jeers and running feet.

The boyish soldier was not to blame. All that anguished way home she told herself that the young soldier was not to blame. They had been trying to protect her, to break up the sudden savage melee, control those maddened men who saw a way of escape and were fiercely determined to possess it. The young soldier had been little more than a boy, frightened by a fearful responsibility, confused and excited. His first shot dropped a black ruffian, blood spurting from a wound in his shoulder.

The second shot, poorly aimed, went wild. In a sick daze Sue saw Jack, saw him falling, a crimson fountain welling from his neck.

The Negroes ran then, some of the soldiers pounding after. The boy in blue stood shaking, his still smoking gun trembling in his hands, staring down, white-faced, eyes bulging, mouth slack.

"You fool! You crazy fool!" the Lieutenant was shouting at him.

"I'm sorry, lady," gulped the boy in a voice that broke and squeaked with horror. "God, I'm sorry!"

She was on her feet in the mud of the road and the green lushness of the spring morning whirled around her. Then a sweet, kind blackness closed in and the day and its ghastly terrors vanished as she felt herself crumpling.

• *Twenty Four* •

ALWAYS AFTERWARD WHEN THE MARKLANDS WERE BITTER SUE REMINDED them that the Union soldiers had been kind.

There was the Lieutenant with his graying hair and tired, troubled face. She was aware of him standing over her as she sat, dazed and trembling in the road with Jack's head in her lap, blood still oozing on her dress.

"This is a dreadful thing, Madam," he was saying. "If you will allow us to help you—"

"You killed him. You killed my papa!" Boone-boy flew at the officer with flailing fists and choking sobs. "You damn ole Yankee you."

"I know, son," the Lieutenant restrained the boy gently, lifting him in his arms. "It was an accident and the army is sorry. Private Wilson there was only trying to help you, to keep those frantic Colored men from killing you all. They wanted to take your rig away from you and they would have killed you all to do it. Now, we will be glad to help you, Madam—" He bent again over Sue, who did not look up at him.

She was trying to press Jack's eyelids down, to cover those dark, dead eyeballs staring so reproachfully at the sky. "Give her some water, Corporal," ordered the Lieutenant.

Someone had unhitched the gelding and tied the horse to a tree. He stood, head hanging listlessly, lame foot off the ground. Someone put a canteen to Sue's lips and she sipped it obediently, looking up with startled eyes to see so many of them. Blue and brass like Billy, like Buzzy. Blue and brass brought terror, brought death.

"I have to take him home," she said faintly. "I have to take my husband home."

"Yes, Ma'am." The Lieutenant snapped his fingers, still holding the child, Boone-boy's head nuzzled into his shoulder. "Get a blanket!" he ordered. "Lay him over there in the shade."

The soldiers jumped to obey. They carried Jack to the shelter of a great gum tree, laid him gently on a blanket and covered his face. Boone-boy struggled down and followed after, tear-smeared, stunned. The Lieutenant lifted Sue, set her on the seat of the buggy and wiped the blood from her hands with his own handkerchief.

"We'll see that you get home, Ma'am," he promised. "And please remember that this was an unfortunate accident. See that boy over there against that tree bawling into his cap? That's the boy who fired the shot. He was aiming at that big black who was pulling you out of the buggy. Your husband moved suddenly and unexpectedly into the line of fire. He's sorry, Ma'am. Private Wilson's about heartbroken over this business."

Sue looked hard at the graying man, her dazed vision clearing.

"You're from the South!" she said abruptly. "From the South and wearing *that!*" Blue and brass. The colors of trouble.

"Yes, Ma'am, I'm from Greene County, Tennessee. A lot of Greene County people are for the Union. That's Andrew Johnson's county."

"My husband was a Confederate captain," she said. "You knew that, didn't you?"

"No, Ma'am, there was no way for us to know. To our boys you were just some travelers in distress. They were doing what they could to protect you when this mischance occurred. There have been a great many travelers in distress, Ma'am, Tennesseans like yourself. I haven't enjoyed seeing the way things are going in my state. Now I want to help you, if you will permit me."

"I have to go home. I have to take my husband home." Her voice rose a bit, hysterically. "Where is my little boy?"

"He's here, Ma'am. The boys are looking after him. I've sent back to our garrison post for a wagon. Where is your home, Ma'am?"

"A long way. A long, long way." Like a monotonous chant her sorrow beat upon one note. "A long way—and the horse went lame."

"I know. He can't travel any further on that leg. We'll find you another horse. We'll see that you get home."

"By the river. The Harpeth River. The Marklands," Sue murmured. "My husband rode with Forrest. His brothers too. All but one. One blue one. Blue and brass like you. Trouble for the Marklands. Trouble in blue and brass."

"Watch her," ordered the Lieutenant, motioning to a trooper. "I'll ride back and get another horse."

Dully she watched the gray-haired man ride off. Under the tree Jack lay very flat, the blanket over his face, and back in the cotton field the Negroes worked in frightened haste, cutting their eyeballs around to watch uneasily as soldiers paced the limits of the field.

Who had won, was the cry in her heart? Who had won this war? Not this sad-eyed officer or the boy snuffling into his cap, not those black men, so disillusioned, once so certain of power and money and freedom, now so frustrated. Not the desolate people who had fled that village they had passed through where the shattered gun lay rusting in the road. Did nobody win wars? Was it all noise and boasting, bugles and banners, thousand upon thousands of marching men—all valiant and all mad? Mad with dreams of glory—and where was glory? Gray Knight's bones bleaching in a gully? Jack lying there, dead eyes searching an unanswering sky? There was blood on her dress. She dabbed at it impatiently, getting her fingers stained again and sticky.

This is the way he came home before, she thought later as the army wagon turned into the narrow road that led to the river and the Markland place.

This is the way Jack came home before, lying prone in the bed of a Union wagon drawn by a Union mule. There were two mules hitched to this wagon and the soldier on the seat beside her was very polite and respectful to the dead. Behind them a strange, tall roan horse with a bony rump pulled the buggy, with another trooper driving and Boone-boy sitting beside him. The army had repaired the wheel, supplied the roan horse, the crude wooden casket in which Jack lay. There was even a flag. A little ragged flag, the Stars and Bars, that the Lieutenant had given to Sue.

"Captured it at Cold Harbor, Ma'am," he said. "Thought maybe you'd like to have it for your husband."

"And where are you from, soldier?" she asked her driver on the second day.

"Kentucky, Ma'am. Morgan County."

All valiant and all mad! And who were they, the great ones, the powerful ones, with the musical voices and the proud words, who were they who could charm men, inflame them, make them drunk with the dry wine of promised glory? Who had blown the trumpets till all the walls of sanity and sense in the land fell down? Shod hoofs, galloping, galloping. Bugles singing, a blood song, intoxicating as alien wine. Jack had worn a red sash when he rode off to war. She had cut it from the widths of a dance dress, hemmed it on her fingers, tears making the eye of the needle dim. So he came home—once in rags and today in thin, worn hunting pants and a borrowed shirt, frayed at all the edges.

She saw the house ahead and suddenly she could hardly bear the sight of it. Miss Annie! How to deal little Miss Annie this last frightful blow? King. King would see only the blue and brass, the enemy. And so would Morgan, the unpredictable. She plucked at the driver's sleeve.

"Let me out at the gate. I'll walk," she said. "Our people were Confederate. I'll have to explain to them how kind you have been to us."

"No, Ma'am." The soldier shook his head. "Captain's orders. I'm to deliver you—and the body—to your door."

I'll tell a lie, she decided. I'll say that Negroes killed Jack, that the troops were protecting us. There mustn't be any more trouble. They were kind and it wasn't that poor boy's fault. I'll tell a lie. God will forgive me.

But she remembered then that it would be no use. There was Boone-boy, who had seen the horrid fight, seen the shooting. Boone-boy would babble out the truth and if she tried to warn him beforehand it would only confuse him and make matters worse. She would let this soldier from Kentucky explain to King and Morgan, she decided, sinking back into an aching apathy of acceptance. The soldier had been blunt and taciturn but he had been considerate all the way. These men were the victors, she kept trying to remember, as Billy had warned her last summer—so long ago—so drearily long ago.

She knew a surge of relief when the door of the house opened and only women came running out. Miss Annie first, twisting her hands in her apron, behind her Winnie tiptoeing daintily over the dry grass, then Angela and black Minerva.

Miss Annie did not faint nor wail. She seemed to freeze, graying into stunned rigidity as she clutched at Sue's hands, pulled Boone-boy close. "I knew it!" she cried, flat-voiced, like a woman in a trance. "I knew it. Three days ago I told them—Jack's in trouble, I told them. Somehow I knew it. Something told me."

"The Union soldiers were very kind," Sue said woodenly, as she would say it so many times, again and again. "But for them we should all have been killed, probably, and our horse stolen."

"Oh, Sue—how horrible for you," cried Winnie when the story had been told. "You were so brave to live through such a ghastly experience."

"She lived through it because she is brave," Angela said. "Come along in, dear. Minerva shall make you some good hot coffee." Angela put an arm around Sue, and gathered Miss Annie close. "You too, Mrs. Markland. Can you gentlemen manage?" she asked the soldiers.

"Yes'm. I'll back the wagon around," said Kentucky. "But you—you get her inside. The mother too. She's wore out. Bad business for a woman. We done our best for her."

"I'm sure you did, and we all thank you," said Angela graciously.

But before the door closed Winnie was querulous. "How could you, Angela? Calling them gentlemen? Those awful Yankees! It was all their fault. I just know it was their fault. If King was here—"

"Thank goodness he's not here," said Angela, "or Morgan either. Sit down, Sue, let me have your bonnet. Hurry, Minerva, get the kettle hot. Mrs. Markland, your hands are like ice. Rub them for her, Winnie. I'd better direct those men. I suppose—the parlor?"

"Angela—in your condition?" protested Winnie.

"Oh, bother my condition! Don't be silly, Winnie."

"Get Boone-boy inside," croaked Sue. "And those men—some coffee—"

Angela came back. "Boone-boy won't come. He's helping. Mrs. Markland, they asked me—would there be a pair of wooden horses in the barn?"

"I'll go." Miss Annie jumped up but Angela pushed her back gently.

"No. Boone-boy will know. He can show them. You're to stay here, both of you. Afterward, when the boys come, we can see about clothes and all that. I'll go with Boone-boy to the barn."

"I can cut some flowers," volunteered Winnie. "The flags and Easter flowers are in bloom. There ought to be some flowers—"

"Yes, Winnie, by all means cut some flowers," said Angela patiently. "You sit still, Mrs. Markland, and when Minerva brings some coffee you drink it. You too, Sue."

"She's good," sighed Miss Annie, when the two went out. "Angela's good and Winnie means well."

"The boys—where are they?"

"King's back in the south pasture mending a fence and Morgan just went off somewhere yesterday. He hasn't come back yet. He said he'd heard about a brood mare down toward Summertown, he thought he could arrange some kind of trade. Sue, tell me—I have to know. All of it." Her small brown hands were shaking again, plucking at her apron. Tears lay in the dry wrinkles on her cheeks.

"It was all so horrible, Miss Annie!" Sue began to cry again. "All those black men swarming over us—it makes me sick to remember. Jack fighting them and the soldiers running and shooting and then Jack fell and there was so much blood—"

Minerva bumped a tray down on a nearby table. "Miss Sue, you hush!" she ordered. "Git yourself all tore up and Miss Annie looks about to faint. Drink this here hot coffee now. You all drink every drop. We got enough troubles."

"I don't know if I can swallow. They tried to make me eat on the road but it seemed like every bite would choke me."

"You kin swallow. Just gulp it down but don't scald yourself, Miss Sue." Minerva leaned to peer out a window. "Oh, misery," she moaned, throwing her apron over her face. "'Nother corpse gittin' toted into this house! Done had three buryin's now since Christmas, countin' Mis' Dory."

Angela came back presently. "I sent Boone-boy to find King, Sue," she said. "He was so upset I thought a run in the sun would do him good. The soldiers are leaving. I asked them to wait and have some coffee but they said they were supposed to report back as soon as possible. They put that strange horse up in the stable and drove away in the wagon. I hope Morgan gets back tonight. But King will know what to do about clothes for Jack and those things."

"Morgan has to come back tonight!" cried his mother. "He has to come. He didn't see his father buried. I don't see why Morgan has to be always dashing off somewhere. The war made them all so restless." She got to her feet weakly, bracing herself on the arms of her chair. "Angela, I want to see him. I want to see my poor boy."

Angela pulled her mother-in-law into a restraining embrace. "Please

—no, Mrs. Markland. Not yet. Not till the boys come. Not till they have him dressed and ready. You mustn't see him now."

"I'm strong. I can bear it. No matter what they did to him he's still my first-born son."

"Jack wouldn't want you to see him as he is now, Mrs. Markland," insisted Angela. She was feeling a little uneasy in her stomach since she had looked at her brother-in-law's body, his drawn face, the ghastly wound, the shabby, pathetic clothes he wore. Old women were always whispering that a mother could mark her expected child if she looked on dreadful sights. Angela pressed flat hands on her rounding body. This was her baby—hers, and nothing must happen to it.

For weeks she had realized that Morgan had an indifferent attitude toward being a father. He had been at first incredulous, then amused, and of late more than a little irritated by her condition, and she saw less and less of him. The baby would be hers and it would be a girl, Angela was determined. Almost hourly she sent up a prayer that was half an ultimatum to Heaven. Make my child a daughter. No more Markland men. No more violence, no more arrogance. She shall be a daughter and she will be mine as Morgan has never been, will never be, mine. Never would Morgan Markland be possessed by anyone, perhaps because he had never been able to possess himself.

It was a relief to the Markland women that the Union soldiers were gone when King came striding in, red-faced and hot-eyed with fury and consternation. Then it all had to be told again, though Boone-boy had babbled the gory tale all the way back from the south pasture. Sue repeated all that she remembered, doggedly insisting that the army had been kind. But King was determined to believe the whole affair had been deliberate.

"They couldn't kill Jack at Shiloh or on any of a hundred campaigns we rode. They had to get him on a little country road, unarmed and helpless."

"They didn't know Jack was a Confederate. Not till I told them," Sue protested. "Then it didn't make any difference. That Lieutenant even gave me a flag for him, a little Confederate flag."

"Very noble! Where's the damn flag? I'll burn it to ashes," roared King.

"You will not!" screamed Boone-boy. "It's my papa's flag and he's going to have it."

"What have we got here?" sneered King. "A young traitor? You want your father to have a captured flag—a flag that's likely been abused, jeered at, spit upon?"

"He's going to have it. Right by his hand." Boone-boy stood his ground, giving his uncle glare for glare.

"Listen, King," cried Sue desperately. "Those troops didn't have to bother with us. They could have let those Negroes beat Jack and throw me out of the buggy and make off with all we had. They could have left me there with no husband and no horse, to get home the best way I could."

"It was their doing that you had a dead husband," persisted King, his obstinacy unshaken.

Angela's eyes began to blaze. "King, shut up!" she ordered. "We'll hear no more of this from you or Morgan either, if he ever comes home. You come upstairs with me right now and find Jack's clothes and help me make the poor boy presentable so his mother can look at him."

"Angela—you can't—" cried Winnie, who had shrunk back, frightened, at King's irate outburst.

"Why can't I? And you come along too, Miss. It will take all three of us. And don't start sniffling, Winnie Markland! It's high time you grew up and now is as good a time as any to begin."

Angela herself was surprised when the two obeyed, King morose and Winnie white-faced, walking on tiptoe up the stairs. It was Winnie who washed the blood from Jack's head and body under Angela's stern eye. Winnie's hands shook and she slopped the water and covered her eyes while King arranged a bandage over the ragged wound in Jack's throat. When they were finished and Jack lay, still and decently clad in one of King's good coats and a white shirt of Morgan's, trousers hastily pressed by Minerva and some shoes that once he had danced in, ages before, it was Winnie who brought a white rose and laid it gently by the dead face. Then she fled weeping and Angela let her go without protest.

"He looks all right now, King," Angela said. "That was really a respectable coffin they sent him home in."

"The devil you say!" King snarled and pointed. "Look over there." On the end, burned into the raw pine board was a charred USA. "Had to put their mark on him at the bitter end," he growled.

"You can bring your mother in now," she said, ignoring his remark, "and then you'd better ride and see about a minister and some people to help with the grave."

"There's nothing to ride," King reminded her. "Morgan took the stud and that colt's not broken to the saddle. What happened to the gelding?"

"He went lame and Sue had to leave him, but they gave her another horse. He's in the stable."

"Some old broken-down plug. Damn it, Angela, can't you keep Morgan at home? Always chasing off on the only good mount on the place!"

"How,"—Angela flung out her hands—"do you hold a Markland? How do you hold quicksilver? Or the wind? With chains? There has never been a chain forged that's strong enough!"

They buried Jack Markland on a breathlessly beautiful morning in spring. Mocking birds sang in the old trees and over the ground pink wild roses swarmed with bees, hovering over every bloom.

Annie Breen Markland clung to the arms of her two daughters-in-law, and Sue held her small son in a passionately loving embrace. King stood alone, still wearing a dark and brooding look.

Morgan was not there.

• *Twenty Five* •

FOR A DAY AND A NIGHT HUNGER HAD GNAWED AT HIM. ON THE MORNING of the last day he scrambled wearily up a rough slope grown to briars and found a few wild strawberries half hidden in the wiry grass. He lay on his stomach hitching himself along, searching with dirty fingers for the tiny globes of sweetness but somehow they did not ease the aching void in his belly.

He had had pockets full of stolen hardtack when he slipped out of the camp and now he turned all his pockets inside out searching for any lingering crumb. A bluejay, balancing on a blackberry briar, tilted and swayed and scolded at him. Buzzy lifted his head on his elbow and tossed a pebble at the bird.

"Git on away from here, you ole jayhawker you! All my guts cussin' one another, ain't no time to fool with you."

He knew exactly how far he had to go. With Billy Markland he had hunted this terrain over many times, with homemade bows and slingshots before Billy was old enough to be trusted with a gun. Buzzy remembered every rabbit and woodchuck hole, every quail cover on the ragged hillside. Just over the fence yonder he had run down a stray yearling calf for Boss Boone and ridden the critter back to the barn, heels drumming on its hard ribs. He should come in sight of the house soon. He should have been here yesterday, and he would have been, but for the riders.

Those riders last night had upset his plan of travel, his getting over the country in darkness and hiding by day. Suddenly, on the road he had heard the thud of trotting horses, the creak of saddles, and abruptly out of the night gloom they had appeared, looking to Buzzy's startled eyes more than twenty feet tall. There must have been a dozen of them although he was too frightened to count. They sat very tall in the saddle and had no faces at all, only white stuff that gave them a ghastly, ghostly look.

They had a Colored man with them, lying across a horse led by one of the riders. Every man in the group was robed, the white stuff hanging below his stirrups, and even the horses had white over their heads. Buzzy, struck cold with horror, had dived into the undergrowth and lay there breathless while the spectral cavalcade ambled by. But he had heard voices, and one voice pricked at a raw spot of dread within him, because it was the voice of Morgan Markland.

Lying quaking, pressed flat against the ground, Buzzy wondered what Mist' Morgan was into, riding in the dark all dressed up like a ha'nt? That it was bad business the limp body slung across a horse made plain, but Buzzy did not concern himself with the fate of that captured Negro, his own fear being too acute for concern about some other black man's trouble. He had stayed hidden till all sight and sound of the riders had disappeared, then on feet winged by terror he had fled till he reached this ground he knew, but dread still had a hold upon him.

It looked now as though things were not going to be too good at home. All the way from Georgia, running, hiding, pilfering, begging when he could among his own color, starving when all else failed, he had been blithely confident, fatuously dreaming about Miss Annie, his Miss Annie. Miss Annie, he had told himself, would be glad to see a boy come back to tote wood and wrestle the churn. With his easy gift for minimizing sinister possibilities he had put King and Morgan out of his mind, remembering only that Boss Boone was dead and Jack gone, and he had comforted himself that the wound that had killed Boss Boone was the fault of that old wore-out gun and not his own.

Now here was the possibility that Mist' Morgan might not be of a mind to let things lie that way. Buzzy decided to be cagey about showing himself till he learned just how things stood. There were empty houses in the quarters to hide in, and although his grandmother was dead he felt he could depend on Minerva to feed him, stealing out food under her apron, maybe slipping a word to Miss Annie that Buzzy was back.

His uniform jacket, buttonless and worn to rags, he had discarded before he crossed the mountains. His pants were thin and his shoe soles flapping. He looked like any one of hundreds of homeless freedmen and though he knew he was a deserter from the army, none of the military he had encountered had paid any attention to him. The danger lay from here on. The Markland men were the danger and unless he was shrewd and quick and ingratiating Buzzy suspected that he could end up flung across a horse with arms dangling limply like that poor boy he had seen last night. Definitely he wanted no men ghoulishly shrouded in white to be dealing that way with him.

Slipping from one thicket to another and along the overgrown fence, he got in sight of the barns and the clustering cabins, seeing no one. The place looked mighty run-down and poor-folksy and Boss Boone would have bellowed with rage to see so many thistles going to seed in the pastures. All the more reason his white folks needed help, if only they could be persuaded to accept it in peace.

There was hay ready to cut and corn sadly in need of hoeing, and although Buzzy acutely loathed the feel of a hoe in his hand, and a mowing blade could give a man a bad backache, no good farm should go to ruin because the Markland boys had never rightly learned how to work hard in the sun. Mist' Morgan, riding that good stud hoss around at night on some kind of low-down meanness, Boss Boone would have roared about that too.

There was a stone wall, swarmed over by a trumpet vine, and Buzzy drew back from that a little, knowing what lay beyond and shrinking from it. Then his eye caught the glimmer of newly turned earth among the Markland graves.

There were old stones, leaning a little, moss-greened, that marked where Boss Boone's people lay and there was a slab of wood already winter-grayed with words burned upon it, that would be Boss Boone himself. But who lay under that fairly fresh mound of soil? Pain surged up through Buzzy's veins, putting iron claws on his throat and stinging his eyes.

"Miss Annie!" he choked. "Miss Annie, she daid?"

Miss Annie could have died without Cap'n Billy's knowing. Buzzy resisted the impulse to go charging off down the slope, back to Georgia where Cap'n Billy was bereft, all unaware. Then prudence stayed him and he dropped behind the wall and lay still. To go back meant the guardhouse at least; they might even shoot him against a wall. He had talked himself out of that escapade in the winter but now he felt that his luck with the military had run out.

His misery was increased by the faint smell of frying meat drifting up the hill, but he knew that he had to wait for darkness, while his belly tore at him with wolf's teeth and growled so much it almost betrayed his hiding place. He saw a sassafras bush near the corner of the wall and worming toward it pulled off some of the greener leaves and chewed them, but their sweet spiciness made a sick feeling in his stomach. He dared not crawl across the slope to the spring. Then he heard the voices.

Two voices. Boone-boy's sharp, quick chatter—and what was Boone-boy doing here? Hadn't he gone off with Mist' Jack and Miss Sue, as the Captain had read in that letter? With Boone-boy came a woman that Buzzy did not know, a yellow-haired woman. Peering through the vine he pondered who she could be, till he remembered that Mist' King had married Mist' Carter Oliver's gal. Cap'n Billy had told him so.

"Look, Aunt Winnie," Boone-boy was babbling, "that little bush you planted for my papa has got green buds on it already."

Buzzy, creeping nearer, saw the yellow-haired woman bend and stir the soil on the new grave with a stick.

"Poor Jack," she said, aloud. "Poor, poor Jack."

Buzzy breathed in relief. Not Miss Annie, then, but Mist' Jack lay in that new grave. Mist' Jack must have gone off some place and come home to die.

"What we plant for the dead always grows, Boone-boy," Winnie was saying. "But I can't plant flowers for my papa. I don't even know where he's buried."

In his thankfulness that Miss Annie was not dead, Buzzy stirred a little and Boone-boy looked with alerted sharpness across the walled space. Then he went back to his solemn job of filling two vases with water from a slopping bucket he carried. "Just a ole rabbit," he remarked. "If I had me a gun I'd git him. I'll cut the stickers off these roses for you, Aunt Winnie."

"There will be enough for your grandpa too." She gathered up the branches of pink bloom. "We'll make them both pretty, then maybe your mama will come out to see them."

"She won't." Boone-boy opened a knife. "She says she can't bear to

[191]

look at graves. But it's kind of nice up here, I think, except in winter when these ole cedars get kind of spooky. Mammy Dory used to say ha'nts come out at night to sit on this wall. I know that ain't so. If my papa could come up out of there he wouldn't sit on no wall, he'd come down to the house and sit with us."

"Mammy Dory was only trying to scare you."

"Uncle Billy said she used to scare him and Buzzy. Buzzy got scared easy. He believed in ha'nts and conjures and things."

"I suppose he still gets scared when he remembers that he killed your grandfather," Winnie said grimly.

Buzzy flattened himself even lower. So they were still mad at him. Could it be that he must just go on being homeless and hungry the rest of his life? Then he pricked up his ears again.

"Aunt Winnie," Boone-boy was saying, "whyn't you ever go home? Don't you ever want to go home and live in your own house again?"

Winnie straightened and through a peephole Buzzy saw her face tighten and grow hard. "I haven't any home, Boone-boy. My home was sold. Your Uncle Billy bought it. It's your Uncle Billy's house now."

"He won't live there. He's a soldier. A Yankee soldier."

"He won't always be a soldier. Some time he'll be out of the army and be old and be glad to have a home. I don't want to live there ever again. I was never happy in that house, Boone-boy. I would have been glad if those guerrillas had burned it to the ground. I hate it!" Her voice rose sharply. "I hate the place. I'll always hate it!"

They went away then, the bucket bumping against Boone-boy's brown, thorn-scratched legs. Buzzy inched himself up after a little, measured the distance to the next screen of bushes, and ran for it. A new thought was boiling about in his head, already a little light from long hunger. Cap'n Billy had a house. That Oliver gal had said so. It was Cap'n Billy's house, he had bought it. Some day he would come back to it.

Buzzy did not wait for darkness. He fled, fleet as a fox across the north pasture, smashing down thistles and sedge grass with pounding shoes, snagging his shirt tail on briars and jerking angrily loose.

At the far gate where the narrow dirt road ran he slowed and dropped under a cedar tree to get his breath. The road was unchanged. Every rut and rock and leaning post he remembered. Even the tumble-bug, rolling his ball of mud determinedly along the washed-out track was an old friend. Once he and Billy had enjoyed the childishly cruel joke of turning a tumblebug around to see how far the stupid insect would push his mud ball before he discovered that he was headed away from his hole.

On this road Buzzy knew a Negro cabin where sometimes in the past he had been made welcome. He got up and trudged on till he came to the fence that enclosed it, relieved to see wood smoke feathering from the chimney and more smoke in the yard where the blackened washpot swung and steamed. He walked boldly in at the leaning gate.

"Howdy, Mis' Drusy," he croaked, dry-throated. "How you?"

The old woman turned, heavy stick in hand. "Who you?" she demanded. "Git away from hyar!"

"Mis' Drusy, you know me. I'm Rinda's boy. Mis' Dory my grandmaw. I'm Buzzy—just got home from the war."

"Mis' Dory daid. She about a hunnerd years old and she daid. You Mis' Dory's kin why ain't you down yonder? Marklands down yonder."

"I'm Union," Buzzy said. "They all Confederate down there. All but Mist' Billy. Cap'n Billy, he a big Union soldier, Union captain. I' been fightin' the war alongside Cap'n Billy."

Drusy flung a billet of wood on the fire. She was old now, Buzzy saw, shrunken and gray like an old, dead tree, with wisps of lank hair straggling about her ears, but her eyes still held a jetty fire.

"You don't look like no soldier to me," she sniffed. "All raggedy, ole tore-up shoes on your foots. Got no gun neither. You look like chain gang to me. Dirty chain-gang nigger. Dogs after you?"

"What dogs?"

"Chain-gang dogs what they catch 'em up with."

"I ain't no chain gang. Never see no chain gang," Buzzy said angrily. "I done walked all the way from Georgy and ain't et nothin' but ole sassafras and stuff, and I about daid." He let himself collapse dramatically on the ground against the cabin wall, rolling his eyes at her piteously. "You ain't got no li'l ole piece of bread layin' around, has you, Mis' Drusy?"

She shrugged a bony shoulder and the gnarled lines of her face softened. "You git yonder and wash!" she ordered. "I ain't feedin' no dirty shackle-hound somebody like you is. I ought to douse you in this here washpot, your head look full of boogers."

Buzzy flew. His flapping shoes impeded him and he kicked them off and flung them contemptuously into the fire. "Ole no-good army shoes! Wasn't never no good. Mis' Drusy, you a good Christian woman to feed a hungry boy."

"Shut your mouth, nigger, so you can wash 'round it!" she snapped.

She gave him cold bread and a dollop of greens, and he mopped the tin plate clean and captured every crumb that fell on his sodden breeches.

"How come you come back hyar?" Drusy inquired. "If you been in the Union army, ain't none of them Secesh Marklands goin' to let you stay on their place."

"I ain't staying on their place. I got me a place, Cap'n Billy Markland's place. I'm goin' there and wait for Cap'n Billy to git loose from that army."

"What place you got, you lyin' black boy?"

"Place up yonder. Mist' Carter Oliver's place."

"That place belong to Mist' King. He done married up with Mist' Carter Oliver's gal. Mist' King, he the meanest Markland there is. He run you off that place mighty quick."

"Mist' King ain't goin' to run me off no place. Cap'n Billy done bought that place. Miss Winnie, she says so. I heared her down yonder at the graveyard. We got us a home now, me and Cap'n Billy, if he come home."

"White men done tore that place all up. Been shootin' and killin' up there. If Mist' King don't git you, them Kluxers'll git you."

"What that?"

"Ku-Kluxers. Rides around at night. They done got plenty a'ready. White and nigger too. Run some off. Run my Lutie off. Tied her up and whup her and run her clear to Ohio," Drusy said.

"I seen 'em. They don't skeer me none."

"If they tie you up in the woods and flog you they skeer you. You keep quiet and lay low, boy. You always was too biggity and brash-mouth," she advised.

He had bragged manfully, but when he approached the old Oliver place at dusk it frightened him. The door was unlocked. He pushed it open and tiptoed into the empty, echoing hall. In the front parlor a bird flew out suddenly from the gaping mouth of the fireplace and Buzzy had to hunt a stubby broom and chase it out, birds being mighty bad luck in a house. Cautiously he explored, holding his breath whenever he entered a dusty, disordered room. There were candles and some lamps with a little oil left in them but he was afraid to make a light. Not yet, not till he had established his proprietary rights a bit more firmly in his own mind.

Some clothing was left strewn around the upper rooms and Buzzy pre-empted a fairly decent pair of trousers and a shirt, but all the boots left were too small. "Mist' Carter Oliver, he got too little foots," he said sadly.

His luck held through a hot May and June. No one came near to protest his occupancy or order him off the place. With the canniness of a pack rat he rummaged the buildings, finding buried silver and once a whole side of meat. This he traded to Drusy for the hot meals she fed him and sometimes he worked her garden patch or cut her wood. In the overgrown Oliver garden he dug some onions that had come up and under them he found a keg of soft soap. With this he cleaned the house and everything in it, sweeping and scouring, even washing the smoke-stained walls and windows.

"All fixed up now, if Cap'n Billy come home." He talked to himself as he worked, and he was muttering angrily, berating the squirrels who had built a nest in the library chimney when he found the money.

It came tumbling down in a shower of grass, sticks, ashes and soot, flat bundles of paper money tied with leather thongs and the whole wrapped in an old saddle blanket, squirrel-chewed and sooty.

Buzzy stared at it, snatched up a bundle and fingered the big, flat gray-and-yellow bills. "We rich!" he cried aloud. "Cap'n Billy and me, we rich!"

Some of the bills fell to pieces when he tried to brush away the ashes, but he hoarded every scrap and packed them again in a flat bundle that he could hide in his bed.

There had been words on the money and he could read a few of them.

"Bank of Mobile." A man's scribbled signature. Buzzy spelled it out laboriously.

"*Judah P. Benjamin*. Who he?"

• *Twenty Six* •

KING MARKLAND HAD BEEN TROUBLED ALL THAT SUMMER OF 1866 BY an uneasy awareness that he felt a growing concern, verging on tenderness, toward his younger brother's wife.

As the hot, golden days of September grew shorter he began to suspect that he was not hiding too well this feeling he had for Angela, nor the increasing irritation he harbored toward Morgan, whose neglect of his wife had become habitual.

It was not Winnie's small acid jabs that worried him. He was used to her prickly jealousies that even at times included his mother. Any lukewarm affection he had had for Winnie had cooled long since into a patient, occasionally exasperated, tolerance. He let her have her way, paid no attention when she tried peevishly to nag and dictate to him. It was Sue's occasional probing glances and frowns, and a nervous sort of concern he could see increasing in his mother's manner, that warned him that he was letting his interest in Angela become obvious and that sooner or later there would be trouble.

"You don't pull out chairs for me or take the water bucket out of my hands," Winnie complained. "Just because that little chit waves her eyelashes at you—"

"You're not having a baby," King snapped back. "Somebody has to take care of the poor girl."

"It's not your baby," Winnie slashed, creeping as far from him as she could in the big bed. "Let her husband take care for her."

"He'd better," growled King. "He'd better stay home from now on. There will be corn to gather too and I'm not doing that by myself."

"He won't stay home and you know it. Tearing around drinking and gambling and probably worse, night after night."

King made no answer. He knew now where Morgan went at night. He had found the robe and masks hidden in the oatbin and had bullied the truth out of Morgan. That tax collector in the county to the west who had been tied up and flogged and left bleeding in the woods all night. The carpetbagger who had seized the Lawson farm from its owner, taken from his bed and carried off stark naked, to be tossed off a horse fifteen miles from home.

"The Philistines," Morgan laughed in King's face. "We're educating them."

"You know what will happen if they catch you," King protested. "Brownlow will have you all hung and you've got a wife, and in a few weeks you'll have a child, to think about."

"You take care of Angela very nicely, dear brother." Morgan had flashed his saturnine grin as he said it and there had been a glint of dry malice in his eyes. How much he suspected King had no way of knowing. With Morgan you never knew. "You can be a godfather to the brat but it had better look like me."

"I'll smash your filthy mouth," King had blazed then but again Morgan had only laughed.

"Gallant lad! Don't be a dramatic fool. Do you think I don't know my little Angela? No matter anyway. All Marklands look alike."

"You stay close," warned King. "It could be any time now and she doesn't look very strong to me."

"October, if she counted right on her notched stick." Morgan pulled down his saddle.

"You're wearing that horse out too," fumed King. "A good stud—only decent piece of stock we've got left but you'll ride him till he's worthless."

"In a good cause. Besides, he likes it, don't you, boy? Know who's going to head up our organization? We're having an election over at Pulaski next week and we're electing old Nathan Bedford Forrest himself as head of the Klan. When this state is restored to decent law and order and all those dirty radicals put down you can thank us boys, Brother Kingman."

He rode off and King stalked back to the house, angry and unsatified.

Angela's body might be growing shapeless but her face kept its bright look of courage, a kind of forced gaiety that twisted King's vulnerable heart. Angela mothered Miss Annie, who had grown tremulous and a little vague from the impact of so much trouble and she petted and encouraged Sue who could not seem to rouse herself from a dull lethargy that the Marklands respected as grief, but which had a hidden anger at its root, a simmering resentment Sue nursed against the blows life had dealt her.

Sue had been born eager and had grown to womanhood thirsting for the one great love girls dream about, secretly hungry to be adored, ultimately restraining her volatile heart. Still, living was an emptiness when no man would ever look at her approvingly any more with the glow of desire in his eyes. She was a Markland widow as was Miss Annie, and to Sue all that lay ahead of her was an endless monotony of being patient and respectable and good.

She did not resent Angela as Winnie did, but Winnie resented every one now but Miss Annie and Boone-boy. Winnie had lately fixed a kind of pale affection on the boy and Angela reminded Sue that this was because Winnie needed a child of her own, which compassionate remark only made Sue jerk her dry, disdaining lips straighter. Sue was the one who saw through King, saw the change that softened his dark, impatient face when he looked at Angela, marked the way he tried to protect the girl from anything that could hurt or trouble her. Sue told herself that she pitied King; that she could be sorry even for Morgan if he were married to Winnie, though the Lord knew that arrogant, self-sufficient Morgan needed no one to be sorry for him.

The weather was hot and dry and Miss Annie worried as the water in the cisterns grew low. "We'll need plenty when we have a baby in the house," she fretted, watching the sky anxiously, frowning with disappointment when every promising cloud drifted away offering no rain.

With the one remaining mule and the sad old roan horse King gathered the harvest, bullying Morgan into helping now and then. Boone-boy, grown sober with responsibility, went about the smaller chores, and of late Winnie had begun to help him, carrying feed to the hens and gathering the eggs.

"The spring's getting low," King worried one night late in September. "May have to start driving the stock to the creek for water and the creek is low too."

"You could haul some barrels from the river," suggested his mother. "Your father had to do that in the dry fall of 'sixty-four when you were all in the army."

"Reckon I could do that tomorrow," King said. "You can come along, boy. You're big enough to tote a bucket."

"I did," said Boone-boy eagerly. "On the road to Texas."

He fell quiet, seeing a cloud move over his mother's face. Sue had walled in that tragic journey in her mind, locked a door against it. Even a chink entering that barrier brought bitter ice back into her eyes.

"We'll load the barrels tonight." King got up. "Where's Morgan?"

"Mist' Morgan already rode out that gate," Minerva said.

King muttered angrily, then relented, seeing Angela's distressed face. "Not your fault, gal," he said. "You were right. No way to hold a Markland if he wants to be loose."

She followed him out into the yard. "But it's different now, King!" she cried, catching at his sleeve. "It isn't just a few of them, it's—"

"I know," he laid a quick hand on her. "Don't talk," he warned. "Not even to me."

"What is it?" asked Winnie, coming up behind them. "What is it she musn't talk about?"

"Morgan's foolishness," replied King quickly. "We don't need any more trouble in this house. Come along, Boone-boy. We'll see how many barrels we can find that will hold water. We'd better decide, too, how many we can load without breaking that old wagon."

The boy trudged after him, but inside the barn he turned and closed the door. "Uncle King," he said in a conspiratorial whisper, "I know about Uncle Morgan. About that white stuff he hides in the oatbin."

Swiftly King laid a hand on the boy's lips. "Keep quiet," he ordered, low. "Don't talk about that to anybody or you could get your Uncle Morgan killed."

The boy struggled free. "I ain't told anybody. Nobody but you. I was hunting for the rifle, thought maybe I could shoot me a rabbit and I found that white thing. Uncle King," his voice sank portentously, "it's got eyeholes in it. And a horse thing with eyeholes too."

King pulled the boy down beside him on a handy box. "Listen, son, does your Uncle Morgan know you found that stuff?"

"No, sir, I never told anybody. I was too scared. Not till I just told you."

"Mind now, Boone-boy, nobody must know about this but you and me."

"And Uncle Morgan. Not even Aunt Angela?"

"Not even Aunt Angela." But King feared that Angela knew or suspected something already. Had Morgan been bragging, as he was prone to do when he had had too many drinks? Was Angela tormented with that dread too? Damn him, damn him, the hurt in King's heart snarled. "You see, boy," he went on quickly, "there are a lot of wicked people trying to make things bad now for all of us. Black people and white people."

"Like those men that killed my papa."

"Just like them. But the sheriffs and the judges and the soldiers are all on their side now."

"Uncle Billy too? He's a soldier."

"He has to be on their side because he's a Union soldier. And the Union is running everything and what they want is to make things mighty hard and mean for anybody who was for the South. So somebody has to fight the bad ones, but it has to be done in secret. No names ever spoken, no talking about it anywhere. The bad men have to be shown that they can't abuse and cheat us forever so your Uncle Morgan and some other men ride out at night and warn them to leave us alone." King finished his exposition and saw by the wan lantern light that the boy's eyes were glittering.

"I wish I was big enough to ride and have eyeholes. Why don't you ride, Uncle King?"

"Ride what?" countered his uncle.

"Yeah, that ole roan horse is pretty slow and got no wind. They'd catch you right off," conceded the boy. "I bet the mean people get plenty scared when they see all those riders coming, all looking like ha'nts."

"You keep mighty quiet about this now," warned King. "It's our secret. Come on and help me load these barrels. I reckon we can haul four of 'em without the wheels breaking down on us. Take us all day. That mule can't move off a slow crawl."

It was late when King slept, muscle weary, and dawn had not yet broken when there came a pounding at his door.

"King," Sue's voice called through the panels. "You'd better get up. Miss Annie says you'd better come downstairs. It's Angela."

King groaned, opening the door a crack. He was trembling nervously. "All right. I'll be right down."

"What is it?" Winnie sat up, lighted the candle, straightening the ribbon-trimmed cap she wore over her hair.

"It's Angela." King jabbed his arms into the sleeves of his shirt. "You go back to sleep. I'll have to go for a doctor, and none nearer than town."

"But it's Morgan's business to take care of his wife."

"He's gone." All the way to Pulaski, King suspected. "Go back to sleep." He pounded out, taking the stairs two steps at a time.

A bed had been put up in Miss Annie's room for Angela and as he crossed the hall a low moan came from that room. He almost collided with Minerva, scurrying with a steaming kettle. The door opened to admit her to a room full of lamplight and the sharp odor of camphor. His mother came out then, her face gray and tense.

"It's been since midnight," she said. "I called Sue down after an hour or two. I think we're going to need help, son. We never have had a birth on this place without Mammy Dory to do everything. I don't know what to do or Sue either, and Minerva is so scared she drops everything."

"I can get Doctor Grimes or that other Doctor Carson," said King. "That is, if I can persuade either of them to come out here. But you know how slow that old roan is, take at least eight hours to ride to town and back."

"I had four children," sighed Miss Annie, "but I just lay there and let Mammy Dory do for me. The same with Sue and Boone-boy. And of course Winnie—"

"Winnie would be less use than nobody," said King, brusquely. "I'll saddle the roan."

Minerva came out, twisting her hands in her apron. "She jest too little bitty," she whimpered, "or that young one too big. She done chawed her lips till they bleed."

"I'd give her some laudanum, but there isn't any left," sighed Miss Annie. "I used it all trying to help your father's suffering."

"There used to be women," began King, and saw Minerva's maroon eyes brighten.

"That Drusy—she been a midwife long time ago. Then she git to drinkin', now she got to wash and iron for a livin'."

"I know Drusy." King felt quick relief. "I'll fetch her first, then I'll ride to town. How about whisky, Mama? Morgan's got some hid in the stable."

"I don't know if she'd take it or not. Sometimes it makes them have fever."

"I'll git a knife," stated Minerva. "Put a knife under her bed to cut them pains."

The roan had only one gait, a lurching, bone-jarring trot. King was aching in every joint when he rode into Drusy's bare yard. The sun had barely risen but Drusy was out, scattering corn to her chickens. She gave him an unfriendly glare.

"I tole you to stay away from hyar, Mist' King Markland."

He swung down, he even took off his hat. "We've got trouble, Drusy," he said. "My mother needs you."

"Marklands always got trouble," she snorted. "Marklands, they ole trouble hisself."

"It's Morgan's wife. Her time's come. She's having a bad time and Miss Annie sent me to fetch you. She said you'd know what to do," King said, very humbly. "Fetch whatever you need, Drusy. You can ride behind me."

She shook the last grains from the pan. "Ain't said I'm comin'. Ain't done no birthin' in a long time." She was crisp.

"Listen, Drusy," King found himself pleading, a trifle startled at his own meekness. "Angela's no Markland. She's a nice little girl and she's young and suffering bad. You've got to come. We'll pay you."

"What you pay?" She was still aloof. "Some old fady dress or old pot got a leak in it? Confedrut money maybe? I ain't workin' for that."

"Morgan will pay you. Hard money. Get your things, Drusy. I've got to ride to town yet and fetch a doctor."

"If you git a doctor you don't need me. Mist' Morgan Markland, he can't pay me nothin'. He bad trouble. He one of them that run my Lutie plumb off to Ohio. I know what Mist' Morgan Markland do." She lifted a bony shoulder, started for the door.

"Drusy," King's voice cracked with desperation. "You've got to come. My mother will pay you. She's got hard money."

"She got five dollars?"

"Yes, she's got five dollars." King hoped that this was true. "Hurry up, Miss Annie needs help right away."

"Got to git me a clean dress," she argued, on the doorstep.

King sighed in relief, then let his breath out in a startled exclamation as a figure shambled in at the gate, a barefoot, ragamuffin shape carrying a hoe and a rusty bucket half full of sweet potatoes.

"Good God!" King exploded. "Buzzy!"

Buzzy squeaked, dropped the bucket and turned to run, sending the hoe flying.

"Come back here," ordered King.

Buzzy halted, scraping his bare feet in the dust. "Mist' King," he wailed, "I ain't done nothin'."

"What the devil are you doing here?"

"Been here all summer," said Drusy at the door. "I told him you'd run him off."

"Where's Billy?" demanded King.

Buzzy came a step nearer, braced, ready to duck or flee. "I don't know, Mist' King. I ain't seen Cap'n Billy since way last spring. Not since us down yonder in Georgy."

"He stayin' at that place up yonder. Oliver place," put in Drusy. "He keep tellin' me Mist' Billy Markland own that place. He jest a lyin' no-good yellow boy. I told him you run him off if you find out."

"Mist' Billy do so own that place!" persisted Buzzy. "Miss Winnie, she say so. I heared her. Down yonder at the graveyard. Miss Winnie say Cap'n Billy buy that place and she ain't goin' back there no more." Buzzy was almost tearful.

King frowned at him uncertainly. "You've been hiding up there ever since you shot my father?"

"No, suh, Mist' King. I' been in the army till li'l while back. Mist' King, it wasn't no way my fault Boss Boone git shot. Mist' Morgan come at me and Boss Boone come at me and I hold that ole gun too tight and it go off. I like to die when I see Boss Boone git shot." Tears were pouring down the boy's face now. "You goin' run me off, Mist' King? You goin' shoot me?"

"I ought to shoot you. I ought to break your worthless neck."

Morgan would do it, swiftly, unthinkingly, savage for sudden vengeance, disdaining consequences. And why had he himself gone so suddenly soft, King was wondering angrily? The Marklands were violent men. He opened and closed his hands, panting, trying to drag forth the fury that should be consuming him. What was it that weakened him, made him aware of a kind of compassion for this shivering creature, this boy who had been his father's slave?

Something had softened him. He felt a kind of disgust for this softness, and a shamed sort of tenderness too, knowing in secret that it was the same softness that lay in a girl's heart-shaped face.

"Miss Winnie tell you you could stay up there at that place?" He bridged the silence awkwardly.

Buzzy was swift to sense advantage. This was reprieve. Mist' King stood there itching to do him violence and somehow could not. He beamed.

"No, suh!" he cried eagerly. "I'm hidin' down at the graveyard and she there and she tell Boone-boy that place b'long to Cap'n Billy, so I git along up there. I clean it all up good, waitin' for Cap'n Billy to come home. You goin' run me off, Mist' King?"

King relieved the embarrassment of his own indecision by yelling at Drusy. "Get a move on will you, Drusy? There's a girl down there needs help mighty bad."

Drusy shrugged and disappeared into the cabin and Buzzy moved nearer, cautiously, bending to pick up the scattered potatoes, to retrieve the hoe. "I tends Mis' Drusy's garden," he explained. "She let me eat here some. What you fixin' to do with me, Mist' King?"

A sudden rash impulse moved King. There was danger. There was Morgan, the unpredictable. He shrugged this aside, hoping that in this emergency he could handle Morgan.

"Know what I'm going to do with you?" he demanded, grimly. "I'm going to send you down home right now. They need help down there. Miss Annie needs help. I've got to ride to town. You get on down there and do whatever Miss Annie tells you to do."

Buzzy's eyes gleamed and a grin split his face. Then it darkened again. "Mist' Morgan come, he shoot me!"

"Morgan's not there now. If he comes, you lay low till I talk him round. Get going. Nobody's had time to milk or fetch in wood or—"

Buzzy bumped down the bucket, cracked his heels together. "Mist' King, I be there before you is," he yelled and was gone like a wisp of yellow smoke.

On the way, pounding hard heels on the dry, crackling sod of the pastures, Buzzy remembered about the money. His conscience nagged him. Probably it was Miss Winnie's money. Maybe he ought to tell Miss Winnie about it, but what if she took the money and bought the place away from Cap'n Billy? Then they would have no home again.

He decided to say nothing about the money till Cap'n Billy came back. And straightway, because so much else was happening, he forgot all about it.

· *Twenty Seven* ·

MORGAN MARKLAND'S DAUGHTER WAS THREE DAYS OLD WHEN HER FATHER returned.

Angela lay white and spent, her eyes sunk in purple shadows, but she could smile again.

"I'm glad she's a girl," she said. "I'm going to name her for her grandmother. She's going to be a second Annie Lou Markland."

Miss Annie glowed happily although she was so exhausted she tottered when she walked and caught herself weeping for no reason at all. She and Sue agreed with the doctor, who had finally arrived at the last moment, that Angela had had a mighty hard time, but to Winnie, who had crept like a wraith through the house, the two days had been sheer horror.

"If that's the way people are born there shouldn't be any more of them, ever," she declared, tearfully.

King felt wrung-out and heart-torn too, but he had had to keep a stoic face and guard against any emotional outburst that could betray the torturing anxieties he suffered. He looked at the baby, when at last Minerva put her on display robed in yards of white stuff that trailed almost to the floor, and poked at her fat, creased wrist and an ear like a shell under a fringe of black hair. Another Markland. Same proud brows, same promise of an aggressive nose. In a few years this Annie Lou Markland would grow into a haughty beauty.

"Lord, what a houseful of women I've got on my hands!" King had laughed with labored lightness. Then, worn by his long vigil, he dropped on the old couch in the front room and fell instantly asleep.

On the third night the house was very still, the lamp burned low and the old clock in the hall had struck one when there was the soft sound of a horse outside and the front door was cautiously opened.

Buzzy, lying awake in his grandmother's cabin, heard the horse and scrambled out of bed, grabbing in the dark for his breeches. Dread made his fingers stiff and clamped his throat with iron fingers. Mist' Morgan! Mist' Morgan had come back.

After five blissful days of being at home, petted and scolded by Miss Annie, fed by Minerva, everybody acting like he'd never been gone at all, now Mist' Morgan had to come busting back and Buzzy would have to hide out again. And today was the day he was to help Mist' King and Boone-boy haul water from the river. Buzzy scrabbled into a shirt, crouching low against a crack in the wall, waiting to hear the creak of the stable door that meant that Morgan was putting up his horse. But the door did not creak.

King was slow to waken. Morgan was shaking him when at last King dragged himself up from the dark well of exhausted slumber into which he had sunk.

"What the—" he mumbled, dragging his eyes open.

"Keep still," hissed Morgan. "Don't wake anybody. Get up and help me. I've got to get away."

"What?" King's feet hit the floor with a thud.

"They're after me," Morgan rasped. "Hurry up. I've got to be on my way. They laid for us at the county line, some troops and some of Jeff Nichols' deputies. Surrounded three of us, riding home with those damn robes bundled up on our saddles. I shot one. I've got to get away. No use to hide. Nichols will search this place. I wasn't masked. Some of them knew me."

"Why the devil did you come home then?" demanded King. "You knew they'd follow you—tear up the place. We've got a sick woman here, your wife. You've got a new daughter. Or don't you give a damn about that either?"

"So she had a girl, did she?" Morgan lifted a sardonic eyebrow. "Well, that's what she wanted. Are they all right?"

"She had a bad time. Doctor said it was a wonder she pulled through. There's been no rest in this house since Monday. Where do you plan to go?" King was on his feet, listening tensely.

"They're far behind me, but I've got to hurry. I want food and all the money you can get together. A blanket and another shirt or two. For God's sake, King, move!" Morgan cried. "I don't know where I'm going. Not Texas—California maybe." He fairly pushed King out to the kitchen where he quickly gathered up all the food available and stuffed it into a saddlebag. "Any coffee left? Wrap some up for me, some salt and flour too. Dammit, I bought most of this stuff, I'm entitled to it!"

"You're leaving—going God knows where, not telling her goodbye or Miss Annie either?" King was incredulous.

"You tell them for me. No time to lose." Morgan took down the old blue sugar bowl where Miss Annie kept her little hoard of money, turned it upside down, grumbled as a few coins fell out. "She ought to have more money than that."

"She had to pay the doctor and Drusy. You weren't here to take care of your own family," growled King. "Now they'll come pounding in here, frightening everybody, making trouble for all of us."

"They probably won't get here till daylight. They'll come by the road. I took off across the fields. I'll leave the same way. Get the other stuff for me and put out that light. Any more money anywhere?"

"Where would I get money?"

Five minutes later Morgan was gone, like a shadow into the pitch darkness, and Buzzy crouching in the corner heard him go. Somebody after Mist' Morgan, sure. Won't never catch him.

King, sitting in the dark listening, was thinking the same thing. Union cavalry had never been able to catch Morgan. The Markland men! Angela had said she wanted no more of them. They belonged to a lost race now, the gallant, strutting, insolent, dangerous young blades who had manned the jaunty cavalry regiments in the war and who now, if they had come home at all, could find no place in life for themselves. Four Markland men, and of them only he was left, sitting alone and listening tautly for the pounding hoofs of his brother's pursuers.

Morgan had killed a man, so he said. But how many had they all killed in the hysterical passion of that fratricidal war? How many dead to be counted against four Markland men? They should stink of death, all of them, reek of it till women turned from them in horror. And no ending—no ending. Morgan would be a marked and hunted man from now on, if ever he set foot on home soil again. He could endanger them all. And Buzzy. Buzzy was a deserter, King knew. If the troops came he would have to hide Buzzy.

Abruptly, in a kind of sick revulsion, he got up and lighted the lamp. A rifle was hidden in the cupboard by the chimney where it had lain since Sue brought it back from Mississippi. King took it out, slid the bolt, took out the load and dropped it into a vase where three limp peacock feathers drooped. Then savagely he broke the weapon across his knee. Now if angry men came he would not be tempted to use it. An end to killing! An end to blood! There had been too much of that already.

In the kitchen he was removing every trace of Morgan's hasty departure when a soft tap sounded on the door. He opened it a guarded crack and heard nervous breathing and a whisper.

"Mist' King?"

He pulled Buzzy quickly inside. "Go back to bed," he ordered. "You didn't hear anything, understand? You haven't heard a thing."

"Mist' Morgan, he—"

"He's gone and you didn't hear him come, you didn't hear him go. Got that through your head?"

"Yes, suh, I ain't heard nothin'." Buzzy's teeth were chattering. "Who after him, Mist' King?"

"We don't know. We don't know anything. He didn't come here. We haven't seen him. We don't know where he went, remember."

"No, suh, Mist' King, I ain't seen Mist' Morgan since Boss Boone git shot." No lie, Buzzy's limber conscience assured him. He hadn't seen Morgan on the road that dark night. He had seen a ghostly shape and heard a voice, that was all.

"Stick to it. And don't wall your eyes and blubber your lips so the sheriff thinks you're lying and beats the truth out of you."

"Yes, suh."

"Reckon Minerva heard him?" King asked anxiously.

"If she do, she ain't talkin' no more than me. You want me to pass her the word?"

"I'll warn Minerva if there's any need. Get gone now and lay low."

"Yes, suh." Buzzy flew on soundless feet. But as he burrowed into his musty tick he felt puzzled. This here now Mist' King, he sure was changed. Mist' King was acting like a different man. Not yelling or cussing nobody, speaking soft and firm like Miss Annie. Something had happened to Mist' King to take the big mad out of him. Maybe that little ole gal Miss Angela got had sweetened up Mist' King. Buzzy approved of Miss Angela although she had disappointed him by marrying Morgan after all the trouble he'd had, toting notes for Cap'n Billy. Mist' Morgan, he decided, he takes what he wants and makes no never mind for nobody. Now, likely, he'd get caught up in this meanness, whatever it was, and get hung.

King announced very early that there would be no water barrels hauled to the river that day. Boone-boy, who had piled out of bed before day ready for the expedition, was indignant and disappointed and voiced his feelings loudly to Buzzy.

"Uncle King says he's got to grease the wagon. What you keep looking off down the road and listening all the time for, Buzzy? I know.

You're scared Uncle Morgan will come home and shoot you. You're scared, Buzzy, I can tell."

Buzzy, maneuvering the new calf's head into a bucket by the ears, wore a queer, quiet face. "Anybody gets skeert of bein' shot."

"I wouldn't let Uncle Morgan shoot you. I'd get me that ole gun of Grampa's out of the oats and make him leave you alone."

"Where at a gun?" Buzzy showed the whites of his eyes.

"I know where it's at. Big ole gun that'll kick you clean across this lot. Grampa killed bears with it. Killed a man too. Blew his head plumb off."

"You stay away from that ole gun!" ordered Buzzy sharply. "We got enough troubles."

"That little ole baby Aunt Angela got is sure a trouble," agreed the boy. "Bawling all the time, and somebody got to rock her. Grandma makes a fuss every time there's a little bitty noise. Girl baby too. Been a boy he might be some good but girls ain't worth nothin'."

But to King Markland, harried and taut on that hot windy day, the second Annie Lou was worth her weight in diamonds. She kept the women occupied, even Minerva, so that there were no questions for which he had no answers. The tormented unease was his alone, his and Buzzy's. Buzzy, wearing a withdrawn face, put the jack under the wagon wheel without being told and stood by ready with the paddle laden with black grease from the bucket. When Boone-boy ran back to the house at his mother's call, Buzzy bent low and murmured, "Reckon they done catch him already, Mist' King? They'd been ridin' in here long time ago if they ain't catch him up yet."

"We'll just have to wait, Buzzy. And quit watching that road. You'll get the women suspicious."

"Reckon if they catch him they just hang him, Mist' King. Mist' King, you turnin' that hub nut backwards! You let me do that."

"No, I've got to keep busy. I'll have to tell the women sometime before long. Miss Annie will miss her little bit of money."

"She bound to think I stole it," worried Buzzy. "Minerva already yellin' at me, I steal all her bread. I ain't said nothin'."

"Could be they've picked up his trail but haven't caught him. He might head north into Kentucky," King said dully.

"That horse mighty fast. Mist' Morgan smart too. They ain't goin' to catch him easy."

It was Sue who faced King later that day. She followed him out to the pasture fence, calling after him. He turned, halter in hand, and from the look on her face he knew that now there could be no more evasion.

She came to stand beside him. "Something's wrong, isn't it, King? It's Morgan. He should have come home long since. Something went wrong, it's written all over your face."

"I hope Miss Annie hasn't seen it in my face. Or Angela," he said lamely. "Your eyes are too sharp, Sue."

"Miss Annie's all taken up with the baby, but Angela's worried. Her eyes look mighty haunted."

King felt his burden lift a little. This was Sue and Sue was fearless, she had good sense. She would help—with his mother, with Morgan's wife. He laid his arms wearily along the fence and she put a hand on his elbow.

"Whatever it is, don't try to carry it alone," she said. "If it's bad news I've borne bad news before."

"Morgan was here last night. They were after him. He shot a man."

"Some brawl?"

"No, no brawl. It was this organization, this thing the hot-heads have got together that they call the Klan. Riders—masked riders, with General Forrest at the head of it. Masked men riding at night to frighten Nigras and punish radicals and carpetbaggers. Morgan had been at a meeting in Pulaski and on the way back a sheriff's gang jumped some of them. They had their robes with them. Brownlow has threatened to hang any man caught with a robe, so Morgan shot his way out and came here. I helped him pack some stuff. He left on the run and God knows when he'll come back," King croaked, relieved that now it was out.

"I missed that blanket from the foot of his bed. It has been folded there all summer. And Minerva was fussing at Buzzy for eating all her cold bread."

"I thought they'd follow him here. I've been waiting all day for them to come riding in. It has been hell—trying to think what I'd tell Angela and Miss Annie."

"But they haven't come so you think they caught him?" she asked.

"I don't know what to think. I thought they'd come anyway. They'd know he had help. They might take me too for helping him escape. But still they haven't come."

Sue looked off across the sun-seared pasture where grazed the one colt left of all the proud Markland horses.

"You didn't help him, King," she said then. "If they come, you didn't even see Morgan. I helped him."

"Sue, you can't do that!"

"I will do it. They won't arrest a woman. I'll swear that you and everybody else were sound asleep—that I didn't know he was wanted by the law. I'll make them believe me, and you keep quiet, you hear?"

"I won't let you do it." He laid an arm around her shoulders. They were shaking a little and her throat quivered.

"You can't stop me. If you try I'll swear you are lying. I will. What could they do—Miss Annie, those helpless women and children, if they took you away? It can't happen. What would become of all of us if you were taken?"

"Save that question for Jeff Nichols. I can't answer it. I can only go on wondering what happened to Morgan," King said.

Her face changed again, drew quickly into a mask of bitterness. "Whatever happens, he deserves it! That little baby—he didn't even see her. He didn't even tell his wife he was going, or where. Nor the mother who has always adored him so much. I can't care what happens to Morgan, King."

"We'll have to tell Angela something, but let's put it off as long as we can and let her get a little stronger. I'm glad you're with me, Sue. It was tough going it alone."

She stood for a little, still looking far off, her slim body as taut as a bowstring, her chin up. Then she faced him abruptly.

"King, you don't ever have to carry it alone. You have a brother. There's Billy. He'll be out of the army this winter. He said as much in that letter he wrote to Winnie. King, you know in your heart that Billy was only trying to help when he took title to Winnie's place. The war's over. Why keep all the stubborn, stupid antagonisms alive?"

"He can have the damn place," growled King. "I told him so."

"Tell him to come home then and take it over and lift some of this load you're carrying. Even if Morgan comes back—and how can he if he shot somebody and has that to answer for?—you know Morgan. Not to be depended upon, ever. More of a liability than a help. If he had any sense or any feeling of responsibility would he have taken all these silly risks, just for the fun of it, just for showing what a reckless hellion he is? That's all it's ever been with Morgan and you know it. That's all the war meant to him, brash Morgan Markland showing off, galloping around on a fast horse, quick with a gun."

"He still has a gun. Lord knows where he got it," worried King.

"You write to Billy, King. Tell him to come home," she urged.

"No, that's for Miss Annie to do. He wouldn't come if I wrote."

"He saved your life once. You don't like remembering that, do you?" she countered acridly.

"I remember. Sue, you'll have to tell Angela something. Just tell her he had to leave. She needn't know any more now," he said.

"If he doesn't come back she'll know I was lying. If I tell her anything," she insisted, "it will be the truth. It will be bitter but it will be kinder that way."

"I suppose you're right." He pulled himself up to the top rail, swung over the fence. "I'm going to catch that colt. He ought to be broken to ride. You could talk to Miss Annie about Billy—if she wants to write to him—"

"She does write. She hides down in the loom house and writes long letters, but she never gets a chance to mail any of them. She's afraid of you, King. She wouldn't dare ask you to mail a letter to Billy."

"Afraid of me?" He stopped still, frowning. "Miss Annie's not afraid of anybody. She's told us all off plenty of times."

"I reckon she thinks you'd never mail a letter to him, King," she said soberly. "You're the one who's afraid. Afraid of being kind, of being generous and gentle. You think it would be weakness. It never occurred to you, it never occurred to your father or Jack—or Morgan either, for that matter—that there can be strength in kindness. In trying to understand other people, helping other people, forgiving their weaknesses. For you, for all the Markland men, strength has always meant conquering something, beating down whatever stood in your way. All but Billy. Billy was never like that. That's why you could never understand Billy."

He slid the halter rope absently through his fingers, looking a trifle stunned. "Why—I do know how to be kind," he protested. "Look at the Olivers. I married her, didn't I? And what did I get? A dead and alive kind of life, that would drive most men crazy."

"That wasn't kindness. That was just another Markland trick. Showing off. You never loved her. You don't even hate her. What does she have from you? Less than nothing. No understanding, mighty little patience, no tenderness at all. A woman can starve on that."

"She doesn't want anything from me, only to be let alone," he said bitterly. "Sue, you could write to Billy. You write and I'll ride in and mail the letter."

But in the end it was King who had to write the letter.

Three weeks went by and inevitably Miss Annie and Angela had to be told. Between Sue and King they softened the blow for Angela as much as they could. Morgan had had to leave the country suddenly on account of a political trouble. When he found a place where he could start over he would send for her and the baby. Miss Annie's optimism came to the fore immediately.

"Likely he's already in California. He'll send for his family as soon as he can. Nothing bad will happen to Morgan. They say California is a good place, people are getting rich there."

Sue was stiffly silent. Where Morgan was concerned, she was thinking, what was bad happened to other, innocent people.

Miss Annie was obdurate however about writing to Billy.

"You drove him away, you Markland men," she cried. "Now you can get him back. You demeaned him, everything he tried to do, even saving my home for me. You can write the letter yourself, Mister Kingman Markland. Now that you need your brother you can be humble for once and ask him to come home. And you can do it right now. I'll make some fresh ink. Buzzy!" She raised her voice. "Fetch me some fresh pokeberries. Right now."

• *Twenty Eight* •

WILLIAM MARKLAND WAS NOT YET TWENTY-SEVEN YEARS OLD, BUT already there were touches of silver in the dark wings of hair that swept back from his temples. Now that his wounded knee had finally stiffened he walked with a hitch and a limp but he could still sit tall in the saddle.

Smoke was drifting warm and gray from the chimney of the old Oliver house as he rode up the brushy hill on a bleak March afternoon. Buzzy would have a fire roaring and in the kitchen there would be a rabbit stew simmering. Buzzy spent his time these wet chilly days contriving rabbit traps. "I figure to plant us some garden sass come spring and ain't havin' all my truck et up by hoppin' tails."

As he rounded the last clump of cedars William saw an old roan horse hitched to the Markland buggy in front of the house. Obviously his mother and Sue had come visiting. William had tried to persuade his mother and Sue to come and live with him now that he had a house, but Miss Annie refused to leave her home and William understood the impropriety of suggesting that Sue should come without her.

On his occasional visits to the home place he saw Angela, but she was withdrawn and aloof, whether from defensiveness or resentment he did not know. She did not relent, no matter how casually friendly his approach and she was obviously not going to allow William to forget that however shabbily Morgan had treated her she was still his wife.

"She's always planning how she'll travel with the baby when he sends for her," Sue told William. "It's pitiful when there hasn't been a word from him in months."

William smiled to himself as he tied The Count to the porch. Undoubtedly, Sue and Miss Annie would be in the house looking over his shirts, scrubbing out cupboards and scolding amiably about the way two old bachelors kept house. As he mounted the steps he expected the door to crash open and Boone-boy to come bounding out, but when he entered it was King who stood waiting in muddy boots and their father's old sheepskin-lined coat.

"Looks like snow," King said without further greeting. "I made a fire and waited for you. Buzzy told 'Nerva last night you'd gone into town."

William moved gratefully to the blaze. "This weather makes my game leg ache. Sit down, King. Buzzy," he shouted, "put up my horse."

Buzzy came pelting through the hall, pulling on a shabby coat that had once been worn by stylish young Carter Oliver the Third. "Yes, suh, Cap'n. Ain't no more corn, Cap'n."

"He'll do on hay but wet it down, you hear?" William stood so near to the fire that his damp clothing began to steam. "After six years in cold barracks and leaky tents I'm just beginning to get warm again. There's a little whisky somewhere. I could do with a drink. King, how about you?"

"It'll help out the weather, I reckon." King was always a bit stiff and self-conscious around his brother although he struggled to relax.

They got out the bottle in silence, poured two glasses and pulled chairs closer to the fire.

"Thought I'd come up and see if you'd heard anything in town," King said, after a little. "I thought maybe somebody might talk to you."

William jabbed at a smoking log with the poker. "She's still waiting and hoping, is she?" he asked. "You've had no news, I suppose. You ever hear what happened that night?"

"I'm a Confederate veteran." King's voice rasped a little. "I've been in town only once since he left. That was when I went in to mail that letter to you in October. I didn't tarry then. I thought like enough they'd be after me too for helping him get away, so I didn't talk to anybody or ask any questions. All I heard was some sour-faced Republicans muttering behind my back."

William relaxed, the whisky warming him. He had come back in February and for a time he had feared that the stiff formality between himself and King would never be eased, although the women had been friendly enough and Sue and his mother were both obviously happy to see him again. But now the guarded look that King had worn for weeks was beginning to soften on his face.

"I got the story in bits and pieces," William began presently. "Morgan had friends in town. A lot of people liked him, he was easy and never what you could call passionately Confederate like the rest of you. Old Squire Armitage seemed to be actually fond of him. He married Morgan and Angela. Lately the Squire has had a shabby deal from some of the radicals in power and he was willing to talk. I'd played poker with him a time or two when we were stationed here and he seemed to trust me, so he talked and laughed about what went on the night Jeff Nichols and some of his gang set out to capture Morgan."

"I've been uneasy all winter, waiting for Nichols to come down on me like a ton of bricks." King drained his glass. "The way he came crashing in down home when they took Pa and Jack. God, Billy, can you realize that they're both gone now? Hard for me to make myself believe it sometimes. All right if I have another? This has been a hard winter."

"Help yourself. But lock that cupboard and bring me the key. I've got a moral responsibility to keep Buzzy out of trouble."

"How are you going to keep the army from nabbing him? That worried me some after he came home."

"I arranged for his dishonorable discharge before I gave up my commission. He doesn't know it, it would hurt his pride, but they could never hold him unless they locked him up indefinitely. Most of the Negro boys we had were homesick and undependable, more of a liability to the service than a help."

"Get on with your story," urged King. "I have to get home before dark."

"Well, when Jeff and his crowd caught Morgan and those other lads that night, Morgan, the hot-headed fool, started shooting and got away. Some trooper who was with the posse got winged in the shoulder but nobody was killed," William said.

"Miss Annie would be glad to hear that. She likes to think we all went bravely through a war without killing anybody."

"If we had been in the same areas we might have killed each other," remarked William. "And if Morgan hadn't gone charging off that night, he would have been rescued. About fifty of them, all masked, caught up with Jeff's posse, overpowered them, roped them up and took them all back to town where they locked them all up in the jail. Then, so the Squire says, they rode round and round that jail till nearly noon, silent and solemn as a parade of ghosts and nobody dared molest them. Had every Negro in town scared green and hiding under a bed. Some troopers rode the country for a while hunting Morgan and the others but they didn't find them."

"If he still believes he killed a man he won't come back," said King. "Not for years anyway."

"Nichols, I heard, is scared and plenty meek. They'll throw him out next election, so the Squire thinks. A sheriff who gets laughed at is a liability. How did it happen that you stayed clear of the Klan business, King?" William asked.

"After Jack got killed I was alone. No depending on Morgan for anything. I had four women and two young ones on my hands," King reminded his brother.

"So you decided to bury the past along with Abe Lincoln and old Stonewall and Beauty Stuart—there was a soldier, King. He gave us more trouble than all the rest of your army put together. And your man Forrest operated about as savagely down in this part of the country, I've heard."

"He's heading up this Klan thing now. I can't think that's the answer," admitted King.

"Violence will never be an answer." William got to his feet. "So," he smiled, "you decided to let me come home. Still think it was a weak thing to do? And that I was doing something weak and expedient to come?"

King rose too, stood almost a head taller than his brother. "I won't deny that there was a time when I hated your guts," he said quietly. "And for about a month when Pa was dying Morgan was hunting you to shoot you dead. I don't know—it was Sue, I reckon, who made me see it was kind of stupid. After all, you believed in what you did and so did I. Events proved my belief was doomed not to win. There was mighty little left—only that we were all still Marklands. Anyway you had a legal right to come, Billy."

"I'm making it definitely legal, King. That was my principal reason for going to town today. I'm buying this place from Winnie. The Squire is drawing up the papers. She agreed to the arrangement when I talked to her Sunday."

"You didn't have to do that. I told her so."

"I wanted to do it. May take me years to pay her for it but I'll pay. And Winnie can take anything out of this house she wants."

"I've never been able to get her to come since those guerrillas were here," said King. "The place scares her to death for some reason. But this"—he fumbled for words—"is mighty decent of you, Billy. After—"

William smiled again. "The last of the Marklands. You and I. Shall we let the war end, for the Marklands?"

King drew a relieved breath. Amenities did not come easy for him. He shifted quickly to the practical where he felt secure.

"Billy, I've been thinking. This is horse country. Once Pa had some of the best horses ever raised in Tennessee. You've still got The Count. He's going on for eight now but he was old Baron's grandson, last of a good bloodline. If we could get hold of a couple of mares—"

"Know where we can find any?" interrupted William, glad of the commonplace again, edging away from emotion.

"Billy, realize this—I'm at a disadvantage. You boys are top dog now. I'm a damned Rebel, ripe to be skinned, a credit to the man who cheats me." Anger flicked scarlet for an instant over King's face. "I've got one good colt. Almost three years old now. All that's left of old Duke's strain. I'll sell or trade him but if I try it I'll be robbed and no recourse. You'll have to handle any deal, and maybe he'll bring enough to buy some mares and we'll be back in the horse business."

"I'll make some inquiries around," said William. "You'd better stay and eat. Buzzy's got a good stew cooking from the smell of it."

"Sorry, got to hurry. It's almost dark. Sue will be out trying to do all the chores with nobody to help her but Boone-boy. That's one grand gal, Sue."

"You should have married her, King. You could have had Sue once," William reminded him.

"I know. My own foolishness. Now—" he did not finish. "You could marry Sue, Billy," he said abruptly.

William stared, startled. "Me?"

"Why not? She's been a widow almost a year now." King hesitated briefly, then held out his hand. William took it and pressed it hard. "The last surrender," said King sadly, then shrugged his shoulders and strode out.

William walked back to the kitchen. Buzzy was waiting there, big-eyed with intention.

"Cap'n," he began breathlessly. "You want to buy some horses, I know where there's a lot of money!"

"Been listening at keyholes, have you? Where's any lot of money?"

"You wait. I'll show you." Buzzy pounded up the stairs, came thundering down again with a soiled and sooty bundle. "Look, Cap'n! I done found it up the chimney in that li'l room where the old books is."

"And you've been hiding it all this time, knowing that it was Miss Winnie's money?" demanded William.

"Yes, suh. I knows. I just forgit when you come home. Reckon Miss Winnie give me some for findin' it, Cap'n?"

William fingered the grimy bills sadly. He counted one pack and estimated the value of the others. At least fifty thousand dollars! Poor defrauded Winnie! Poor deluded South!

"It's nobody's money, Buzzy," he said soberly. "True, it was good money once. Back in 'sixty-three, maybe, when that poor old man probably exchanged all he had for it. He must have given good gold coin for it. It's rebel money, Buzzy. You couldn't buy a forkful of hay with it, much less a horse."

"Rebel money? Ain't no good at all, Cap'n?" Buzzy's face was a stark mask of woe.

"No good at all. Worse than no good. In this state with things as they are it's risky to own it, much less to spend it. And you couldn't spend it. Nobody would give you a rusty pin for all there is here."

"What I do with it? All that there wouldn't even buy one ole horse, Cap'n?"

"Not even a dead horse, Buzzy. It's filthy now. Toss it into the fire. It's tragic that Miss Winnie hasn't got what that money cost her grandfather. She could have bought half this county now if she had it and all the horses to be found anywhere. All wasted as so much was wasted."

Buzzy went sadly to where the log fire still burned hot in the fireplace and heaved the dusty bundle into the flames. It smoldered slowly.

"Don't even burn good!" he grumbled. "That ole Judah man he make mighty sorry money."

• *Twenty Nine* •

ALL THROUGH THAT LUSH AND BURGEONING SPRING WILLIAM WAS haunted and a little troubled by King's casual, half-joking remark about his marrying Sue.

When Sue had married into the Markland family, a volatile spark of a redhead at seventeen, William had indulgently regarded his brother's wife as a restless little coquette, married too young, but he had watched her settle down and grow in strength and self-discipline. That her self-control may have masked a cheated sort of loneliness had never occurred to him until now.

Looking back over the years before the war William could see now that Jack had been possessive, with quick angers and an impatient attitude, but had Jack ever really been the lover Sue's hungry heart yearned for? That she had been entirely faithful, William was certain.

Trouble had brought out the strength in Sue, and along with it a refining and inflexible goodness that had grown into a power upon which all the Marklands depended. William caught himself watching her, whenever he returned to the home place, seeing his mother's dependence upon Sue, the way King relied upon her, her quiet ignoring of Winnie's spoiled temperament and tearful moods, her gentle understanding with Angela. In Sue's dark time of trouble it had been Angela's gentle patience that had brought Sue out of her dour broodings, and now Sue strove to reinforce Miss Annie's continuing determination to await cheerfully a reunion with Morgan about which William himself was dubious.

Angela had grown stronger but her courage and gaiety had not returned. William suspected often when he saw her that Angela had spent a tearful night, but because she was so continually on guard against him he kept his attitude casual and remote. It was Boone-boy who finally brought matters to a climax in William's mind.

Boone-boy had attached himself to Buzzy in the weeks before William's return. Now as the days lengthened in June Boone-boy was continually running away from the Markland place to come flying barefoot across the fields. He followed William and Buzzy over the pastures where the two new mares grazed, followed watchfully by The Count. He even shouldered a hoe to help chop out thistles and sprouts before they had a chance to bloom.

Buzzy grumbled at field work but Boone-boy was a dogged hand, helping Buzzy spread lime and paris green on his young plants in the garden patch, dropping corn in the furrows that King and William turned with the slow mule and the old roan horse. He helped Buzzy rig his traps and bait a ragged piece of undergrowth with old wheat they scraped out of the bottom of a bin to entice quail to nest there. Boone-boy's pointed, dark little face was growing almost as dark as Buzzy's, and his slim body was taut with muscles that he loved to display.

"I'm most a man ain't I, Uncle Billy?" he gloated. "When can I ride that Count horse, Uncle Billy?"

"You stay away from that horse," ordered William. "A stud can be savage when he has mares in the lot with him or when he's penned up alone."

William was seeing himself again in Boone-boy, seeing that skinny small boy who had tagged after Buzzy, taunting old Baron through the bars, climbing every tree on the home place. And Buzzy approved of Boone-boy.

"He mighty smart, Cap'n. He do most as much work now as me."

"Part of the time he does more than you," William said. "He hoed two rows of corn yesterday before you finished one."

"Cap'n," Buzzy sighed, peeling onions for another stew. "We ought to git us some field niggers. Miss Annie, she raise me to be a house nigger. I don't like this field-hand business too good."

"She didn't raise me to be a field hand either," William pointed out. "I happen to like eating. Nobody eats these times unless they work. You don't hear me grumbling because the sun is hot, do you? And where would we get any field hands? How would we feed them if we had any? It's mighty slim scratching here sometimes just for the two of us."

"Them Freedom niggers, they git paid, Cap'n. Four bits a day they gits."

"You want to work for the Freedmen's Bureau, Buzzy? You're free. There's the road. You can take off down the road any time you feel like it."

"Who goin' carry water for them horses, if I hit the road? Who goin' wash your shirts and cook you sump'n t' eat?" whined Buzzy.

"All right, you've got a point there. I'll pay you fifty cents a day.

Next fall if we sell some corn or if we get a good colt later that will bring a decent price. You make a mark yonder on that wall every day you do a full day's work and in the fall we'll reckon up and see how much I owe you," agreed William.

"Hot dam!" exulted Buzzy, flying to the hearth for a charcoal stick to mark with. "Now I buy me a solid purple shirt. Maybe git me a pair of yellow shoes too."

Boone-boy, intrigued by Buzzy's bookkeeping arrangement, had to have a marking place on the wall too. "But if you pay me any money, Uncle Billy, I ain't buying no yellow shoes with it. I'm buying me a colt."

"A Markland!" William gave the boy a playful scuff on his shaggy head. "Another real Markland. Maybe that Flossy mare will have twin colts. If she does, one of 'em is yours."

"You goin' to give me a colt too, Cap'n?" Buzzy asked eagerly.

"I'm paying you, remember? You can buy your own colt. But it will cost more than a pair of yellow shoes. And mind this—if a boy who hires out to the Freedmen's Bureau doesn't work, he gets fired. Any time you get to loafing on us here, you can lose your job," teased William.

Buzzy looked aghast for a moment till he detected the twinkle in William's eye. "Cap'n, you know mighty well you ain't never goin' fire me. We been together ever since we a infant baby, you and me."

"I know where there's a saddle." Boone-boy was excited. "Down home hanging up high. It's all dusty and mildewed but I know how to soap it good, Uncle Billy."

"Fine. Get it ready for when you get around to breaking your colt."

If William and Buzzy were pleased with Boone-boy's shifting loyalty however, it was becoming evident that Sue was not.

The roan horse, weary from a day in the field, became a familiar sight plodding up the hill ahead of the Markland buggy at dusk, with Sue sitting sternly in the seat.

"I don't know what to do with him," she complained, the fourth time Boone-boy was dragged, protesting loudly, away from Buzzy's intriguing activities in the kitchen. "He's jealous of that baby, Billy. Always he was Miss Annie's pet, now little Annie gets all her attention. It's fine for Miss Annie, it keeps her from worrying, but I don't think it's so good for Angela. It gives her more time to brood. What do you believe happened to Morgan, Billy? He must have been killed some-where."

"He wasn't killed. Not around here at least. I found out that much. Morgan got clear away."

He could not tell Sue of the rumors he had picked up in town. He had not yet told King, debating whether it would be wise, whether King's impulsive and undisciplined tongue might not some time let the rumor loose to hurt Angela still more. He had not mentioned the artillery major who had lately returned from Memphis with a story about the newly rehabilitated steamboats that were being put into service on the Mississippi.

"Rode one of them north from Port Gibson, Captain, and there was a gambler on board I thought for a few minutes was you. A little taller than you, I noted later, but as far as looks go he could have been your twin brother. Crew told me he'd been going up and down the river every trip."

"Poor Angela," Sue said now. "Not really married and not free. You were in love with her once, weren't you, Billy? She told me a little, then I remembered you and Morgan having a fight about her that awful night they took Pa and Jack to jail."

"That was long ago, Sue," William said evenly. "A very long time ago. She married Morgan."

"Come along, Boone-boy," ordered his mother patiently. "King says I'm going to have to put hobbles on him, to keep him at home."

"Why don't you let him stay?" asked William.

"Let me stay, Mama," begged the boy. "I work. I help. Don't I, Uncle Billy? I work right along with Buzzy and Uncle Billy's going to give me a colt if Flossy has twins."

Sue's eyes brimmed suddenly. "But he's all I've got," she cried. "All my people—my husband, all gone. There's nobody else that belongs to me any more but Boone-boy! Don't you love me any more, son? Is that the reason you run away from me all the time?"

"I don't run away from you," insisted the boy. "I just like being up here with Uncle Billy and Buzzy. There ain't any aunts up here nor any baby yelling. Mama, I know"—his face brightened and he danced a little step—"you come and stay here too. You come and live with us men."

Sue's sudden flush of flaming color startled William. Suddenly he saw how pretty she was, with her hair like a wreath of coppery fire around her head, her amber-green eyes and the rich glow in her cheeks.

"I couldn't do that, Boone-boy." She got him by the arm hastily. "It wouldn't do at all. Now, you scamper out and get in that buggy and the next time I have to come here after you I'll bring a big switch, you hear?"

William raised an interposing hand, as the boy darted out the door. "That isn't such a wild thought, Sue," he said gravely. "You could come here—"

"Stop, William! I won't listen." She tried to laugh, giving her hair a quick push back, and he noticed there were tears in her eyes.

"There may be a time when you'll listen," he persisted. "Next time —I'll bring Boone-boy home. The Count needs to be ridden now and then or he'll get insolent too and above himself—like all the Marklands."

"That Miss Sue, she a mighty fine woman," commented Buzzy, when the buggy had rattled off down the hill and William had walked back into the kitchen. "Miss Sue, she had a hard time too. Mist' Jack, he your brother, but you knows and I knows that Mist' Jack git mad mighty easy."

"Jack is dead," said William. "Let him rest."

"Yes, suh, Cap'n suh! But if you git married to Miss Sue, we git us a cook. I don't cook so good."

"Hold your tongue, boy!"

"Yes, suh!"

Buzzy held his tongue but he grinned slyly into the pot he was stirring. He grinned still wider when on Sunday he was ordered to press a pair of William's prewar trousers and observed his captain ruefully surveying a Buzzy-ironed shirt.

Cap'n goin' courtin' and he don't even know he is, chuckled Buzzy to himself. Hot dam, you ole skillet, I'll git shut of you yet.